First published 2018

First printed edition published 2023 by Drollery Ltd.

Copyright © Alice Coldbreath, 2018

ISBN 978-1-916736-02-3

More books available by Alice Coldbreath:

The Vawdrey Brothers Series:

Book 1: Her Baseborn Bridegroom

Book 2: His Forsaken Bride

Book 3: An Ill-Made Match

The Brides of Karadok Series:

Book 1: Wed By Proxy

Book 2: The Unlovely Bride

Book 3: The Consolation Prize

Book 4: Her Bridegroom, Bought and Paid For

Book 5: An Inconvenient Vow

Book 6: The Favourite

The Victorian Prizefighter Series:

Book 1: A Bride for the Prizefighter

Book 2: A Substitute Wife for the Prizefighter

Book 3: A Contracted Spouse for the Prizefighter

This book is dedicated to Leslie Carter, my own personal cheer squad. Thank you, Leslie, for all your encouragement. It is much appreciated! Love from Alice.

Prologue

The Solstice Eve Feast, the Winter Palace, Aphrany

"The King's champion," announced the Lord of Misrule, "must kiss the girl who finds the silver token."

Roland lowered his tankard as his friend Ned Bevan smote him between the shoulder blades, and the hall erupted into laughter and excited chatter. He inclined his head to show his willingness to carry out the King's fool's pronouncement. "By all means," he said, wiping the foam from his upper lip.

"Pray to the gods she's pretty," rumbled James Attley from the other side of the table, and Roland shrugged. Did it really matter if she wasn't? A brief peck would suffice if some old dowager unearthed it, or even a kiss on the hand if she was truly hideous. Meanwhile, a commotion had started at the other end of the table.

"You lucky bastard," swore Attley. "Fair Lenora's found it!"

"Nay, wait a moment," cautioned Bev. "She's saying it's her cousin that found it." He chuckled. "The Lady Eden wasn't going to admit to the fact either."

"Bad luck," commiserated Attley, but for some reason Roland found his interest perking up. Eden Montmayne? He glanced up the table and saw the briefest glimpse of wide-eyed panic on her face. Then, just as quickly, she had herself back under control, and gave a tight smile of acknowledgment. Roland almost laughed at her obvious displeasure. How she would hate giving him a taste of those lips, he thought with satisfaction, for he knew at once that he had no intention of kissing her hand. The opportunity was too good a chance to squander.

He smirked, looking around in acknowledgment of the calls of his friends, the encouragement of the crowd. "I claim my prize," he said, flinging a look of challenge Eden's way. *Now what would my Lady Propriety make of that?* Not pausing to take stock, he swung his leg over the bench and swaggered his way toward where she was seated. As he drew nearer, he watched her turn her proud head and gaze down the length of the hall with an appearance of outward calm that impressed the hell out of him. She was a haughty piece, but he knew he had not imagined her discomfort. She was so prim and proper, chances were that this was her first kiss. For some reason, that thought made the breath catch in his throat.

He watched as she flung back her shoulders and pushed back her seat, standing on her two feet to meet him, and his pulse raced in anticipation. By rights, Eden Montmayne should taste as dry and dusty as the book pages she pored over, but somehow, he knew she would not.

He blocked out the raucous clamor and the bawdy jests as he stepped right into her space and stood a moment looking down at her slender figure, dressed all in modest black velvet with scant ornamentation. She blinked, then appeared to steel herself, tipping back her head to look up at him. Their eyes met, and he realized his own mouth was suddenly dry, as if he were parched for her. Instead of grabbing her waist as he had intended, or swinging her around in boisterous play, acting up for the crowd, he kept his hands respectfully to himself. Her eyes widened a moment as she seemed to realize she wasn't about to be manhandled, and he saw surprised relief flit across her delicate features.

2

No doubt it was gratitude that prompted her to aid his progress by rising up onto her toes to receive his kiss. What it didn't explain was the jolt of fierce pleasure that shot through him at her participation. Stunned, he lowered his face, his mind turning blank, as he forgot exactly why he was in this position, where Eden Montmayne found his overtures permissible, and instead reveled in the fact she did.

Like some ardent, respectful lover (a role he had never played), he found himself touching his lips to hers in the softest of featherlight kisses, his eyes drifting shut to savor the sensation. In the darkness and the silence, where all he could hear was the beating of his own heart, he sensed rather than felt the answering tremor that ran through her at their achingly tender kiss.

Gods, what was happening to him? He didn't want to draw back. He wanted to stay like this, suspended in time, feeling her breath mingling with his, her lips pressing against his with the same sweet pressure his own were exerting. His chest throbbed. She was kissing him back. Eden Montmayne was kissing him. The thought was equally as shocking as it was pleasurable.

He drew back with a startled exclamation. The spell was broken. How long had he hovered above her like that? Not long enough, though it might have been an eternity for all he knew. He had forgotten himself and all thought of time or their surroundings. He felt hot color slash across his cheekbones as he watched the answering blush spread across her face. He was breathing as if he'd run a race.

It took an effort, but he managed to drag his gaze from hers to scan the company at large. Had they witnessed his undoing? No, they were drumming their heels against the flagstones and hooting in approval. He could not have made such a bloody fool of himself as he had imagined, he thought awkwardly, transferring his weight onto his back foot and clearing his throat.

He couldn't even speak, let alone leer or throw a jest her way. On unsteady feet he turned and lurched back to his seat like some bashful bumpkin who had just kissed his promised sweetheart. His ears burned. Gods! What had the wench done to him? He suffered the slaps on his back and the tankard pressed into his hand as he sank back onto his bench, feeling winded as if by a fall.

He did not dare glance back in her direction until everyone was distracted by the fool's next jest. To his irritation, Eden had not one hair out of place. How could she look so calm when the blood was still pounding in his ears? He wanted to touch his lips and relive the feeling of hers, but ruthlessly suppressed the impulse. What the hells? He took a large draught of ale.

Doubtless it was just some excess of Solstice merriment that made his head reel, he told himself uneasily. He had not even tasted her, and even as he bitterly regretted the fact, he realized he was grateful for it all the same. For if just pressing his lips to hers in the most innocent of kisses could result in this intense longing, what havoc would it have unleashed on his peace of mind if his tongue had actually tangled with hers? He gave a small groan. Hells, he must not even think of it!

"Ah, the roast meats!" announced Bev, noticing the servers trooping in with laden platters. "Now we feast!"

But it wasn't food Roland hungered for. That kiss had awakened the strangest longings deep down inside of himself. Unable to stop himself, he stole another glance at Eden. He had the most terrible foreboding that for him, nothing was ever going to be the same again.

The Royal Summer Tournament at Caer-Lyoness

Roland gazed through his visor at the noble's box and saw her straightaway. *Eden Montmayne*. In a sea of fluttering pretty gowns, she sat there all in black, like a crow among a crowd of doves. Why then, did his traitorous pulse pick up at seeing her there? He spat into the dust. Doubtless it was that bloody dream he woke from in the early hours, breathless and hard with need. The same dream he'd been having for a sixmonth now. His loins didn't seem to care one whit that she was a sour-faced bitch with more airs and graces than the King and Queen combined.

He shook his sweaty hair from out of his face as his squire led his horse toward him, decked out in his colors of red and black. So intent was he on his horse that the blow to his shoulder from behind made him wheel round in surprise. But it was only his comrade in arms, Sir Ned Bevan. "Bev," he murmured.

"You've seen her then?" his friend said with a nod in her direction.

Roland stiffened. "What of it?"

"Well, I'm just guessing that's who you'll be giving the Summer Queen's crown to when you beat de Bussell."

Roland nearly choked on his own tongue. "Her?" he spluttered. "Hardly! Why in god's name would I give the tribute to her?"

Sir Ned blinked at him, taken aback by his vehemence. "Steady on, Roly," he said in bewilderment. "Everyone knows she's the most beauteous maid in all Karadok."

Roland stared at him a moment. Then glanced back at the box to see Eden seated next to fair Lenora, her cousin. He hadn't even noticed Lenora sat there with her blinding beauty. Because the only one he could focus on was Eden Montmayne with her nose stuck in the air and her mouth pursed up like a maiden aunt! What the fuck was wrong with him?

Luckily, Cuthbert arrived with his horse, so he turned from his confused friend to mount the large charger's back as his squire passed him up his lance. The crowd grew louder with excitement, and Bavol moved his feet uneasily and tossed his head.

"Steady boy," he murmured. The fact was, he couldn't dismiss the Lady Eden nowadays, not now he knew how those prim lips tasted and made desire curl low in his belly. Unable to stop himself, he glanced in her direction again. She rarely graced the tourneys with her presence. Too lowbrow an entertainment in her book, no doubt. Well, he'd give her something to look at, better than her pet poets, he vowed with a curl of his lip. He'd let her see him in all his glory, lifting the victor's cup.

*

"He's looking at you again," said Lenora matter-of-factly.

Eden froze. "Whoever do you mean?" she asked, though she knew full well who her cousin was referring to. Roland Vawdrey, the bane of her existence.

6

"Roland Vawdrey," said her cousin, speaking aloud the name that Eden had deliberately left unspoken.

Eden repressed the urge to scream. "I'm sure he's just looking at you, dear," she forced herself to say, though her breathing quickened. She steadfastly refused to look in the direction her cousin was placidly gazing.

"No, he isn't," said Lenora tranquilly. "He hasn't looked my way once since you kissed him."

Eden had to bite back the childish retort that sprang to her lips. *I didn't kiss him, he kissed me!* Only the ruthless self-control she had exerted over herself from a young age saved her.

Taking a calming breath in and out, she focused on the hazy blue sky and ignored the fact she was sat watching jousting, which she hated, specifically Roland Vawdrey jousting, who she hated even more. And that she was starting to perspire, which was her biggest hatred of all.

Discreetly, she lifted her veil from the back of her neck to allow the breeze to cool her. The midday sun was really starting to make itself felt. Briefly, Eden considered explaining to her cousin just how much she disliked anyone referring to that Solstice Eve when Roland Vawdrey, in answer to a jester's forfeit, had kissed her, tasting of spiced wine and hot sin.

But that would mean confessing that she thought of it at all, and Eden never liked admitting to weaknesses. So instead, she folded her lips and did her best to look indifferent as the two great hulking brutes thundered toward each other on their destriers and collided with a great clash of lances.

The crowd roared as their lances splintered on impact. Eden winced faintly at the thud of bodies hitting the ground. They'd both been unhorsed, she noticed with distaste. What happened

7

in that event? Eden never attended the lists if she could get out of it. She watched now as they both rose from the dust, groping for their long swords.

Eden sighed. *Really?* As if they hadn't wrought enough damage on each other's bodies. Roland Vawdrey was beating down on the other's sword with a sudden burst of furious strength. The other knight—Eden had forgotten his name—who had seemed for a while equally mighty, fell to his knees under such a vicious onslaught.

His sword was knocked from his nerveless fingers, and Roland stuck his own blade point under the wretched loser's throat. They both turned their heads toward the royal box where the King and Queen sat watching. "Rise!" bellowed the King, coming to his feet and standing with his hands on the edge of the box. He nodded to the crowd as they drummed their heels against the wooden stands.

Both combatants were now on their feet. "You've much improved, de Bussell," said the King. "But you're not yet strong enough to rival the best." The King's gaze swept the crowd. "I give you your champion and mine. Sir Roland Vawdrey!" The crowd roared. Roland swaggered toward the royal box, and the King passed him down a golden chalice and a purse of gold as prize. Then the final item—a floral wreath for the champion to bestow on the most beauteous maiden in attendance.

His own lance broken, Roland had to take up another to loop the flower ring over. Eden's eyes narrowed as she saw him walk toward the noble's box where they sat, and she inched away from her cousin's side so he could hold up the floral tribute to Lenora. Sure enough, the lance tip hovered before her fair cousin, and composedly, Lenora took it from the end with a smile and a wave to the cheering crowd before slipping it over her pretty blond hair.

8

Roland had already turned his back and walked away as soon as Lenora put her hand to it. He did not wait to see her crowned. Eden glanced at her cousin to see if she was put out, but she looked as serene and placid as ever. In Eden's opinion Roland should have waited for Lenora's smile. He ought to have bowed when he offered tribute to the prettiest maiden in all Karadok. But no, he was an arrogant boor to the very last!

Eden's lips pinched tight. She had no idea why the crowd adored him so. Doubtless it was those Vawdrey looks that were to blame. The black brows and the strong jaw, the warm brown eyes and that curling dark hair. And there was the fact the crowd liked a winner. Otherwise, she told herself with a sniff, she could not account for it.

"He only gives it to me because I'm the prettiest," said Lenora.

Eden looked up in surprise. For a second, her cousin's voice had sounded almost wistful. "Of course you are," said Eden, at a loss. "It's your due."

"No, I mean—" Lenora broke off with a frustrated sigh. "He doesn't—" She bit her lip. "Never mind. It doesn't matter."

"Are you feeling well?" Eden asked her cousin. "Only it is very warm today and Uncle Leofric said—"

"Yes, don't fuss," said Lenora, reaching across to clasp Eden's hand. "You know I like to watch the jousting."

"I have no idea why," grouched Eden. The idea her serene cousin liked to watch sweaty men grapple in the dirt was bizarre to her.

"Because no one expects you to converse with them," said Lenora. "And I love the anonymity of a crowd."

9

"Anonymity?" repeated Eden in surprise. "You've just been crowned the Tourney Queen!"

Lenora shrugged. "Look around you," she said calmly. "Does anyone look like they care? All focus is on the combatants, not me. This," she said, pointing to the floral wreath in her hair, "is merely one of the trappings of the tournament, and soon forgotten."

Eden scanned the audience. Her cousin was wrong. It was only in the noble's box that no one batted an eyelid at her crowning. In the masses below, she spied many a woman casting an envious or admiring look Lenora's way. But perhaps her cousin meant that no men were looking at her? In that respect, she was quite right, for once no men were staring. They were all looking at their idols who were now receiving runner-up tokens.

Eden saw one mother pointing Lenora out to her child. She fancied she could almost hear her words. *Look at the beautiful princess, my darling*. The little girl waved, but Lenora was oblivious.

Eden elbowed her. "You're wrong. Wave to that small child."

Lenora raised a surprised hand. "Where—?" she asked. Eden pointed her out. Lenora waved obligingly, and the small child jumped with excitement, turning back to her mother.

"Lenora," said Eden heavily. "You really need to make more of an effort to connect with other people."

Her cousin looked startled. "Why?" she asked.

"Because…" Eden took a deep breath. "Try to understand. That woman probably had to work for weeks to earn these few hours of respite from hard labor. They queue for hours, too, to occupy those spectator seats. This is a treat for her daughter, to see the pretty ladies on display and the noblemen compete. She will remember this day through the rest of her life. And the moment when you waved at her will be the high point. It's such a small thing to you, but—" She broke off when she heard the embarrassing throb of emotion in her own voice. "The childhood of a peasant is very short-lived," she said brusquely. "That little girl will be expected to earn a crust before 'ere long. Surely you do not begrudge her a mere wave of your hand."

Lenora's eyes were wide. "I never thought of it that way," she said, and leaned forward to look down from the box. To Eden's surprise, Lenora raised her hand again and gave a hesitant wave and a nod. "Should I throw them some coin?" she asked nervously. "I have my alms purse."

"You might start a stampede," said Eden, ever sensible. Instead, she beckoned to one of the royal pages who lined the steps. He darted forward obligingly, in hope of a tip. "Lady Lenora would like to bestow some coin on that child and her mother," she said, pointing them out. "And will give you a penny for your pains."

The page held out his palm obligingly, and Lenora tipped her alms purse into it.

"That's rather a lot," said Eden, looking at the pile of coins. The page was now cupping it in both his hands.

"I want them to have it," insisted Lenora.

"Send the purse then," said Eden. "'Twould be easier for them to carry. Wait," she said, eyeing Lenora's gold brocade purse with tasseling. "My purse is much plainer," she said, reaching for her own black purse, which was suspended from her belt.

"No, give them mine," said Lenora. "They can keep it as a memento of this day."

They would probably sell it, thought Eden, but held her tongue as the page skipped off.

Lenora put her hands on the edge of the box and watched the page deliver her purse. She smiled and nodded again.

Eden watched the woman's astonishment and delight at the gift. She curtseyed and then hid the purse about her, without opening it. *Sensible woman*, thought Eden approvingly. She would do much better to open it in privacy at home. "Now they will remember that the princess was benevolent, as well as beautiful," she said aloud.

"I'm not a princess," Lenora pointed out.

"To that child you are," Eden answered. She kept her face forward, though she could feel her cousin's gaze on her profile.

"I wish I was like you, Eden," Lenora burst out at last.

"Me?" She turned her head at that, and the force of feeling in Lenora's words. Her cousin was not known for speaking her mind.

Lenora nodded. "I'm selfish," she said unhappily. "And I don't really like people." She turned her troubled gaze on Eden. "I'm not a good person," she finished. "Not like you."

Eden opened and closed her mouth. "Nonsense," she scoffed, but Lenora was holding up a dainty hand.

"I did not mean for you to placate me," she said quietly. "I just wanted to—to be truthful for once. You probably know me better than anyone, except for Grandmother. Yet even you…"

"What?" asked Eden, feeling lost in the conversation.

"Don't realize…what an empty shell I am. Or perhaps you do, but you do not wish to own it," she added painstakingly.

12

"Lenora…you are too harsh on yourself," said Eden awkwardly. While it was true that her cousin could be vacuous, she was never unkind.

"Am I?"

"Yes," Eden insisted. "And I don't approve of…people just making statements like that and then moping about it a day or so before reverting to their old ways," she said, rallying herself. "If you wish to be less selfish, then espouse a cause. If you don't like the people around you, then…" She cast about. "Try spending time with someone else. Someone you admire."

"I already spend more time with you than anyone," Lenora pointed out mildly.

Eden, who had never before realized she was an object of her cousin's admiration, blinked. "Someone who could benefit from your society then," she persisted doggedly.

Lenora sighed. "I tried sponsoring one of your impoverished artists before, and they just fell in love with me and made things awkward."

That was true enough, thought Eden. Men fell in love with Lenora at a glance. Her cousin gave them no encouragement, but it happened all the same. "How about taking up the cause of a lady then," suggested Eden heartily. "You never trouble to make any female friends of your own, and I believe that to be a great misstep. Female friendship is a great source of solace, comfort, and joy. You could befriend some newcomer at court and help her on her way…"

"Oh, but I'm hopeless with women," objected Lenora matter-of-factly. "They are not merely content to sit and look at one's face. They expect you to have…opinions and stories to tell. And I have none," she said with a little shrug.

Eden looked at her cousin critically. "Of course you do," she argued. "That's an absurd thing to say, Lenora."

Her cousin shook her head. "No, it's the truth," she said calmly. "I have nothing to offer as a friend. It's because my growth was stunted."

Eden's jaw dropped. "Whatever do you mean?" she demanded. "We're—we're the same height, for heaven's sake!"

"Not my physical growth," Lenora corrected her. "It's like that wise woman told me that time outside Hallam Abbey. Don't you remember?"

Eden suppressed a snort. In her opinion, Lenora set far too much store in what fortune tellers told her. She always had. "Was that the one who said there was a curse on your pretty face?" she asked sarcastically as she eyed the crowd. They were starting to disperse now and filter out of the stands.

Lenora flinched. "Yes," she said hollowly. "That was her."

"Well, I hardly think—"

"She said you and I were two branches of an old and venerated tree. Though my branch was higher up with superior views, your branch was flourishing and putting forth leaves, while my branch was stunted and withered and bore no buds."

Eden rolled her eyes. "Lenora—"

"Don't you see?" said Lenora again, lighting up with unaccustomed enthusiasm. "I've thought it through, and she was right! All anyone ever told me as a child was how beautiful I was and how well I would marry—at least a duke or an earl, if not a prince!"

"Well, yes," agreed Eden. "But I don't see—"

14

"There you have it," said Lenora, sitting back in her seat. "That kind of talk stunted me." She shrugged her shoulders. "All that was ever expected of me was to sit and look pretty. While you were devouring books and concentrating on your studies, I stagnated. I never…grew, as I should. At the end of the day, I'm only half-made."

Eden stared at her cousin. Where had this come from? She had *never* heard Lenora speak in such a way. "I—but, if that's the way you feel then there's still time, Lenora," she tried to reason with her. "There are still books to read, and dancing masters, and music lessons, and—"

"No," her cousin said simply. "No, there isn't. The opportunity is quite gone. My father expects me to marry before my twenty-first birthday. He would be appalled if I told him I wanted to engage tutors and to study at this late stage. Besides," she said hopelessly, "my mind is quite formed, and it is just a sad blank. I have no conversation. I have only this." She pointed to her face. "The wise woman was quite right about that. Only now I think we must have misremembered her words. I don't think she said there was a curse *on* my pretty face. I think she meant that my pretty face *was* the curse."

Eden tried and failed to hide her concern. She had never dreamed that Lenora had such thoughts or, if she was truthful, that she was even capable of thinking such things. Lenora was, well…not a deep thinker. She mostly seemed to daydream her days away and seemed happiest of all left in peace with her cat or with old, decrepit suitors who posed no threat. That she could have been having such thoughts was disturbing to Eden. She struggled to think of what to say.

"Do not fret yourself, cousin," Lenora told her, placing a hand on her sleeve. "I did not mean to pose this as a thorny knot for you to unravel. There is nothing to be done about it now. I must

15

simply tread this path that has been laid out before me. I must," she said, "marry well and soon."

It was some three hours later that Roland, accompanied by his squire, returned to the Vawdrey quarters in the summer palace. He booted the door open and dropped his arms inside the door with a large clatter. Cuthbert started gathering up the various pieces of his armor and making a pile of it. They were both surprised when they noticed a quiet, tall figure sat at the table examining the pile of trophies and cups stacked there.

"Oswald!" exclaimed Roland, straightening up. "Didn't see you there."

"This place," said his older brother, turning with a frown, "is starting to resemble a miser's cave."

Roland snorted and flung his latest acquisition onto the pile. "I haven't got around to getting this lot melted down yet," he said airily. "Besides, you and Mason haven't stayed here in months."

"So, you and Cuthbert have been letting the place go to merry ruin!" Oswald tutted. "It's frightening what the lack of a civilizing influence can do."

Cuthbert grinned, but Roland scowled, throwing himself down into a chair opposite him.

Oswald picked up the latest gold trophy. "You won then?" he said, examining the prize.

"Who else?" asked Roland arrogantly.

Oswald tipped his head. "I had heard that some of the northern barons had lately entered the lists. And were not to be taken lightly."

"What of it?"

"Sir Garman Orde's the best of them," piped up Cuthbert, settling himself down on a footstool with a polishing cloth. "He's beaten Roland twice this year so far."

"And how many times have I beaten him?" asked Roland belligerently.

"Twice," answered Cuthbert serenely.

"Three times!" Roland corrected him hotly.

"Twice," insisted Cuthbert. "You were disqualified at Kellingford."

"*Everyone* was disqualified at Kellingford," Roland explained to his brother. "Total farce. Whole melee was declared null and void. I beat him though."

"Not officially," said Cuthbert. "Lord Kentigern's good too. He beat Roland at Roget's Ford."

Roland exhaled noisily.

Oswald's eyebrows rose. "Dear me!" he tutted. "The playing field seems to have leveled off of late. Perhaps I'll have to start attending again. It got rather tiresome just watching you win."

"I bet," said Roland sarcastically.

"Garman Orde didn't compete today," carried on Cuthbert helpfully. "So Roland had an easy win."

"De Bussell is considered to be a fair competitor," Roland told him in exasperation before turning back to his brother. "Remind me why I let you persuade me to take this little swine as a squire again, brother?"

Oswald smiled. "You're twenty-five years of age, Roland. It's only right that you start taking on some responsibility," he said. "Even you agreed it was high time."

"When the devil did I say that?" Roland frowned.

His brother waved a hand airily. "I've come about that little matter you wished me to approach Sir Leofric Montmayne about…"

"Oh yes," said Roland hurriedly. He darted a gaze at Cuthbert, who was bent over the armor and seemingly absorbed in his task. "I forgot about that. Did you speak to the old man already?"

His eldest brother regarded him impassively. "Yes," Oswald agreed lightly. "I spoke to Sir Leofric of your matrimonial prospects."

"And?"

"And," his brother replied unhurriedly, "he agreed that with your country estate, good name, connections, and fine lineage you have much to offer as a prospective bridegroom."

"Oh," said Roland blankly. He'd been girding himself for more of a battle as a younger son, without title. He had expected Lenora's father to need more buttering up. Still, he thought, eyeing his brother, Oswald's negotiating skills were meant to be second to none. "I'm obliged to you," he said grudgingly.

"Not at all." Oswald smiled urbanely. "Merely doing my duty as head of our house. I must say though…" He paused. "You don't look particularly happy at the prospect of winning her hand."

"Course I am." Roland bristled. "Just didn't expect it to be so…easy, that's all." He brooded a moment in silence. "What happens next?"

"Sir Leofric proposed that we travel to his place, Hallam Hall, in a month's time for a betrothal banquet, with appropriate fanfare."

"A month's time?" echoed Roland, feeling again rather unpleasantly jarred at the prospect.

"Too long?" tutted Oswald. "Dear me, I forget how ardent you young lovers can be—"

"Not too long," Roland interrupted him impatiently. The small smile playing about his brother's lips told him the bastard was well aware of his feelings on the subject. "Young lovers, my ass. I've walked in on you and Fenella more times than I can mention."

Oswald grinned. He was totally unabashed by his passion for his own wife. It was downright indecent, in Roland's opinion.

"Will you come?" Roland asked abruptly. "To the betrothal feast?"

His brother looked shocked. "To see the last of us brothers married? Of course! Mason will, too, I have no doubt." He clapped a hand on Roland's shoulder.

"I was thinking of Fen's condition," Roland pointed out. Fenella, Oswald's wife, was currently big with child and due any day now.

"Fenella's presence is unlikely," his brother conceded. "But we will cross that bridge when we reach it. Hopefully, my heir will have made an appearance by then. If not, my head will be entirely gray."

Roland glanced at his brother's hair, but it looked black as any Vawdrey's to him. "All is well though?" he asked with a flicker of concern. He had grown fond of his sister-in-law. He had even been to visit her at the large townhouse she and Oswald had purchased in Caer-Lyoness. They had a matching one in Aphrany, the winter capital. For some reason, they seemed to prefer town life to the living quarters afforded to courtiers in the royal palaces. The old family seat, Vawdrey Keep, Oswald had gifted to Roland six months previously.

"So she assures me," said Oswald. "She's as contented as ever. It's me that's harried to death with worries."

"You don't need to be worried, milord," Cuthbert said, raising his head and dropping the metal gauntlet he had been cleaning. "I already did her a reading with the bones. Nothing but good omens for her delivery. Twin golden suns with long rays and no shadows."

"So she told me, Cuthbert," said Oswald. "She was much reassured."

"Cuthbert," said Roland severely. "How many times do I have to tell you? You're a knight's squire now. You can't be running around reading palms and telling fortunes like some old hedge crone."

Cuthbert spat onto his breastplate and then calmly polished it with his cloth.

Roland narrowed his eyes. "Is he trying to be impudent?" he asked his brother. "Because I can't quite make up my mind."

"Don't annoy him," recommended Oswald quietly. "His granny's a witch."

"Wise woman," Cuthbert corrected him, not even looking up from his task.

21

"And he has excellent hearing," added Oswald.

Roland rolled his eyes. "You're no more superstitious than I."

"I have nothing but the utmost respect for Mother Ames," said Oswald. "She's still journeying up for Fenella's lying-in, isn't she, Cuthbert? Only I thought she'd have arrived by now."

"Aye, she's well," said Cuthbert, looking up. "She'll be here by Wednesday."

"Wednesday next week?" echoed Roland. "What if Fen drops tomorrow? She's big as a house!"

"Next week," repeated Cuthbert sagely, nodding his head. "She'll be here in plenty of time. You'll see."

3

One Month Later, Hallam Hall, Seat of the Montmayne Family, Vetchfield

"I thought you'd be wearing the blue gown," exclaimed Eden in surprise as her cousin turned from the looking glass in a dusky rose damask. "Is the blue not your current favorite?"

Lenora shrugged. "It doesn't really signify."

Eden regarded her beadily. "It's your betrothal feast," she pointed out.

"I thought you might wear the blue," said Lenora with a studied casualness which made Eden's spine stiffen.

"Me?" They hadn't worn each other's gowns since they were girls, and then not in public. "Why on earth would you think such a thing?" Eden looked down at her own gown, which was her customary black. "I am very well as I am." Her gaze sought out Hannah, the maid she and Lenora shared, and she rose her eyebrows speakingly. Hannah shrugged as she started to comb through Lenora's blond locks.

"Of course you are," agreed Lenora calmly. "I just thought, as it was a celebration, you might make an exception." She shrugged. "Will you at least let me lend you my pearls?"

"Your pearls?" echoed Eden. "Certainly not. I am very well with these glass beads. It is you who will be the focus of all attention, as the bride-to-be. I am merely your attendant."

"I'll just braid the front sections and leave the back down loose, like the pretty maid you are," said Hannah with satisfaction.

"Will you pass me up Griselda?" Lenora asked Eden, ignoring her maid's words and holding out her arms for her cat.

Eden looked down and found Lenora's white cat rubbing herself against her skirts. She scooped her up and deposited her on her cousin's lap.

"Where are her kittens?" asked Eden. "Did you leave them at court?"

"Oh no," said Lenora, looking shocked. She waved a vague hand in the direction of her bed. "They're all sleeping."

Eden glanced over and saw the four little balls of fur snuggled up inside Lenora's best hat. "I hope you weren't planning on wearing that pearl-encrusted toque," she said dryly.

"Oh, milady," tutted Hannah, following the direction of her gaze. "You didn't ought to let them ruin your nice things."

"Leave them be, Hannah. They're quite comfortable there after the long journey home," said Lenora. "Unless you wanted to borrow it, Eden?"

"No, thank you," said Eden, feeling bewildered. It wasn't that her cousin wasn't usually generous with her possessions, for she was. It was just that she wasn't usually so persistent when she got an idea in her lovely golden head.

Eden regarded her cousin, feeling troubled. This last month she had really tried to encourage Lenora in the pursuit of more substance, but it had all come to naught. All of her suggestions for personal improvement had been rejected. Especially when Lenora's father, Eden's uncle, had proposed this wretched match with Roland Vawdrey. The whole of the Montmayne household had been overtaken with talk of the betrothal and nothing else. It was all very frustrating to Eden. She felt helpless.

Why did Lenora not struggle against this awful fate she saw unfolding for herself? How hard could it be to reform your ways and turn your life around? Finally, Eden had been forced to accept that Lenora was determined on this course of action and would duly marry the King's champion. But now she found herself feeling irritated by even Lenora's attitude toward this!

In Eden's book, if you commit to something, then it should be completely. This was the attitude that had made her the best dancer in all of Karadok. It had also made her a fine musician and songstress. She had applied herself to her lessons as if her life depended on it. There were no half measures for her. So, this lackluster attitude of Lenora's was infuriating.

Where was the excitement that a bride-to-be should exhibit? Why didn't Lenora care to wear her best dress or jewelry? Eden wished now that she had not backed right off about this betrothal. Mayhap her cousin did not wish to marry the boorish Roland Vawdrey after all. And she had offered her no moral support.

"It's not too late, you know," she said, dropping down onto a seat opposite Lenora. "If your heart is not in this betrothal…I could speak to my uncle and explain—"

"Oh no," said Lenora, opening her blue eyes very wide. "This is absolutely the right step. I am convinced of it."

"Really?" asked Eden skeptically. Then she decided to bring out the one thing she knew Lenora felt strongly about. "What about your prediction from that street hawker in Bonebartle? How does Roland Vawdrey fit in with that?" If Lenora's composure and placidity had one weak point, it was her devotion to superstition. And cats. "Have you even asked Sir Roland how he feels about cats?" Eden added slyly. "Only I had heard he didn't care for them."

25

Lenora turned very red. "Did you really hear that about the cats?" she whispered. Eden experienced an inner struggle with herself. Reluctantly, she shook her head. Lenora breathed out. "You yourself told me that prediction was a great piece of nonsense," Lenora said, rallying bravely.

"You know I set little store by such things," Eden replied, lamenting her own honesty.

"And in the last ten years, I have never yet met a knight whose emblem was a weeping heart."

"So you've given up waiting for him?" Eden asked her. "When you were twelve you vowed you would marry none other."

"Eleven," Lenora corrected her, but her eyes were dreamy again and she was stroking the purring Griselda. Eden could tell the opportunity had passed, and she was to be lumbered with Roland Vawdrey for a family member.

With a bitter taste in her mouth, she made her way down to seek out her uncle and find out if there were any particular duties for her that evening. Officially, her grandmother would act as hostess, but Lady Dorothea Montmayne had been sticking to her rooms all day and had refused to be prized out of them, even for the arrival home of her two granddaughters.

After only one day, Eden was already feeling the strain of being back at Hallam Hall. And she hadn't even *seen* Lenora's mother, her aunt Gwenda, yet. They had arrived back the previous night to prepare for the betrothal party, but from what Eden could see, Hobson, the steward, had everything well under way.

The kitchens were well stocked, extra staff had been brought in to serve at the tables, and the hall had been scrubbed from top to bottom. She wished her uncle had not insisted on her

26

attendance at all. She had been raised as Lenora's companion, that much was true, but surely being a bridal attendant at the wedding would suffice as far as duty went? Did she really need to drink a toast to Lenora's ill-advised betrothal?

Everyone knew she thought Roland Vawdrey was a poor choice of bridegroom, and she really hadn't wanted to leave the summer court. Several events were coming up that the Queen would be depending on her to organize. Without her there, Queen Armenal would invariably fall back on her new favorite, Jane Cecil. Eden pressed her lips together with vexation when she thought of it. She had worked so hard for her position at court!

She found her uncle in the Great Hall, which was being decked out for the feast.

"My mother's being awkward, Eden," her uncle fretted, hurrying over to her. "I am depending on you to ensure she behaves herself tonight."

Eden shot a look at him. No one could make Lady Dorothea do a thing against her will, as well he knew. "I will do what I can, Uncle," she assured him.

"Good, good," he said. "Is my daughter yet dressed? The Vawdrey party will be arriving around sundown."

"Yes," said Eden. "She was having her hair arranged when I left her."

"And my wife?"

Eden grimaced. "I have not yet seen my aunt," she admitted. "But Paulson said she had taken to her rooms with a headache and did not wish to be disturbed until strictly necessary." In her youth, Aunt Gwenda had been a golden beauty like Lenora. She found it hard to see her daughter the center of attention, even though she thought it her rightful place. It was probably for this reason that she was seldom at court.

"And has my brother, Christopher, arrived with his demon spawn, your cousin?" Uncle Leofric asked with a shudder.

"I have not seen hide nor hair of Uncle Christopher or Kit," Eden replied. Kit was her fifteen-year-old cousin who would inherit Hallam Hall on Sir Leofric's demise. His father, Uncle Christopher, was Uncle Leo's younger brother and an insufferably pompous bore. Every chance he got to crow that it was he and not his older brother who had sired a son and heir, he took it. Thankfully Uncle Christopher's wife was not coming to tonight's betrothal feast as she had fallen out badly with Lady Dorothea and been banned from Hallam Hall the previous winter.

Her uncle fidgeted. "Is that the gown you're wearing?" he asked, looking her up and down with a wince. "This is an occasion of joy, child."

"Is it?" said Eden dryly. She could not imagine what he was about, marrying her beautiful cousin off to Roland Vawdrey. At the very least, she had thought Lenora would marry foreign royalty. What was the point in squandering her beauty on a mere third son?

Her uncle gave her a sharp look, and she returned his gaze unflinchingly until he at last looked away.

"Roland Vawdrey is a fine match," bleated Sir Leofric. "He has excellent connections and is the King's own champion."

"What about when his sword arm fails?" asked Eden. "What then?"

28

"And why should it fail?" her uncle bridled. "His sire was a fine, strong man, well into his sixties. No one would dare challenge him! He was a great bear of a man."

"Does Sir Roland even realize the jewel you are bestowing on him?" Eden asked pointedly. "He is arrogant and proud. To my knowledge, he has not sought out my cousin once to woo, or have some private speech with her—"

"And why should he? That is most proper!" blustered Sir Leofric. "Whispering with ladies in corners is not the act of a gentleman, but of a scoundrel! I am shocked, Eden. Shocked at your attitude! You speak to me of pride and arrogance," he railed, "but you are the one who needs to bend your neck! Since you have been at court these last three years you seem to have grown a good deal too pleased with yourself, I think!"

Eden drew herself up but remained silent. Her uncle had turned quite purple. In the main, her uncle's moods were fairly even; he usually only blustered and shouted when he was feeling ill at ease about something. In truth, he *was* under a lot of stress and his wife, Eden's aunt Gwenda, usually only added to his burdens rather than supporting him. That was usually Eden's role. She felt a pang of conscience at making things difficult for him now.

"Well!" he huffed. "I have said enough, I think. I hope you will consider my words. Since your father died, I have tried to do my best by you, I think you will admit."

Eden felt herself stiffen under the mention of her ne'er-do-well father. "You have, Uncle," she agreed in her most colorless voice.

"Have I not sponsored you at court and raised you in my own home?"

"You have provided for me most handsomely, Uncle."

"There now," he said, climbing down off his high horse. "I hope you know I am fond of you, child."

"Yes, Uncle," she said, for it was true. In his own way, Leofric Montmayne had acted very handsomely by the wife and daughter of his younger brother Godwin. No one could claim any differently in all conscience.

"Run along now," he advised. "For Hobson has everything well under way here. Make yourself useful by rousing your grandmother from her self-imposed exile. Unless," he added doubtfully, "you wish to try and raise your aunt."

Eden could think of nothing she would like less. Instead, she hurried off in the direction of the north tower.

4

Eden found Lady Dorothea Montmayne ensconced in her private rooms and surrounded by her tapestry looms.

"What say you to this match?" her grandmother asked after suffering a kiss on the cheek by way of greeting. "Will he do for her?" she asked. "Is he enamored of her?"

Eden sank down into a seat and pondered how to reply diplomatically. "He admires her beauty greatly," she said at last.

"My own instinct tells me he is not the one for her," continued Lady Dorothea with a sigh. "He is handsome to be sure. But I predict they would be living in separate abodes by this time next year. Lenora barely tolerates court."

Eden looked up, startled. "Oh, but…"

Dorothea turned a gimlet gaze upon her. "You think because she is the toast, she enjoys the adulation?"

Eden frowned. It seemed their grandmother was far more insightful where Lenora was concerned than she had been. "She rides out," she said stubbornly. "Her company is much sought after…"

"She does not enjoy the society of young men," said Lady Dorothea dismissively. "She never has. She dislikes being fawned over or pawed."

Eden hesitated. "I do not think Roland Vawdrey is the fawning type," she said slowly. "His admiration has barely taken any physical form that I have seen." She thought a moment. "I am not sure they have even spent much time in each other's company," she said with a helpless shrug.

"And yet, you are sure he admires her?" asked her grandmother sharply.

"Of course. He asked for her hand after all," pointed out Eden, feeling uncomfortable.

"There are some men," said the older woman, "who see a wife merely as a possession. They want the most sought-after, the most beauteous, the most admired. They do not see her as a helpmeet or even as a person, simply as a way of triumphing over others." She looked at Eden shrewdly. "Could it be that the youngest Vawdrey is such a one?"

"I barely know him," Eden said, not adding that what she did know, she did not like. "I am not qualified to answer such a question." She cast about her. "His older brothers both seem happily wedded. Mayhap, once married to Lenora, he would come to appreciate her finer points, her sweet nature—"

"Pffft!" Lady Dorothea interrupted abruptly. "Not he! He is his father all over again. Did you ever meet Baron Vawdrey?"

"Not formally."

Her grandmother's lip curled. "He was a great churl of a man, much given to shouting and railing. He rode roughshod over both his wives and was more considerate toward his hounds than his spouses!"

Eden sat quietly a moment. "Then what is to be done?" she asked hopelessly. "Lenora insists this is the right step for her."

"She said that?"

"Yes, not even an hour ago." Lady Dorothea seemed much taken aback by this. "Don't misunderstand me, Grandmother," Eden said painstakingly. "She was far from enthusiastic—"

"Lenora is never enthusiastic about anything," cut in her grandmother despairingly. "Except for soothsayers and cats!" Sadly, this was nothing but the truth, and Eden could make no argument. "Well, there is precious little we can do," she said heavily. "Except watch events unfold."

"At least," said Eden, perking up, "this is a betrothal and not a wedding feast. There will be some time afterward for both parties to recant."

"True enough," pondered Lady Montmayne. "And after the betrothal, they will be expected to associate more closely…"

"And familiarity may breed contempt on Lenora's behalf," finished off Eden hopefully. They exchanged a look.

"That is the most we can hope for," said her grandmother at last. "Though it pains me to say it. And my son is strangely determined on this course."

Eden looked up sharply. "My uncle could not have coerced Lenora," said Eden with a frown. "She would have told me!"

"I did not mean that precisely. Perhaps he has heard some inside information." She shrugged. "That young Vawdrey is to be granted a peerdom? And he feels he is stealing a march by snaring him now before it is common knowledge."

"Do you really suppose that could be it?"

"Stranger things have happened, and I would not be at all surprised," intoned her grandmother. "The King has promoted many a man for stupider reasons than being a good fighter." Eden murmured in agreement. "And let us not forget that his brother is in a position of great power. Both his brothers," she added. "The Vawdreys are not a family to be trifled with." She shrugged again. "Perhaps, after all, Leo knows what he is doing allying us with them."

33

Eden eyed her doubtfully. In her opinion, Roland Vawdrey was nothing more than a well-muscled brute. He had an insensitive nature and a callous, shallow outlook on life. But what was the point in voicing that opinion now? Women married such men all the time. Very likely her opinions were out of step with general thought. She knew the King's champion to be much admired among the court ladies. She just wished to goodness he wasn't marrying her cousin!

5

Three Hours Later, the Betrothal Feast, Hallam Hall

It was very strange, thought Roland, frowning down at his plate. His head was swimming although the last course had not yet been cleared, and he held a half-full cup of wine in his hand. He was commonly known to have the constitution of an ox and could drink into the early hours before he got addled.

This stuff they were serving was damnably strong though. He tried to reckon up how much he had consumed but kept losing his train of thought. He knew he had something he urgently needed to impart to his brother Oswald, who was sat at his right, although it kept slipping sideways out of his mind.

Catching sight of the ladies who were setting up their instruments for the entertainment, he remembered it again. "Oswald," he said with urgent conviction, and reached across to catch hold of one of his brother's silver buttons.

Oswald looked at him in polite enquiry. "Yes, Roland?" he said, angling his face toward him.

"Can you hear me?" Roland asked, suddenly doubtful. His own ears felt very muffled.

"Perfectly," his brother assured him, although he did inch closer. "What is it? You look troubled. Be at ease. You are among family and friends."

Roland held up his finger. "Wrong one," he said, forming his words carefully. "She's the wrong one."

"Well, well," said Oswald, looking amused. "Alcohol is generally held to muddle the senses, not clear them."

Roland frowned at him. "What?" His gaze returned to where Eden Montmayne was in the act of strumming her harp with her slender white fingers. He didn't really like skinny wenches, but for some reason, she drew his eye like no other. He liked the way she moved too, so gracefully, and almost…sinuously.

'Twas a pity she wasn't dancing tonight instead of playing at her harp. The odd thing was that he couldn't hear any music, although all around him the other guests were tapping their feet or nodding their heads as though in enjoyment. "Think I'm going deaf," Roland said aloud.

"Try not to shout, brother," Oswald murmured in reproof as heads turned to look at them censoriously.

Roland looked up to find Eden's annoyed face glaring at him across the room. "Why do I want her so much? Answer me that, if you're so clever," he said thickly.

Oswald's mouth twisted into a smile. "How refreshingly candid you're being, Roland. Although you have left it a *little* late in the day." He leaned forward to look at their other brother on Roland's left. "Mason, can you hear him?"

"It's too late for cold feet now, Roland," said Mason bracingly.

Roland turned his head and nearly pitched forward onto the table.

"Steady," warned Oswald, his hand suddenly at Roland's neck, pinching him there.

"What's wrong with him?" asked Mason. "He can't be sotted already."

"Ah, but he is," murmured Oswald. "It must be nerves."

36

But that couldn't be right, thought Roland. He'd drunk no more than his companions, and everyone knew that Oswald had no head for drinking. He caught sight of Eden and Lenora side by side again and felt frustrated. "Can't do it," he said, shaking his head. "Wrong one, damn it. Need to call it off."

"My dear Roland," tutted Oswald indulgently. "You'll be getting a reputation as a jilt at this rate. After all, this is not the first prospective wedding you've cried off."

Mason's head turned to spear Oswald with a vicious glare. "You're speaking of my wife." He scowled.

"I didn't even know Linnet," Roland objected unevenly, throwing out a hand which thudded oddly against the table leg. He felt like he had pins and needles all over.

"What possible objection could you have to this one?" Mason asked.

"She's not Eden," Roland slurred and fell forward facedown onto the tabletop.

6

Something was tickling Roland's nose. He scrunched it up and blew out of his mouth to try to dislodge whatever the irritation was. It drifted away before settling again across his mouth this time. With an annoyed murmur, he tried to reach up to drag it away, only to find both his hands were already occupied, palming the charms of his current bedmate.

He glanced down in surprise to find one hand full of buttock and one of breast. She was lay sprawled atop him and was gently snoring into his chest. His eyebrows shot up as he tried and failed to remember how this one had ended up in his bed.

He must have gotten steaming drunk, he realized, as his last memory was sat between his two brothers at the betrothal feast. He must have picked up some serving wench, he thought uneasily, though he had done precious little of that in recent months. Not since that witch Eden Montmayne had kissed him and tied his libido up in knots.

He frowned down at the top of his companion's hair, which was black and shining, but he didn't remember a damn thing. Eden's hair was black. Maybe that was why this one had caught his eye. He released her perky breast with faint reluctance and reached up to brush her long hair from his face.

It was straight and long and smelt faintly of roses. That was when he felt the first frisson of alarm. Most serving wenches did not smell of flowers the morning after. He reached down and gently lifted her hand from where it lay on his mattress. Slender and soft with clean, rounded pink nails.

Holy fuck. He'd bedded a highborn lady yester e'en. If she was married, he'd cuckolded some poor bastard, and if she was a virgin, even worse! He lay staring at the ceiling in horror a moment as he absorbed this. He prayed to the gods she was a horny widow who had fallen into his bed like a ripe plum! But even widows could be troublesome, he thought with distraction as he released the soft hand and absently recupped her breast.

What if she demanded he made an honest woman of her? He'd finally pledged his troth to most beauteous woman at court— Lenora Montmayne. It would not go down well if he'd swived some friend or relative of hers at the betrothal feast! He cleared his throat, and the wench gave a muffled groan which made his dick perk up with interest.

"Thirsty," she whimpered and lifted her face to gaze at him through blurry blue eyes. He knew those eyes, though usually they were sharp as gimlets. He knew those delicate features too.

Fuck.

They both stared.

The moment stretched.

Then an insistent hammering started on the door.

Eden yelped, and he sucked in a sharp breath as they drew closer to each other in mutual confusion. Roland slid his hand from her bosom around her back to cradle her body against his.

There was a splintering sound, and then suddenly the door burst open, and they found themselves confronted with their host, Sir Leofric Montmayne, his brother, Sir Christopher, Roland's own two brothers, and an astonished-looking man he vaguely recognized as the steward.

"Ah, there you both are," said Oswald. There was a glint in his eye that Roland didn't care for.

Eden gave a strangled scream and bounced off him, dragging the covers up to her neck, exposing his naked body and very hard cock. When he had realized his naked bedpartner was Eden Montmayne, it had gone from half to full stand. He sat up with a muffled exclamation and dragged a cushion over his crotch.

Oswald coughed, and Sir Leofric made a strangled noise in his throat. The steward's eyes opened so wide they almost fell out of his head. Sir Christopher's face turned an outraged purple color as Mason rolled his eyes.

Oswald looked like he was struggling to keep his face straight, the bastard. "Tsk, tsk, brother!" he said, shaking his head. "I didn't like to speak out of turn, Sir Leofric, but I could see how things were brewing when I saw them together yesterday." He gave a heavy sigh. "Roland has seduced your poor niece."

"You—you—blackguard, sir!" shouted Sir Leofric. "If I had not seen this with my own eyes, I would ne'er have believed such infamy!"

His words seemed to rouse his brother Christopher's ire too. He took a hasty step forward and pointed at Eden. "You've certainly shown your true colors and no mistake!" he wheezed. "The apple never falls far from the tree. You have nurtured a viper in your bosom, Leofric. She's nothing but a little wh—!"

Mason's arm shot out and pinned Sir Christopher to the doorway. "Who the fuck is this again?" he asked Oswald over his shoulder. He dwarfed the other man, who was dangling feebly from his fist.

"I forget," said Oswald. "Some cousin of yours?" he asked Sir Leofric, turning to him.

"My brother, Christopher," said Sir Leofric awkwardly.

40

"Tell him to shut the fuck up," said Roland from the bed. "I've got a pounding head."

"Yes, do," said Oswald. "His shouting isn't really contributing to the matter at hand."

"Shut up your racket, Christopher," said Sir Leofric irritably. "You're not master here, I am."

Sir Christopher opened and shut his mouth like a fish. "Very well," he uttered on a wheeze. Mason released him and he landed on his feet with a yelp.

"This is an outrageous business," agreed Oswald, cutting in smoothly. "You have every right to be incensed at his behavior, Sir Leofric. Let us not sink to his level, however. Let us remember that we are gentlemen."

Eden, who was sat rigidly at Roland's side, tried to speak. Roland thought she said "Uncle," but then went off into a coughing fit.

"Get your bride-to-be some water, boy," said Oswald mildly.

Roland's head snapped up, and they locked eyes a moment. He experienced the oddest feeling of... He didn't know how to describe it. Something blooming in his chest. He'd never felt anything like it. Whatever it was, it seemed laced with something very close to relief.

He exhaled noisily and climbed from the bed, dropping the cushion. There no longer seemed a reason to shield her from his nakedness. After all, she was going to have to marry him now. He sauntered over to where his clothes were neatly folded onto a chair. Dragging on his braies, he then turned to a small table with a glass pitcher full of water and some cups. He downed a cup himself before pouring a second for Eden.

41

Oswald, he noticed, was talking in a persuasive and smooth voice to Sir Leofric. "Shall we repair into the adjoining room to thrash out the details, my dear Sir Leo?" he said. "After all, the damage is now done. Let us attempt to pick up as many pieces as can be restored." Sir Leofric mumbled something, passing a shaking hand over his brow, before allowing himself to be ushered into the sitting room. He looked a broken man. Mason turned and followed them.

Roland crossed swiftly to the door and shoved out Sir Christopher and the steward, who were still stood there staring. Then he shot the bolt. He was surprised to see it hadn't bust off its hinges at the ill treatment it had suffered. He turned back to look at Eden, who was as white as the sheet she was wrapped in. "What happened?" he said simply.

She drew in a sharp breath. "Are you saying you don't remember either?" she asked shakily.

He narrowed his eyes at her before returning to the water jug and picking up the cup he'd poured. Walking over to her side, he sat heavily on the bed beside her, holding it out.

Eden released the edge of the sheet she was white knuckling to take it, and then took a deep draught. Her hand trembled as she drained the glass. He took it from her and set it down.

"Did we...?" He let his gaze travel over her shrouded form.

"Do not speak of such things," she begged. "How could this have happened?"

Roland's brain felt like muddled fog, interspersed with pinpricks of pain. It hurt to try to think. He also had a raging thirst. Fetching the jug of water, he returned to the bed, filling both their cups again. "I don't remember a damn thing," he admitted, rubbing his temple. He stole a sideways glance her way. Eden was sipping rapidly at her water, a pained expression on her face. Her hand was shaking so badly, she was sloshing water onto the bedsheet wrapped around her.

"I remember…playing my harp and speaking afterward to my cousin," she said, sounding bewildered. "She handed me her wine to drink, as she didn't like it. I don't remember much else." The last part was nothing more than a whisper.

"Do you remember me at the feast?" Roland asked. A thought had pierced through the mist for a moment, but then just as quickly disappeared.

"I remember you talking loudly through our performance," said Eden with a hint of resentment. "I thought I should give you a piece of my mind."

"Looks like you gave me a piece of something else," he said.

Eden sat up. "Are you being crude?" she asked uncertainly, clearly unfamiliar with the vulgarity.

He ignored her, glancing around the room. "This is my room, Eden," he said and noticed her start when he said her first name. "Which means *you* accompanied *me* back to my bedchamber." She clutched her cup so tightly, he reached across and prized it from her death grip. "Ring any bells?" he asked.

She turned bright red. "No," she said in a strangled voice, but looked suddenly guilty as hell.

"What?" he asked. If she remembered being underneath him, and he did not… Well, it hardly seemed fair, that's all.

"I think—I think I remember you kissing me," she said, staring past his left shoulder.

Suddenly, Roland felt parched again. He poured more water. "And?" he asked huskily.

43

She gave her head a quick shake. "Maybe…holding me," she added quietly. "Unclothed."

Roland spat out his mouthful of water. "Well," he said, wiping his mouth with the back of his hand, "that's that, then."

Eden's scarlet face gazed back at him with horror. "Yes," she said helplessly. "That's that."

There was a discreet knock on the door, and Roland crossed the room. It was Oswald.

"I believe we have now come to a suitable agreement," said Oswald from the doorway. "The priest will be here within the hour."

Roland heard a groan, but wasn't sure if he'd uttered it, or Eden.

Oswald smiled urbanely. "You're welcome," he said.

7

Eden spoke her vows through lips that felt numb. She was in the midst of a nightmare, a living *nightmare*. She simply could not believe that this was happening to her. The past three years she had worked so hard at her advancement at court. She had practiced her harp until her fingers bled. Read so many books her eyes felt strained. Sat so many hours attending the Queen that her back ached. And all for naught!

She had trampled her own carefully earned reputation and honor into the dust! And for what? One or two overly strong goblets of wine and a mad impulse to find out what came after Roland Vawdrey's kisses? She shuddered at the thought, glancing at his handsome profile. For in the secrecy of her own heart, she *had* been curious. Far too many times her errant thoughts had returned to that Midwinter kiss.

Her cheeks burned at the recollection of her foolishness. In the privacy of her own bed, she had let her fingers trace her mouth and remembered the sensation of his firm, well-shaped lips on hers. *Stupid girl!* Well, she was certainly paying the price now. She would have cried if her pride did not force her to hold her head up high.

Here she was, a once righteous and virtuous maiden of impeccable repute, now completely besmirched. How her rivals at court would delight in her disgrace! She thought fleetingly of the Queen's newest favorite, Lady Jane Cecil. Jane's star would certainly ascend now, without Eden there to check her progress.

Eden's stomach lurched. And what would Queen Armenal say when she heard that the attendant she always relied on had behaved so ignominiously? Stealing her own cousin's bridegroom? The thought of it made her feel sick. How could she have behaved so wickedly?

There could be only one explanation, and the thought of it made Eden so horrified she felt faint. She had always been an uneasy sleeper, tossing and turning, mumbling snatches of conversation in her sleep. From a young age, her cousin and the servants, anyone who prized their uninterrupted sleep, had refused to share sleeping quarters with her.

There had been periods during her life when in times of trouble or anxiety she had been a prolific sleepwalker. After her parents died, and she was first brought to live with her aunt and uncle. When she had first entered into womanhood.

Many a night she had woken in the middle of the Great Hall, surrounded by pitch black. And once she had even awoken up to her knees in the dark water of the ornamental lake on the south lawn. She asked herself now, candidly, could she have sleepwalked herself into Roland Vawdrey's chamber? The thought made her stomach lurch alarmingly. But she had not done it for the whole three years she had been at court! Not once!

But, whispered a voice in her head, she was now back at Hallam Hall. The scene of all her previous somnambulant forays. She would, of course, have known full well which bedchamber he'd been put in, the best guest chamber. She could walk herself there now blindfolded.

But even in her sleep, she asked herself, how *could* she have behaved so improperly? Had her slumbering conscience been unable to prevent her from acting immorally? What if her sleeping self had wondered what came after Roland Vawdrey's kisses?

Unbidden, the images had flashed into her mind's eye when Roland Vawdrey had asked her if she remembered anything of the night before. Lying in his arms. Feeling his warm body against hers. So, it must be true. She had acted with wicked abandonment.

Feeling herself sway slightly, she hurriedly corrected her stance. And what of Lenora? What would her cousin think of her? They had been raised together from childhood. Eden thought of her as a sister. Would Lenora hate her now?

Her tumultuous thoughts were rudely interrupted when Roland Vawdrey reached across and took her hand in his. She almost jumped out of her own skin. Before she could snatch it back, she realized he was merely following the priest's instruction, so she lowered her accusatory gaze.

Luckily, her hands and feet were afflicted with a strange case of pins and needles, so she couldn't really feel his large hand engulfing hers. Still, she could scarcely believe she was even now being bound in matrimony to the greatest boor in all Karadok!

Roland Vawdrey was the opposite of every virtue she admired in a man. He was a swaggering, uncouth brute! If he hadn't been steaming drunk, he would never have given her a second glance! Eden knew only too well how highly Roland prized physical beauty, to the detriment of all other accomplishments.

She knew, too, that he thought her a stuck-up prude with too much book-learning. She'd heard him say as much to his group of laughing cronies. She swallowed, grateful that he'd had no humiliating recollection of her from the night before. *Please, gods, let that continue!* She made a vow to herself that if he had any flashbacks, she would vehemently deny there was any truth to them!

Grudgingly, she had to admit to herself that Roland had behaved rather well about the whole business, all things considered. He hadn't even tried to worm his way out of his obligation to marry her. No recriminations or accusations had fallen from his lips. Other than pointing out she had been in his chamber, he'd not tried to allot any blame for their shocking predicament.

She darted a glance at his blank face, but his eyes were half-closed, and he looked pretty grim. She hurriedly looked away. They both were so far from the ideal couple on their wedding day that it was painful. She glanced down at the wet patch on her hem, which smelled like spilled wine.

She had quickly dressed in her gown from the night before. Other than the wet hem, it seemed none the worse for wear, despite the fall from grace its owner had suffered. She had scrubbed it vigorously, but that was one of the many virtues of wearing black. It never showed any stains.

She had dressed and braided her own hair, as her uncle had not sent Hannah to attend her. She had been ushered straight from the room of her disgrace to the chapel adjoining Hallam Hall. The ceremony was rushed through with none in attendance save her uncle Leofric, and Roland's brothers, the Duke of Cadwallader and Earl Vawdrey.

Eden wondered with a pang if her grandmother or Lenora had been told of her downfall yet. She'd bet Uncle Christopher would be complaining bitterly to anyone who would listen. At least he had not been allowed to attend, so that was one saving grace.

As soon as the priest pronounced them married and stepped back, Eden swiveled smartly on her heel and started back up the aisle alone, her head held high. She did not wait to see what Roland intended to do, but was instead focused on her escape.

In the vestibule she heard a footfall behind her and thought for one horrible moment that her bridegroom was pursuing her, but when she glanced over her shoulder, she found it was only her uncle Leofric and halted.

"Where do you think you're off to, young lady?" he puffed.

"My room," said Eden.

"Oh-ho! Your room, is it?" He huffed. "I think not. Your place lies at your husband's side now, my girl."

Eden gasped. "He will not—neither of us want that, Uncle!" she protested. "We have gone through with the formalities for decency's sake but should now surely be permitted to go our separate ways."

Sir Leofric drew himself up to his tallest height. "I had not realized," he said coldly, "that it was your place to decide what is considered decent behavior under my roof."

Eden felt her cheeks flame. "I apologize, Uncle, I did not mean—"

He waved a hand, angrily brushing aside her words. Eden swallowed a lump in her throat, seeing the Vawdrey party approaching. Roland was walking between his two brothers. They did not pause when they drew level, but simply carried on making their way out of the church.

"You'd best run after him, my girl," her uncle told her.

"Please, Uncle," Eden begged. "Don't make me do that."

"He intends to leave us within the hour."

"Good!" she burst out angrily. "I would happily never set eyes on him again!"

"Ungrateful girl!" her uncle scolded. "Is this the thanks I get for pleading your cause with Lord Vawdrey?"

Eden caught her breath. "I—no. What do you mean?"

"Do you imagine he was ecstatic to see his brother palmed off with the poor relation, rather than the daughter of the house?" he asked harshly.

Eden felt her mouth tremble. "No," she whispered, and lowered her gaze.

"Or perhaps you think I was happy to rob my own child of her prospective bridegroom, and give him to the cuckoo in our nest?"

Eden's eyes flew to meet her uncle's. Suddenly it was hard to breathe. She felt herself turn light-headed.

"Run after him now!" her uncle thundered at her. "If my Lenora forgives you for supplanting her, we will send your possessions on to follow you. You will take no horse, nor stitch of clothing with you now, save for that you wear on your back."

Unable to look anymore upon his unyielding expression, Eden grabbed up her skirts and ran from the dark chapel into the light.

8

"I think it would be expedient," mused Oswald in that infuriatingly calm manner of his, "if we Vawdreys made ourselves scarce."

"Suits me," grunted Mason. "Damned awkward business, all said."

Roland shook his head to clear it and took a few gulps of fresh air. His lucidity came and went in the oddest manner.

"He looks fit to drop," Mason observed critically.

"I am here," Roland complained irritably, focusing on his brothers' faces with an effort.

"Of course you are," agreed Oswald, who was a smooth-faced bastard at the best of times. "What say you, brother, to leaving now? We can do no more here this day. Indeed, our tarrying would probably only prove problematic to the Montmaynes."

"You mean after Roland seduced the bride's cousin?" put in Mason sarcastically. "Funny that."

Oswald gave a sad sigh. "What's done is done, brother."

Roland scowled at Mason. "If it comes to unscrupulous bridegrooms then you're not one talk!" After all, it was well-known that Mason's wife was betrothed to him originally.

Mason snorted. "You're swaying on your feet," he pointed out.

"Now, now," said Oswald hastily, "let us not fall out among ourselves…"

"And neither are you!" added Roland, pointing a finger at his oldest brother, though for a minute Oswald seemed blurred and he had to move his finger to track him. "Stop moving, damn you," he murmured. He couldn't remember at this precise moment what Oswald had done to trick sweet Fenella into wedlock, but he remembered it was dastardly!

"Oswald's standing stock-still," thundered Mason. "What ails him?"

"He'll be right as rain this time tomorrow," Oswald replied soothingly. "There, there." Roland found himself bolstered on one side by a firm shoulder.

"Is he still sotted?" piped up a curious voice.

Roland groaned, recognizing his plaguey squire was now making an appearance.

"Ah, Cuthbert," said Oswald, sounding relieved. "I need you to go and pack up your master Roland's things…"

"Already done it, milord," said Cuthbert, kicking a pack he'd dropped at his feet. "His and mine. Could see the way the wind was blowing, couldn't I?"

"Well done, lad," said Mason, clapping him on the shoulder.

"Cuthbert, if you would only remain down here with Roland whilst Mason and I collect our own belongings and then we can be on our merry way."

"Will he be able to ride?" asked Cuthbert.

"I am here," repeated Roland wearily, raising his head from Oswald's shoulder. He hadn't even realized it, but he must have been dozing off. He felt terrible.

Cuthbert's arm threaded around his waist. Lucky the boy had put on some muscle these last six months or he would never have been able to support him.

Oswald extricated himself. "We won't be long. Now, Cuthbert, you proceed slowly with your master to the stables and ask the groom to saddle our horses."

"Aye, milord."

"Now, what else?" mused Oswald, tapping his chin thoughtfully. "I have a feeling we have forgotten something…"

A discreet cough sounded, and Roland blinked blearily to find Eden Montmayne hovering nearby. She was white as chalk and wearing the most uncertain expression he had ever seen on her face. Usually, she wore a look of irritating superiority. He wasn't quite sure how he felt about this mortified look. It didn't suit her.

"Ah yes, of course." Oswald beamed. "Our party of Vawdreys would not be complete without its newest member! Come join us, Eden. We are rounding up our numbers."

Now Roland did feel a certain malicious satisfaction when Eden blanched at this. After all, why should he be the only one feeling like death warmed up?

The next thing Roland knew, he was being jolted out of a stupor by his brother Mason. "Wha—?"

"Up with you," his brother grunted, hauling him off a hay bale. "We're ready to depart." Before he could respond, a bowl of water was thrown in his face, making him gasp. "Look lively, lad," his brother recommended.

"You bastard!"

"Up you get," Mason said, pushing him toward his horse. "You're to have your lady up before you."

Roland glanced round at that and found Eden looking almost as exhausted as he felt. She was leaning against one of the horses' stalls, looking fit to drop. "Where's her cloak?" he asked with a frown as he swung himself up into the saddle. His head spun, but he managed it. Just.

"Her uncle has declared, in time-honored fashion, that you're to take her with the clothes on her back, and nothing else," responded Oswald drolly.

"Has he, by the gods," muttered Roland without much heat.

"She'll have to share yours," Oswald told him cheerfully and lifted Eden up in his arms. She made no protest, and Roland felt a prickle of annoyance at that. Before he could voice it, Oswald was approaching him with her. "Here you go," he said. "Your lawfully wedded wife." And he hefted her up onto the horse before Roland.

He closed his arms around her at once. To Roland's surprise, she melted right into him without even a murmur. Hers was the slender and lithe body of a dancer. He felt a flicker of recognition that had him cursing his faulty memory anew. That she should remember something of their tryst, and he not at all, struck him as extremely unjust.

"Think you can manage not to drop her?" asked Mason, leading his own horse out of the stall. "Maybe she should go up before me?" he said, turning to Oswald.

"No," Roland found himself saying with more force than he'd expected. "She sits up before me."

"Very proper," said Oswald. "You see, Roland? You're acting like a husband already!"

9

It was a two-day journey from the Montmayne seat to Caer-Lyoness, the King's summer palace, but they had not ridden for much more than a couple of hours before Roland realized he was not fit for the journey. And he was not the only one. At one point they had stopped so their party could relieve themselves. Eden had disappeared scarlet-faced behind a mulberry bush. Five minutes later she had still not reappeared.

"Maybe she's given us the slip?" suggested Cuthbert, scratching his head. "Shall I go and look?"

"You most certainly will not!" Roland flared. He himself had gone in search of her, and after fruitlessly calling her name, had proceeded cautiously, only to find her curled up fast asleep in the dirt. When he had shaken her awake, she had looked so startled to see him that he had almost expected her to slap his face.

She was wilting in the saddle before him now, and truth be told, he was not much better. The arm he had wrapped around her waist was the only thing he felt certain of, that and the jolting horse beneath him. He was just wondering how to broach the subject with his brothers when Oswald pointed out an inn along the road. "That's where we'll put you lovebirds up for the night," he said with satisfaction.

"What?" Roland turned in his saddle to squint at his brothers. "Where will you be?"

"We'll carry on to Caer-Lyoness," said Mason.

"We need to pave the way before your return, Roland," said Oswald with a meaningful look. "Break the news at court. Smooth things over as it were with the King." Roland blinked at him. "You're his champion, after all," Oswald reminded him. "It's a courtesy to ask permission before marrying." He glanced at Eden quickly and lowered his voice. "The Queen will also need appeasing."

Roland frowned. "The deed is done," he said. "What purpose is there to cutting up rough about it?"

Oswald waved a hand airily. "You know how royals are. As you say, it is mostly tokenistic, but you may have some forfeit or penance to perform before the Queen is reconciled to her favorite's wedded state."

Roland glanced down at Eden's dark head resting against his chest. She'd never dream of doing such a thing unless she was in a deep slumber. "If there's a price, I'll pay it," he said with casual indifference.

"Admirable," responded Oswald briskly. "Now, let us get you settled into your own chamber forthwith. Once you're settled, we can go and spread the happy tidings."

Roland peered at his brother suspiciously, but there wasn't even an ironic inflection in his voice. You could tell Oswald was a leading courtier and powerful politician, damn his eyes. "What will you tell everyone?" he asked with sudden unease.

"That your affections were engaged elsewhere, and the plans were duly altered," his brother replied swiftly.

Mason snorted. "We'd best get in fast before that dolt Sir Christopher starts spreading his version."

"That is my intention," said Oswald dryly. "Never fear, we shall have Fenella and Linnet espouse Eden's cause at court. They will be keen to admit their newest sister-in-law into their circle."

"Fenella is not long out of the delivery bed," Mason reminded him. "After bearing your twin sons."

"Well, I was expecting Linnet to carry out the lion's share of work at court," admitted Oswald. "But Fenella is lately receiving guests at home. Lady Schaeffer visits with us almost daily. She is proving to be a most devoted godmother." His tone was rather dry.

Mason laughed. "You needn't sound so happy about it. Now you've children of your own, you'll find it much harder to monopolize your wife's attention. You'd best get used to it."

"I don't mind sharing her with my boys," said Oswald. "But Hester Schaeffer always swore she detested children! Now I find her fawning over them at all hours!" Mason chuckled again. "Meldon's even worse!" complained Oswald about his aged manservant. "I caught him singing to them the other night. *Singing!*"

Roland found his eyes drifting shut as his brothers rambled on about domestic matters involving their offspring.

"Roland!" He opened his eyes. "We're here. Pass her down." Mason had his arms reaching up for Eden, and begrudgingly, Roland eased her off the horse and into his brother's grasp.

"Where's Oswald?" Roland asked, dismounting and peering around as Cuthbert led the horse toward the stables.

"Gone in ahead to secure you a room."

"Oh. Pass her to me," he said, but Eden was already struggling to be put down. Mason set her on her feet, and Roland passed an arm around her waist. She suffered this, but he noticed the faint color that spread to her cheeks. At least her pallor was improving.

They made their way toward the inn, and for Roland, every step was an effort. He recognized Eden was not doing much better than him. She almost tripped on the threshold, but his arm steadied her. Oswald greeted them, directing them toward the stairs.

"One moment, sirs!" cried a concerned-looking patron rushing forward. "But the lady is not ill, is she?"

"Ill?" repeated Oswald in seeming surprise. "No, no, my good man. These are newlyweds and only suffering from an excess of good spirits."

The landlord peered at them doubtfully one after the other. "Your pardon, sirs," he said after letting his eyes roam over their pale, tired faces. "Only I did hear," he whispered hoarsely, "that's there's summer plague in some parts." He glanced nervously over his shoulder. "An honest businessman can't be too careful."

"Understood," Oswald agreed genially and slapped him on the back. "But as you can see their countenances are completely unblemished."

"Indeed, milord, indeed," he said with a bow. "I can see that now."

"What they desire from you, good sir, is some washing water for their travel dirt, some repast for their empty stomachs, and the key to secure their room. We shall be leaving their squire to attend to their horses. No doubt you can supply him with bed and board when he comes in."

"Very good, milord," the landlord said, drawing a large key from his apron.

"Excellent."

They trooped up the stairs, Roland practically hauling Eden, and though the slight wench should have been light as air, she felt to Roland like a sack of grain at this point. Mason carried in his belongings, and Oswald swiftly unpacked for him as Roland set Eden down on the edge of the mattress. She looked a little green around the gills. It crossed his mind that she might imagine he was going to demand his conjugal rights, but nothing could be further from the truth at this point. He would be as harmless as a kitten in the bed beside her!

A chambermaid knocked on the door and entered with a jug of water and a basin for washing. She left and another maid appeared with a trencher of bread and cheese which she set on the side, and then departed.

"Now," said Oswald. "Let me hear you turn the key in the lock behind us," he said, inserting it into the door. "This seems a respectable establishment, but you can be none too careful."

Roland moved to the door and placed his forehead against it as Mason and Oswald walked out onto the landing.

"I have left you directions on the side," said Oswald, nodding to a dresser by the window. Roland glanced at it in surprise. When the hells had his brother had time to write him a missive? "Don't bother trying to read it now, you need to sleep. Twelve hours should do it. Maybe a little longer," he added with a shrewd glance at Roland's face.

Roland shrugged tiredly. He knew Oswald had always suffered after imbibing, but that seemed a little precise even for him. He yawned.

"Oh, and congratulations," said Oswald, squeezing his upper arm.

"Get some sleep," recommended Mason with a nod.

Their footsteps didn't move away until he'd closed the door and turned the key, locking them in. When he turned back, Eden was already curled up on the bed, her arms wrapped around herself, her eyes closed. Was she cold? He couldn't even muster the energy to undress, but instead flung himself down on the bed beside her as sleep closed in and everything turned mercifully dark.

10

Eden woke suddenly in the midst of a bad dream where she had been falling from a great height. Her heart was racing and her mouth was dry. She lay blinking a moment as her senses returned. Everything seemed in confusion. As her eyes grew accustomed to the darkness, she realized the shadowy room was laid out all wrong.

She could make out the great chest and the small table, but they were in the wrong place. And where was the cupboard by the door? Feeling the breath of a companion on the back of her neck, she realized she must be sharing a room, with her cousin maybe? Of course, she was back at Hallam Hall!

Then the body at her back shifted and muttered a smothered oath. The whole bed creaked. That was not her dainty cousin. The moon at the window slipped out from behind a cloud, and she saw the illuminated room in all its simplicity. Unpleasant memories crowded into her brain, and with a feeling of dread, she turned her head and gazed on the sleeping face of Roland Vawdrey. Her husband. She felt nauseous. It hadn't been a bad dream after all.

Panicked, she started to inch her way off the mattress, only to find a brawny arm anchoring her to his side. His arm was wrapped around her waist! Eden felt herself break into a sweat. It took every effort not to lose her composure altogether as she levered his heavy arm off her.

He muttered again in his sleep, and she held her breath. When he rolled onto his back, she slipped off the bed and crouched on her knees beside it until he quieted. Then she creeped over to the washstand and poured a trickle of water into the bowl, enough to wash her hands and face.

The cool water felt good against her fevered brow. Her gown was all twisted and uncomfortable. It wasn't meant for sleeping in, she thought ruefully as she unlaced the front and then her wrists to facilitate washing. The moon was still high in the sky, she realized, glancing from the window. It would not yet be time to rise for several hours.

She hesitated, biting her lip. Should she take it off? She glanced over at the bed. Roland Vawdrey was lying still, the rise and fall of his chest steady. He had one arm bent now and draped over his face. He would likely continue oblivious if she stripped down to her shift, and she would be a lot more comfortable.

Making a swift decision, she loosened her laces further until she could maneuver the dress up and over her body. With economical movements, she wriggled out of her gown, draped it over a chair, and then removed her stockings and added them to the pile. Returning to the bowl of water, she added some more and then washed her neck and armpits. Cloths had been left out for their use, though there were no soap leaves. She could find no comb on the shadowy dresser, so instead she quickly tidied her hair into one long braid over her shoulder.

Then she turned back to gaze at the bed. Could she climb back in without disturbing its sleeping occupant? Apparently, she hesitated too long.

"Come back to bed, for lord's sake," Roland grumbled. "If you need to take a piss, the pot's likely under the bed."

Eden stiffened. Did he imagine her some chambermaid to speak to her thusly?

When she didn't move, he rose onto one elbow to scrutinize her. "Eden?"

"I thought you were asleep," she blurted.

"Hardly," he said. "You wriggle around in your sleep like a worm on a hook."

Eden felt her face redden. "I was having a nightmare," she told him coldly. Would she have walked again if he had not anchored her? The thought made her break out in a sweat.

He made no reply, and the moon drifted behind a cloud again, plunging the room into darkness.

"You'll take a chill," he said gruffly. "Get under the covers." He rolled onto his side, turning his back to her.

Eden approached the bed with reluctance. "Separate chambers would have been nice," she muttered as she slid under the sheets.

He snorted. "Bit late for that."

"It's never too late for niceties," she corrected him, folding her arms around her waist. She lay still, staring up at the shadowy ceiling. Now they had spoken, she had a terrible fear she would not find sleep again.

He rolled onto his back, and Eden shrank back from the physical contact in alarm.

"Well, if you're feeling so inclined," he said, "I wouldn't deny you."

Eden stared at him, unable to make out his features. "What do you mean?"

"We are married," he reminded her. "And you spoke of niceties." He let his words sink in as he patted the mattress. "We're in the marriage bed…"

Eden breathed in a sharp breath. "That is not what I meant! And you know it!"

63

He gave a sigh, and to her alarm, the bed lurched. As she tensed, she realized Roland was climbing out.

"What are you doing?"

"Getting comfortable," he said irritably.

The clouds drifted, revealing the moon again, and in its light, she saw he was still fully clothed too. Something he was swiftly remedying by stripping down to his own undergarments.

Eden screwed her eyes shut in alarm, turning her head sharply.

"We were both naked as babes this morn," he reminded her, obviously aware of her discomfort.

"Do not speak of it! Do not think of it, even!" she implored him.

He huffed out a breath, and she felt the blankets lift. Now he was climbing under the covers, she realized with horror. Eden lay rigid.

"Relax," he told her. "You're wholly resistible. I'm not about to force myself onto you."

She took a deep breath. Of course. She fell far short of his standards regarding women. She expelled a relieved breath. "Are you going back to sleep?" she asked after a moment or two of tense silence.

"Why? What are you offering?"

"I just thought we should have some discussion," said Eden, turning on the pillow to face him. The moon had appeared again, shining bright. Roland was alarmingly close. And his chest was bare. Eden tried not to stare at the smattering of dark hair on that muscular expanse of tanned skin. Even so, she was sure her eyes were wide.

64

"I'm listening." His voice sounded a little thick. Maybe he was tired, she thought distractedly, though when her gaze darted to his, he looked alert enough. He propped himself up on one elbow.

She wished he wouldn't do that. In an effort to be on the same level, she struggled into a seated position facing him. Noticing the direction of his gaze, she hurriedly pulled the blankets up and over her chest.

Her shift was made of the very finest linen and was quite thin. Though why Roland Vawdrey should have any interest in her bosom was beyond her. She was quite sure it was nothing special. Still, it was practically in his face, she conceded. And everyone knew men were base creatures when it came to the flesh.

He looked away a little guiltily and cleared his throat. "Let's hear it then," he said huskily.

Eden eyed him suspiciously. It dawned on her that he was probably remembering that very morning when she had woken sprawled on top of him. His hands had been in such shameful places that she felt herself turn scarlet. "I want you to stop thinking about that, Roland Vawdrey!" she whispered primly.

"I told you, I can't even remember it," he retorted, sounding indignant.

"You remember where your hands were, I suppose," she snapped. "When we awoke!"

His gaze darkened. "Aye," he said hoarsely.

"Well…" said Eden lamely. She had thought he'd have the decency to deny it! "I want you to forget all about it!"

He snorted. "I'll forget it alright. When you give me something better to remember, wife."

Eden gasped. "Don't call me that. Why are you making everything so hard?"

A strange look passed over his face. "I could ask you the same thing," he said, shifting about under the sheet. "Though I doubt very much you'd know the answer!" Eden regarded him suspiciously. He groaned. "Just say what you need to say, Eden."

"Very well, I will," she said with dignity. "What I have to say is this. We have, one way or another, ended up in this predicament." She gulped and plucked at the bedsheet. When she looked back up, he was watching her closely, though he uttered not a word. "The only sensible thing we can do now is find a way to make this situation bearable with as little disruption to our daily lives as possible." She forced herself to meet his gaze. "Would you agree?"

He tipped his head to one side. "That doesn't sound very realistic. There's bound to be disruption."

"Why? Think about it," she urged him. "We both have so much to occupy our time already at court. Why need we let this...this fleeting lapse of judgment ruin the lives we have so carefully carved out for ourselves?" He frowned. Before he could give voice to his disagreement, she placed a palm on his chest. "Think about it first, Sir Roland," she said imploringly, though in truth, she wished she sounded slightly less breathless. His chest felt warm and naked. She pulled her hand back, but he had caught hold of it by the wrist before she could withdraw altogether.

"Just call me Roland," he said in a rough voice. He closed his eyes briefly and cursed. When they fluttered open again, she was startled by the expression they held. Turning his face away with a muttered oath, he released her hand, and she quickly placed it on the mattress beside her, out of harm's way.

Truly, men were slaves to their physical impulses, she marveled. Her proximity alone was enough for him to let his precious standards slip! "The fact remains," said Eden a little squeakily. "That we need a strategy to tackle this…"

"Marriage?" supplied Roland gruffly.

"Peculiar set of circumstances," Eden carried on painstakingly. "You must agree?"

"There's bound to be a lot of talk," he conceded. "However our families try to suppress it."

Eden thought of court gossip and felt her stomach lurch. "Precisely." She pursed her lips. "Did your brother tell you exactly how he intended to break the news to the King?" she asked wretchedly. "Only I wasn't able to give him my full attention when he mentioned it earlier."

"Well, no, you were asleep in my lap," Roland pointed out.

Eden glanced at him with annoyance. Manners were completely squandered on Sir Roland. Then another thought occurred to her. "Don't you think that's a little odd," she said with a frown, "how we're both unable to recall the events of last night?"

"At least you remembered something," he said, sounding resentful.

"Yes, but…nothing substantial. Like how we ended up—"

"In bed together?"

"That predicament," Eden persisted doggedly. "I mean, it's so unfathomable!" Her thoughts shied away from her suspicions of sleepwalking into his bed. The idea it could all be her fault made her feel profoundly unwell. Oh gods, he had said she was wriggling around her sleep…

Roland snorted. "It's not that unusual," he objected.

"To you, maybe!" Eden wheezed. "What lady would be fool enough to sacrifice her good name for…for…" Words failed her as she faced up to the fact this was all her fault.

"A quick tumble?" he suggested. She broke out in a cold sweat. "Eden?" Roland swore and disappeared a moment. When he reappeared, he shoved a basin at her chest.

She pushed it away. "I'm not going to be sick," she uttered faintly, and lifted her head to stare at him as the horrifying realization set in that he was probably far more of a victim in all this than she was. Should she confess her deepest fears that she was likely to blame?

"You're sure?" Roland asked her doubtfully. "You look sick as a dog."

Eden folded back against the pillows, exhausted by her own bitter self-recriminations. She nodded her head distractedly.

"Why are you staring like that?" Roland asked her as he replaced the basin on the stand. "Like you've seen a ghost. I'm flesh and blood, I assure you."

And muscle, thought Eden, gazing at him despairingly. *Lots and lots of muscle.* She wished he'd put some clothes back on. "I suppose it's just starting to sink in," she said, feeling oddly disconnected from events. "That we're well and truly…*married*." She whispered the offending word as if it were a profanity.

Roland shot her a quizzical look. "Not the fastest on your feet, are you?" he asked, sliding back into the bed, but mercifully sticking to his own side.

Eden lay brooding over this. "Are you saying you've adjusted already?" she asked a little testily. She found that quite difficult to believe somehow.

"Men are better at reacting to circumstances," he boasted with an arrogance that came near to banishing Eden's nagging guilt. "And you're the one who said it need not change things overmuch," he reminded her. "Anyway, what's the point in lamenting over it? What's done is done."

And just like that, she was back to feeling guilty again. He really was facing up to this with a lot more equanimity than she would have done if she was the injured party. Of course, that would all change if he knew she was the cause of their disgrace and downfall.

"Go back to sleep," he told her with a yawn. "There's about five hours till dawn. We'll decide what course of action to take then."

"Very well," she murmured, closing her eyes. Strange to say, she thought she probably would sleep now. Not that awful dark sleep that engulfed and dragged you under like a frightening wave. But a more refreshing, natural sleep this time. She would feel better in the morning, she told herself. And more able to cope with this awful turn of events. After all, she could hardly feel any less.

11

Roland awoke to the sensation of sunlight on his face. The birds were singing outside the window, and he was feeling languorous and well rested. For once, he wasn't a mass of aching limbs and muscles. Slowly, he became conscious of a warm body tucked into his side.

A warm body that curled into his in slumber. His eyes flickered open, and he gazed down at the dark head resting on his stomach. Eden was a cuddler. He had no idea why that amused him so much. Maybe because her personality was so prickly and aloof.

One of her arms was wrapped around his hip. He could feel her breath against his belly button. It was strangely stimulating. That could be an issue, he thought, feeling a stirring in his loins. No doubt his bride would not appreciate such a rude awakening as his hard cock in her face. *More's the pity.*

He sighed, trying to get his rampaging urges under control. At least there would be no breaking down of doors this morning, he thought, remembering the previous with a frown. That day, too, had started this same delightful way, to him waking with a sleepy Eden on top of him.

She had not been so frosty when she first awoke, as he recalled. At least, she had not recoiled from him until their kinsmen had appeared in the doorway, blustering and posturing. He lay contemplating the fact when suddenly she lifted her head and gazed blearily up at him.

He cleared his throat. "Morning."

Eden dropped her head, then seemed to realize what her pillow comprised of. His body. She drew back in alarm and blinked at him.

"Remember?" he prompted her confused face.

To his irritation, she rolled over, showing her back to him. *Well, good morning to you too!* After a moment's pause, she craned her head back at him over her shoulder.

"Still here," he said wryly.

At that, she huffed out a breath and sat up. Roland let his eyes wander over her disheveled state. She looked good all mussed up. Frankly, he wouldn't mind being the cause of such disarray. She rubbed her eyes and swung her legs over the side of the mattress.

He watched as she opened the casement window and threw the water from the basin out before refilling it from the jug. Every move she made was graceful and decisive. She washed her face and hands and dried herself off with a cloth before turning back to him. "Do you have such a thing as a comb?" she asked.

Roland nodded toward his pack. "Help yourself."

She balked a bit at going through his things, but when he simply placed both hands behind his head and stretched out on the bed, she seemed to realize he wasn't going to get it for her. "Where should I look?" she asked, unfastening the cords with nimble fingers.

"I'm not very tidy when it comes to packing," he admitted as she flung open the lid and winced, casting him a reproachful look.

"I did warn you." He smirked.

She peered inside. "Is it wood or bone?" She lifted out a penknife and discarded it, then a dice cup, followed by a pack of cards. "Ah, here 'tis." She turned it over in her hands before sitting in an uncomfortable-looking wooden chair and loosening her hair braid.

He guessed she did not want to sit on the bed and pulled a face. His stomach rumbled. "I'm hungry," he commented and supposed he must be feeling much improved.

Eden glanced over at the table by the window. "There's the bread and cheese the servants left last night."

Roland eyed it with disfavor. "It looks stale." He rose from the bed and walked over to pick up a hunk of the bread. It was hard as a rock. "It must have been stale when they brought it in," he said with disgust and crossed to the basin to wash.

Eden did not respond. Her hair was now a black shining veil down to her waist almost. He tried not to stare, but in truth he found it hard to tear his eyes away from her. She was too pale and slim to be comely, but for whatever reason, she pleased his eye this morn. *Elegant.* It was never a word he thought he'd use to describe a woman, but that was the only one that fitted her.

She sat in only her shift, in a common tavern chamber, and still managed to look like a queen. Her eyes were a deep royal blue. How had he never noticed the color before? He wanted to object when she started to neatly braid her hair again but managed to still his tongue.

Instead, he looked about him for his clothes and set about getting dressed. He'd almost forgotten Oswald's letter when he noticed it out of the corner of his eye. When he'd fastened his tunic, he walked over to the window and perused its contents, turning his back as Eden donned her black gown.

Dear Roland, Oswald had written.

Hopefully this letter finds you mostly recovered from the aftereffects of your nuptials. Few know so well as I the unpleasant repercussions that have to be endured before one is restored to full health. After some deliberation, I believe it would be better if you allowed me to prepare the ground for you at court for a month or so before you and Eden return. By that time the talk of your marriage should have died down somewhat. You can also be assured that I will do my best to reconcile the King and Queen to your unsanctioned union.

I can put it about that you have taken Eden on a tour—perhaps to compete in a tourney or two along the way and display your prowess in the field to your bride. You might even decide to journey as far as Vawdrey Keep to show Eden the property she is now mistress of by rights. I am sure you know best how to conduct yourself in a manner that your new wife will find agreeable.

I remain, as always, your affectionate brother.

Oswald

Roland's eyebrows shot up as he read the letter through twice and then passed it wordlessly to Eden, who had finished dressing. He watched her gaze travel over the page. Her eyes widened and then grew thoughtful as she neared the end of the missive.

"Perhaps your brother is right," she sighed as she passed it back to him. "These scandals are usually only a three-day wonder after all."

He murmured some agreement as his mind ticked over. There was a tournament close by that he had meant to attend once the betrothal feast was over with. It was being held at Sir Aubron Payne's estate in nearby Tranton Vale.

He had his armor and weaponry, provided Oswald had not taken any of it back with him to court. Somehow, he doubted that his brother had taken such a misstep after suggesting as much in his letter. In any event, he could check with Cuthbert after they had broken their fast.

"Shall we venture below stairs and see if we can find some repast?" he suggested absently and held his hand out to her. Eden looked a little flushed as she took it, and he led their way out of the room and down the stairs in search of food and his squire.

12

Eden started her third piece of toasted bread with a slightly self-conscious air. She hadn't realized just how hungry she was. Glancing at Roland wolfing down his second plate of roasted fish, she comforted herself she was not the only one suddenly ravenous.

"Regaining your strength, like as not," commented the landlord's wife with satisfaction as she tucked her hands behind her apron. "Millie, bring another dish out for these gentlefolk," she bellowed in the direction of the kitchen. "Starting to get a bit concerned about you, we was," she confided with a shake of her head.

"I mean, we knew you was newlyweds, but there's overdoing a thing, you know." Eden shot a startled glance at Roland, who looked as blank as she felt. "Depend upon it, I says to my man. The poor little maid will be as wan as a bowl of curds by the time he lets her out of that there bedchamber!"

Roland's mouthful of cod was suddenly choking him, and the good lady thumped him obligingly on his back. "Better, sir?" she asked solicitously. "You needs to learn to control your appetites," she said with a sly wink at Eden. "I'm sure your good lady wife will agree to that."

Eden sat up very straight. "Quite," she said in a stifled tone, unsure how else to stem the tide of the woman's words.

"There now, don't take on, that squire o'your'n explained how it was to us," said the landlady cheerfully. "How mad the young sir was for you that he wouldn't rest until he'd stolen you out from under your uncle's hand. Even if it meant he had to ruin you first."

Now it was Eden's turn to nearly choke. Her eyes watered as she swallowed her dry mouthful of toast.

"Cuthbert told you that, did he?" asked Roland grimly. "What an obliging lad he is." His head turned sharply as the sound of a whistled tune grew closer. "Speak of the devil," he muttered.

This must be Cuthbert, thought Eden, who had only the vaguest impression of Roland's squire. He was a good-looking youth, she thought, though clearly not a Vawdrey with that head of golden hair and clear blue eyes.

"Good morrow." He grinned, sauntering up to their table. "Risen finally, have we?" He gave a bow, which was more of a nod in Eden's direction.

Roland glanced at the window in surprise. "The hour is surely not more advanced than eight." He frowned.

Cuthbert cleared his throat. "Aye, true enough, but you've missed a full day and a night in entirety."

"What's that?" Roland asked, thunderstruck.

"Today's Wednesday," said Cuthbert. "And the pair of you took to your bedchamber on Monday e'en."

Eden's eyes widened in astonishment. She had been unwell and exhausted from grief and guilt, which might account for her deep sleep, but all Roland Vawdrey had by way of excuse was a sore head from too much wine.

"Well," Roland said after a moment's pause, "I'd better settle the bill."

"Nay, good sir, for his lordship paid that. Your kinsman. The one who spoke so fair." The landlady beamed.

"Oswald," said Roland hollowly. "But surely he only paid for the one night?"

She shook her head so hard her chubby cheeks wobbled. "No indeed," she replied. "He said as you'd be with us at least two nights before you'd be ready to leave."

"Did he, by gods?" He turned to Cuthbert. "You have all my armor still? My brothers did not take it with them to Caer-Lyoness?"

Cuthbert shook his head. "It's all here." He looked from one of them to the other. "Are we bound for Tranton Vale?"

Roland looked at her. Eden shrugged helplessly. "Aye," he said. "We are."

13

When Roland had said that Tranton Vale was in the locality, it was still a good four hours hence. Oswald had kindly purchased her a horse from the inn, so she now had her own steed, a rather nice sandy-colored mare she had promptly named Christobel.

They rested the horses at the midway point and Eden sat on a felled tree trunk, worrying about Lenora and if her cousin despised her now and blamed her for stealing her bridegroom. *I need to marry well and fast*, Lenora had said. Who would she wed now that Eden had stolen her husband of choice? So deep in thought was she that she almost jumped when Roland sat down beside her.

"Penny for your thoughts," he murmured.

Eden doubted he'd care for them. She glanced over at where Cuthbert was tending the horses. "When we reach your friend's, the host's, place..." she started hesitantly.

"Sir Aubron Payne's," he supplied.

"I do not think I've ever met him."

He winced. "He's not really what you'd call a courtier."

"I see." She mulled this over, guessing the tournament crowd was not going to be her usual kind of people. The only tourneys she had attended had been very few and far between, and they had always been royal tournaments either held at the winter or summer court.

"What were you going to say?" Roland prompted her. His eyes looked a little wary.

"How are we going to approach this?" Eden asked him forthrightly. "I mean, are we going to admit that we were forced to marry or...?" Her words trailed off.

"We don't have to say that," Roland said after a heavy pause.

"What other reason would we have?" she asked, turning to him doubtfully.

"We could say that you were madly in love with me," answered Roland with an audacity that took her breath away.

Eden nearly choked on her own tongue. "No one would believe that for an instant!" she replied more shrilly than she'd intended.

"We could say you came to me, confessed your ardor, and I took pity on you."

Eden felt her color ebb away. "I see," she said stiffly.

Roland Vawdrey lolled back on the log, stretching his long legs before him. "Or maybe I could say I wanted another taste of that pert mouth of yours."

Eden sat up even straighter, staring fixedly ahead of her. "If you do not mean to take this seriously, then I see no point in continuing this conversation."

"Everyone could tell I enjoyed your kiss on Solstice Eve," he said calmly.

Eden's color flowed back. "You kissed me," she pointed out, wishing she didn't sound quite so petty.

"Maybe we should try it again."

"I thank you, but no. I have no desire for your pity, or your kisses."

He was silent a moment. "Has no one *ever* teased you, Eden?" he asked.

Thrown, she turned to look at him. "Is that what you're doing?"

He pulled a face. "I'm attempting it, but not getting very far." She screwed her eyes up and tipped her head to one side. "Not even as a child?" he asked incredulously.

"I was a very serious little girl," she answered briskly. And besides, she'd had duties. Running around fetching and carrying for her aunt Gwenda. Keeping Lenora amused.

He frowned at her. "You can tell you haven't any brothers," he said at last, his answer surprising her.

"I have a cousin, Kit," she said. "He will inherit Hallam Hall on my uncle's death. But he is somewhat younger than myself and Lenora. We did not see much of him growing up."

He made no comment on that, but instead stared into the distance. Eden turned her own attention back to the view, and they sat side by side, in almost companionable silence for a few minutes.

In the end Roland spoke again. "We'll just tell them I had a change of heart," he said abruptly.

Eden started. "What?"

But he was already coming to his feet. He held his hand out to her, and without thinking, she took it and he pulled her to her feet. Holding it fast, he drew it through the crook of his arm and led her back toward the horses.

Eden pondered his words uneasily for the next stretch of the journey. If he meant to tell everyone he'd simply decided on her instead of Lenora, then it was vastly unlikely anyone would believe it.

For starters, her cousin was dazzlingly beautiful. Quite apart from that, she was also the heiress to a considerable private fortune. As for herself, she was neither an heiress nor a beauty and possessed nothing that would have caught the eye of a man like Roland Vawdrey.

Eden knew she had her good points, but none of them would have served to tempt a man like the King's champion. He had no interest in the arts or ingratiating himself in intellectual circles. When she had thought of marriage in some distant, hazy future, she had imagined her husband as a diplomat or polished courtier who might attend the Queen as she did. Not as the King's champion, who earned his gold through brawling with other knights. She huffed out a sigh before noticing that Roland's squire was watching her curiously. "Cuthbert, isn't it?" she asked, pulling herself together.

"Aye, milady." He drew his horse on a level to hers.

"Have you been Roland's squire long?"

"Only for a sixmonth," he answered. "Before that I was his brother's squire. And before that, the Duchess of Cadwallader's page."

"The Lady Linnet?" asked Eden in surprise. "So you are acquainted with all the Vawdrey family then?"

He nodded. "Oh aye," he said airily. "I'm well in with the family."

"And how do you like being Sir Roland's squire?"

"Well enough," he answered cautiously. "I get to see a good bit of the country, traveling from tournament to tournament."

She nodded thoughtfully. "I daresay, most knights do not travel with their ladies," she said, thinking about future tournaments, when she could remain at court while Roland trampled his unfortunate rivals.

Cuthbert appeared to consider this a moment. "Depends," he said. "Plenty of them take their doxies, but wives only tend to come to the bigger events."

Eden's eyes widened, but before she could press him for any more detail, Roland called something from ahead, and Cuthbert spurred his horse on to join him. Doxies, thought Eden. So her life had come to this. If someone had told her she would be consorting with doxies before the month was out, she would never have believed them!

They did not arrive at Tranton Vale until midday and approached Sir Aubron Payne's timbered manor house by way of a moat. The sun was bright and the clouds cleared from a blue sky.

Cuthbert twisted in his saddle to look around at her. "Looks like a good day for it," he called back as attendants approached Roland. Eden smiled weakly and wondered if the activities would have already begun.

When he'd finished giving their names to the attendants, Roland turned his horse to bring it alongside hers. "Do you want to go up to the house first or straight to the field?" he asked.

"Why would I want to go up to the house?" Eden asked him blankly.

"To…" Roland waved a hand vaguely. "Change your dress, or arrange your hair," he suggested, looking uncertain himself.

"I don't have anything with me," she reminded him. "And besides, I do not know the host's family. 'Twould be most awkward indeed to thrust myself upon them with no introduction."

"You're in the country now, Eden," he reminded her dryly. "Court manners will be wasted on these folk."

"I'll come to the field with you," she said decisively, not caring if he was embarrassed to have her trailing behind him. She suddenly felt filled with a sort of horror of letting him out of her sight. After all, he was the only person she knew here. The idea of having to tell strangers her new married name brought her out in a cold sweat.

Strangely enough, instead of looking irritated by this news, Roland looked if anything rather pleased. She would never understand him, she thought as he directed the attendants to which baggage they could take up to the house, and which would be accompanying him to the field.

She wondered sourly whereabouts she ranked in his list of possessions. Rather lower than his horse and his armor, she fancied, though perhaps marginally higher than his hair comb. She followed behind him on Christobel as they rounded the house and headed toward a large field that was fluttering with brightly colored tents in the breeze.

Cuthbert bobbed around on his saddle, pointing out various standards and pennons. "Lord Kentigern's here!" he exclaimed with satisfaction, gesturing at a large banner of a portcullis against a blue background. "I thought we would not see him till Vettell."

Roland nodded absently but was clearly scanning the colors for someone else's. "There," he said, pointing to a tent set to the far left. "There's Bev and Attley's pavilion." He set off in that direction, and Eden surmised these were his friends Sir Edward Bevan and Sir James Attley. She knew them by sight but did not think she had ever exchanged more than three words with either of them.

Her heart sank a little at the prospect of Roland breaking the news to his closest acquaintances, but she braced herself and urged her horse forward nonetheless. It must have been their standards he recognized, for the tent flaps were down and no one was in sight except for a sulky-looking boy with a head of coppery curls.

"Ancel's still around then," Cuthbert said as if he took no pleasure in the fact.

"Who is Ancel?" asked Eden when Roland took no notice.

"Sir Ned's new squire," Cuthbert answered without enthusiasm. "There he goes," he added with a snort as the boy slipped around the side of the tent and scarpered. "Scared he'd be asked to help rub down the horses, likely as not, lazy beggar!"

Eden did not get the chance to respond for Roland had swiftly dismounted and, before she knew it, was plucking her out of her saddle.

"I can dismount myself," she objected rather breathlessly as he set her down in front of him.

"Newlyweds, remember?" he murmured, crooking an eyebrow at her.

Were they supposed to be playing a role? Eden wondered with a frown. If so, he had not filled her in on the plan! Before she could voice any reservations, he had wound an arm around her waist and was steering her toward the opening of the tent. "See to the horses," he flung over his shoulder at Cuthbert. Eden took a deep breath as the woven jute fabric was brushed aside and she found herself pulled through the entrance.

84

Inside the tent, all was in disarray. Eden's eyes fell first onto the wooden table strewn with armor, and then on the two surprised males in varying states of undress.

"Roly!" shouted the taller one jovially. "Didn't expect to see you here, you young brute!" His eye wandered idly to Eden and then widened. "What the—?"

The blonder one yelped and scurried behind the other side of the table to secure the ties on his braies.

Roland sidestepped in front of Eden, obscuring her view. "Why the hells aren't you two dressed at this hour?" he complained. "I've been up for hours!"

"Not really fair, Roly," protested Sir Edward. "Bringing spectators into this area before noon!"

"Did you bring *all* your prospective in-laws?" asked Sir James with pointed disapproval.

"She's not a spectator," answered Roland mildly. "She's my wife."

Eden, who was still stood behind his bulk, closed her eyes even though she couldn't see their reactions. The stunned silence that greeted his words spoke volumes. Roland picked up an overturned goblet and poured some ale from a jug into it. He took a swig, and then passed it back to Eden. So thirsty was she that she happily drained the rest of the cup.

"Y-your wife, you say?" stammered Sir James, still clad only in his white linen underclothing.

"Aye," agreed Roland, taking the empty cup back off Eden and calmly refilling it. She shook her head when he reoffered it to her. He tossed back the contents in one gulp. "Take a drink with me," he suggested to his dumbstruck friends. "And you can toast our health."

"You surely jest?" ventured Sir Edward.

Eden, thinking she had cowered long enough, stepped around Roland to stand squarely at his side. His hand slid around her waist to draw her closer still. She suffered this without comment and returned Sir Edward's stare.

"But...surely that's the wrong one?" pointed out Sir James in a hoarse whisper, looking from one to the other.

"I changed my mind." Roland shrugged and sat down easily on one of the benches. His heavy hand on her hip compelled her to follow him down until she was sat squarely in his lap. Eden flushed. "Pour three cups, sweetheart," said Roland, seemingly oblivious to the shocked disbelief in the room.

Eden sat frozen a moment, but then reached for the tray of cups in the middle of the table. *Sweetheart?* She could feel at least two pairs of eyes trained on her disbelievingly as she awkwardly poured the foaming ale into three goblets. She pushed two of them in the direction of his friends and then picked up the third, which she offered uncertainly to Roland.

"We can share," he said. "Bev, you toast us first."

Sir Edward picked up the cup and cast about him wildly. Considering he was dressed in a pair of green woolen hose and had a bare chest, Eden was impressed when he cleared his throat and struck a dignified pose. "To the bride and groom, worthy among your friends," he said gravely. "Your very good health."

"Hear, hear," joined in Sir James hastily.

Eden took a sip and passed the cup to Roland, who drained it.

"Another," he said to Eden, and she picked the jug back up as the other two slammed their cups down on the table. After she'd poured again, they all turned to Sir James Attley.

He straightened up and raised his goblet. "Drink! May you live your wedded days in plenty."

This time, Roland took one swig, then passed the cup to her. Eden took a hearty draught and then passed it back to Roland for him to finish. He slammed it back down on the table when it was done. Eden wiped her mouth with her kerchief in the absence of a napkin and looked up to find his friends still blinking at her as if not quite able to believe their eyes.

"It's…er…the Lady Eden, isn't it?" asked Sir Edward, giving her an awkward bow. "Your servant, Sir Ned Bevan."

"We just call him Bev," Roland added.

"Sir Edward," said Eden, who could not imagine addressing him as Bev or even Sir Ned anytime soon.

"And I'm Sir James Attley," said the other, who now pulled on a tunic and was looking a lot less discomforted. "At your service."

"Sir James," said Eden coolly. She inclined her head, unable to curtsey from her current position in Roland's lap.

"Bit of a turn up for the books," said Sir Ned with a questioning look on his face.

"As you say," Eden responded dampeningly. She hardly wanted to encourage this line of enquiry.

"If we'd known it was to be a marriage feast, we'd have accompanied you, Roland," piped up Sir James plaintively.

"Didn't know myself." Roland shrugged. Eden felt her face grow tight. As if aware of her tension, Roland slid his hand from her hip to her lower back and rubbed her there reassuringly as he spoke. "It was a spur-of-the-moment thing. You know how impulsive I can be."

Eden tried not to notice the way Sir James's gaze was riveted to Roland's hand massaging her lower spine, or the skeptical look on Sir Edward's handsome face. Instead, she concentrated on breathing steadily and not going into hysterics.

She'd known this part would be excruciatingly embarrassing, and it was nothing less than she deserved, she told herself savagely, for getting herself into this mess in the first place! Her cheeks burned, and she could only imagine how pink her face must appear.

"What's the order of events today?" Roland asked calmly. While Sir James eagerly filled him in, Sir Edward donned the rest of his clothes and Eden found herself able to breathe easier. Roland's hand continued to circle at the small of her back until she found herself relaxing back against him. To her surprise, when Sir James had finished the rundown of events, Roland turned his head and kissed her cheek. She gave a slight start but managed not to squeak.

"Time for us to go and find our hosts," he said. "I'll introduce you to Sir Aubron and find you a vantage point to watch from."

"Will you compete?" Eden asked in dismay at the idea of being left in the company of strangers.

"Aye," he said. "But don't fret. Sir Aubron's bound to have some womenfolk you can sit with."

14

Sir Aubron Payne turned out to be a portly man in his fifties with high coloring and a very fluffy head of iron-gray hair. He was delighted that Roland had brought his new bride along to his tournament. "Delighted, my dear Lady Vawdrey," he enthused, bowing over her hand. "Allow me to introduce you to my wife, Elizabeth, and daughter, Gunnilde. We would be very honored if you would sit along with us and watch the proceedings."

"I would be very happy to," Eden lied, eyeing his giggly wife, who looked far younger than his daughter, and seemed to be making eyes at Roland.

"You must sit with the family tonight at the high table, Sir Roland," said Lady Payne, reaching across to touch the back of his hand flirtatiously. "In the position of honor, as befits the bridegroom."

Eden watched as he absently rubbed his fingers on his tunic. "I'd rather sit with my friends," he said rather bluntly.

"Of course he would, young rogue," broke in Sir Aubron cheerfully before turning to Eden. "But your tender young bride might prefer to sit with us, rather than among the rank and file."

Roland did not look best pleased with this suggestion. Before she could accept the well-meaning offer, he said abruptly, "My wife sits with me." He drew off to one side, tugging her along with him. "You'll sit with the Paynes awhile now, and I'll collect you after the melee."

Eden nodded, feeling the gazes of their hosts burning into the back of her head. "Yes, that's fine."

"And will you watch, wife?" he asked with a gleam of challenge in his eyes.

Eden was taken aback a moment. "I thought that was the plan," she said. "Sir Aubron said they have set up benches along the far field—"

"I meant," Roland interrupted her heavily, "will you look for me in the field?"

Eden's puzzlement grew. "Well, I doubt I'll even know anyone else here," she pointed out. His brows snapped together abruptly, and he frowned at her a moment. Eden blinked back at him, wondering what misstep she had taken now.

"Just give me a token, Eden," he said abruptly.

"A token?" *What for?*

"A kerchief or a sleeve or something."

"A sleeve?" Eden repeated. "I only own two in the world, and I am hardly likely to give one of them to your safekeeping! I'd be walking around with one cold arm for days!"

He rolled his eyes in exasperation before startling her by tapping the brooch on the front of her bodice. "Give me this."

Eden considered arguing. She only owned two good pieces of jewelry. A bracelet of turquoises her grandmother had given her, and this pearl brooch which Queen Armenal had graciously bestowed on her. "Don't lose it," she said with a sigh as she unpinned the brooch and held it out to him.

Now in all likelihood, it would probably end up being trampled into a muddy field before the day was out! Instead of taking it from her, he held out his arm for her to pin it to. Eden considered a moment, and then whipped out her kerchief, wrapped it around his arm and then used the brooch to secure it

90

in place. She was just surveying her handiwork when his finger under her chin tipped her head up so he could meet her gaze. "Now," he said in a murmured undertone, "get on your tiptoes and give me a good-luck kiss that our audience will appreciate."

Eden forced herself not to stiffen, though it wasn't easy. Instead, she lifted slowly up onto her toes and puckered her lips in anticipation. Roland looked down at her a moment with an unreadable expression. Just when she was considering asking what he was waiting for, he leaned down and took her lips in a strangely tender and lingering kiss, his hands resting lightly on her hips.

When he drew back, she swayed a moment, trying to catch her breath. His grip on her tightened, and he didn't release her until she was steady on her feet once more. Eden braced herself, waiting for him to make some comment, or tease her for her reaction, but he did neither. He simply took hold of her elbow and steered her back toward their hosts.

"I know I can trust you to keep a watchful eye on her," he said, and took his leave of them.

Eden could only hope her face was not as red as it felt.

"I'll take Lady Vawdrey along to the seated area, Father," said Gunnilde Payne eagerly. She was an amiable-looking girl of about eighteen, with tow-colored hair and rather large teeth. Eden let herself be led away, grateful to escape Lady Payne's avid stare.

"What a piece of luck for us that Sir Roland brought you along to our tourney," she enthused. "So far nothing interesting has happened except for Lord Kentigern breaking Sir Renlow's nose in the preliminary joust."

"Oh dear," murmured Eden, who'd never heard of Sir Renlow. "Poor fellow."

"And I didn't even see that," admitted Gunnilde, sounding aggrieved. "For my stepmother sent me on an errand to fetch her second-best veil. She fancied the sun was catching the back of her neck in her new steeple-hennin headdress."

Eden clicked her tongue sympathetically, though in truth she could not imagine the girl had missed much by being spared such a spectacle. "They do say it spurted blood like a fountain," Gunnilde confided in a rush of ghoulish fascination.

Belatedly, she noticed Eden's disapproving expression. "I hope you do not find me unduly bloodthirsty, Lady Vawdrey. You see, I have heard it said that a knight has not proved his mettle until he's suffered a battle scar or two," she added hastily.

"I see," said Eden politely. "I was not aware of that fact." Seeing Gunnilde's eyes widen, she added, "As a rule, I do not follow the tournaments."

"Oh," said Gunnilde with dawning understanding. "*Oh!* So you've come to our little tourney to learn the rudiments?" she asked, looking pleased. "To ensure you do not embarrass yourself at one of the royal events? Never fear, Lady Vawdrey," she said, seizing Eden's hand and patting it reassuringly. "I can help you with that!"

The girl looked so happy to be of service that Eden didn't have the heart to tell her she didn't care a rush about tournaments. "That is very kind of you," she answered instead and was repaid with a radiant smile.

"Will this spot do, do you think?" Gunnilde asked, gesturing to a section right in the middle of the length of benching and in the front row.

"I'm sure it will do very well, thank you." They sat down next to one another. "How close will the knights be to us?" asked Eden with trepidation as she eyed the wooden barriers. At Caer-Lyoness the spectators had been on raised platform seating that seemed well away from the violence. Here it seemed a lot closer.

"Oh, you needn't worry on that score, Lady Vawdrey," Gunnilde assured her. "You'll be able to see the whites of their eyes from here."

That was what she was afraid of! "Call me Eden," she responded after a moment's pause.

Gunnilde flushed. "Thank you," she said, looking unspeakably flattered. "And I would be very honored if you would call me by my given name also."

Eden inclined her head to show she was agreeable. "Do you think it might be advisable to move to the second row, Gunnilde?" she asked, glancing over her shoulder.

Her new friend looked shocked. "Oh no! We couldn't do that, Enid!"

"Eden," she corrected her, but Gunnilde had her hands clasped before her as if in prayer, and a faraway look in her eye.

"I'm sure your good knight and true will be looking for you. And when he sees you here, he will be inspired to great feats of valor and chivalry!"

By knocking someone off their horse with a big stick? It hardly seemed to make any sense to Eden, but she forced a smile and nodded her head nonetheless.

93

"It was just wonderful to see how highly he regards you," said Gunnilde shyly. "I would love to have someone view me one day with such a gaze."

Eden struggled to keep her face blank at these startling words. She wondered if Gunnilde would think Roland so respectful if she'd heard him bluntly tell her to use the chamber pot that morning. "Are you betrothed, Gunnilde?" she asked instead politely.

Gunnilde blushed and shook her head. "No, for Father has had other things on his mind of late with his own remarriage. I had hoped…but alas, it was not meant to be." She huffed out a sigh, and Eden deduced she had lost her heart to someone along the way. It was not that surprising when you considered how fanciful the girl was.

"Indeed?" asked Eden encouragingly, leaving an inviting pause for confidences.

Sure enough, Gunnilde plucked at her skirts a moment before taking a deep breath. "Mother always said I was informally matched with our neighbor Sir Giles Conway's eldest son, Arthur. The Conways should be attending today's festivities, so you may even meet him later on." Gunnilde patted her hair distractedly.

"But no mention has been made of a contract since you have come of age?" asked Eden with a small frown. "How old is Arthur Conway?"

"Two and twenty, so high time he took a wife," Gunnilde supplied readily. "But their family came into some money unexpectedly and they have expectations now at court, and so…" She winced. "Stepmother says I am no longer sufficiently grand enough for the Conways."

"Expectations?" asked Eden, her ears pricking up. "Do the Conways now have connections at court?"

"Yes indeed." Gunnilde nodded. "For Arthur's sister has lately married Sir Christopher Lelland, a very prominent man. And they do say that he may sponsor Arthur, which would be a very grand thing for the Conways." Gunnilde's voice had dropped to a reverent whisper.

Eden's mouth twisted. She knew Sir Christopher Lelland. He held the position as an usher in the King's retinue. She supposed, around these parts, they might think him an elevated member of court, though he did not move in the first circles and was rather staid in reputation.

"I know of Sir Christopher," said Eden cautiously.

"Oh!" Gunnilde reddened. "I hope you do not think I spoke out of turn…"

"Of course not," Eden assured her. "You have said naught amiss."

"I wonder if he and his new wife are still staying with the Conways," wondered her new friend aloud. "If so, you may even see him here today."

Eden's heart sank at the idea of crossing paths with a fellow courtier. Still, it had to be done. And no doubt several of the knights attended court. "Have you met Sir Edward Bevan and Sir James Attley?" she asked. "They are both friends of Roland Vawdrey's. My husband," she added belatedly, trying it out. It sounded stiff and awkward on her lips.

"Not officially," replied Gunnilde, who had not seemed to notice. "But I saw them when they arrived yesterday, for my brother, Hal, and I were watching from the ramparts. They both looked so very handsome and distinguished. I am sure I would

95

be far too tongue-tied to ever utter more than two words together in their presence!"

"Nonsense," responded Eden briskly. "You need not be shy and must have some conversation with them at this evening's feast. You are a young woman with a great deal of presence and rational conversation. I will be glad to introduce you myself."

Gunnilde gasped. "Would you?" She bit her lower lip. "Your pardon, I did not realize that you were so well acquainted with royal court. Is that where you met your husband, the King's champion?"

Eden nodded. "Yes, for my uncle Sir Leofric is a member of the King's bedchamber, and I myself am a lady-in-waiting to Queen Armenal."

The girl's jaw dropped. "L-lady-in-waiting? To the Queen herself?" she stammered.

"Yes," answered Eden. "Though I may not be when I return." She winced. "The Queen's ladies are supposed to ask permission before they marry. And I did not."

Gunnilde was staring at her now with so much astonished admiration that Eden was a little alarmed. Belatedly, she remembered how romantic the girl was in her notions.

"To risk losing your position at court for love," breathed Gunnilde, covering her mouth with her hands. Her eyes filled with tears. "It should be made into a ballad!"

"It is largely just a matter of courtesy these days," Eden hurried to reassure her. "And the Queen will likely not care overmuch."

"I think you're wonderful," said Gunnilde in a choked voice. "I really do!"

To Eden's relief, she spotted a crowd of people heading their way and realized more spectators were arriving. "It seems we have company," she said brightly.

Gunnilde wiped her eyes and blew her nose. "Oh no," she whispered. "'Tis the Conways already. Is my nose very red?"

"It looks fine," Eden assured her. "I think I see Sir Christopher. Which one is Arthur?"

"The fair one with the lordly bearing and the blond moustache," said Gunnilde with a very clear bias.

Arthur Conway was of middling height with wavy blond hair and a moustache. He had a slightly self-conscious swagger in his walk, which Eden thought might have been for Gunnilde's benefit as he seemed to look everywhere except directly at her new friend.

"Is that his mother and sister with him?" Eden asked, looking at a middle-aged matron in blue and a younger woman with a rather large headdress on, and an even larger air of self-importance.

"Yes," said Gunnilde, sounding a bit crestfallen. "Muriel and I used to be great friends, but in recent years…well…" Her words trailed off miserably. "Not so much." They waited as the Conway party approached.

"Goodness, is that you Gunnilde, child?" said Lady Conway as they drew near. "I would hardly recognize you. You look quite changed. Have you been ill?"

Gunnilde flushed as she bobbed a curtsey. "I have not," she said with a quiet dignity that impressed Eden.

"She doesn't look ill, Mother." Sir Arthur Conway frowned. "Looks very well, i'faith!" He made a bow to Gunnilde and then to Eden.

"May I introduce our neighbors," Gunnilde started her introductions. "Sir Arthur Conway and his mother, Lady Conway. And this is his sister, Lady Muriel..."

"Gracious me, you silly child! You seem to forget I am lately married!" cut in Muriel Lelland with a high, rather false laugh. "I have not been Muriel Conway for at least a month and a half!"

Eden took an instant dislike to Muriel, who must be of a similar age to Gunnilde. She guessed it was her recently married status that caused her to now act so condescendingly to her childhood friend. Eden slipped her arm through Gunnilde's in a silent show of solidarity.

Gunnilde started. "Please allow me to introduce my friend Lady Eden—"

"Yes, yes," cut in Lady Conway rudely. "Hurry now, girl! My dear son-in-law approaches, and you will both need to move along the bench. Muriel and her husband are sure to be the most distinguished guests here this day and deserve the best spot."

Eden pursed her lips and looked over her shoulder to see Sir Christopher and an older man approaching. When she had turned back two bright spots of color had appeared on Gunnilde's cheeks. "I'm afraid that won't be possible," she answered in a surprisingly loud voice. Before she could continue, a cry from Sir Christopher Lelland interrupted her.

"By all that's holy! Is that you, Lady Eden?" He swept a very graceful bow. "I hardly expected to see the Queen's favorite sat among our humble company this day! What a pleasant surprise!"

A silence had fallen over the rest of the Conway party, who simply turned and stared at Eden in open-mouthed horror.

"Yes, it is," said Eden in a composed voice. She gave a curtsey, but did not release Gunnilde's arm. "May I introduce my friend Gunnilde Payne to you, Sir Christopher?"

"Delighted," he said, giving Gunnilde just as reverent a bow as he had to Eden. "Have you met my wife?" He held his hand out to Muriel, rotating his fingers hurriedly. She rushed over to his side.

"Just this moment," said Eden. She looked coldly at the scarlet-faced Muriel before resolutely turning her back on her. "Shall we be seated, dear Gunnilde? I mean to point out anyone of interest to you." They sat themselves back down in their original seats as the Conway party stood about in mortified confusion.

"But whatever has happened?" Eden heard Sir Christopher asking his wife in an urgent undertone as he led her to one side. Muriel Lelland was wringing her handkerchief and remonstrating with her mother in a slightly hysterical manner. Luckily Eden could not make out the babbled words.

"I think you've had a lucky escape," she murmured to Gunnilde. "Though Sir Arthur does seem to be the best of the bunch. Imagine having to contend with his mother on a daily basis."

"I can't believe they were so rude," Gunnilde whispered back. "I can only apologize, I was mortified!"

"'Tis not for you to apologize," Eden told her, squeezing her arm. "Why, Gunnilde, you're trembling!"

99

"'Tis with anger," her friend admitted. "My stepmother was right all along. They do think themselves far superior to the likes of me. I can't believe I was so foolish as to still…" She choked on her words.

"Do not let it spoil your enjoyment of your father's tournament," Eden urged her. "After all, you are a great admirer of knightly prowess, are you not?"

Gunnilde dabbed her eyes with her scarf. "Y-yes." She gulped. "You are right. And I have so been looking forward to it."

"Sensible girl," said Eden approvingly. "Now, tell me, who is this party of people approaching?"

Happy to be distracted, Gunnilde pointed out the guests, who were made up of various pillars of local society. These included the abbot from nearby Tranton Abbey, a few well-heeled merchants from the nearest city of Greater Tranton, and assorted friends and neighbors.

"Your family must have lived here in Tranton Vale for a good many years, I think?" Eden asked, taking care to keep the conversation flowing. That way her new friend did not have the chance to feel awkward before the festivities started.

"Oh yes," Gunnilde told her. "My great-grandfather built Payne Manor." She chattered away happily, explaining the improvements various generations had made to their home. "Here comes Father now…" She broke off a few moments later as the family party approached.

"That's my brother, Hal," she said, pointing out a lad of about fourteen who bore a strong resemblance to Gunnilde with his yellow hair and amiable manner. "We must be getting close to starting for the day." She waved. "Hal! Father!" She stood up to show them where they had saved them seats.

Hearing someone click their tongue disapprovingly to her left, Eden turned her head sharply and narrowed her gaze at Lady Conway, who turned red and looked away. *Awful woman*, thought Eden. Just then, she caught sight of Arthur Conway, who was gazing rather wistfully at Gunnilde.

He did not seem to find anything amiss with the way her friend was bouncing on her toes in excitement and beaming all over her face. Her sweetness would no doubt prove a strong contrast to his own mother and sister, who were extremely sour faced.

A blast was given by a rather motley crew of buglers. Eden turned her head and found knights on horseback had entered the field and were arranging themselves into two lines, facing each other. A murmur of excitement ran through the crowd. Hal Payne sat hurriedly down on the other side of her. "We only just arrived in time," he said, sounding out of breath. "Father *would* keep talking to that prosy bore, Father Clements!"

"Hal," Gunnilde whispered urgently, leaning around Eden. "Father Clements is a highly respected and moreover venerable—"

"Yes, yes, for the lord's sake don't start with that now!" said her brother hastily. "Hello," he said belatedly, realizing he had not met Eden before. "I'm Hal. Would you like some marchpane?" He was unwrapping a piece of cloth in his lap, which was full of sticky treats.

"This is the Lady Eden," said Gunnilde, leaning forward again with a frown. "Show some respect. She's married to the King's champion."

Hal's eyes nearly started out of his head. "That one?" he asked, pointing to middle of the line in the group to the left.

Eden was grateful he had pointed him out. She recognized Roland's black and scarlet shield at once. "Yes," she agreed, noticing with a start her kerchief wrapped around Roland Vawdrey's arm. Never had she thought to see the day when Roland Vawdrey wore her favor on the field!

On his other arm he wore a yellow scarf along with all the other knights in his formation. Looking to the other group, she found they all wore blue scarves. "Is the melee the mock battle?" she asked, trying to remember the last tournament without much success. "Is that why they're in two groups?"

"Mm-hmm," agreed Hal Payne, his cheeks bulging with sweets. Looking at his sticky fingers, Eden was suddenly glad he had not offered a handshake. The bugles sounded again, and suddenly, the horses were all spurred forward, and the two sides rode at each other, leveling their lances.

There was a thundering of hooves as the two lines charged each other. Eden winced at the clash of lances against breastplates. For a moment, all seemed in confusion as several bodies hit the ground and rolled around perilously close to the horses' hooves. Eden held her breath as she sought Roland out.

After a moment or two, she found him still sat astride his horse. She breathed out and noticed that the lines seemed to be slowly reforming and galloping apart again, before wheeling around to face one another again. A bunch of squires ran forward from the edges of the pitch.

"What are they—?"

"The squires are allowed to refurnish their masters with lances up to three times," Gunnilde told her obligingly.

Eden looked back and sure enough found the squires were passing up lances to those knights who were still seated. It seemed Roland had held on to his lance as Eden noticed Cuthbert's blond head glinting in the sun on the sidelines. Rather than running forward with the rest of the company, he was still lolling on the edges as if he had not a care in the world. When the squires fell back and the horses started forward again, Eden let out a strangled cry. "But what about the men who are fallen?"

"They'll be fine," Hal assured her, licking his fingers. "Look, even now they're drawing their swords."

Eden looked, but while that was true of most of them, at least two of their number were being dragged from the field. One of them merely looked dazed and was mumbling. The other, though, was being dragged by his heels and looked to Eden's eye completely dead to the world.

"Oh, poor Sir Renlow!" exclaimed Gunnilde, and Eden surmised this must be the unfortunate who had suffered a broken nose.

Why on earth would he not retire from the lists after suffering such an ignoble defeat the day before? The crash of lance against shield made her jump, dragging her from her thoughts. Again, several bodies were rolling in the dust. Eden's eyes sought their crests to make out who was who in the bewildering throng. "I can't quite—"

"He's there," said Hal, pointing a finger to a knight on horseback.

"Oh yes," she said, relieved, before frowning. "Though he's lost his lance this time." Her gaze swept to Cuthbert, who was looking alert now and already had a replacement in his hand ready. The horses were reforming and galloped toward the other side of the field where the squires were already running forward. "How long does this go on for?"

"Until they're all unseated and there's a clear winning side."
Hal shrugged.

"Well, how long does that usually take?"

"Depends," said Hal, selecting another sticky piece of
marchpane with great deliberation. "I did hear tell of one melee
that went on for three whole days."

"What?" Eden could not keep the note of horror from her voice.

He grinned. "But there were over four hundred knights
competing in that one."

Eden breathed out with relief. To her eye there were no more
than twenty on each side today.

"There's a fair few knights on the ground now," Gunnilde
pointed out, nudging Eden in the side.

Eden looked and indeed there were. They had been hacking and
slashing at each other a few minutes ago but now they had
fallen back to gaze at the enemy line with their swords held
ready for the next charge. "It seems very dangerous to be in the
thick of it like that, amid all the charging horses."

"See how they've started forming into groups," pointed out
Gunnilde. Surely enough, they were now stood in threes and
fours. "They'll start trying to pull the knights off their mounts
now likely as not."

"What?"

"You'll see," said Gunnilde complacently.

"Surely you jest?" quavered Eden. She was sure there had been
none of that at the royal tournaments.

Gunnilde shook her head, her eyes glued on the field. "See that one there," she said, pointing to a large knight in black armor. His helmet was horned and somehow quite monstrous to look at. Her voice lowered to an awed whisper. "That's Lord Kentigern."

"I think I heard someone mention his name earlier, but I don't think—?"

"He's one of the northern lords, and a very fearsome fighter. He was apparently of great renown in the north, but only just earning his fame in these parts."

Eden gazed at him in some trepidation. He was on the opposing side to Roland. Then her eyes turned back to the side of the field where the fallen knights had been dragged. To her horror, she found they were being bound hand and foot by the squires. "Whatever are they doing?" she asked faintly. "Surely, they should be having their wounds being treated to, rather than being handled so roughly?"

Hal glanced at her face and then the direction of her gaze. "Oh, them? They'll be ransomed tonight at the feast."

"Ransomed?" Eden stared at him.

"Aye, for prize money," he explained calmly.

Eden suddenly realized that these rural tournaments were a lot more rough and ready than the court ones she had attended.

"Eden," said Gunnilde, shaking her arm. "You'll miss the next charge!"

Roland had wheeled his horse around again and looked poised to charge. To Eden's trepidation he looked exactly center in the lineup now, which meant his direct counter was the ferocious Lord Kentigern.

Eden felt a sense of foreboding stealing over her. Roland's tall, muscular physique was impressive, but Lord Kentigern looked like the stuff of nightmares. Eden found her fingernails biting into her palms and had to force herself to uncurl her fingers. This was *brutal*! How could people find this entertaining?

"There's a hair on this piece of gingerbread!" complained Hal, sticking out his tongue.

"It's probably *your* hair," tutted Gunnilde. "Father keeps telling you to get it cut."

Eden winced as the shields and lances met in a loud splintering and a dust cloud went up from the horses' hooves. Her eyes blinked at the ensuing confusion. "Is he down?" she muttered, her eyes scanning the chaotic scene. Then she spied Roland's horse, and it was riderless. "Oh!" She covered her mouth.

"His horse has trampled him!" squeaked Gunnilde in dismay.

Eden gasped, seeing Roland's prone form lying under his horse. A few of the previously unseated knights were darting forward, ready to pounce on him, but Bavol tossed his head and lunged at anyone who approached, snapping his teeth together as if he would bite. "Nay, wait," said Eden. "I think he is protecting his master."

Hal whistled. "I believe you're right. That's one good beast."

"What is his name?" said Gunnilde, clapping her hands together.

"Bavol," Eden told her, grateful she knew at least one piece of Vawdrey trivia.

"Most noble steed!" choked out Gunnilde, dabbing at her eyes again.

106

Eden watched Roland roll onto his side, and then swiftly climb to his feet. He paused a moment to pat Bavol's neck and then drew his sword. Slapping his horse on the rump, he dispatched him to the edge of the field.

She watched him roll his shoulders as if testing for injury as two knights on foot simultaneously charged him. He beat their attacks aside as effortlessly as if he were swatting mere flies. Then, suddenly, they fell back and were reforming their ranks again as the last remaining mounted knights wheeled their horses about.

Eden watched Roland gesturing with his hands as he spoke to his allies. "Is that his friend?" she muttered aloud as one clapped him on the shoulder. She was speaking to herself in truth, as it was unlikely that her companions would even know.

"The yellow stag?" asked Hal, withdrawing a list from his belt and unfurling it. "Sir Edward Bevan of Knollesley," he read aloud.

Eden nodded. "That is him." At least he was among friends, though she would rather he was still on horseback than in the midst of the fray.

"They're about to come around again," said Gunnilde, bouncing in her seat.

Eden felt a sense of dread as the horses charged. Roland looked perilously prominent to her eye and positioned too far forward. Suddenly, she realized he was poised to spring and to her disbelieving eye, she watched him leap up and drag Lord Kentigern from his saddle. "He's mad!" she uttered faintly as Hal yelled and cheered in her ear.

"Not for nothing is he the King's champion!" the boy whooped, leaping out of his seat.

Lord Kentigern came crashing down like a lead weight, and the two of them rolled around in the dust as Kentigern's massive horse reared and plunged like a crazed thing, eyes rolling with fear. Sir Ned Bevan ran forward and caught it by the head, pulling it away with dogged determination.

"Oh, that was well done indeed!" marveled Gunnilde. "What did you say his name was, Hal?"

"Bevan, Sir Edward Bevan," her brother replied, sinking back down onto the bench.

Eden was sat ramrod straight, her hands clenched so hard together she had lost all sensation in her fingers. Roland sprang to his feet and drew his sword, waiting as Lord Kentigern staggered about, shaking his head jerkily as if to clear it.

"That grotesque helmet surely does not help?" murmured Gunnilde. "Why, it has probably turned from back to front and he cannot see!"

"Good!" fired back Eden, surprising herself along with her friend. "Why does he not attack him now? While he is incapacitated?"

"Because he is the King's champion perhaps?" suggested Gunnilde, looking taken aback. "It would hardly seem chivalrous…"

"Chivalrous?" blurted Eden hotly. "How is *any* of this remotely chivalrous? Just strike him!" she shouted furiously, leaping out of her seat. "What are you waiting for?" As if he had heard her anguished cry, Eden watched Roland's helmet snap up to look in her direction. She drew a ragged breath. Surely, he had not heard her? Clapping her palms to her overheated cheeks, she dropped self-consciously back down into her seat.

Hal chuckled, but Eden did not have the chance to feel any more embarrassed as a terrific clanging of blades could now be heard above the clamor. She refocused on the fighting and found Roland and Lord Kentigern were now trading blows with their broadswords. In her opinion, Roland should have forced his advantage while he still had it. Lord Kentigern looked to wield a freakish strength. Even though Roland was giving as good as he got, who knew how long he could keep this terrible pace up?

"The knights are coming back around!" yelled Hal excitedly.

Eden felt sick to her stomach as she looked from the two combatants to the charging horses. How could they be oblivious to the fact they were about to be mowed down by a mass of horses' hooves? She closed her eyes. The crowd bayed, and Eden felt herself go hot, then cold all over. Feeling her hand squeezed tight, she realized Gunnilde had hold of her nerveless fingers.

"All is not lost," her friend was assuring her. "Look. They still stand."

Eden blinked as the dust settled. By some miracle, their two figures were still stood, swords swinging, oblivious to the fact there was now only one knight left astride his horse. A bugle sounded. A cheer went up from the crowd.

"Wait—what is happening now?" asked Eden urgently.

"The melee is over," explained Gunnilde. "See?" She pointed. "Only one knight remains unseated."

Eden spared a glance at the knight with his arm raised in triumph. "But who is going to tell *them*?" she asked impatiently as Roland and Kentigern continued locked in their private battle.

One of the buglers approached them cautiously and raised his horn. When the bugle blast rent the air at such close quarters, they both staggered back, looking around in seeming confusion.

"Oh dear," said Gunnilde. "I do hope poor Sir Roland will not be too disappointed to be on the losing side."

After all that, he'd lost? thought Eden in bewilderment. Sure enough, the seated knight was wearing a blue armband.

"To my eye there seems to be more blue hostages though," said Hal. "So I'd say it probably works out that the yellows will receive the fatter purse, all told."

"This—this melee makes no *sense!*" Eden complained tightly. "No sense whatsoever!"

"Do you think not?" asked Gunnilde, sounding surprised. "To me, it seems to imitate actual battle quite closely."

"How?" demanded Eden irritably. "To my mind, there is no clear winner. It is chaotic. It is unfair. It's hard to even tell which side anyone is on and—" She broke off distractedly. "Oh," she said, catching Gunnilde's meaning. Clearly there was a lot more to her new friend than met the eye.

Gunnilde gave her a sad little smile. "Yes," she said with a sigh. "My father was taken as a hostage for three years after the battle of Oskirk. And yet, to all intents and purposes, our side was the victors."

Eden huffed. "But why should anyone want to celebrate anything so...so *nonsensical?*" She broke off in agitation.

"Is it not better to have pretend battles where there are far less casualties than actual battle?" asked Gunnilde so sensibly that Eden felt guilty for feeling so irritated by her words.

110

Why did she feel so wound up about it all? she wondered and took a deep breath. "In any event, I found it very hard to watch," she said in a muffled voice.

"But you weren't bored," pointed out Hal, nudging her in a familiar manner she really ought to discourage. "Bored people do not jump out of their seats at tournaments and shout."

Eden gave him sideways look. "A momentary lapse, I assure you."

He sniggered and Eden pursed her lips.

"'Tis likely you found it hard to watch because you have a loved one in the field," said Gunnilde, kindly patting her on the shoulder. It occurred to Eden that she'd had more physical contact with other people in the last few days than she had for the rest of her twenty-two years in entirety. She felt her cheeks color. Gunnilde's theory didn't really hold water, but she could hardly say as much.

Servers filed onto the field carrying trays of ale and mead and small pastries.

"Oh good," said Hal, perking up. "I'm half-starved."

"What happens now?" asked Eden, watching the various knights still milling around the field.

"Well, that's today's main entertainment," Gunnilde explained. "This afternoon there will be a Challenge to Arms, but otherwise…"

"What's that?" asked Eden, accepting a cup of ale from a passing page.

"Last night at the feast an open invitation for any challengers was issued by a group of knights who did not enter the melee. Their shields will be hung shortly from that tree over there,"

111

said Gunnilde, pointing to a large oak. "Any knight who wishes to take them up on it will ride up and hit their shield with their lance. That will take place around three o'clock," Gunnilde explained. "But those taking place in tomorrow's jousting will likely take it as an opportunity to rest up in preparation."

"I see," replied Eden. She was wondering uncomfortably where she was to be put up for the evening. She had noticed bunks in the tent Roland's friends were occupying. But surely, she would not be expected to bed down in such a communal arrangement? Then she remembered Roland had sent some of his baggage up to the house.

So deep in thought was she, she nearly jumped out of her skin when her shoulders were seized, and she was spun around to face Roland Vawdrey, who seemed to have shed half his armor, and must have vaulted over the barrier.

"Well, wife?" he asked, sounding in high good humor. Why did he look so pleased with himself? She scanned his jubilant face. Did he not just lose? He walked her backward until the backs of her knees hit the bench, and she was forced to put a hand to his forearm to steady herself.

Ale sloshed over her other hand, but for the life of her she could not look away from his gaze. "I saw you out of your seat, cheering for me," he said in a low, intimate voice that turned Eden's face quite scarlet. She could see he was pleased by the idea and could not quite bring herself to correct him.

"I—er—yes." She gulped. "It was all most—um…" Words failed her as his gaze focused on her mouth. Oh gods, he wasn't going to kiss her, was he? Eden's wits scattered even further. It would be just like Midwinter all over again! She made a strangled noise in her throat and at that, his eyes snapped to hers. There was a question in them. Eden darted her eyes meaningfully to the left and right. He frowned but tore his

112

attention from her to take in the sea of faces all around them. Reluctantly, it seemed to Eden, he dropped his hands from her shoulders. There was almost a collective sigh of disappointment from the crowd.

She cleared her throat. "Allow me to introduce my new friends, Harold and Gunnilde Payne." She wished to goodness she did not sound so breathless. "My husband, Sir Roland Vawdrey," she said as Gunnilde dropped into a curtsey and Hal performed a rather wooden bow. Roland returned a perfunctory nod. "They have kindly been explaining the melee to me," she added somewhat desperately.

"May we wish you joy on your recent marriage," offered Gunnilde politely. She jabbed her brother with her elbow, no doubt hoping to jolt him into offering his congratulations, but he was staring up at Roland with a starstruck expression on his face.

"Congratulations," Hal said squeakily. "The way you brought down Lord Kentigern was masterly!"

Roland's gaze flickered to the boy with a little more interest. "Liked that, did you?"

"The Lady Eden did not think you struck soon enough," Hal confided. "But I saw naught amiss with your attack."

Eden inwardly cringed at Roland's startled glance in her direction. Mercifully, the hurried approach of Sir Aubron forestalled any further discussion of Roland's technique in the field.

"Sir Roland." Their host beamed. "What a display! What an *outstanding* display you have treated us to this day! We are honored to see the King's champion in action, positively honored! I declare the loudest cheer of the tournament so far went up when you unseated Lord Kentigern in your glorious act of valor!"

Roland heartily returned Sir Aubron's congratulatory embrace, and they slapped each other's shoulders a few times. Eden was surprised to see the older man had tears of sentiment in his eyes.

"Never did I dream to see such feats on the grounds of my humble home. Entertainment fit for a king! A veritable king!" A smattering of applause ran through the audience at his words, and Roland nodded and smiled in response. "How proud your father, the old baron, would have been to see it! And such a treat, indeed, for your new bride to see your manly skills on display," he said, turning his benevolent gaze on Eden.

"Quite," she agreed after the tiniest pause. It seemed there was cause for celebration after all, she pondered, hoping she did not look as confused as she felt.

Gunnilde sidled up to her discreetly. "They award a prize to the most skillful fighter on both sides at tonight's banquet," she whispered.

Oh! Well, that made a lot more sense. She cast a grateful look at her friend.

"Will you join us now for some refreshment up at the manor before the Challenge to Arms?" asked Sir Aubron hopefully. "I have some friends and neighbors here this day who would be very happy to converse with the King's champion himself."

"Mayhap later," said Roland absently, reaching out and capturing Eden's hand, drawing her to his side. "I'll take Eden back to our tent for now, while I wash and change." Eden blinked. Why would he expect *her* to return to the tent for that? Then she noticed the Conways hovering close with Sir Christopher.

114

Suddenly the tent seemed preferable to confronting that bunch, so she decided to meekly go along with it, squeezing his fingers in a mute show of support. He lightly returned the pressure and cleared his throat. "We'll take our leave of you for now, Sir Aubron," he said with a nod.

"I'll look for you later, Eden," called Gunnilde above the clamor of well wishes toward Roland.

"Yes," agreed Eden, flashing a quick smile over her shoulder as Roland whisked her from the tent. "And I for you!"

15

Roland cast a sideways glance at his new wife as he strode across the field with her hand firmly in his. She was facing forward, with her nose stuck in the air as always, and even though she had to be taking three strides to his every one, she managed to keep up with him, far too haughty to ask him to slacken his pace. For some reason he could not fathom, it warmed his blood.

He knew not why, and did not care to examine it too closely, but the fact Eden Montmayne was now his made his chest tight and his pulse quicken. She was his. He felt it again, that overwhelming *something* that he'd felt when Oswald had first called Eden his bride. It rushed over him, fair taking his breath away, and he found himself exerting a slight pressure on her fingers.

He'd liked it when she'd squeezed his fingers when old Sir Aubron was talking to him. Making him aware of her presence—not that he needed reminding. His attention had been inexorably drawn to her for the last six months. Since he'd felt her breath mingle with his at that Solstice feast. His feet had been set on this path to her, and now he'd arrived at his destination. *Finally*. It was a good feeling. Almost like coming home.

They arrived at the tent, and he threw open the flap. "Out!" he said without much heat to Bev's squire, who was lolling on one of the benches. The lad scowled but jumped up and made himself scarce. "Boy's bloody useless," Roland murmured, seeing he had not cleared away the remains scattered all over the table from the last meal taken there.

He turned hearing the tent flap open again, but this time it was Cuthbert, carrying a bucket of steaming water for him to wash. Roland took it from him without comment and poured it into the basin. "Help me unbuckle," he directed, pointing to the pauldrons still strapped onto his shoulders. His squire swiftly unfastened the leather bands and Roland stripped to his waist to begin his ablutions.

Cuthbert moved around the tent swiftly, fetching him soap leaves and clean cloths. From the corner of his eye, Roland could see Eden hovering uncertainly. "Sit down," he told her. "I won't be long."

She trailed over to the bench and sat down. "Shall I pour us a drink?" she asked.

He shook the water from his eyes and picked up the soap. "Good idea."

"Ancel's disappeared again," complained Cuthbert, laying out his mail hauberk and hood ready for the morrow.

Roland frowned. Who the fuck was Ancel?

"Roland just dismissed him," explained Eden.

Oh.

"Am I to wait on all three of you then?" asked Cuthbert with irritation. "You know Sir James doesn't have a squire of his own at present."

"Well, you're dismissed for the rest of the day also," Roland growled at him. "Make yourself scarce."

"Really?" Cuthbert's spirits picked up immediately.

"Aye. The others can shift for themselves when they get in." Cuthbert, who didn't need to be told twice, was already halfway

117

across the tent when Roland called after him. "Take some coin with you. There's sure to be entertainments and such."

Cuthbert grinned and made for Roland's saddle bag, where he extracted a couple of coins, whooped, and showed a clean pair of heels.

"You didn't tell him how much to take," commented Eden.

Roland looked up from where he was drying off his neck and shoulders. "No, I didn't," he agreed, throwing down his cloth. He donned his tunic, walked over to the table, grabbed her hand, and pulled her in the direction of the bunks.

16

"Whose bunk is this?" asked Eden, sounding slightly panicked as he pulled her down onto the mattress beside him.

"Mine," he answered huskily, drawing her against him with his hands at her waist. They would not have long before his friends showed up, but he wanted a taste of those lips again.

"But how do you—?"

"I always have the bunk to the right," he interrupted her, anticipating her question.

He lowered his head, but Eden ducked hers. "I surely won't be expected to sleep here though?" she asked, an edge of desperation to her voice.

"Nay," he agreed, running a hand up the back of her neck in a soothing motion. "You'll sleep up at the house." *And so will I,* but he did not feel the need to say that aloud. She was already skittish as a colt. At his words, she slumped in relief, and he took the opportunity to claim her lips, half rolling on top of her.

She squeaked when he licked along her bottom lip, and he slipped his tongue into her mouth. There was no way in hells he should find kissing Eden Montmayne as exciting as this. He wished someone would tell that to his heart, which was pounding almost out of his chest. She made a strangled sound into his mouth, and he slid his hand down between her shoulder blades to her slender waist.

"Kiss me back," he said huskily, tearing his mouth away for an instant. "Give me your mouth." She huffed, and guessing she was about to say something disagreeable, he forestalled her by crushing his lips to hers. He almost groaned when he felt her hesitant hands land on his upper arms in what he guessed was her approximation of an embrace. He broke off again. "Put your arms round my neck, Eden."

"But your—?"

He stopped her words again with his lips, and after a few seconds, she removed her hands and wrapped them tentatively around his neck. Shit. Why did it feel so good? He groaned and felt her gasp beneath him in alarm. He shifted over her, insinuating one leg between hers. Her heavy skirts were in the way, but still, he was breathing heavily through his nose like a godsdamn bull.

It was only supposed to be a taste, he reminded himself, suppressing the impulse to toss up her skirts. That was out of the question, even if he only wanted to feel her legs tangle with his. To comfort himself, he palmed her breast over her dress. Eden was a modest dresser and wore her necklines rather higher than fashion dictated. At his touch she jumped so hard, it startled even him. He drew his head back to look at her quizzically. "What?" he asked.

Eden stared up at him in confusion instead of answering, and her gaze dropped to his mouth. That was invitation enough for Roland. He returned to her pretty lips but was less demanding this time. Ravishing her mouth was just getting him hot and bothered, and he could hardly bed her here, like a camp follower.

When his hand covered her breast again, she whimpered, but did not bridle. He stroked his thumb gently over where he guessed her nipple would be and coaxed her lips teasingly with his. As it was, he was aroused beyond all reason. Mayhap the six months of celibacy that had afflicted him was partly to blame.

For whatever reason, he was at risk of embarrassing himself if he did not calm things down. One thing was clear, he thought, his head reeling as he was overtaken by desire. His instincts had not led him astray at Midwinter. Eden Montmayne was his, and his alone.

Someone coughed behind them. Roland stiffened, turning his head to look over his shoulder. Eden immediately turned as rigid as a board beneath him. His friends Bev and Attley stood gaping at them in astonishment. At the murderous look in his eye, they both fell back, clearing their throats and scratching the backs of their necks.

"Do you want us to try and rig up a curtain as partition?" asked Bev uncertainly as Roland levered himself off his mortified bride. "Only we need to wash and…"

"No," Roland answered shortly. He held his hand out to a scarlet-cheeked Eden, and after a moment's pause, she took it, and he hauled her off the bunk to stand beside him. Strangely enough, his overwhelming impulse was to soothe his affronted wife.

He deliberately stepped in front of her, obscuring her from view as she tugged this way and that at her dress, trying to right herself. He eyed her headdress, which was hanging off to one side at a rakish angle. She picked up his cue, her hands flying to right it.

"Is it on straight?" she muttered, looking uncertain and seeking assurance.

Why the fuck that made his chest squeeze, he had no idea! It was straight, but he reached out anyway to lightly touch her silky hair beneath the beaded band and gauzy scarf. Was this what it was going to be like from now on? Forever looking for excuses to touch her? The thought unnerved him, but at least it

121

served to dampen his ardor sufficiently so that he could turn around and face his friends.

Attley was staring like a fool, but Bev was studiously looking anywhere but at them.

"We're going to watch the Challenge to Arms," Roland said coolly, feeling anything but. He stretched out his hand, but Eden slipped her arm through his more formally. He frowned but bent his arm anyway to accommodate her.

"Mayhap we'll join you later," suggested Bev.

"Aye," Roland agreed readily. "We'll look to see you." He grabbed his doublet off the bench and flung it over his shoulder before leading Eden from the tent.

"I should probably warn you, Sir Christopher Lelland is here," she said haltingly as they made their way back toward the main field.

He turned his head. "Who?"

"He is one of the King's attendants."

"What of it?" asked Roland sharply. Who the devil was this fellow to her?

"Naught, save that he is a courtier," explained Eden with raised brows.

Her words sank in. "Oh." He shrugged. "Well, my brothers will be informing the King as we speak, so it little signifies."

"It appears he has lately married one of Sir Aubron's neighbors," she elaborated.

Roland frowned. On the one hand, Eden was talking to him, which he felt he should encourage. She did not strike him as the naturally voluble type. Indeed, she had been entirely silent for large stretches of their journey there.

On the other hand, he couldn't care less about Sir Aubron's neighbors, or the King's attendants for that matter. He made a noncommittal noise, which he fancied struck the middle ground he required. From the frown on Eden's face, it seemed he had aimed and missed. "Indeed?" he added lamely. Perhaps he should have attempted this polite conversation thing at some point prior to now. He'd never realized he would need such a skill in his arsenal. "What did you think of the melee?" he asked, steering things into safer waters.

A pained expression crossed Eden's face. "It was very difficult to keep track of you," she said. "Amid all the chaos." There it was again. A warm feeling spread through his chest at the idea of her looking for him in the crowd. Since his father died, he had not had anyone watching in his corner. Not family anyway. "I fancy I will find the joust tomorrow easier to stay abreast of," she added awkwardly. "They have an announcer, do they not?"

"Aye," he agreed, covering the hand in the crook of his arm with his. She looked up startled at his touch. "Best you get used to it," he said.

"Tournaments?" asked Eden.

"My touch," he responded, shooting her a wink. She colored up and looked away, biting her lip. He grinned to himself as they crossed the field.

"Are you really not as bothered as you seem?" asked Eden suddenly as they neared the observational benches.

"By what?"

She hesitated. "All the people staring at us," she said at last.

Had they been staring? Roland glanced around at the milling crowds of people. A fair few did look hastily away at his confrontational stare. "Why should I be?" he asked, returning his attention to her. Her gaze skittered away. "Eden?" He wanted those blue eyes trained back on him.

"No reason. I suppose I envy your composure," she said lightly, but he wasn't sure he believed her answer.

"You have no reason to be self-conscious," he found himself telling her as he led her to a vacant bench. "Are not brides usually a source of interest?"

"Brides?" She sounded startled again. "More than half these people will be completely unaware of our marriage!"

He cocked an eye at her. "I wore your badge in the field," he said, reminding her. "I've never worn a lady's favor before."

Eden's expression wavered. "Oh!"

"They may not realize we are wed, but all will know you're my sweetheart."

Her step faltered. "Cuthbert said these rural tournaments are not overmuch attended by wives," she blurted.

"True enough," he agreed, wondering at her blush.

"Well, I hope no one thinks—"

"What?" he asked curiously as she plunked down onto the bench.

"That I'm not respectable!" she huffed, straightening her veil.

He longed to point out that they'd woken up in bed together three days previously, but he already knew Eden was ill used to teasing and likely to react poorly. Managing to hold his tongue, he summoned an attendant over with some drinks.

"Will you have ale or wine?"

"Watered wine, if you please."

After selecting their drinks, he sat beside her, clearing his throat. "Has anyone explained the Challenge to Arms to you?"

"Yes," she said, straightening up. "Is that the tree Gunnilde spoke of?" she asked, raising a hand to shield her eyes against the sun.

Roland looked to the large oak. Shields were hanging from the lowest branches. "Aye, that's the one."

"Do you recognize any of the coats of arms?" she asked, taking a sip of wine.

He glanced back. "The white shield with the black tree is the strongest competitor today," he said after a moment's appraisal. "Sir Jeffree de Crecy."

"If he's so good, why would he not have joined the melee or the joust tomorrow?" asked Eden.

"He may have arrived too late today to make the melee. And the joust is likely oversubscribed already."

"I see."

With irritation Roland noticed approaching figures. Would they not be given a moment's peace together?

Eden clicked her tongue with annoyance. "'Tis Sir Christopher with his wife, Lady Muriel."

The fact Eden was not happy at the interruption either pleased him inordinately. He turned a heavy frown on the interlopers.

125

"Sir Roland," the newcomer hailed him enthusiastically. "Well met!" Roland nodded warily. Now that he saw the fellow, he did vaguely remember seeing him about court. "I believe congratulations are in order," Lelland carried on genially. "I understand you have lately joined our newlywed ranks. May I introduce you to my bride, Lady Muriel." He turned to the insipid-looking woman at his side.

Roland flickered uninterested eyes over her. Muriel Lelland, he noticed, was eyeing Eden nervously. Now what had happened there?

"I do hope you will forgive me for the misunderstanding earlier," she twittered obsequiously. "I—er—I did not realize that you were a fellow courtier of my husband's."

Eden regarded her stonily, her blue eyes suddenly as hard as flint. "I see," she said briefly, and turned back to regarding the shield-covered tree. It was amazing how haughty her features could turn in the mere blink of an eye. Roland was dimly aware he should not find it as entertaining as he did.

Sir Christopher hovered uneasily, his wife looking anguished.

Roland found himself clearing his throat. "You—er—staying for the Challenge to Arms?" he asked.

Sir Christopher cast him a grateful look. "Indeed!" he agreed. "Indeed, we are. My wife knows a couple of the local entrants, is that not so, my dear?"

"Er, yes," said Muriel, who was still regarding Eden with unhappy eyes. "No one of consequence, you understand. Not court folk."

Eden looked up at this and pursed her lips. "Is that your criteria for determining who of your company are important and who are not, Lady Muriel?" she asked caustically.

126

Lady Muriel's eyes flew wide with alarm. "Oh! Well…"

"I'm afraid my wife expressed herself ill," interjected Sir Christopher hastily. "She is very fond of the Payne family. Is that not so, my dear? Indeed, you and Gunnilde Payne were like sisters growing up by all accounts."

"Yes, oh yes!" agreed Muriel. "Quite like sisters!"

"I find that an extraordinary statement," said Eden. "In light of the manner in which you greeted her not three hours ago."

Muriel Lelland's face was scarlet. She opened and closed her mouth without managing to utter a single word.

Roland glanced warily from Eden to Sir Christopher. He had not the faintest notion what was going on, but it seemed this Muriel woman had somehow managed to offend Eden. And it appeared his wife was not the forgiving type.

"Could you possibly intercede for us, Sir Roland?" asked Sir Christopher, wincing. "I'm afraid my wife's behavior has caused yours much offence."

It was on the tip of Roland's tongue to ask what the devil he was expected to do about it, but he managed to squash the ignoble impulse. After all, he was a husband now, so he supposed these sorts of things were bound to occur. Sort of like owning a hound and it attacking someone else's. "Maybe yours should apologize?" he hazarded, stretching out his legs before him.

"She already did," Eden pointed out. "But I am a great subscriber to the notion that actions speak louder than words. Lady Muriel's future behavior toward my friend shall determine whether I accept her apology or no."

A silence greeted her words. Roland found himself uneasily hoping he did not incur his wife's stiff-necked wrath anytime soon. She was making it damned hard for the wretched woman. It didn't help matters that he was entirely confused as to who this friend was that Eden referred to. Was there someone else here from court then? "Ah, here come our hosts now," said Eden mildly. "And your opportunity to redeem yourself, Lady Muriel."

Roland looked up to see Sir Aubron approaching with his family party. Sir Aubron was nodding and smiling and waving at everyone as they took their seats in the center of the front row. Muriel Lelland stood in frozen indecision for a moment, and then walked forward jerkily toward the plump blonde on the outskirts of the group. Roland vaguely remembered her from earlier. He cast a questioning look at Eden, but she was watching with her lips pressed firmly together.

The two young women seemed to be in earnest conversation. Suddenly Muriel put her hands to her face and seemed to be dissolving into tears. The shorter girl crowded in sympathetically and soon had an arm around her, patting her back.

"There, there," said Sir Christopher awkwardly. "All seems well between them, in any event. Would you not say so?" He cast an anxious look in Eden's direction.

Eden stuck her nose in the air. She was not so easily mollified.

"Aye, all seems to have worked itself out," Roland found himself agreeing, catching the gleam of desperation in Sir Christopher's eye.

"Excellent, excellent," murmured Sir Christopher, rubbing his hands together. "I felt sure it would be so."

"I believe," said Eden after a moment's pause, "that there was an understanding between the Conways and the Paynes as to Sir Arthur and Gunnilde eventually marrying. Have you ever heard anything of that nature, Sir Christopher?" she asked, bestowing her first agreeable smile on him.

Sir Christopher blinked and Roland found himself frowning. Why the hells was she giving him her smiles now?

"I—er—that is, no I had not, Lady Eden."

"Perhaps you have not yet had the chance to accustom yourself with your brother-in-law's affairs," she said kindly, but with a trace of reproach that made Sir Christopher wince.

"It's true I have not as yet, as you say, Lady Eden."

She inclined her head graciously, and Roland found himself thinking that his wife would likely grow into one of those very stern matrons who struck fear into the hearts of men. For some godsforsaken reason that did not seem to put him off one damned bit. He must have rocks in his head!

"I will just go and ask my wife to introduce me to the Lady Gunnilde," said Sir Christopher, earning another smile from Eden. It was an approving one this time.

"How long have you known these people?" he asked a little testily as he watched Sir Christopher hurry over to his wife and Gunnilde Payne.

"The Paynes?" She sounded surprised by his question. "Only since my introduction today."

"Then how the devil do you know all about their betrothal arrangements and such?" he demanded belligerently.

"Well, naturally Gunnilde and I had some conversation while we were waiting for you to enter the field."

"Mmm." For some reason he was put out. He had a vague notion it was because she had smiled twice at Sir Christopher and not once at him. But that was damn ridiculous. What did he care for Eden Monmayne's smiles? He stretched out on the bench. Mayhap it was because she was Eden Vawdrey now, and they belonged to him, he thought moodily as he mulled it over.

The sound of horses' hooves and a dull thud roused him from his thoughts to the realization that the first challenge had been issued. Sir Jeffree's shield was rocking from the lance buffet it had received. A cheer went up from the crowd.

"Oh dear," said Eden. "Is that not poor Sir Renlow again?" She turned to Roland. "But I thought he had been taken hostage after the melee."

Roland shifted uneasily in his seat. "Someone must have paid his ransom already." *Damn.*

"Why on earth is he challenging the white shield? Did you not say de Crecy was the best?"

"Because he's a bloody young fool," seethed Roland. "He must have suffered a worse injury than a broken nose yesterday. He must have had his brains scrambled!"

17

Eden gazed around the carousers with disfavor. The afternoon had passed in something of a whirl. Roland had sat beside her explaining who the various knights were in the Challenge to Arms. Not that she could remember any of the finer details, save that poor Sir Renlow had been rendered quite insensible again by Sir Jeffree de Crecy this time. It was evening now, and they were sat in Sir Aubron's banqueting hall. The hostage ransoms had all been paid off, and the trophies awarded. Roland had won the prize for the most valiant member of the yellow side in the melee. Sir Kentigern had won the same accolade from the blue. Without his helmet on, Sir Kentigern somehow looked even more savage. He had the most dreadful scar down the left side of his face and the eye on that side was white as a boiled egg. It had to be blind. Was that why Roland had not struck him when he was dizzy and disorientated? He seemed a sullen and moody figure and stumped off as soon as he had received his winnings and the ransom for the four knights he had knocked from their seats.

Eden snuck another look at the terribly bruised and battered face of Sir Renlow. She had no idea how he could look so cheerful as he supped his ale through a split lip. Both eyes were purple, and his nose was doubtless broken. Yet there he sat. She glanced toward the high table where the Payne family were sat dining on a platform well away from the common herd. She heartily wished she was sat among them rather than the competitors where it was so rowdy. She noticed wryly that Gunnilde and the Lady Elizabeth gazed back rather enviously at her. Really? They'd rather be sat where she was?

The men were mostly drunk, and she suspected that the few women present on their long trestle table were not respectable.

They sat on laps. Eden tried not to look at them. She glanced sidelong at Roland, who had an arm draped along the top of her chair. She felt sure he was testing her in some way. Did he mean to outrage her? To shock her prim sensibilities? She could see his friends darting looks at her every so often in silent appraisal.

"A toast to you, Sir Jeffree," announced Sir Aubron loudly from the dais. "The victor of the Challenge to Arms!"

Sir Jeffree was a rather arrogant-looking male with a short blond beard and very blue eyes. He nodded at the acknowledgment, though it was clear he thought it nothing but his due.

"The victor of the Challenge to Arms!" repeated the table obligingly.

"Hear, hear," cried another.

Eden raised her goblet for the toast, when to her surprise, Roland leaned forward and sipped from her own cup, tipping the bottom, though she held it still in her hand.

"A loving cup!" yelled one reveler, nudging his companion in the ribs. They laughed uproariously, and Eden felt herself flush. She looked up at Roland in reproach. "Why do you drink from mine?" she asked. He shook his head and pointed to his ear as if he could not hear her above the clamor.

When Eden leaned forward to repeat her question, he surprised her by kissing her soundly on the mouth. She squeaked, but it was drowned out by the loud cheer that went up from their table. Eden sucked in a deep breath to let him know what she thought of his antics, but Roland's lips were suddenly at her ear.

"We're newlyweds," he murmured. "'Tis customary to share plate and a cup for at least a month."

"What?" She stared up at him in confusion. "That must be peculiarly customary in this part of the country, as I've never heard of it." She looked to his elbow, and sure enough he had no cup of his own. Had he not been drinking all evening? And if not, why not?

"A toast to the bride!" yelled Sir Aubron, holding his cup aloft. There was a deafening noise as the revelers dragged back their heavy chairs and stood with their goblets aloft. "To the Lady Eden Vawdrey!"

"May she be always warm and willing!" roared one of the uncouth northern lords.

Eden felt herself tensing as the raucous laughter turned to bawdy jests. Roland's arm slipped round her waist and rested there like a heavy, warm anchor. She felt herself relax slightly.

"Shall we to bed?" he muttered against her brow. Eden had been shown the bedchamber she was to use earlier when she had freshened up before the feast. Roland had not joined her then, and she did not know if he meant to join her later.

"Not now," Eden replied tightly. "They'll all think—" She broke off wretchedly.

He squeezed her hip. "Let me know when you've had enough."

"I could retire, and you stay down here with your friends," she pointed out, but he didn't appear to hear. It was very loud at their table, Eden thought despairingly. She didn't like to lean in close to him again, in case he took it as another invitation to kiss her.

Feeling flustered and out of place, Eden clutched at her skirts and hoped her smile wasn't turning too glassy. Roland nodded meaningfully at her cup, and before she'd even thought about it, she was raising it obligingly to his lips.

One of the knights sat to her right chuckled. "Thought you said his wife was a sour-faced scold," he said overloudly to his neighbor. "The lass seems amenable enough to me!"

Eden stared hard at Roland to see if he'd heard it too, but he just wiped his lip on his sleeve and smacked his lips in satisfaction.

The next hour was a very trying one for Eden. The roast meats were brought out, and sure enough, she and Roland were expected to share a plate and *feed* each other. Her cheeks burned, but luckily, everyone seemed to expect a rosy-cheeked bride, so it was not remarked upon.

"'Tis very different from the feasting at court," she answered when Sir Ned Bevan, sat at Roland's left, tried to include her in their conversation.

"A lot livelier," he agreed with an uncertain grin.

Eden could tell Roland's friends were ill at ease in her company, but what could she do? Their society would hardly be her first choice either! She racked her brains for some common ground, but in truth they had none, save Roland. "Have you known one another for many years?" she asked with an air of desperation.

"We were squires together, as youths," Sir Ned told her.

"I see." She glanced at Roland, who seemed content to simply sit back and watch her rather than facilitate the conversation. "You must have had many adventures together, I think," she hazarded.

She watched an uneasy look flit over Sir Ned's good-natured face. "Just boyish scrapes," he assured her with an air of anxiety.

134

Roland rolled his eyes. "She's my wife, Bev, not my aged aunt," he told his friend dryly.

Eden tried to not to react to the casual way Roland was slinging the word *wife* around. He certainly seemed a lot more comfortable with the married terminology than she. Then she found herself worrying Sir Ned thought her too prim and stern to share boyhood tales with. "I am not so far removed from my own youth, I hope," she joked feebly.

After all, she was not yet three and twenty! Truth was that she had been the most obedient and well-behaved child in all Karadok, and had never had a hair out of place, let alone put a foot wrong. She braced herself for Roland to guess as much, but he said nothing. Merely trailed a hand down her side in an absent caress that would normally have had her jumping out of the chair.

He had given her a fair few swallows of wine this evening, though, so she sat there and allowed it. She presumed it was for the benefit of his companions in any case, so it would be a shame to ruin the effect.

Thus encouraged, Sir Ned launched into a lengthy and rambling set of stories involving apple scrumping, fist fights, and youthful feuding which made very little sense to Eden, except to realize that squires at court were a lot less hemmed in than young noblewomen were. A couple of times Ned started a tale and then seemed to collect himself, breaking off to change his mind about telling it to her. Deemed them rather too colorful for her ears, she guessed. At one point, he got distracted by the way Roland was playing with her fingers, his eyes nearly starting from his head.

"Your tales are boring Eden," Roland drawled as Sir Ned lost his train of thought.

"No, no," she said weakly.

"Well, he's boring me," he said, raising her hand to his lips. He kissed her fingers. "Let's go to bed." Sir Ned coughed and averted his eyes as Roland stood abruptly from the table and all eyes swiveled in their direction. Before the first jest had even been uttered, Eden found herself scooped up out of her seat and into his arms. "Bid the company good night, wife," he prompted her.

Eden held up her hand in farewell as he swept her out of the hall to the accompaniment of whistles and catcalls. "Why on earth do grown men behave like that without civilizing company?" she puzzled aloud. Roland didn't bother to answer her, simply scaled the staircase with seemingly little effort. "You can put me down now, you know."

Again, he didn't give any indication of having heard her. Eden tipped her head back to look at him. He crooked a quizzical eyebrow in return. "You're being very high-handed this evening," she told him, wondering why she wasn't more incensed about it.

"Mayhap you should get used to it," he said thoughtfully.

She frowned. "That's not what you said before," she reminded him. "You said we would not disrupt one another's lives overmuch."

"No, you said that," Roland corrected her. "I just didn't argue with you."

"That's commonly taken for agreement," she pointed out as he opened the door to their chamber for the night.

"And I'm not arguing now either," he added mildly. "I've something else entirely in mind."

136

Eden's brow puckered as he shut the door behind them and walked toward the bed. She felt a twinge of apprehension. He laid her down on the bed and gazed down at her a moment. She couldn't fathom the expression in his eyes, which were dark and full of…something. "Can you please lock the door?" she asked in a strangled voice. "I've never relished sleeping in strange places." And if it was bolted, it would likely guard against her sleepwalking again.

He walked back to the door without a murmur and shot the bolt across. Then he crossed to the dresser and performed a perfunctory strip wash. Eden stared up at the ceiling, trying to remind herself that they had, in all likelihood, done this before. Even if she could not remember it, and anyway it was far too late for maidenly nerves. She was glad she'd had some wine now, or she'd probably be tense as a block of wood.

She had realized somewhere along the way that Roland was not going to settle for a marriage in name only. Even she, oblivious as she was to men's foibles, had picked up on the fact he liked to touch her. Indeed, he couldn't seem to stop. Tonight, at first, it had crossed her mind he was doing it to salve her pride, by letting it be seen that they were on terms of supposed intimacy. But after a while that suspicion had faltered.

Roland Vawdrey did not strike her as a good actor or hider of feelings. As mind-boggling a notion as it was, it seemed he was touching and stroking her because he actually wanted to. She swallowed as she heard his footsteps approach the bed. She should get up and wash, but suddenly she felt as heavy as if she were made of stone. The bed dipped as he climbed in but instead of settling on his side, he reached for her immediately.

"I should undress," she muttered as he rolled into her and began kissing her, running his hands up and down her sides.

"Don't trouble yourself," he said thickly. "I want to do it."

137

Eden blinked. "You want to take my clothes off?" she asked uncertainly.

"Gods, yes," he breathed, though he seemed in no hurry, his lips lingering on hers as he placed very soft kisses on her mouth. And not just kisses. He nipped her bottom lip, only gently, but she definitely felt his teeth. When he did it again, she jolted and tried to draw her head back, but suddenly, his tongue darted out and licked along the seam of her mouth, and when she tried to draw a shuddering breath, he did that shocking thing where he slid his tongue right into her mouth!

Eden squirmed under him as he rolled right into her, his heavy body pressing into her and *rubbing* against her. Her head reeled. His hand was in her hair, tugging her head back as he thoroughly ravished her mouth. She heard a strangled groan and wasn't sure who had uttered it. She had a horrible feeling it might have been her!

Her eyes flew open as she felt his hands at her front laces, unfastening her bodice. And not only that, his big warm hands were shaping and kneading her breasts, slipping inside the fabric and gently squeezing and stroking her sensitive skin there. Hurriedly, she closed her eyes again, unable to watch something so indecent! She panted and twisted as he tugged down the fabric to gain greater access.

As he palmed her breasts, she bit her lip and realized she was not trying to escape his groping hands, but actually trying to assist them! What on earth was she doing? Now he had lowered his head and was covering her bosom with soft kisses. Was that even normal? When he added his tongue, she gave a cry that would have embarrassed her if he had not simultaneously robbed her of the ability to think by taking her nipple into his mouth.

Eden gave up. She was not in control of her own body's reactions, let alone his. Collapsing back on the mattress, she simply gave herself up to sensation as he roamed over her with his shocking hands and wicked mouth. Roland Vawdrey was consuming her alive. His appetite was ravenous, but what was her undoing was his consummate tenderness.

He was being so careful with her that it brought a lump to her throat. Why was he being like this? Acting like she was the most delicious and precious morsel that he'd ever tasted? It was bewildering. She couldn't get her whirling thoughts together. Then he backed off a moment, throwing his head back to catch his breath, and his eyes glittered down at her.

Eden tried not to imagine the view he was getting of her, on her back, her breasts spilling out of her unfastened gown, her face red, her chest heaving. Still, she couldn't break eye contact as he reached for her skirts and started hitching the fabric up. Her legs fell apart as his fingers brushed the insides of her thighs, and when she hurriedly tried to correct this, it was too late as his hand was already between her legs, rubbing and fondling her there too, in a manner which shocked her so much, she could barely think straight. "R-Roland!" she gasped, squeezing her eyes shut.

"Yes, Eden," he murmured huskily, his fingers circling her and his thumb pressing against her so intimately that she felt herself violently trembling. Why did everything feel so…*wet* down there?

"W-wait!" she quavered. "Oh! *Oh!*" The last word was a shriek. Suddenly his fingers plunged so deep inside her that she winced at the sensation. *"Ouch!"* It wasn't enough pain to stop her quivering, delicate flesh from luxuriating around the invasive press of his fingers though. She bit her lip and strained against his big fingers as he moved them in such a way that the tremors intensified until pleasure shot through her, jolting her in waves, and she found herself moving against him, desperately seeking more.

He gave it to her, his circling thumb, his fingers deep, drawing out unspeakable gratification from her body until she gave herself completely over to the sensation, her head flung back, and her body taut like a bow. Finally, she collapsed, spent, her chest heaving, and her cheeks wet with tears.

He moved back up her body, and kissing her again on her mouth, gently at first and then with his tongue. He moved his fingers inside her again and Eden whimpered; everything still felt so fluttery down there and sensitive. She winced again as she felt him add another finger.

"Sore?" he asked huskily. She nodded and watched a pained look cross his face. "I don't want to hurt you, Eden." She blinked up at him. His expression was so regretful that she found she believed him.

She tipped her head and felt the oddest inclination. Reaching out, she hesitantly touched his cheek. He turned his face into her hand and kissed her palm. Eden watched with fascination as he closed his eyes briefly, and then opened them again. He shifted over her, urging her thighs apart. Eden's arms fell to her sides. She clutched the bedsheets as he aligned their bodies so they would fit. She felt his male appendage, heavy and bobbing against her stomach, then the tip of it was pressing at her entrance.

Her eyes flew wide with alarm. One of Roland's hands planted on the mattress by her shoulder. The other was still between her legs, guiding himself into her. She tried not to show her discomfort, her alarm as he pushed in. No wonder he'd been worried. His staff was monstrously huge and unwieldy!

140

She wanted to push him away from her but managed to stifle the unwifely impulse. Her eyes watered as he sank slowly into her, inch by painful inch. Feeling his gaze on her face, she tried to make her expression a blank, but could not help but flinch when she felt him lodged deep.

Her depths burned, and she took a deep breath to fortify herself. Surely there could not be much more of this she was supposed to bear? Nature could not be that cruel! Then he groaned deep, as if in pain, and her eyes flew to his face. But it wasn't pain, she realized, for Roland's expression was rapt as if in the throes of some kind of ecstasy.

"You feel so—" he whispered. "I can't stand it—" He shuddered, and she had barely the chance to wonder what he was trying to express when she was shoved back into the mattress, his whole weight crushing into her as he bore down on her, digging his knees into the bed to brace himself against her.

Eden's hands flapped to his sides in alarm as she tried to hang on for dear life. His hips shifted over hers fitfully. Each time he jolted against her, she winced, feeling him deep within her. She could feel his manhood throbbing, and the sensation was so strange it took her mind momentarily off the pain.

"Eden," he muttered thickly. Was she supposed to answer him? She felt scandalized that he should want speech with her when he was doing something so dreadfully intimate. To her discomfort, she realized he was looking directly into her eyes now. She turned her head aside, and to her dismay, he dropped his face into her neck and groaned against her sensitive skin there.

She could feel his every breath as he cursed and moaned and even kissed her there as he thrust again and again. Eden found herself devoutly hoping no one was in the bedchambers on either side, he made so much noise! And the bed was nearly as

141

bad, creaking and squeaking and knocking against the wooden paneling. How long did this act usually take, for heaven's sake?

"Gods, I can't—" he repeated brokenly, raising his head from her neck.

Can't what? thought Eden, gritting her teeth and sinking her nails into his warm skin as he redoubled his efforts to drive her into the mattress. There was simply no dignity to this act of coupling, she thought as he finally bellowed and collapsed against her, his breathing hard and raspy. Eden lay beneath him, stunned. Was this to be her lot in the bedchamber for the next fifty years? It was too much! They were still physically connected, for lord's sake! When did that indignity end? She struggled to catch her breath.

"Am I crushing you?" he asked in a low gravelly voice that unnerved her. Had all that groaning taken its toll on his vocal cords?

"Yes," she answered hastily. "I can scarce draw breath." She still didn't think it was right, engaging in conversation while they were like this.

He huffed out a breath and withdrew, rolling off her. "I'm going to get a cloth. Don't move."

She nodded and he padded across the floorboards, but she closed her legs all the same, wincing at the sensation. Her muscles, too, were sore from having her legs splayed out like that. She tried to pull her skirts down from where they were bunched up around her waist, but she was hopelessly entangled.

In the background she could hear him pouring water into the basin and then swirling a cloth and wringing it out. Seconds later he returned, shoving her skirts aside and urging her legs apart again. Eden gave a muffled sound of objection, but he

142

ignored it, passing the wet cloth between her legs. Was that blood?

She tried to sit up, but he'd already returned to the water bowl, and was washing out the cloth. She gnawed on her lip, hoping he hadn't done her any damage. Unless of course—cogs turned in her head—that had been her virginity. Which would mean they had been innocent of any wrongdoing the night of the betrothal feast.

She cast a look at Roland, but far from looking in any way shocked or conflicted, he was simply now wiping a cloth over his own intimate areas. She hastily averted her eyes and started trying to wriggle out from her half-fastened gown. She had no sooner managed to get the skirts up and over her head than she felt firm hands dragging the sleeves and bodice off her.

Finally, she was left in her shift alone as he draped her gown over the back of a chair. Eden pulled the bedsheets up to her chin. When he returned to the bed, to her consternation, he curled around her, pulling her firmly back against him. Eden tensed as he leaned into her and kissed first her brow and then her cheek.

Thoughts clamored into her head. Why was he kissing her now the act was over with? Was he not angry that they had so needlessly been wed? One of his arms curled around her middle and rested on her stomach. She felt his eyelashes flutter against the back of her neck. Gradually, it dawned on her that far from lying in the dark feeling wronged and betrayed, Roland Vawdrey was instead soundly dozing off to sleep!

18

The next morning, Eden woke as she heard someone fumbling with the door latch. She hurriedly rolled away from Roland's body and made haste to fling the door open to the maidservant who was carrying two pitchers of hot water.

"Your pardon, miss," said the girl, who was craning her neck to look over Eden's shoulder into the room behind her. "I didn't mean to wake you. Just to slip in like, but your door was locked." She fixed a vaguely accusing look at Eden.

"Yes, that's right," said Eden briskly. She found herself stepping directly into the wretched girl's line of vision, obscuring her view of Roland's sleeping form. "Let me have the water and I'll spare you the task."

The maid shot her a resentful look as she passed the jugs over. Eden shouldered the door shut in her face and carried them over to the washstand. Why anyone would want to stare at Roland Vawdrey was beyond her. Especially when he was not dressed and fast asleep!

She poured one jug of hot water into the basin and only then permitted herself to glance over her shoulder at her sleeping husband. He lay on his side, the blankets covering him from the waist down. That still left his impressively muscled chest and arms on display. Eden's eyes roamed over him distractedly.

His chest was covered in a fine smattering of dark hair, and she remembered how it had felt against her own skin the night before, her face growing warm. Then, too, there had been his warm, hard body. Hurriedly she turned away, biting her lip. He had been a horrid, rampaging beast, she told herself sternly. But, she thought, plunging her hands into the warm water, he had also shown himself quite caring and concerned for her well-being.

Eden grabbed for the soap flakes that had been set out for her use and rubbed them between her fingers. He could easily have slouched back down to the tent he shared with his friends after having his way, she thought. And quaffed a few tankards of ale. He had scarcely drunk anything at the feast, save what sips he'd had from her own cup.

She washed her face and shook the droplets away before pressing a cloth to her damp skin. But she would have preferred it, if he had left her to sleep soundly by herself? her inner voice persisted. "Liar," Eden surprised herself by whispering soundlessly. She would have felt wretched, indeed, if he'd slunk away and left her. There had been something oddly comforting about his solid presence next to hers in the darkness, his hand at her hip.

Not that she'd enjoyed having a bedfellow precisely. Far from it! But still, it could have been a lot worse. If he'd been a crude, drunken sot, for instance. Her hand froze in the act of replacing the cloth on the stand. Was that why he had not overimbibed?

The thought of Roland Vawdrey being a considerate bridegroom was such a strange one that she had to flick a quick glance over her shoulder to check he still slept on. Her stomach fluttered strangely as she regarded him. In all good conscience, he had been solicitous of her for a good deal of yesterday, she thought slowly. But marital relations gave no quarter when it came to dignity.

Her cheeks burned as her mind dwelled on the things Roland Vawdrey had done to her the previous night. She had never dreamed the marriage bed would be so... Words failed her. Swiftly, she drew down her shift and rubbed the wet, soapy cloth over her neck, bosom and shoulders. To her surprise, as

145

she rinsed and patted herself dry, she noticed reflected in the mirrored glass a red rash spread right across her décolletage.

It went right across the tops of her breasts and down the valley between them, marring her pale skin. What was that? Surely Roland's tongue could not have wrought such an effect, she puzzled. It had not been raspy like a cat's! Hearing him stir in bed behind her, she hurriedly pulled the neckline of her shift up and rinsed out the cloth.

She wanted to wash below her waist too and wondered if she might be permitted a bath. She still felt stiff and a little sore this morning. She turned back to the bed reluctantly, sure that he would now be awake.

Sure enough, Roland's eyes were open and focused on her blearily. "Come back to bed," he grouched. "It's too damn early."

"I'm an early riser," Eden said, clearing her throat. "Besides, I'd like a bath." To her annoyance, she blushed hotly. Roland eyed her a moment in silence. Then to her surprise, he rolled out of the bed entirely naked. Eden hastily spun around. He made no comment at her prudishness, but instead pulled on his braies and walked barefoot across the room before disappearing out of the doorway.

Eden bit her lip. Why did she feel vexed that whatever servant he happened across would see her husband's half-naked body? Shaking her head to dispel her strange thoughts, she seized Roland's comb and started on the snarls and tangles in her hair. Once that was dealt with, she stole one of the blankets from the bed to wrap around her shoulders like a stole.

The sun was already shining in a clear blue sky, but there was a chill to the morning air, and her thin shift did little to ward it off. Besides, she felt highly immodest clad in such a transparent garment in front of Roland.

He was back in a few moments, shutting the door behind him. "The bath will be along presently," he said, then something seemed to catch his eye.

Eden looked down, following the direction of his gaze. The blanket had slipped slightly but was not indecently low.

"Come here, Eden," he said. When she looked up, he crooked a finger at her.

A quizzical look on her face, she crossed the floor to close the gap between them, and he gently drew the blanket aside. Eden's eyes shot to his, but he was looking down ruefully at her cleavage.

"How far down does that extend?" he asked softly.

"What?"

"The redness?"

"Oh, that. Just"—she gestured to the top of her ribs—"to about here."

"I shall have to have a care of you in future," he murmured. At Eden's quizzical look, he took her hand and placed it against the bristle on his jaw and rubbed it.

"Ohhh!" she exclaimed as enlightenment dawned. The rash had been caused by his stubble. Her face heated to think of him kissing her in all those tender places.

He cleared his throat and released her hand. "I'll shave," he said shortly.

"Let me just empty the basin," said Eden practically. Her fingers were still tingling from where she'd touched his face. She wanted something practical to do to shake off this strange feeling. "There's fresh water for you."

By the time Roland was shaving, the servants had arrived with the tub and several pails of steaming hot water. They set it in front of the fireplace and emptied the buckets into it until it was half-full.

"Thank you," said Eden, reaching into the water to feel it nice and warm. They duly filed out, and Eden waited patiently as Roland dragged the razor down his soaped face.

Becoming aware of her still figure, he turned with a frown. "What are you waiting for? The water will get cold. Hop in."

Eden's jaw dropped. Surely, he jested? "I thought… That is, are you not almost ready to go below stairs?"

Roland looked down speakingly at his undressed body. He still wore only his braies and an undershirt. "No," he said firmly, turning his back to her. "Get in the tub, Eden."

She spluttered, but realizing he was ignoring her, felt she had no choice. He was right, the water would quickly become lukewarm. She hovered a moment in frozen indecision. She would have liked to climb in with her shift still on. She could easily have washed in it, but for the fact she did not have a clean one to put on for the day ahead. This meant she could hardly get it soaking wet.

Biting her lip, she drew it quickly over her head and stepped into the tub, sinking down into the water. It only came up as far as her waist, so she drew her knees up for decency's sake, obscuring the view of her top half.

"Do you have soap?" Roland asked lazily as he lowered his straight razor.

Eden gazed around wildly before closing her eyes briefly in vexation. "No," she said tensely.

"What about a cloth?"

Eden tutted. In her anxiety about her nakedness, she had not thought about the bathing necessities. "Neither," she admitted, watching the back of Roland's head. Seemingly in no great hurry, he wiped the suds from his face before collecting a clean cloth and some soap leaves from the side.

Eden drew her knees up until they pressed against her breasts as he approached, holding out the items for her to take. "Thank you," she said in a stifled voice, and he nodded before returning to his own ablutions. She released a breath she hadn't realized she was holding.

Roland whipped his shirt over his head and began running a washcloth over his body. With a gulp, Eden returned to the business of her own bath. Silence fell over the room, except for the gentle lap of the water against the side of the tub and random splashes of water as they washed.

A knock on the door made Eden squeak and shrink back against the side of the tub, her hands over her breasts. Roland crossed to the door and opened it just a crack. Eden heard a low murmur of voices. Then Roland opened the door a little further and took a bundle from whoever was in the corridor. "Wait a moment," she heard him say. Then he dumped the bundle on the bed and started gathering up Eden's clothing.

"What are you doing?" Eden asked sharply.

"Lady Payne has sent you a clean set of clothes. Her maid will wash yours."

"Oh, that is kind of her," said Eden, taken aback. Mayhap she had misjudged the youthful Lady Payne. "Pray, thank her for me," she called after him as he carried her things to the servant waiting at the door. He muttered some words of thanks and shut the door with his foot before crossing the room to dress.

"You must be turning wrinkled in that water," he commented, his back to her as he pulled on a tunic.

Eden cleared her throat. "I am almost ready to emerge," she agreed, sounding far too formal even to her own ears.

"Waiting for me to go below stairs? You'll have to get used to me being around, wife." Despite his words, he turned around and grabbed her a large drying cloth. He approached the tub with it and Eden drew up her knees again for modesty's sake, reaching up her arms to take it. He handed it over, but stood looking down at her a moment in consideration.

Eden clutched the cloth to her chest. "What is it?" she asked in strangled tones.

"Naught. Just"—his mouth twisted—"if someone had told me four days ago that I would have Eden Montmayne wet and naked in my bedchamber…" His words trailed off a moment as he eyed her. "I would scarce have believed them."

Eden stared at him. "Well," she said weakly. "It's a good thing we know not what the fates have in store for us, I suppose." He made no comment, his eyes roaming over the parts of her that were on view, and sudden realization washed over her that Roland Vawdrey, at this precise moment, would like nothing better than to lift her out of the tub and have his wicked way with her. *Again.*

The knowledge flooded her cheeks with color and made her shrink back as far as possible into the water. How could he want

150

to repeat such an indignity in broad daylight? She gazed back at him, frankly appalled. She had only just got clean!

Abruptly, he turned away, and Eden let out a sigh of relief. "I'm going to break my fast," he said shortly. "The jousting's today. I'll look to find you with the Paynes."

Eden watched Roland let himself out of the room and finally relaxed. While she was used to sharing a royal apartment with her family, most of the time it was just herself and her cousin as her uncle divided his time between Hallam Hall and court.

Eden had not shared a bedchamber since she was a child and was accustomed to spending a good deal of her time alone, either reading or practicing her music or dance. Nothing had prepared her for these intimacies, let alone the manner of man she had somehow thrown her lot in with.

She stood up from the bath and wrapped the cloth about herself. Her hair was damp, but she had washed out the soap and would pat it dry once she had donned her nice clean shift. Padding over to the bed, she unrolled the bundle and felt her first pang of misgiving.

The dress that Lady Payne had sent along was all wrong for her. It was an icy blue of a very eye-catching nature. The material was very silky and gossamer fine. Had she sent Eden her best dress? Eden shook it out and noticed the low neckline with the puffed sleeves and fussy trim detail that looked like garlands of flowers. She blanched. She had never worn such a dress in her life!

Biting her lip, she debated sending for a servant to return it and asking for a plainer one. She knew that would be a gross insult to her hosts. Thrusting the dress away from her, she picked up instead the shift, and realized that she had not been mistaken. Lady Payne had sent along her very finest clothing.

151

This shift was fit for a queen and would have cost Sir Payne a pretty penny. With a sinking heart, Eden drew it over her head and then donned the fine white stockings and scarlet garters. Still avoiding the dress, she wrapped the drying cloth about her damp tresses, patting them dry.

A light knock on the door surprised her. "Who is it?"

"'Tis Martha," came the reply. "Lady Payne sent me to help lace you into your gown."

Eden sighed. "Come in, Martha."

The maid bustled in with an air of efficiency. "There now," she said. "You're half-dressed already! I had no idea fine court ladies could dress themselves."

"I'm not royalty, Martha," Eden said mildly. "I just attend the Queen."

But Martha was already making for the bed where the dress lay. "Well now!" she exclaimed in surprise. "I never!"

Eden looked up from detangling her damp hair. "What is it, Martha?"

"My lady only went and sent you the dress she was married in!"

Eden blinked. That would explain the sumptuousness of the gown.

"Mind you, I daresay she couldn't fit in it now," said Martha, sucking in her cheeks. "She's put on some flesh since she was wed. I daresay she thought it would be as well to get some more wear out of it. Her father paid a fortune for her wedding trousseau."

"Well, it's extremely generous of her," said Eden. "Though I fear it will become me most ill. I don't suppose the Lady Payne has any black gowns…?"

"You're a bride," said Martha firmly. "It is most fitting you should wear it."

Eden gave up. Instead, she cast aside the drying cloth and straightened up. "Very well then."

"And you're as slender as a faery maiden," said Martha approvingly. "We'll soon have this on you."

Eden grimaced as she stepped into the confection that was her outfit for the day. Martha maneuvered the full skirts and fussy sleeves until she was surrounded by it.

"Oh yes," said Martha with satisfaction. "We won't have to force *you* into this bodice!" She pulled it around Eden's waist and ribs and began on the lacing at the back. "My poor lady couldn't eat a morsel all day."

Eden thought of Lady Payne's voluptuous figure and thought she must have looked a good deal more alluring in it than she. She glanced down and was surprised to see a lot more of her breasts on display than usual. "Um, Martha…" she started.

"Just a minute, my lady," said Martha, who was tying the laces. "I'll be with you presently. Just let me secure this. We don't want your dress falling off you in mixed company."

"No indeed," agreed Eden fervently. "But I'm a little worried that it's gaping at the front."

Martha moved around to her front. "Where?" she said. "It's supposed to be like that…" Then her eye seemed to catch something, and she placed a finger to her lips.

153

Eden looked down and realized the servant must have noticed the unsightly rash. "What can I do?" she asked despairingly.

"Never fear," said Martha. "I shall fetch you some rosehip oil. 'Twill soon soothe it."

"Really?"

"Don't move a muscle." She hurried out of the door and Eden crossed to the small, mirrored glass, trying to crouch down to view the offending area. There was far too much of it on display. And it was still blotchy and pink. Eden groaned. The low neckline was not scooped, but began from her half-exposed shoulders, so it wasn't like she could try to add in a modesty panel of some kind. She turned this way and that trying to catch a glimpse of what the wretched dress looked like on her, but the small rectangle of glass did not allow much of a view.

The door opened again, and Martha held up a small glass vial. "I have it," she said. "This will soon calm your sensitive skin. You apply it while I arrange your hair," she suggested, and Eden sat on a low stool.

"As a bride, it might be nice to wear it loose?" suggested Martha, running the comb through Eden's black hair.

"Certainly not," said Eden firmly. "I was married some four days ago now."

"Wedding feasts are known to go on as a long as a sennight," the maid pointed out.

"Not mine," retorted Eden, her cheeks pinkening as she remembered the hurried ceremony followed by the subsequent flight of disgrace from Hallam Hall. She shivered slightly.

"It's nice and sunny outside," Martha assured her. "A fine day for it."

154

Eden looked down and started rubbing the oil into the pink rash across her chest. "How soon before it starts to work?" she asked.

"Depends," admitted Martha with a shrug, her quick fingers braiding a coronet in Eden's hair. "It's different on different folks. But my sister, she swears by it. Her Jed has a great stubbly chin, wreaks havoc on her skin, it does."

Eden's face turned redder as she realized Martha knew the cause of her rash. "I see. Thank you, Martha."

"You can keep it," the maid continued as Eden set the small bottle down. "Unless he grows his beard out longer, it'll likely happen again."

"He said he'll have a care in future," Eden rejoined without thinking.

"Did he, by gods?" Martha sounded impressed. "Well, that's gentlemanly of him. But I'd take it all the same, if I was you. They have these intentions, the menfolk," she said complacently. "But then the mood takes 'em and they're more beast than man."

Eden felt her face must be glowing like a beacon by now. "Thank you, Martha, you may be right," she said in a stifled voice.

"You'm very welcome, my lady."

19

Fortunately, Gunnilde Payne was hovering at the foot of the stairs waiting for her.

"Oh, don't you look pretty!" her new friend cried, clapping her hands together with delight.

"I feel rather uncomfortable out of my customary black," Eden confessed in an undertone. "Are you sure I don't look a sight?"

"Oh, quite sure!" responded Gunnilde with admiration. "If I looked like that, I would expire of happiness on the spot! You look like a faery princess!"

Eden was a little taken aback at such effusive praise. "That is very kind of you to say," she ventured uncertainly. A faery princess? She glanced at Gunnilde's happy face wreathed in smiles, and noted, not for the first time, that her friend was a little fanciful.

"Shall you take a little something to break your fast now?" her friend asked, gesturing toward the main hall where even now Eden could hear the murmur of conversation and the clatter of plates and cups.

She shook her head. "I'm not at all hungry."

"There will be pastries and such brought out in an hour or so, in any case," Gunnilde said reassuringly, and Eden linked her arm through hers. "Shall we go forth?"

"Let us." They proceeded at a leisurely pace down to the far field where the spectators were filing into the benches.

"Hie!" shouted a familiar voice. It was Hal Payne. He waved his arm vigorously. "I've saved you seats!" And good seats they were too, roughly in the same spot as the previous day. They joined him, and Eden sat between the two Payne siblings as before. Hal twisted in his seat and looked at her curiously. "You look different today," he said finally, blushing and scratching his ear.

"It is naught but my borrowed finery," Eden replied firmly.

"And your hair," said Hal, glancing up again, but not quite meeting her eye.

Eden self-consciously patted her hair. Despite the fact she'd told Martha she did not want to wear it loose, the maid had taken up only the front and sides of her hair and plaited it into a braided coronet. The rest of her hair hung down almost to her waist, and instead of being covered by a serviceable veil, she wore a short, frippery piece of gauze pinned below her braided crown. It fluttered ineffectually, concealing nothing, but rather, Eden thought, drawing attention to her locks. "Yes, I suppose," she conceded. How funny, she thought. She had never dressed as a marriageable maiden until she was neither a maiden, nor marriageable.

"Have they announced the order of the jousting?" asked Gunnilde, leaning forward.

Hal nodded. "The first pair is Kentigern and de Bussell, followed by Vawdrey and Linley, followed by Bevan and Renlow."

"Sir Renlow?" said Eden startled. "Surely not! How much more damage can that young man sustain?"

Hal grinned. "We'll soon find out."

Eden pressed her lips together with disapproval. "It ought not to be permitted."

157

"Oh, but…" Gunnilde broke off, looking embarrassed. "Your pardon, but I thought he was quite your husband's protégé?"

"Roland's?" asked Eden in surprise. "What gave you that impression?"

"Oh! 'Tis only…" Gunnilde fidgeted in her seat.

"She's been listening to gossip," said Hal. "Depend upon it. She always gets that look on her face when she has."

"Hal!" his sister exclaimed reproachfully.

"What gossip?" asked Eden, curious despite herself.

"Well, my father's steward told me—"

"Henderson?" interrupted Hal.

"We only have one steward!" his sister pointed out in exasperation. Hal shrugged.

"Yes?" prompted Eden, placing a restraining hand on Hal's forearm. He seemed to be deriving great pleasure from tormenting his sister. He fell still at once.

"Well, Henderson told me that Sir Roland paid Sir Renlow's ransom, after the melee, so that he was free to join the banquet from the outset and did not have to sit with all the other captive knights."

"Oh." Eden recalled Roland's frustration when Sir Renlow had ridden up to the Challenge at Arms the next morning. That must have been why. He had perhaps wanted Renlow to rest up and not fling himself straight back into combat, she reasoned, sitting back in her seat.

"Why Hal!" said Gunnilde suddenly. "Your face is as red as a beet! You must have had too much sun yesterday."

20

Roland knocked down his visor and Bavol danced beneath him. "Easy boy," he cautioned. Was his horse picking up on his own distraction? he wondered. His mind had been otherwise preoccupied since he'd left his wife in her bath that morning. Of course, he knew he owed her some consideration after taking her maidenhead the night before, but still, it had gone against the grain, leaving her like that.

He scowled behind his helmet. He had thus far resisted looking for Eden in the crowd. Only now, he allowed himself a quick scan of the sea of faces. She would be sat near the front, with the Paynes, he thought, his eyes seeking her out. And then he spotted her. Or was it her? He did a double take. It looked…rather like her, but then again, it also did not.

Bavol whinnied, but he ignored him, staring at this female in the pale blue dress, with her eyes of sapphire and her black hair loose. She turned her head, listening intently to that yellow-haired son of his host. A bolt of pure jealousy shot through Roland, winding him. Why the fuck was her hand resting on his arm with such familiarity?

Bavol jolted and struck a hoof against the ground. Roland leaned down to pat his neck. "Easy now." Soothing his horse was the last thing he felt like doing, and in all honesty, he knew he was not doing a good job of it. Not when he was feeling so disordered.

With a start, he realized what it was that was bothering him. This Eden he could see now in the crowd was not wearing her customary drab disguise. This Eden looked like the same Eden he had woken up in bed with five days ago. And now everyone could see her. He swore, and Bavol skittered sideways in the enclosure, throwing back his head.

"What ails him today?" yelled Cuthbert, jumping back a few paces to a safe distance.

"It's not his fault," said Roland grimly. It was his. The horse was picking up on his own inner turmoil. He needed to rein them both in if this morning's jousting was not to be a complete disaster.

*

Five minutes later, it was all over. Roland was rolling in the dust, and Bavol had bolted to the far side of the field. He groaned. Everything, but everything, had felt off this morning. From the balance of the lance in his hand, to the direction of the sun in his eyes. Kentigern was not the opponent to face when you were not on your best form. He tentatively flexed his limbs as he rolled to a seated position. Nothing felt broken in any event. The thud of footfalls heralded Cuthbert's approach. "Go after Bavol," he directed him.

His squire showed him a clean pair of heels, disappearing after the steed. Roland lifted off his helmet, shaking his head to clear it. Two servants appeared to help him to his feet. He let them haul him to his feet and staggered a little before shrugging them off to walk unaided from the area.

He was stiff and his ribs hurt, but that would hopefully wear off as he kept moving. The impact had dented his armor but did not look to have pierced it. Breathing hurt, but with a bit of luck, his ribs were bruised rather than broken. He grimaced as other knights slapped him on the shoulder, commiserating him.

160

"I'd beat that horse if I were you, Vawdrey," recommended one.

Roland ignored him, heading for the physician's tent.

James Attley fell in beside him. "What the hells happened?" he demanded.

"Wasn't my day," answered Roland shortly.

"I'll say! Never seen you go out in the first round before!"

Roland bit his tongue rather than point out his draw had been against the mighty Kentigern. Attempting to justify his poor performance was beneath him. At least he hadn't lost to some nonentity. He'd have been capable of even that today!

"You're going to have a devil of a job getting that armor off," predicted Attley.

Roland glanced down at the battered suit. "Very likely," he growled. Sensing he did not feel much like conversing, Attley took off when they reached the tent promising to go and check on Bavol. "Send Cuthbert to attend me here, if you see him," Roland shouted after him.

The physician tsked and tutted and had to call in two fellows to help remove the armor, a painful proceeding which had Roland gritting his teeth.

*

The business with his armor and the physician took a lot longer than Roland had anticipated. He limped back to the tent he shared with Attley and Bevan to wash and change. Cuthbert

161

caught up with him there and assured him all was well with Bavol. Roland went along to check for himself anyway, and spent some time reassuring his spooked horse.

It was while he was there that one of the squires ran in excitedly. "It's all over!" he shouted. "They've been tumbling off this morn like I've never seen before! It won't even go to a third round!"

Roland looked up in surprise. "Who won?" he called.

"Lord Kentigern, that's who!"

Roland grimaced. It ought to be a consolation that he had lost to the eventual winner, but somehow it was not. Damn his eyes. He emerged from Bavol's stall box and decided on impulse that he may as well start packing up. He'd be damned if he'd sit through another night's feasting, toasting to that bastard Kentigern's victory!

He was rolling up clothing when Bevan and Attley strolled into the tent some half an hour later. He'd already secured his armor into a pack, although the breastplate did not look salvageable. Both his friends broke off abruptly from their conversation when they spotted Roland and looked extremely awkward.

"What is it?" he asked, looking up at them and narrowing his gaze. Attley coughed and scratched his neck.

"Naught's amiss," said Bev hastily. "We were just discussing Kentigern's choice of tournament queen, that's all." Bev reddened, and Roland felt himself turn cold.

"He didn't," he said in an ominously quiet voice. "Tell me he didn't."

"Now, now, it's not as bad as you're thinking," protested Attley, throwing up his hands.

"Did he give the crown to my wife?" barked out Roland.

"Well…yes," admitted Attley, "but—"

"Now, Roly, don't for the lord's sake go flinging off in a temper!" appealed Bev, but it was too late. Roland had already bolted from the tent, muttering foul oaths and dire punishments.

The pain from his ribs shot through him like short knife blades being plunged into his sides as he hurried across the field. He locked the pain into another place, small and dark, as his temper overrode all, pushing him forward. By the time he reached the tournament arena, the spectators were out of their seats and milling around, taking refreshment.

Roland scanned the crowd for the ice-blue, slender figure of his wife, and located her stood next to the dumpy little Payne girl at the far end of the crowd with her back to him. He strode toward her, people hastily falling away as they caught sight of his thunderous expression.

Her friend saw him before Eden. She turned a little pale, her animated conversation breaking off. Eden only appeared to notice her riveted gaze directed over her shoulder at the same time as he grabbed her elbow and swung her round.

"Ah, there you are," said Eden. "I was starting to worry you might have been injured."

Roland gave a short mirthless laugh. He was just about to launch into a blistering tirade at her behavior, when he caught sight of the flower garland sat squarely upon the Payne girl, and not Eden's head.

He opened and closed his mouth and shot a suspicious glance at Eden's composed face. Had he misunderstood? But no, his friends had definitely said that Eden had received the honor. As he looked from one to the other, Gunnilde reached up to touch the garland perched atop her hair.

"I can scarce believe you awarded it to me," she said dreamily, and Eden smiled back at her.

"You were by far the most deserving," she said, and shot a challenging look Roland's way.

"And how is it, wife," he asked, rallying, "that you were in a position to bestow such a favor on Miss Payne?"

Eden fixed a cool look on him with her deep blue eyes. "Lord Kentigern's choice fell inappropriately," she said with a shrug. "So I simply reassigned it."

Her effrontery almost took his breath away! "It is no mere maid's place to award such a prize," he retorted.

Eden's eyebrows rose. "As you well know," she responded, "I am no maid. Not anymore."

Roland felt the tops of his ears turn scarlet. Though why her words should put *him* to the blush he had no bloody notion! "It's a knight's honor to bestow," he bit out doggedly.

"You would have preferred it then," she answered, "if I had accepted Lord Kentigern's gesture? Curious! I had an idea you would not care for it. I shall be sure to bear that in mind, should it occur again."

Roland stared at her in helpless indignation. His chest heaved. She was tying him in knots. Was she doing it deliberately? "Did he place it on your head?" he ground out, unable to stop himself.

"No, he did not," she replied crisply. "He tipped his lance toward me. The garland fell into my lap, and I promptly placed it at Gunnilde's brow. That is all."

The gods alone knew why, but that did appease him a little. He tore his eyes from Eden's infuriatingly calm face to look at the Payne girl again. She was watching them both anxiously.

"If Sir Roland thinks I should give it back—?" she started.

"No—" he began, only to be cut off by Eden's firm "Nonsense!"

Gunnilde looked extremely relieved. "Oh good." She beamed. "For it is quite the most exciting thing to have ever happened to me!"

It seemed to Roland that the fact it had been given to her by another woman did not lessen the distinction for her in any way. He turned to his wife. "We're leaving," he told Eden abruptly.

"Leaving?" she repeated.

"Now," he clarified.

She stared at him. "Why?"

"You vastly overestimate yourself, wife," he told her bitingly. "Your place is where I say it is. No more, no less. You are merely required to obey my will."

Eden stiffened, then turned back to her friend. "I must have some speech with your family before I leave." She glanced down. "Your stepmother's dress—"

"Oh, do not trouble yourself on account of the gown," Gunnilde assured her, glancing nervously at Roland. "For it does not even fit her anymore. I am sure she will be happy for you to return it to her when 'tis convenient." Eden pursed her lips and looked as if she might argue, but Roland turned on his heel, refusing to wait. "Go now," he heard her friend urge her. "And I will let Father know directly that you are departing."

165

He did not hear Eden's reply, but only her hurried footfalls after him. He just knew somehow that her nose would be in the air— stubborn wench!

Once they got back to the room, he wasted no time in slamming trunks and throwing his things into his bag. Eden, of course, had nothing to pack, but busied herself tidying her appearance. He could feel her eyes on him as he fastened the ties, and almost forbade her to even speak. He already knew whatever she said was going to infuriate him. Sure enough, it was not long before she spoke up.

"I didn't even wear that garland, why are you so out of reason cross about it?" she started patronizingly. "Lord Kentigern likely did it as a courtesy to you, or perhaps because I am lately a bride…" Her reasonable tone was like a red rag to a bull.

"You know nothing about it, Eden," he said angrily. "He did it to rile me and for no other reason than that, so don't fool yourself!"

Eden stood very still a moment. "I did not flatter myself it was because I was the most beauteous there," she said in an ominously quiet voice. "So, you need not worry I have any illusions on that score."

"That's not what I meant, and you know it!" he snapped, and she turned her back on him.

They were packed to leave within twenty minutes and neither of them spoke a word until they descended the stairs and were bade farewell by the Paynes. Sir Aubron was disappointed, but not surprised by their impending departure. "Too bad m'boy, too bad," he tutted. "But we will remember for many a long day the magnificent way you unhorsed him in the melee yesterday. Is that not so, my son?"

166

He turned for confirmation from his son and heir, but instead of standing worshipfully by to speak to the King's champion, young Hal was bent over Eden's hand. Roland regarded the brazen youngling with a jaundiced eye. Hal's cheeks were flushed, and he lingered a few heartbeats too long before relinquishing her hand.

"Young puppy!" snorted his father. "Growing up too fast," he sighed.

Roland struggled a few moments with this. "You should squire him out," he retorted. "That would soon knock some sense into him." *And see to the boy's puppy fat*, he thought. Every time he looked at him, he was either fawning over Eden or some sticky treat.

"There may be something in what you say," murmured Sir Aubron. "But I'd miss the lad, sending him off to Wymer's court."

"It'd be the making of him," said Roland callously. "You should give it some thought."

"I will, my boy. I suppose you're—er—quite happy with your own squire?"

Roland's jaw ticked. Cuthbert was an impudent knave, but at least he had shown no propensity to hang after his wife. "Quite happy," Roland lied. "You could do worse than speak to Attley," he suggested grudgingly. "He's currently without squire."

Sir Aubron looked thoughtful. "Sir James," he said, nodding slowly. "I knew his father."

Roland shot a look over at Eden, who was now embracing Payne's daughter, who was crying copious tears and hanging about her neck.

167

"Of course I will write. We will maintain a correspondence and you must come to court," Eden was saying soothingly. "I shall speak to the Queen."

So, the wench could be placating when she chose to, thought Roland bitterly. Just not to him! "Eden," he said sharply.

Lady Payne and Gunnilde were now babbling excitedly at the idea of a court visit.

Eden looked over. "I am ready," she said coolly. "Lady Payne has kindly made me a gift of her gown."

Roland nodded toward Lady Payne, who now only had eyes for Eden.

"A royal visit," she twittered. "Auby, what say you to that? We will need new gowns of course!"

Sir Aubron turned a vaguely reproachful look on Roland. He shook his head. "There will be no peace to be had now," he sighed. "Until we have journeyed to Caer-Lyoness." Roland grunted. "Ah well, such is the lot of us married men," said Sir Aubron with resignation. "You must take the rough with the smooth, eh?" He nudged Roland with his shoulder and gave a short laugh. "Good journey, my lad. Good journey, my lady."

"Thank you for your most kind hospitality," said Eden politely. "You have been exceptional hosts."

You really couldn't fault her manners, thought Roland. Except, for some reason she chose to give him the sharp side of her tongue! *Court.* He had no great desire to return there with all its damn gossips and troublemakers. He had half a mind to take her to Vawdrey Keep instead.

There at least they would be walled up together and she could not avoid him, running off to the Queen and her damned poetry readings! Then he remembered his brother's letter. What was it Oswald had written to him? He had suggested something about delaying their return until he had been given a chance to smooth their path with the King and Queen.

"I would not hurry to Caer-Lyoness if I were you," he said aloud. "For we go now to my place, Vawdrey Keep, for a month, and will not return to court until August at the very least."

Eden's head turned sharply, but she said nothing.

"Oh, but that will be ideal and give us chance to plan," carried on Lady Payne, quite unperturbed.

21

Eden had preserved a stony silence for over an hour. They were riding easterly and would not arrive in Vawdrey Keep for at least a day and a half. The worse thing was, he knew he was being a moody, unreasonable prick.

He was angry at losing the jousting, his best event, in front of her. He was furious at that bastard Kentigern. Hal Payne had been nothing but an irritant, but in the moment, he could not be rational. He was experiencing something he had never even come across before.

He, Roland Vawdrey, the King's champion, was being eaten alive by jealousy. And it didn't even matter that it made no earthly sense. Impulsively he tugged on his reins and let Bavol drop back. "You take the lead," he muttered to Cuthbert. The lad nodded and urged his horse to the front.

"Let's have it then," he said tersely to Eden as he drew level with her. "You do not approve of the plan to proceed to my estate?" He crooked an eyebrow at her.

She regarded him haughtily. "I am surprised you have been able to draw any such a conclusion, as my opinion was not consulted in any way."

"I'd have to be blind not to, the way you've been carrying on," he said dryly.

"Carrying on?" repeated Eden icily. "I fail entirely to catch your meaning, Sir Roland."

Sir Roland? He pulled a face. "I mean," he said with deliberation, "the way you've been sat on your horse like a marble effigy." If she could have sat up any straighter, Roland was sure she would have, but she was already ramrod straight. Gods, she was a proud piece.

"I am sorry if my style of riding offends you," she said stiffly, staring off into the distance. Clearly, she did not wish to engage with him in conversation. For some reason, that irritated him too. He wanted to poke her with a stick until she wheeled around and bit back.

"You have nothing else to say to me, wife?" he said, casting about for something to torment her with. "Your behavior at the jousting today, for instance?"

He heard her sharply indrawn breath. "My behavior? *I* have nothing to reproach myself with, I assure you!" she flung back, her color rising. "*Your* behavior on the other hand—" She bit back her words, her cheeks aflame.

"Aye, what of it?" he asked arrogantly.

"I am astonished by it, quite frankly," she said with a toss of her head. Her silky black hair flew and distracted him a moment. He remembered how it had looked spread over his chest that first morning.

He snorted. "What aspect?" Was he enjoying this? Roland wasn't exactly given over to analyzing his feelings, but to his surprise his irritation seemed to be, if anything, trickling away as he conversed with her.

"I would have thought that the King's champion would have been gracious in defeat."

Roland nearly fell off his horse. Where the hells did she get an idea like that? "Gracious in defeat?" he scoffed. "I'm a competitor. I don't like losing."

"Most people don't," Eden pointed out tartly. "However, part of being a civilized adult means learning to tamp down such emotional excesses."

Roland squinted at her. "Is that what you do?" he asked mockingly.

"Of course." She inclined her head. "What you ought to have done is stayed for the rest of the tournament and applauded Lord Kentigern on his win at the banquet tonight."

"Like hells," growled Roland.

"*That* would have been the noble thing to do."

"I'm not noble."

Eden glared at him. He wondered if any of her pet poets had ever written about those eyes. "Do you mean to tell me that you always fling off like that if you do not win?"

"Not just me." He shrugged. "Kentigern, de Crecy, Orde. None of us would stay to watch the other celebrate a win." She stared incredulously. "This is real life, Eden. Not *The Tales of Maurency of Jorde*."

"Well, maybe you *should* take a leaf from that book."

"Not bloody likely," he laughed, genuinely amused.

She shot a curious look at him before looking hurriedly away.

"And what about the spectacle you treated me to?" he asked lazily. "Have you nothing to say of that?"

"What spectacle?" asked Eden suspiciously.

"Hal Payne hanging off your every word, while you clung to his arm. You seem unaware that he eyed you with the same greedy gaze he bestows on a sugared plum!"

172

Eden gaped at him. "Hal Payne is the veriest child!"

"He's a lad of fourteen years and believe me did *not* regard you with the eyes of a mere babe."

"You're being ridiculous!" she scoffed, then seemed to consider before rallying. "And even if he was dazzled by this dress, and the pomp and ceremony of the occasion, it was a passing whim which would have faded as soon as I was out of his sight."

Roland snorted derisively. "You know absolutely nothing of the male animal." The truth of this shut her up a moment. "And thanks to your espousing them, the Paynes will all be showing up at court at some point," he added dryly. "And no doubt, I'll be subjected to the same maddening display all over again!"

Eden pursed her lips and stuck her nose in the air.

Almost, he had to hide a grin. "So, you have no apology to make me, wife?" he asked, shaking his head in mock disappointment.

"You're not really angry anymore," she said forthrightly, surprising him. "You're just amusing yourself at my expense."

"Not exactly," he said slowly. He watched as she took a deep breath.

"Are you suggesting you lost because I distracted you, by appearing in a borrowed dress and sitting next to an attentive youth?" she asked pointedly, turning in her saddle to face him.

Roland blinked. The thought hadn't even occurred to him. "No," he answered. "Today is not the first occasion I've lost to Kentigern. He's a strong opponent." Her eyes widened at that before she turned back to face front again. Now, why had she looked so surprised by his words? Immediately he missed her eyes on him.

173

"We'll have to stop presently, and I'll have you up before me," he said.

"What?" Her tone was far from pleased. "Why?"

"Your horse is going lame." It was a bald-faced lie, but Eden swallowed it, leaning forward to murmur sympathetically to the horse she had named Christobel. Seeing the concern on her face, he added: "If she goes riderless for the afternoon, likely it'll pass."

She looked relieved, and he didn't even feel guilty. He noticed Cuthbert turn in his saddle and glance back at them with a speculative look on his face. Roland stared back at him, daring his squire to contradict him, but the little swine only smirked.

22

They did not reach an inn until night was falling. Eden had been sat up before him for the past three hours, and the bitter taste had long since receded from his mouth. How could it linger when her sweet-smelling hair tickled his chin and he had one arm wrapped securely about her waist?

His ribs hurt like the devil though. Every movement of the horse seemed to jolt them. He longed to just lie still for a few hours.

"This is a large town. Where are we?" asked Eden, breaking her silence.

"Pryors Naunton," he answered. "It's the nearest city to our estate."

"Pryors Naunton? I've heard of it," she said with surprise. "Is there not a very fine cathedral hereabouts?" She turned her head to look over her shoulder at him.

"Well, there's a cathedral at all events," he conceded. "Whether it's fine or not is anyone's guess. I've never set foot in it."

Eden tsked under her breath as he steered Bavol into the inn courtyard toward the stable. "I should like to see it," she announced as Cuthbert reached up for her and Roland suffered her to dismount. "Shall I have time in the morning before we depart?" Roland rolled his eyes and started to climb stiffly off his horse.

Cuthbert cast a quick glance at him before answering. "We've half a day's ride still tomorrow and will likely leave at daybreak."

"Well, what about if I went now?" she asked, glancing out of the stable door at the failing light.

"It's getting dark," said Roland shortly. "I need a meal, a bath, and a bed." Then, he heard himself add, "It's not far from Vawdrey Keep, I can take you another day."

Eden looked as surprised as he. "Thank you."

He shrugged, which immediately pained him. He fancied both she and Cuthbert noticed his discomfort, for they seized on their packs and started carrying them toward the timbered main house.

Soon, they were settled in a comfortable chamber, and a full table provided of cheeses, roast meats, and wine. After seeing to the horses, Cuthbert ate with them, which seemed to surprise Eden, though she made no comment. A bath was then brought up for their use, and they bathed one after the other. Neither one of them spoke until they were lying side by side in their bed. Roland's eyes were just drifting shut when Eden surprised him by starting a conversation.

"I saw Cuthbert just now, out of the window," she said. "He was illuminated by one of the lamps in the courtyard." She paused. "It looked like he was making off into the town."

Roland grunted. "Very likely he is, young villain."

"Are you not concerned by him going out unattended?" she asked in surprise. "After all, he is so very young."

"He is fifteen, or thereabouts," he corrected her. "Besides, he is not gently reared and has plenty about him."

He heard her pillow rustle and guessed she had turned to face him. "I had wondered as to his position," she said. "I mean, he

176

seems very closely affiliated to your family. The way you treat him…" She hesitated.

"Wondering if he's a by-blow?" Roland asked her bluntly. "If he is, then he would be a Cadwallader. He was raised as Linnet's page on her family estate."

Eden was silent, and he squinted across at her, though he could make out only her outline. "Are not squires usually from noble families?" she asked at last.

"Yes," Roland agreed. He hadn't ever really given any thought about Cuthbert's elevation. "He is my sister-in-law's favorite."

"I suppose Linnet would know his parentage."

"Doubtful," snorted Roland. "Linnet had an extremely sheltered upbringing. His old granny is the local witch. I don't recall anyone ever mentioning his father."

Eden was quiet and still for a while. Instead of falling thankfully asleep like a sane person, he found himself lying awake. "Shall I blow out the candle?" she asked eventually.

"Aye." Still, he did not close his eyes. "What of yours?" he found himself asking gruffly instead.

"Mine?" Eden sounded startled in the dark.

"Parentage."

"Oh." She shifted on the mattress before starting briskly. "Well, as you know, my uncle Leofric is the head of our family. My father was his youngest brother, Godwin. He died very young."

Roland waited, but it seemed nothing else was forthcoming. "He was sickly?" he ventured.

"No not sickly, no," she said stiffly. "Just…full of vices."

177

"Vices?" Now it was his turn to be startled.

"Drinking, gambling, women," Eden continued with clear reluctance. "My mother was very unhappy in their marriage, by all accounts. She did not outlive him by many years."

Roland digested this surprising news. "Do you remember them?"

"Not really. My mother, a little."

"So you were raised by your uncle then?"

"Yes."

Dimly, Roland had some idea that womenfolk in the main were supposed to be more talkative than Eden was about herself. "And do you like him?" he persisted. "Your uncle."

Again, she moved around restlessly. If his ribs did not hurt so much, he'd throw a leg over her to stop the fidgeting.

"Yes," she said, then seemed to realize she was not giving him much. "Of my cousin Lenora, I am very fond."

He waited, but she did not ask him for any return of confidences. He had no idea why that bothered him so much. Maybe that was why he found himself saying suddenly, "It should have been me that gave you the tournament crown." He heard her surprised intake of breath, her head turn.

"I would not at all have been happy if you had," she said after a heavy pause. "In fact, my reaction would have been just the same. I would have awarded it in turn to Gunnilde."

He stared at the space where he imagined her face was. "And why is that?" he asked testily.

"Because the crown is for the prettiest girl present. Not the cleverest girl, or the most talented girl, or even the worthiest girl. The rules are very simple."

Roland opened and closed his mouth. He was wary of taking a misstep now he had her talking to him again. "It's not that straightforward," he said after a moment's pause.

"Yes, it is," Eden corrected him.

"No, it is not," he contradicted her patiently. "In your eyes Payne's daughter was the fairest, but many would not agree with your view."

"She is young and fresh and eager to please. That is pretty in my eyes."

"Exactly," said Roland. "In your eyes."

She chewed this over for a moment. "Very well, I agree that if you are going with conventional attractiveness then her stepmother, Lady Payne, would likely be the more popular choice. But I wanted to give my friend a day to remember."

A day to remember? Frustrated by the dark bedchamber, Roland stared instead at the ceiling. He had not really thought overmuch of how the recipient of the tournament crown felt about it. Well, if he was honest, he had not considered it at all. It was a mere detail, a footnote to the real business of the tourney.

Was it really such a matter of distinction for a girl to receive it? He cast his mind back, remembering how Gunnilde Payne had kept reaching up to reverently touch her head and check it was really sat there. Certainly, she had seemed so proud she might burst at any minute.

Over the course of his career, he had cavalierly handed it over only to the most beauteous maiden present. Mostly, this had been Lenora Montmayne. She had never seemed overly thrilled by the distinction and had received it merely as her rightful due. But then, he thought judiciously, she must have received dozens of the things over the three years she had been at court.

Maybe, her very first had meant something to her, but after that… He cast a look toward Eden, who was obscured in darkness, but seemed for once to be lying very still. He wanted to ask if she had never received the garland, but he already knew the answer. Suddenly, the taste in his mouth was bitter.

He felt a ridiculous longing that he could turn the clock back and—what? Crown Eden Montmayne tournament queen when he'd had the chance? It was stupid. He could no more turn back time than anyone. What was the use in thinking such thoughts? And if he had done such a thing, everyone would have been in uproar at such uncharacteristic behavior.

"Eden," he said heavily, concentrating on the throbbing ache in his sides.

"What is it?"

"You weren't mistaken."

She hesitated. "About what?"

"I would not have taken kindly to you accepting the crown from Kentigern. Or anyone else for that matter," he added. Somehow it was easier to confess such a thing in the dark. Suddenly, he was glad he couldn't make out her expression.

She didn't speak for a long while. Then she said simply, "I see."

But he didn't think she could see. Any more clearly than he.

23

By the time Roland woke around six, Eden was already sat on the edge of the bed, braiding her long hair. She had pursed her lips at the idea of donning the ice-blue dress but had washed and dressed in it all the same. Roland washed gingerly; his ribs had turned black and purple overnight. He noticed Eden wince when she glanced at him while he dressed.

"Will you be able to ride?" she asked.

He crooked an eyebrow at her. "Of course." They hurt, but not as badly as the day before.

Below stairs, they found Cuthbert already tucking into roasted fish with bread and butter. He hailed them cheerfully, and they joined him. "Got something for you, milady," he said, nodding toward a bundle of something on the floor.

Eden peered at it doubtfully. "What is it?"

"Take a look and see," replied Cuthbert with a wink.

She reached down and unfurled the soft material to find an exquisite cape of a dark berry color, a matching hood, and long mittens made of the finest silken wool. "They're beautiful!" she exclaimed. "But where—?"

"Dice cup?" asked Roland knowingly.

Cuthbert grinned and nodded. "I'm always lucky in towns that don't know me."

Remembering Eden's words about her father's gambling, Roland cast a wary look her way, but she was still stroking the material. As if aware of eyes on her, she looked up. "Cuthbert you really shouldn't have—"

"It's a bride gift," Cuthbert said, and waved a hand dismissively. "Tell her," he said, looking at Roland, "while I fetch you more dishes." He was already out of his seat when Roland nodded at Eden.

"As you observed last night, Cuthbert is practically one of the family. Besides, you'll need a cloak to approach the Keep." She looked up in surprise. The sky was blue and already the sun was breaking through the clouds. "Our lands lie in dense forest," he added, pushing away his plate. "There's usually a nip in the air, even when the sun shines."

24

They set off immediately after breaking their fast. Eden was relieved to see that Christobel showed no sign of lameness and Roland's ribs seemed a little easier, even though they had looked horribly bruised in the glimpse she'd caught that morning. She didn't ask again, as he seemed irritable about admitting any weakness. Maybe that was a male thing, although her own uncle frequently complained about his gouty foot. They had soon left the bustle of Pryors Naunton far behind them, traveling down country lanes and over fields until they seemed to be entering into a wood populated with huge oak trees. Roland turned in his saddle. "This is Ryder's Oaks and marks the outer boundary of our lands."

Eden nodded, raising a hand to shield her eyes as she peered up to the tops of the trees. "These oaks must be hundreds of years old," she ventured.

"At least," Roland agreed. "My father said in his boyhood, the country folk still used to tie charms and prayer ribbons to the lower branches. A leftover from olden days."

"This was a sacred place?"

"So they say."

"Still is," said Cuthbert. "Look." He pointed to a silver bell that gave a faint chime as if on cue as the breeze ruffled through the branch it hung from.

"That's probably been there for years," scoffed Roland.

"What difference does that make?" asked Cuthbert with a shrug. "Trees mark time different to people."

Eden glanced at him curiously, remembering Roland's words about his granny being a wise woman. "Do we pass through the village to reach Vawdrey Keep?"

"No, the village is that way, about five miles," Roland told her, pointing westerly. All Eden could see was trees.

"The village of Sitchmarsh?" she asked. Roland shot her a surprised look. "You seem to forget that Fenella is a good friend of mine," she explained, naming another of his sisters-in-law. "She is from this area, is she not?"

"Oh aye," he said, his frown clearing. "Sitchmarsh Hall, her brother's place, is the other side of the village."

"Walking distance?" she asked.

Roland gave a brief laugh. "Fenella would likely say so, but she's country bred."

"Unlike me?"

"A fine court lady like yourself would likely go on horseback," Roland retorted.

"Fenella is a countess," Eden reminded him.

"She is now," he agreed. "But she's ill at ease at court. Unlike yourself."

"And I was raised at Hallam Hall, not Caer-Lyoness."

He ignored this, but for some reason, Eden was not content to let him lapse into silence. "Are you acquainted with Fenella's brother?"

"Gil Bernard?" grunted Roland after a moment's pause. "He's years older than me."

"You know him though?" she persisted.

"By sight," he admitted cautiously.

"And has he not now married Fenella's previous sister-in-law?"

He shot her a look of exasperation. "What?"

"Fenella's former sister-in-law married her brother—I remember her telling me."

Roland frowned heavily at this.

"So," piped up Cuthbert, who had clearly been following the conversation. "Her previous sister-in-law became her sister-in-law once again?"

"Precisely."

"You've probably got that wrong," said Roland disparagingly.

"I have not."

"Sounds damned unlikely."

"Fenella was married to Sir Ambrose Thane before your brother had that marriage annulled," huffed Eden. "Then *his* sister married Fenella's brother, so that means—"

"You sure Thane had a sister?" he asked off-handedly.

"You're hopeless," Eden told him roundly. "I feel sure Fenella would have said as much to you, and you likely paid scant attention!"

"It little matters." Roland shrugged. "She's a Vawdrey now. As are you."

Eden caught her breath as her wits scattered. She still had not accustomed herself to that fact. Now it was her turn to go quiet. She trained her attention instead on the surrounding green wood which seemed to be growing thicker and denser with each step they took. Strangely enough, it was a long-forgotten story their old nurse used to tell her and Lenora that sprang to mind. A tale of warning against marrying dark, handsome strangers who might carry you off to places dark and forbidding from whence you might never be seen again. She glanced at her husband, who very much fit the description, and shivered.

Roland sat up straighter in his saddle. "There," he said, pointing ahead.

Eden looked up. A series of hills, maybe even mountains, loomed in the distance. Standing out starkly, sat atop the central hillock stood a dark, sinister-looking tower. She turned back to Roland with a sense of foreboding.

"Vawdrey Keep," he said. "It's never been breached," he added with apparent pride.

Eden blinked, glancing around. Who on earth would want to? It was in the middle of nowhere! Wondering where any invaders were supposed to emerge from, she murmured, "I see." No wonder he was amused at the idea of her walking on foot to the village. Getting to the bottom of the hill itself would take her a good hour.

Their horses started the climb up the narrow path, and she fell in line behind Roland with Cuthbert bringing up the rear. Luckily, Christobel was sure-footed. Eden pulled on her new mittens, feeling the chill in the air, as they climbed higher. Somehow, the brooding keep did not grow any more welcoming the closer they grew to it. Instead, it seemed to grow bleaker still, with its uncompromising gray stone and fortress-like features. Eden started to wonder what kind of a homecoming they would receive when they reached the summit.

"Have you many staff in residence?" she asked as they reached the top, without any signs of life stirring from within. Roland frowned, but did not speak. Instead, he dismounted and ran up a rickety wooden structure which led to a single large, studded door set surprisingly high off the ground. Seeing Eden's confused look, Cuthbert leaned over to explain.

"It's set that high so a battering ram can't be used on the entrance."

"A battering ram?" repeated Eden. Again, she wondered at the Vawdrey preoccupation with invaders.

"Ho!" Roland was shouting, beating his fist against the door. "Fulco? Baxter? Who's within?"

A tremendous baying and barking of hounds started up, which even the heavy door could not muffle. Eden winced and noticed a flash of white fur in one of the windows above. A ferocious, broad white head appeared there, glowering down at them with a malevolent stare and sharp teeth.

"Castor, you villain!" Roland yelled in recognition of the large dog. It redoubled it efforts to drown out the racket of the other dogs, throwing back its giant head and howling. "M'father's favorite hound," he said, turning back to them by way of explanation.

If that was his favorite, Eden found she did not overly relish the idea of meeting the rest of the pack.

Finally, it seemed the cacophony had roused someone. A bushy-bearded giant rounded the side of the tower with a huge axe over his shoulder, and a forbidding expression. He looked thunderstruck at the sight of Roland, and staggered back a pace or two before righting himself. "Master Roland! As I'm alive!"

"Fulco!" Roland descended the steps, and they seized one another by their right forearms, gripping each other in some form of welcome which Eden had not observed before.

"Quiet, ye evil pack of devils!" Fulco roared at the dogs within. So startled was Eden that she nearly fell off her saddle. Luckily, Cuthbert reached across and had caught Christobel's head before the mare had a chance to rear. The dogs' barking died down at once, and Roland strode across and held his arms up for her.

With little other choice, Eden dismounted into his waiting grasp, and found herself borne over to the alarming Fulco for his inspection. She wondered if Roland's ribs were really up to carrying her, but if they hurt, he gave no sign of it. Fulco regarded her a moment from beneath bristling brows. Eden stared up at him. Neither one of them seemed equal to the occasion.

"My bride," said Roland by way of explanation. Fulco gave a nod, and a growl. Eden wasn't sure if he cleared his throat or spoke. "Fulco's served at the Keep some twenty years, man and boy," continued Roland, seemingly oblivious to her discomfiture. "And his father before him."

"I see," said Eden, struggling to find words. "How do you do?" She felt disadvantaged not being stood on her own two feet but could hardly ask to be set down without seeming churlish.

Fulco stared at her as though she was some strange creature the likes of whom he'd never seen before.

"Is there anyone to attend her?" Roland asked.

Fulco snorted and shook his head. "There's been no womenfolk at the Keep, not for a twelvemonth."

Now it was Eden's turn to stare. *No womenfolk?* What kind of a household was this?

Roland swore. "Cuthbert will have to play the page until we sort someone out."

She thought she heard Cuthbert mutter darkly at this but did not turn her head to dignify it.

"You sent no word ahead," Fulco rumbled in reproach, lowering his axe. He cast another uneasy look at Eden. "Wife, ye say?" He squinted at her suspiciously.

"Aye, wife." She was surprised by Roland's tone, which was not unlike the one he'd used earlier when speaking of the Keep. "Of five days now."

"Six," she corrected him.

"Six?" He frowned down at her. "Oh aye, I always forget that day we lost in bed."

Fulco coughed, and to her annoyance, she felt her face turn bright red. Roland was now striding toward the rickety-looking steps. Eden sat up in alarm. "The steps will surely break if you carry me up them!" she objected. "And bearing my weight must surely be paining your ribs."

"You're slim enough and weigh no more than a decent-sized dog," he said absently.

"A dog?" Eden looked at him in exasperation. "Don't you mean a feather?"

He smirked. "Sweetheart, you're not that light."

She was still spluttering indignantly as he mounted the swaying steps. They creaked ominously.

Eden grabbed for his broad shoulders. "Do not drop me, Roland Vawdrey," she warned him fretfully, and squeezed her eyes shut. Almost, she could imagine herself on a storm-tossed ship. "These steps are treacherous."

"Faint-heart," he mocked, though he held her a little tighter. "I'm not about to drop you. And these steps have been here many a long year."

"Then it's high time they were replaced," she told him, her eyes still shut.

"Stop ruining tradition, wife."

Eden cracked an eye open. "What tradition? Making your wife seasick?" By her reckoning he had already ascended a good five steps. How many more could there possibly be?

He ran up the last five steps nimbly enough. "Carrying you across the threshold," he murmured, shouldering the huge studded oak door open. It creaked in a sinister fashion.

Eden peered into a bare room with a large wooden table in it and a window seat. Other than that, the room was strewn about with a good deal of what looked like either farming or battle implements.

He seemed to notice her puzzlement. "The disarming room," he explained.

"Disarming room?" Eden repeated blankly.

"Aye, wife." It seemed to Eden that he had, of a sudden, a gleam in his eye that she regarded with misgiving.

"Ready for what comes next?" he asked.

Not caring for his manner, she pointed out, "I'm not armed," with dignity.

"You can't expect me to take your word for that," he said, letting her slide down his body to her own two feet.

"You know full well—" Eden began hastily, stepping back, only to nearly trip over a pair of boots. "Ow!"

He caught her about the waist and yanked her back into his arms.

"Roland!" she protested breathlessly as his lips sought hers, but before she knew it, she was being pushed back against the door and soundly kissed. *Not this again!*

Suddenly the inner door was shoved back and what looked like a half dozen large dogs burst into the room, swarming and jumping around them, barking and knocking things over. Roland tore his lips hastily from hers. "Down, you brutes!" he roared.

Eden eased past him in the confusion, and nearly lost her footing again as the heavy tail of a huge barrel-chested dog struck the backs of her legs, nearly buckling her knees. For a moment, she was even grateful for Roland's arm at her waist, keeping her upright. "Down, Hector!" Roland bellowed.

Eden clutched at him helplessly in the midst of the chaos of writhing dog bodies. She scrambled to stand on her own two feet, seeking to put some space between them. "Is this part of tradition in these parts too?" she asked stiffly. "Savaging your bride with the hounds?"

Roland grinned, and slid a finger under her jaw, tipping it up. "Only if her performance displeases her groom," he said, his eyes dropping to her lips again.

Performance? Thankfully the big white dog bounded up again with a loud bark, and Roland was forced to release her and remonstrate with him. "Cease, Castor!" he boomed before seizing the animal and wrestling the large beast to the ground. Eden backed up a few steps in alarm, but after a moment, noticed the dog was wagging his tail even though he was snarling in a terrifying manner.

"Daft cur!" Roland laughed as Castor bestowed a lick to his face. As if to some unspoken signal, the other dogs all pounced en masse, and Roland disappeared under a wave of wagging dog bodies. "Let me up!" he groaned after a few minutes of rolling on the floorboards with them. "Parnell, you rogue, you've grown damned heavy."

Eden regarded him speechlessly. Her uncle kept a housedog, a civilized old thing, but the hunting dogs were kept separately in a pen well away from the hall, and they were kept as working dogs, not pets. "Come here," he said, holding out a hand to Eden. "I want them to know your scent."

He was crouched now among a sea of large dogs. Eden approached, determined not to show that she would be much more at home with Lenora's cats. "Castor!" Roland called and the big white dog he had called Baron Vawdrey's favorite stepped forward. "Meet Eden."

Roland took her hand and placed it on the dog's broad head. The dog emitted a low growl, and Roland rebuked him sharply. Castor tossed his head, dislodging her hand, and wheeled around to sniff at her fingers. "Aye, that's it," Roland said, though she was not sure if he spoke to her or the beast. "Good lad, very good."

The dog, thought Eden. "Now pet him," he said, still not lifting his eyes from the dog's face. Oh, now that was directed at her. Hesitantly, Eden extended her fingers toward Castor's wide brow. He gave a rumble in his throat, and Roland seized his scruff, holding him tight. "This is your mistress," he said sternly.

192

Castor looked up at her with a proud, scornful look. Of course, the animal did not comprehend the words, she told herself uneasily. "Let him sniff you again," Roland recommended, loosing the dog, who lunged forward and glared up at her tensely before barking loudly at her.

Eden froze as Roland hauled him back again. "You always were a stubborn wretch!" he scolded. "That's probably enough for now," he added, straightening up. "It won't happen overnight."

Eden nearly jumped out of her skin as a wet doggy nose pushed into her hand. "Hello," she said to this dog, who had a coat of curly, sandy hair and a much friendlier aspect. "Who's this?"

"Parnell," said Roland. "Hie, Parnell! You've a fancy to be a lady's lapdog, have you?"

A lap dog? The animal was the size of a sheep! Eden patted his neck and he panted, his tongue lolling out. The other dogs milled around but didn't get any closer to her. Clearly, they followed Castor's lead and not Parnell's. "An independent thinker, I see," she murmured, noticing the strong smell of dog that was assailing her nostrils.

"It's good you like dogs," said Roland airily. "We Vawdreys have always kept dogs at the Keep."

Eden could think of no answer to this; instead she turned back to scanning the mysterious objects in the room. Now she noticed it, the large table's surface was covered in dust as well as an assortment of daggers.

Noticing the direction of her gaze, Roland reached into his belt and then his tunic, extracting two knives which he slung on to the table. "I'll show you the rest of it," he said, holding out a hand to her. Mindful of the dogs, she took it, and he drew her in the direction of a side door which revealed a winding staircase.

193

He shut the door firmly behind them, which caused a few barks from the dogs, who were shut on the other side of it. "Don't want them tripping you and breaking your neck."

Eden frowned. "These steps are quite steep," she admitted, navigating her way around the curving stairwell.

"Not just that," he told her, gripping her firmly by the elbow. "Just when you hit your stride, you'll find a trip step."

"A trip step?" Eden asked, looking back over her shoulder. Her foot hit the next step and she would have stumbled if he had not been there to support her.

"You've just found one."

Eden looked down and found the step that had caught her out was of a different height and breadth to the others.

"It's a stumbling block for any strangers to the Keep."

"Intruders again?" Eden asked in exasperation.

"You notice how the staircase runs clockwise?" he asked. "They're all like that here. It's so any invaders could not swing their swords." He placed a palm against the gray stone. "Their blades would strike against these walls, while we defenders would have our right arms free to fight."

Eden looked down at him in surprise. "I've never heard of such a thing."

"Your uncle's place, Hallam Hall, was built as a country residence. This is a fortress."

"I see."

"Keep going, but cautiously. In five steps you'll hit another trip step."

Eden did not object when he kept a firm grip. He bade her to ignore the first door they encountered, for they were servants' quarters. The second door they passed through, emerging into another large gray stone chamber.

This one had two large scarred wooden tables, an assortment of benches, and a floor scattered in stale, grubby rushes which had likely not been replaced in an age. The windows were mere slits which meant the room was dark and gloomy. Various shields were mounted on the walls which bore the scarlet field and black panther of the Vawdreys. They looked old and battered as though they had all seen service.

Seeing her stare, Roland pointed. "My father's," he said. "Oswald's, and Mason's."

Eden noticed that Mason's shield was the plainest, with the same colors, but no heraldic animal, merely the slash of the bar sinister denoting his bastard status. It did not look like that anymore, she thought, now he bore a ducal title. He now had not one, but two beasts on his shield—the leopard of the Cadwalladers as well as the Vawdrey panther.

Of course, their older brother Oswald Vawdrey's shield would not look like this either, she reflected, now he had been elevated to the role of Earl Vawdrey. His panther would wear a leafy coronet, where his father's had been bare-headed.

These must be relics from the civil war that had torn the country apart some years ago. She turned back to Roland. "Why is your shield not hung here?"

"I did not fight in the war. Was just a boy." He crossed the room and flung open another door. "Through here."

"But you have been a knight now for several years," Eden pointed out, walking toward him. "Why do you not hang your first shield?"

"I'm still using it," he said shortly. He seemed reluctant to discuss the subject, but Eden was loath to let it drop so easily. His current shield was surely not his first, for she had seen how battered it had been from just one tournament.

"Just a boy, you say," Eden mused, calculating Roland's age. "But you must have been on the verge of manhood. Did you not serve as one of your brothers' squires?"

Roland tensed, and she wondered if he was sensitive about not having seen genuine battle. It seemed odd that the old baron should have shielded a mere third son from the war. To Eden's eye, Baron Vawdrey had not looked the nurturing type.

"I was fifteen and served as Oswald's squire in several battles," he said after a heavy pause. "And failed spectacularly. It was the only time I ever incurred my father's wrath." He spoke without meeting her eye, and Eden could see he was telling her something he seldom spoke of.

"How did you fail?" she asked before she could stop herself.

He did not answer for a moment. "I saw my brother cut down at the battle of Adarva," he admitted on an outward breath. "I thought I watched him die." He shook his head. "I was not stoic about it, as my father thought I should have been." He grimaced. "I suffered...bad dreams, disturbed sleep for months afterward."

Watching his face, Eden felt indignation rise in her breast. "Your father was cross with you for this? For mourning a brother you thought dead?" Baron Vawdrey must have been a monster!

196

"Aye," Roland admitted, scratching the back of his neck. He pulled a face. "I wet the bed too, for a while. So, you see he had some cause for annoyance." Before she could speak, he added. "Mercifully, as it turned out, Oswald had only been taken captive and returned to us in one piece."

"Captive?" Eden asked with horror.

"They demanded a ransom for his release, but as it turns out…my brother was not a model prisoner."

She nearly let the subject drop, seeing his unease, when a sudden thought occurred to her. "Is that why you take no hostages?" she asked. "After what happened to Earl Vawdrey?"

There was no other way to describe what happened next. Roland *blushed*. Hotly. "No," he mumbled in what Eden could plainly see was a lie. Seeing his discomfort, she finally let the matter drop, though she thought he had nothing to be ashamed of and *every* right to hang his shield in the chamber alongside those of his brothers. At some point she would tell him so.

"Come along," he urged, leading her on, and passing through another door, she found herself in another large chamber. This one was dominated by a large fireplace full of ash and soot. There were no other furnishings, save a few scattered chairs of gloomy, dark wood. No tapestries or pictures were hung on the walls to break the monotony of the gray stone. There were no books or musical instruments to be seen. The only cushions were of a dirty gray and were squashed flat on the floor and covered in dog hair.

Eden worked hard to maintain a neutral expression, while her heart plummeted into her slippered feet. *Our estate*, Roland had said, which had been generous considering the way she had been foisted on him. She didn't want to be ungrateful. As a Montmayne, she had only ever been a poor relation, a

197

dependent. Yet here, at Vawdrey Keep, she would be mistress, which would be a new experience indeed. She could not deny however, the heavy pang of homesickness she felt for the mellow brick of Hallam Hall, or the comforts of life at court. "It's a fine big hearth," she said aloud.

"You should see it with a roaring blaze in it," recommended Roland. She just about bit her lip to stop herself from commenting that no one had apparently cleaned up after the last one. "Come, I will show you the next floor with the bedchambers."

"I don't understand," said Eden as they returned to the staircase. "Where are the kitchens?"

"Below the disarming room," he explained. "There are steps that lead down. I did not bother to show you the pantry or the buttery. You're mistress here after all, not a servant."

Eden pondered this. "I see. But surely Fulco cannot be the only staff here?"

"There used to be others," Roland said vaguely. "I'm not sure how many remain." He held his hand out to her and she took it, following him back out to the winding stairs. They climbed upward once again. "Watch this step," he said.

"How is it that Vawdrey Keep passed to you, the youngest son?" she asked curiously.

"I'm the only one that has any affection for the old place," he replied after a slight pause. "Oswald has no desire to live here. Too far from court. And Mason gained an estate through his wife. Though," he added with a shrug, "I suppose he could not have inherited it by right. My father never married his mother." The next door up opened into a small passageway with several doors off it. "This will be ours," Roland said, leading her into a large bedchamber furnished only with a large carved bedstead and a rather battered-looking trunk. He exclaimed in annoyance.

"What is it?" asked Eden before noticing that the bed wore no mattress, blankets, or quilts. "Oh, well, likely we can have it made up before night falls."

He shot an irritated look at her, and the unwelcome thought occurred that he might have had more immediate plans for it. He crossed the room and inspected it, looking underneath the bed, and then lifting the lid of the trunk. Eden stayed by the door in case he got any ideas about lying her down on the bare ropes slung across the bedstead.

Or worse still, he found some old dog blanket which he expected her to lie on. "Let's check the other rooms," he grunted at last, seeming to give up. They went back out to the corridor and into another bedchamber, which was still decent-sized though rather smaller.

There was a large box cupboard in the far corner which Roland crossed to, while she went across to the window to look out at the valley below. It was a great view, she conceded, from atop the Vawdreys' hill. There was a bird's-eye view of the green forest they had ridden through that morning.

Looking back over her shoulder, she found Roland flinging the doors open to the cupboard. To her surprise, there was a good-sized bed inside it, with a mattress, though the blankets looked sparse, and she could see no pillows.

"How curious," she said, moving closer. "I've never seen a bed inside a box like that."

"It's Oswald's old bed," said Roland disparagingly. "He always was a secretive bastard."

Peering inside, Eden thought she could see a pile of books in the far corner, though it was hard to make out without a candle.

"Forget it, I'm not sleeping in there," said Roland. "You can't see your hand in front of your face it's so dark."

"But why should you need to when you are sleeping?" Eden asked him irritably.

Again, he cast another look at her. "I mean to see what I'm doing."

Eden flushed. Could he think of nothing but his conjugal rights? she thought crossly. It was ridiculous!

"Come," he said. "There's always my old room." He led her to a third smaller bedroom which had only a pallet bed low to the ground. "Damn, I had forgotten," he muttered, "just how small my old bed is."

"When were you last home?" asked Eden, trying to distract herself from the thought of having to sleep on such a narrow cot with Roland Vawdrey. Why, she'd have to lie fully on top of him! She felt her chest swell at the indignity of marital relations. Why had no one warned her how it would be? No wonder so many women took themselves off to a nunnery! The fact he was so handsome somehow made it ten times worse!

He leaned down, pressing on the thin mattress. "The dogs have been sleeping on this," he said with displeasure, ignoring her question. "We can't sleep here."

Thanking the heavens for small mercies, Eden followed him back out into the passageway. "What's on the top floor?" she asked.

"Naught but the attics. Although…" He broke off, brightening up. "Mason's old room is up there. Wait here." He bounded up the last flight of stairs, while Eden wondered if she would be allowed her own bedchamber once he had tired of her. If so, she would surely choose Oswald's old room, which undoubtedly had the best view.

She wandered back into the largest bedchamber again to look out of that window. But this window faced the mountains and the aspect was not half as picturesque. She heard Roland's footsteps and hurried back out to meet him. She did not want him to think she was poking and prying around his home.

"A straw mattress, would you believe," he said with disgust. "Half eaten by mice."

"Oh dear," said Eden without much conviction.

He glowered at her. "We'll just have to use Oswald's until we get a new mattress."

"Can we have it aired before tonight?" Eden asked, wondering when the last time was that it would have been slept on.

"At least being in a cupboard means the dogs couldn't get on it," he murmured, opening the door to the staircase. "Mind your step. Put a hand to my shoulder." Eden followed closely behind him, lifting her skirts with one hand, so she should not trip, and placing the other on his muscular shoulder.

He warned her each time they were approaching a trip step, and she marveled at how quickly she had heard him run up to the attic. Even with this cautious approach, she felt herself stumble at least twice, and was grateful to have Roland's back to brace against, preventing her from falling headlong down the steep stone steps.

She only breathed easy again when they emerged once more from the staircase into the disarming room, although two of the dogs still stood guard in there and immediately glued themselves to Roland's heels. He glanced back at her uncertainly. "I'm going down to see if I can find Fulco."

"I'm not staying here on my own," Eden found herself retorting. "Castor could return at any point and resume hostilities!"

He laughed. "He'll be outside now very likely, or with Fulco." He reached down and fondled the ears of the brown-haired dog she thought was called Hector. The other dog was black and white, and she had no idea of his name. Without Castor around they seemed determined to ignore her. Well, that was fine with Eden. "Follow me down then," said Roland. "But stay close and mind your footing."

Eden followed his directions and found herself in a large kitchen and scullery area with two big fireplaces, a number of cavernous cooking pots, and two large spits for roasting meats. A vast table stood in the center, covered in pots and pans. Not a soul was in sight, but the kitchen at least looked lived in. There was no dust or soot lying around and the floors were swept clean. Roland strode across the floor and opened another door leading into a vast storeroom which Eden guessed was the pantry. "No one," he huffed, shutting the door again. "Where the devil is everyone?"

Eden pointed to a large bowl of eggs. "Someone collected these," she said. "And very likely this morning." The black and white dog jumped up, setting his two paws on the table to sniff for any meat.

"Down, Seth!" Roland roared, and the dog complied, looking a little sheepish.

Seth, thought Eden. *Castor, Parnell, Hector, and Seth.* That just left two she did not know the names of. The ginger dog who looked like an overgrown fox and the gray one who looked rather like a gargoyle.

Just then they heard footsteps on the stairs, and both turned to look as Cuthbert sauntered down the steps. "I'm half-starved, anything worth eating?" he greeted them.

Roland shrugged. "There's eggs, if nothing else. Where's Fulco?"

"He showed me the stables and disappeared."

"Damn," swore Roland. "I'd better go in search of him. Will you stay here with Cuthbert?"

Eden frowned at him. "If that's what you want," she said, sounding annoyed. Why did he keep trying to shake her off? A smile seemed to tug at his lips a moment, and she wished she had not said it. He was conceited enough to think she craved his company, and she had not meant to give that impression in the slightest.

"I only mean to get a fire lit and make things comfortable for you as soon as possible," he explained. "I can do that quicker by myself."

"Of course," she said stiffly, folding her arms across her chest.

He hesitated and then came right up to her, tipping her face up to his with his fingertips and brushing a kiss against her lips. "I won't be long," he said in a low, intimate voice. "Cuthbert can get you some refreshment in the meantime."

"As long as it's eggs," she said waspishly to hide her flustered state. He pinched her chin but made no further comment. Emitting a sharp whistle, he ran up the stairs with Hector following him close on his heels.

"Don't worry," said Cuthbert, who was cheerfully clattering around with the pots. "I learned how to make a tasty posset for my Lady Linnet, with egg and nutmeg. Roland will be back before you know it."

Eden sniffed. "I am not remotely concerned about his return," she said, then spoiled it entirely by adding, "I only hope he does not break his neck on those steps."

"He may seem like a great, clumsy oaf," said Cuthbert sanguinely, "but he's actually pretty light on his feet."

Eden pulled out a wooden chair and sat on it, drawing her cloak in close around her body. She still wore her mittens too, for it was chilly in the Keep. "It's a good thing you gave me these gifts, or I would likely soon perish here," she commented as Cuthbert broke four eggs and niftily separated the whites from the yolks using the shells. He set the yolks aside and beat the whites.

He nodded thoughtfully. "There is that," he said, and, humming a tune, made his way over to the fireplace. He made a few passes with his hand, and she heard almost instantly the crackle and flare of a fire.

"That was fast!" she said, startled.

"It wasn't really out, just damped down," Cuthbert said modestly. He set a pot of water over the blaze before rising from his knees and making for the pantry. He reappeared carrying a large stone jug and a pot, which he took straight over to the heating water.

"What are you adding?" asked Eden, cupping her chin in her hand.

"White wine," said Cuthbert, pouring from the jug. "And spices." He added three liberal pinches from the bowl before sniffing it. "Nutmeg and cloves." Then he stirred the pot, replaced the lid, and left it to heat, returning to rifle the pantry. When he emerged, he was carrying honey and milk.

Eden felt her stomach rumble. "This is Linnet's favorite, did you say?"

He nodded. "She used to say it could revive her even from the depths of despair."

Eden looked up sharply. "It's not as bad as all that," she mumbled, hoping her face had not shown too clearly her dismay at her new home. Cuthbert merely shrugged, intent on his task.

"Have you been here before?" she asked. "With Linnet and her husband?"

He shook his head. "The old baron, he practically moved to Cadwallader after his grandchildren were born. This place was shut up and forgotten."

"Odd that Roland's never brought you here." Eden frowned. "He seems so proud of the place."

"He's got his fortune to make in the tournaments," said Cuthbert sensibly. "He's the youngest son. They never inherit."

"Roland inherited Vawdrey Keep."

"Only cos no one else wanted it," answered Cuthbert smartly.

Rather like me, thought Eden. Then she caught herself. Was she becoming melancholy? That would never do! Sitting up straighter on her stool, she cleared her throat. "The pot's bubbling."

Cuthbert crossed to the hearth and inspected the mixture. He fiddled with the height of the hook before returning to the table and mixing the egg whites with the milk.

Eden sat brooding over the fact Roland had been forced to marrying a dowerless girl when he needed to make his own way in life. If he had wed Lenora as planned, no doubt Uncle Leofric would have awarded him a handsome sum.

She frowned a moment as her uncle's outraged countenance swam into her mind's eye. She didn't want to dwell on how much disgrace she must be in with her family. If she thought about her uncle, then her cousin and her grandmother would surely follow.

A sudden weight on her knee made her look up. The black and white dog's large head was lying there, his eyes gazing up at her soulfully. "Seth?" she said in surprise. His tail wagged. Eden cast a furtive look around the room. Cuthbert was crouched over his pot again, adding the dairy mixture to his concoction.

She reached out and stroked Seth's ears as she had seen Roland do to Hector earlier. He huffed out a breath and leaned against her legs. Eden smirked. "I have your measure, dog. If Castor were here, you would not fraternize with me." He wagged his tail harder. Eden lightly tweaked his ears.

Somewhere above them a door banged shut. There was a heavy thud of boots on floorboards. Seth sprang back from her guiltily, and they both looked up as they heard Roland's voice conversing with Fulco. It sounded like they were coming down the steps together.

"You cannot keep them for love nor money!" Fulco boomed. "They say the place is haunted. No maid will stay here after dark."

"Haunted?" repeated Roland in surprise. "By who?" There was an awkward silence. "My father?" suggested Roland when

Fulco did not speak. "He'd be more likely choose Cadwallader to haunt in death, like he did in life!"

"Not the old baron," admitted Fulco. He had arrived at the bottom of the steps now and cast a startled look at Eden as if he'd forgotten her very existence. Or maybe he just did not expect to see her there.

"Who then?" demanded Roland, clattering down behind him. They both stood in the kitchen now. "Answer me, damn you!"

"His wives," said Fulco, scratching the back of his neck and looking a picture of abject misery.

"What?" Roland was visibly taken aback.

"You know how superstitious country folk can be," mumbled Fulco, red-faced. He darted an embarrassed glance at Eden.

"Bloody fools!" Roland swore. "I notice they didn't start with this horseshit while he was alive."

Then he, too, seemed to notice Eden sat perched on her seat and fell silent, though he was still scowling. Seth skulked over to the hearth, and with a rather ostentatious yawn, settled himself down in front of the fire.

"Posset's ready," said Cuthbert cheerfully. He poured some into a large cup and brought it over to Eden.

She took it from him and took a tentative sip. "Delicious!" she exclaimed with surprise. "Truly." She turned to Roland. "You should try some. Apparently, it has restorative powers."

He ignored her words but gave a start. "Which reminds me," he said accusingly, turning back to Fulco. "There is barely any bedding above stairs!"

Fulco shrugged helplessly. "It all fell into disrepair and we've had no need of it."

"Well, we have need of it now," said Roland pointedly. "I'm newly wed."

Eden bristled. Did he have to be so obvious?

"I could ride to the village," said Fulco uncertainly. "But new bedding would likely have to come from somewhere like Pryors Naunton, not Sitchmarsh!"

Again, Eden felt her lack of dowry keenly. Most brides would bring such things with them as embroidered sheets and coverlets to their marriage bed. She had never prepared a trousseau like girls with expectations did.

"I can restuff an old mattress," offered Cuthbert, "in the meantime."

Roland grunted. "We're going to have to use the one on the box-bed, in the second largest bedroom. What will you stuff it with?"

"I'll go take a look in the outhouses and see what there is. Maybe fresh grasses or feathers?"

"There's nothing like that out there," said Fulco, shaking his head. "Though we can likely get some materials such as those in the village."

"Let's for the village then," said Cuthbert. He looked at Roland, who nodded.

"Aye. No time like the present," he agreed. "Fulco, you take Cuthbert in with you to Sitchmarsh for provisions." He reached into his tunic for his purse and tossed it to Cuthbert. "Get whatever is needed."

Cuthbert nodded and made for the stairs. On the bottom step he hesitated and turned back toward Eden. "Milady?" he said. Eden looked up. "Have you any commission for me?"

"None," said Eden simply. "I'm sure you will think of everything." She listened to their steps ringing out as they headed up the staircase.

Roland walked to the fire and threw some more logs on it. "I want you to stay in here where it's warm for now."

"Very well."

He came over to her. "Hold up your cup." She looked up in surprise to find he'd brought the rest of the posset over to her.

"Are you not trying any?"

He shook his head and refilled her cup. "Stay here with Seth." He touched his hand briefly to her cheek, then he, too, mounted the stairs and was gone.

Eden wasn't sure how long she'd spent staring into the fire when she heard grumbling and faltering steps descending down toward them. Seth raised his head from his front paws and glanced around, but then resettled himself, looking unconcerned. Clearly, he recognized the owner of those scuffling feet.

Eden drained the last of her posset and set the cup down. She turned her eyes expectantly to the doorway, and sure enough at last there appeared a hunched old man carrying a brace of dead birds. He started a moment when he saw her, but other than a sharp breath in and a hunch of his shoulder, he gave her no other greeting and shuffled over to the kitchen table where he slammed down the birds bad-temperedly. Eden cleared her throat. He stiffened. "I see ye," he muttered. "I see ye well enough! But be ye sprite or harlot, I'll have none of ye!"

Sprite or harlot? "I am neither of those things!" Eden told him loudly. "I am…Lady Eden Vawdrey," she said with only the slightest hesitation over her new name.

He made a quick gesture which Eden recognized was to ward off evil spirits, but otherwise refused to look her way.

"I am lately married," she said, starting again. "To Master Roland."

He muttered under his breath and started tearing out the feathers on the uppermost bird.

"Perhaps you know his older brother, Oswald, who is now styled Earl Vawdrey?"

He turned his head sharply at that. "Don't ye be trying to tell me you'm married to Master Oswald," he said, pointing a small bladed knife at her. "He married a local lass. Sitchmarsh born and bred, and you're none of her!"

"I never said I was married to Oswald," said Eden. "I am married to his brother Roland, who is now master here."

"Master here, you says?" cackled the old man, shaking his head. "That he b'aint!"

Eden gazed at him irritably. "He most certainly is," she stated firmly. "And I am not going to sit arguing here with you about it. What is your name?"

He gave a snort. "I knows better'n that, I'm country-raised."

"What do you mean?" asked Eden, momentarily thrown despite herself.

"Give a spirit your name and you gives 'em power over you."

"A spirit?" Eden pursed her lips. Still, Fulco had said the village girls all thought the Keep was haunted. "I am no more spirit than you." Another thought occurred to her. "I suppose you know Fulco? He recognizes me as mistress here."

"Fulco?" the old man spat. "Ah, you're one of his slatterns, are you? Might have known. Shameless! Giving yourself airs and graces and coming into my kitchen!"

"That is quite enough!" said Eden, drawing herself up. "You go too far!"

The old man gave her a hard look and puffed out his cheeks. "Well," he conceded. "You're done up fancy, I'll give you that. Fine as the Faery Queen herself."

Eden glanced down at her finery. The fur-lined cloak and mittens from Cuthbert, and Lady Payne's wedding dress. Maybe she did look rather frivolous sat among his pots and pans? She lapsed into silence, cupping her chin and leaning her elbow against her knee. She'd waste no more words on the stubborn old buzzard.

The old man carried on dressing the birds in silence, and Eden's eyelids began to droop. The fire was hot at her front, but her back felt chilly. In spite of that, she was feeling sleepy. The old man was ignoring her, and she would return the favor. If anyone looked like a bad faery, it was him. A hobgoblin or brownie. She frowned. She was thinking of her old nurses' tales again! Weren't brownies paid for household chores with a bowl of cream on the hearth? Insulting them was said to bring bad luck. Perhaps she ought not to have spoken to him so harshly. How did you free brownies from labor? Was it them you had to sew a smock for or was that elves? And which ones turned into boggarts when they went evil?

The next thing Eden knew, she was being carried in a pair of strong arms.

"It's me," said Roland when she started.

"A boggart runs your kitchen," she murmured before dropping her head back to his shoulder.

"A boggart?" repeated Roland. "That's funny. He accused me of wedding a wicked faery. Said I must have found you sat in a rowan tree."

Eden considered this a moment. "They must be very superstitious parts around here."

"The boggart's name is Baxter," said Roland. "He's been here for years. Before my father's time even."

Eden thought this over. "Maybe he's more of a goblin than a boggart. Boggart might be a bit harsh." She glanced at one of the narrow windows that they passed and gasped. "Has night fallen? How long was I asleep?"

"It's late afternoon," said Roland. "It looks darker due to the thunderclouds."

"And now it's raining," observed Eden, catching another glimpse through an arrow loophole.

"It rains a lot round here. That's why it's so green."

"Are Cuthbert and Fulco returned from the village?"

"Hours ago. We've tidied up a bit since then."

"I can't believe I was so tired," she yawned. "Did Baxter put a blanket over me?"

"No," said Roland dryly. "That was me. Baxter threw salt over you."

212

"Salt?"

"It's said to counteract malevolent beings."

Eden digested this. "Boggart was not too harsh after all," she said darkly. Roland smirked, but said nothing. "Did Cuthbert restuff the mattress?" she asked, determined to fill any silence. Being cradled against his body like this was creating a false sense of intimacy she just was not comfortable with.

"Yes. He used hay, and a good quantity of wool from the village."

"I see. He is a very useful boy, is he not?"

Roland's gaze flickered. "He can be, when it suits him," he said cautiously. He shoved the door open on the second landing. "We have covered a fair few miles the last few days, likely more than you're used to riding," he reminded her.

They were in the dining room, which had been tidied and swept out. The floorboards were now bare instead of strewn with dirty rushes, and the benches were arranged tidily around the tables. Four of the dogs were lying under the benches. Castor, Hector, Seth, and the gray gargoyle one. They all raised their heads at their entrance but did not make a sound.

Roland strode right across to the table next to the fireplace, and deposited Eden there. "We're about to eat," he told her, and sat down next to her. Eden looked about the room in approval. The scuffed table looked a lot better covered in a plain linen cloth. It was already set with heavy silver candlesticks and platters and goblets of pewter.

Reluctantly, she reached for her cloak fastening. She should really take it off now, though she did not feel thus inclined. She wished she had her wool mantle with her. She had a lovely one in dark green that she would give her eyeteeth for right now.

Doubtless it was lying unused in the bedchamber she used at Hallam Hall.

Eden dropped the cloak from her shoulders and gave a little involuntary shiver. Lady Payne's ice-blue gown was not designed for warmth. As she was drawing off her mittens, the door opened, and Cuthbert sailed in, carrying a large soup pot, and a platter bearing two small loaves.

"It's barley beef," he announced, setting down the pot. "And there's two types of bread. Maslin," he said, referring to the darker rye and wheat loaf, "and manchet," which was the round white loaf. He sat down opposite Eden and started ladling the soup into the bowls as Roland poured the wine.

The door opened again, and in came Fulco, looking rather ill at ease and bearing a platter of fried cheese curds with some flat cracker-breads and a garlic dipping sauce. Once he'd set the dish down, he seated himself next to Cuthbert.

Eden perked up at the appetizing fare. "Did Baxter cook all these dishes?" she asked with surprise. For some reason she had imagined him to be a rather basic and unimaginative cook.

"Yes," piped up Cuthbert. "Baxter says if you're tricked into eating human victuals, you'll be stuck in the human realm."

"Tricked? I'm ravenous," said Roland, accepting his bowl of soup and tearing off a large hunk of bread.

"Oh, he knows *you're* real enough," continued Cuthbert blithely. "He just thinks you're ensorcelled."

Eden, who was in the act of buttering her bread, put down her knife. "Is Baxter…sane?" she asked carefully.

"He's alright," said Cuthbert heartily. "It's normal for folks to hold the old beliefs in the country."

214

"He's not going to throw salt in my face every morning or strike me with a birch wand?"

Cuthbert chuckled, but Roland didn't look nearly as amused. "He'd better not," said her husband with a heavy frown.

"He'll calm down," said Fulco awkwardly. "He's not used to having people about the place. He's gone a little peculiar, that's all."

Eden refused the soup but helped herself to some of the fried cheese and dipping sauce. It was delicious, as were the crunchy crackers. Cuthbert watched her with approval.

"Baxter said I was to make sure you ate a little from every dish. He means to ensure you're trapped here to 'keep Master Roland happy,'" he quoted.

Roland's brows rose at that, but he turned to Eden. "In that case, you'd better take a sip," he said.

A week ago, she'd likely have refused the gesture, but now, Eden merely bent her head and put her lips to the soup spoon he offered her. The soup was flavorful. She could taste shallot and parsnip as well as barley and the meat. "It's good," she said with a nod.

Roland cleared his throat and took a swig of wine. "In fairness, my father always kept a good table. Is that not so?" When no one answered, Roland lowered his goblet. Eden looked across at Fulco, who was the only one qualified to say. He was watching her intently. Oh no, did he think she was a faery too? thought Eden with misgiving.

Fulco flushed. "Oh aye, he was a great man, the old baron," he said hoarsely, and started hastily tucking into his soup.

215

Eden relaxed, though she thought Roland seemed to tense beside her. He sat up straighter and plunked his cup down rather heavily. For a few moments, the only sounds were of chewing or swallowing and the clink of knives against trenchers.

Cuthbert nudged the plate of cheese and crackers toward her and she helped herself, though she eschewed more of the sauce, of which a little went a long way. Roland, she noticed, ate three bowls of soup and at least half of the small dark loaf before turning to devour what was left of the cheese. When that was gone, he had a large slice of the manchet loaf and dipped it in the garlic sauce for flavor.

Cuthbert and Fulco both excused themselves and removed the empty platters, descending below stairs to fetch the next course.

"We'll have to get some womenfolk up here and soon," said Roland heavily. "You're driving Fulco to distraction."

"Me?" asked Eden in surprise. "Why? What have I done?"

"Nothing," he admitted. "Save sit there, eating daintily. You're likely the prettiest thing he's seen in a twelvemonth."

Eden raised her goblet to hide her discomfiture with this kind of talk. Was he trying to flatter her? "I doubt it," she said without thinking. "I don't think he has been as starved of female company as you suppose."

"What?" His brows knitted together in a frown.

"At one point, before he decided I was otherworldly in origin, Baxter thought I might have been 'one of Fulco's slatterns,'" she admitted.

Roland went off into a coughing fit. Eden was just wondering if she might need to thump him on the back when the others returned with a dish of roasted birds stuffed with garlic, grapes,

216

and herbs. Roland poured himself another cup of ale and pulled himself together, although his eyes were still watering.

Fulco excused himself before the final course, no doubt cowed by Roland's beady eye on him, putting him off his food. Eden fancied the dogs received quite a lot of the meat, for all four of them crept closer as the meal progressed. She wondered at one point if she was the only one not feeding them.

Only Cuthbert seemed to enjoy the dessert, which was baked eggs with apple in a pastry shell. Eden ate a mouthful to satisfy Baxter's absurd superstitions, and Roland pushed his around his plate a while before shoving it away from him.

"Shall we?" he asked, standing abruptly as Cuthbert finally dropped his spoon, having consumed his third bowlful. Eden rose and took the hand he offered to find herself led the through the door into the adjoining sitting room where a fire blazed in the huge hearth.

This room had also been dusted and cleaned, and the remaining two dogs dozed there by the hearth, including her old friend Parnell, who rolled over onto his stomach and barked in greeting. She nodded in response and looked about her.

It was still a rather bleak and uninviting room in all. It needed curtains and wall hangings and cushions, thought Eden, in reds or blues to complement all the dark wood interior. Roland halted and looked around, seeming to deliberate which of the chairs looked the most comfortable. Eden eyed them doubtfully. They all looked equally uninviting.

Apparently, Roland came to the same conclusion, for he simply hooked his foot around the nearest and dragged it toward the fire. Then he dropped into it, with Eden sat squarely in his lap. She ought to protest, of course, but what was the point? Instead she looked sidelong at Roland, who was looking back steadily at her. "Yes, wicked faery?" he asked, raising his eyebrows. "Something to say?"

Eden tilted her head to one side and steeled herself. "Perhaps there are some matters we ought to discuss," she said gravely. "Now we are no longer on the road."

Roland stirred uneasily beneath her. "Such as?"

*

Even before she spoke, he could tell he would not like her chosen topic of conversation. *Damn the woman.* Could she not pick up on his mood? Now she was safely under his roof, all he wanted to do was cosset her. It was a strange impulse, which threw him a little, in truth. Never before had he had such an inclination toward a woman.

He wanted her to like his home. Their home. Her opinion of Vawdrey Keep, whose superiority to all other places had always been a matter of fact to him, strangely counted. She was accustomed to court life, and all its attendant luxuries, and Hallam Hall, which was a country residence, not a harsh fortress.

He wanted to know what things he had to add to the Keep to make it acceptable to her as her new home. But he could tell from her expression that it wasn't about home comforts that she wanted to speak now. He sighed. "Let's hear it then." Eden rose from his lap and resettled herself into the chair directly opposite him. He suffered this, although it irritated him.

"Don't you think it's odd that we've never actually discussed what must have happened that night?" she asked, turning to him, her expression serious.

Oh gods. Why now? Roland spread his hands wide. "What's done is done. I see no point in crying over spilt milk."

"Spilt milk?" repeated Eden, her expression so blank that Roland immediately cast about for a turn of phrase she'd find more palatable.

"Things didn't turn out as intended," he said carefully. "But what's the point in cutting up rough about it after the deed is done?" A heavy silence greeted his words, and he rolled his eyes. "Quite frankly, I have no desire to discuss it now," he said bluntly. "What would be the purpose?"

"To clear the air perhaps?" she suggested gravely. "To try and promote some kind of understanding between us at this point." She paused heavily. "It seems to me that we are poised at a critical juncture. Would it not be best to clear up any confusion now?"

Roland snorted. "I'm not laboring under any misunderstanding," he said dismissively.

Eden took a deep breath. "Really? What about the fact we clearly had *not* engaged in any...premarital relations?" she asked with a directness that took him aback. "Despite what everyone assumed. Ourselves included." When he continued silent, she fixed him with a stern look. "You know as well as I that I was still a virgin that night at Tranton Vale. Yet we've never discussed it."

Roland felt his face grow hot. "What of it?" he demanded.

"So clearly, we were innocent of any wrongdoing that night at Hallam Hall!" she cried, losing her calm.

219

Roland stiffened. "I was drunk," he said bluntly. "I may not have breached your virginity, but we could still have done other things."

"What?" Eden looked startled.

"We were both naked," he pointed out. "When I woke up, my hands were all over you—"

"I know that!" Eden interrupted him. "But still, we had not gone beyond the bounds of decency!" Her face flamed.

"Of course we had, Eden!" he replied scathingly. "You may have been intact, but we had slept in a naked embrace that was far from innocent on my behalf. Or had you forgotten my state when your uncle interrupted us?" He gestured to his crotch.

Eden glared at him. "Why must you always be so crude?" she huffed. "Do you really mean to tell me that you have *no* curiosity about how we ended up in such a predicament in the first place?"

He shot her an incredulous look. "Eden," he said with exasperation. "Let's just drop the pretense, for once and all."

"What pretense?"

"That you were as injured a party as I." She went so still, he thought she must be holding her breath. Uneasily, he added, "I know full well the scheme would not have been of your devising."

Her eyes flickered to his face. "Scheme?" she repeated hollowly.

He nodded, strangely reluctant to continue. "Aye."

"Pray say what you mean, Sir Roland," she said so formally that he felt slightly alarmed.

"Why do I need to say it?" he asked. "It's obvious enough."

She shook her head. "Not to me."

He sighed. "It was my bedchamber we woke up in, Eden."

"Yes," she said, two hot spots of color appearing on her cheeks.

"And so…?" he prompted. He waited until the penny dropped. He did not have to wait long.

She drew in a shuddering breath. "You're saying… You think…that I snuck along the corridor and let myself into your bedchamber. And then, while you were insensible, that I slipped under your covers. To entrap you." She slumped in her seat a moment, breathless and glassy-eyed. He said nothing. "But if not of my devising…?" she began hesitantly. "Then who is it you imagine was behind such a scheme?"

"Your uncle, of course," he answered brusquely. "Probably thought a younger son wasn't good enough for his only daughter."

She stared hard at that. "But an unwanted niece was? You really have thought this through," she marveled. "Down to the last detail." Her lip trembled, and she bit down on it. "When?" she asked harshly, making him jump. "When did you decide I was complicit?"

"Eden…"

"Before we consummated our marriage?" she asked. "Before you wore my favor on your arm at Sir Aubron's tournament?"

"Eden…"

"No!" she said in a choked voice. "You wore my brooch, introduced me to your friends… You made me think… You

221

pretended that you *liked* me. But all the time, you thought…you thought…"

"Eden!" He started out of his chair toward her, but she jumped to her feet and ran to the door, wrenching it open.

"If you come near me right now," she said shakily, "I will hate you forever." He halted, seeing she was trembling all over and pale as chalk.

Something turned over in his chest. "Don't go near those steps!" he warned. "Not in that state."

"Don't come near me, Roland Vawdrey." She shook her head for emphasis. "I need you to leave me alone." Tears were rolling down her cheeks now.

For some reason, the sight of her tears incapacitated Roland. He felt like he couldn't gather his wits. Where the fuck had this storm blown up out of nowhere? All was well with his world just a short while ago! She had been sat in his lap as meek as a lamb. He was reeling. "I can't," he said with utter truthfulness, and was out of his seat and at her side before she'd managed to even take another step. "Eden—"

She shoved at his chest with both her hands, trying to push him away from her. "No!" she said in an anguished voice.

"I won't touch you," he promised. "Just let me accompany you upstairs."

She fell back at that. "I want to sleep in a different room to you," she said woodenly.

"Too bad," he said harshly. "That's a step too far."

"I won't share a bed with someone who thinks I'm a thief!"

"A thief?" he echoed in bewilderment. "Who the hells ever called you a thief? Not I."

Eden shook her head angrily. "You think I willfully stole you from Lenora!"

He gave a crack of laughter at that, and all color leeched from her face. "Eden," he said, bending down so his face was close to hers. "I was never Lenora's. And for all I know, she could have been in league with the plot. What do I know of her wishes?" Eden's chest heaved indignantly, and she stared at him. "Besides, you're not bedding down anywhere else," he told her arrogantly. "I'm not complaining about you being in my bed, so why the hells should you?" Her expression went from devastated to outraged in a second. He must be losing his mind, because for some reason he could not fathom, that was a relief to him. "Now, let's to bed."

*

Why the hells, he thought crossly as he rolled over in the bed, dutifully turning his back to wife, had he thought he could speak frankly with a woman? He should have known better. They didn't like plain speech. Eden certainly didn't, with her airs and her graces and her sheer bloody-mindedness. He listened carefully to her ragged breathing. Was she still crying?

She'd even managed to twist things around so that *she* was the injured party! he thought with disbelief. Alright, so she was probably mortified that he knew she had climbed into his bed that night. But he had never complained about the substitution of bride, so why did they need to dwell on it now?

After all, he was the one who had the wool pulled over his eyes. *He* was the one who had fallen prey to her uncle's subterfuge. Had one word of reproach passed his lips? No! Even during their dispute just now, he had no desire to reproach or scold her for her part in the deception.

Instead, he had given her an excuse, intimated that she had just been a pawn in her uncle's ambitions, much like him. She was Sir Leofric's ward and dependent on his goodwill. Roland's jaw tensed. For some reason, he didn't like to think of Eden being at the mercy of her uncle's schemes. And he certainly didn't like to remember that she had been sent from her childhood home with only the clothes on her back.

What had she called herself just now? An unwanted niece? He felt slightly sick remembering those words. But there had been worse. Her face when she cried, *You pretended that you liked me.* Remembering that made him catch his breath. Why the fuck had she looked so hurt when she said that?

He forced himself to go back over her words in the dark. She'd extinguished the candle as soon as she'd climbed into the box-bed, and it was pitch black in there now. It had been the thought that he had worn her token, had shown her off to his friends and bedded her, all the while thinking she was a deceiver which had cut her to the quick. But he didn't even care about the deception!

He swore under his breath. Why was she making so much of it? Pride, stiff-necked pride, he told himself angrily. Her damn reputation. But deep down, he knew that more than her pride had been hurt by him bringing the whole mess out into the open. *Hells.* He half wished he'd played along and just lied. *Yes, it is very odd how we neither of us have any recollection of how you ended up in my bed, sweetheart. Ah well, 'tis doubtful we'll ever get to the bottom of the business now!*

It was contemptible to lie just to please a woman, and such an idea would never even have entered his head before today. But perhaps if he had lied, he'd be lying in her embrace right now, and any tears she would be shedding would be of ecstasy, not misery. He tugged at his pillow, unable to get comfortable.

The thought of her crying silently beside him was an oddly disturbing one. He almost turned over, to pull her into his arms, when he remembered, *If you come near me, right now, I will hate you forever*, and stopped dead in his tracks. That was more than disturbing. That was simply something that could not be allowed to happen. Ever. He closed his eyes again briefly and consigned himself to a night of broken, uneasy sleep.

25

Eden woke on a gasp. She'd been underwater. She flailed a moment in confusion, still half-asleep, before she noticed half of her was pinned underneath a big male. Roland Vawdrey was lay across her lower body. His face was buried in her stomach, his arms wrapped around her waist. She blinked down at him in consternation a moment before the memories of the previous evening set in.

Roland Vawdrey must think himself married to a hysteric as well as a liar, she thought bleakly, after the tearful scene she subjected him to last night. She turned first hot then cold all over. What a contemptible mess. She felt heartily ashamed of her emotional outburst. What on earth had come over her? It just wasn't like her to act in such a way. And really, she had no cause. Roland Vawdrey was not her friend. He was not her confidant. He was just someone who was trapped in this travesty of a marriage along with her.

In reality, she should be relieved that he had realized it was all her fault, she thought resignedly. Because she *must* have done everything he had accused her of. The fact she had been asleep when she had done it made very little material difference. What astonished her the most was that he must have thought this of her all along.

It was extraordinary. He must despise her, have thought her character the lowest of the low. Yet he had not shown any discernible anger or resentment toward her. He had not flung blame in her face even once. She was frankly astonished by how magnanimously he had acted toward her all this time. When you consider he believed himself to have been duped at the outset, it was nothing short of miraculous.

Eden lay staring up at the plain wooden roof of the box-bed feeling numb. This was to be her lot in life. Married to a man who thought her a schemer and a fraud. She closed her burning eyes again briefly. At least she had no tears left to cry. All would be well, she told herself firmly, once she managed to get back to court.

Once back as part of the Queen's inner circle, she would be back on firm ground again, and sure of her step. In the past, she had even had occasion previously to sleep on a truckle bed in the Queen's dressing room. There may be no need for her return to her husband's quarters at all, she thought, perking up. He could hardly insist. Not when it was by royal appointment. Feeling him stir, she stiffened as he rubbed his brow against her stomach, then exhaled noisily. Was he awake?

"It can't be morning yet," he groaned, his words tickling her skin. "I've barely slept a wink."

Eden held her tongue, wondering if she could slither out from under him, but his arms seemed to tighten on her as if he'd heard her thoughts.

"If you're awake now," she said coolly, "perhaps you'll permit me to rise."

He murmured something disparaging that she couldn't quite make out. "Back to this again, are we?" he asked, raising her head and looking up at her blearily. "As it's your fault I'm so damnably tired, the least you can do is let me use you for a pillow."

"My fault?" Eden blurted before she could stop herself. Was he saying he had trouble sleeping after their altercation?

"Aye, yours, wife!" he said belligerently. "Who else would be kicking at me, and trying to climb over me in the night?" Eden gasped. "You're like a little eel, wriggling about."

Without thinking, she answered tightly, "I can't control my impulses when I'm asleep." Of course, she thought afterward, he was wholly unaware of the magnitude of what she'd just imparted.

"You don't need to tell me that!" Roland grumbled. "I'm thinking this box-bed is a damned good idea for you. At least you can't seem to find your way out of it."

There was something in that, she thought. "My sleep is only disturbed in times of…upset," she said dismissively. "It'll pass. Can you please let me up?" She felt him turn his head and lay his cheek against her stomach but gave no other sign of having heard her request.

She was just wondering how to insist when he murmured, "This bed is too hard."

Eden sucked in a breath. "Personally, I think Cuthbert did an admirable job with the materials at hand. The mattress is fine." She paused. "I fancy 'tis the choice of bedfellow that vexes you rather than the bedding."

He raised his head at that. "I've got no complaints on that score," he said dismissively. "You can put that out of your head."

She gave a short laugh. "You can scarcely expect me to believe that."

His eyebrows rose, and his gaze narrowed. "And why the hells not?" he asked coolly.

"Because of your opinion of me!" she huffed. "My gods, I am astonished that you even thought to bring me home with you. I wouldn't have, in your position."

Roland snorted. Then abruptly he levered himself off her and hauled her down the mattress until he loomed over her. His hands at her waist anchored her beneath him.

His eyes roamed over her at leisure, and Eden felt herself grow hot and bothered. "While it's true I've never previously admired resourcefulness in a woman," he said thoughtfully, "I find I'm not too angry that you decided to win me."

Eden gaped at him. "I beg your pardon?" she spluttered.

"You heard me, wife."

"Of all the egotistical…" Eden broke off distractedly. *Resourceful?* She stared at him as if unable to believe her own ears. "You astonish me!"

"I'm sure," he said, running his forefinger across her collarbone. "That's only fair, seeing as you astonish me too." Eden gulped. What was that expression on his face? "I think Baxter may be partly right, and you've bewitched me," he said huskily.

"Baxter's mad," she pointed out, wishing her own voice didn't sound so breathy. "And so are you if you think that."

"I don't know," he replied softly. The direction his finger brushed against her changed, and Eden swallowed. "Round these parts all the faery maidens are reputed to look like you. Black locks, soft skin as pale as milk," he said. "And eyes like jewels that bewitch a man."

Eden frowned. *Eyes like jewels?* He made her sound much more alluring than she knew herself to be. "No one has ever thought me bewitching before."

"Maybe you've only just come into your powers?"

"You're being nonsensical," Eden objected, but she knew her voice lacked sternness.

"You fit here," said Roland with conviction.

Eden forgot to breathe. *What?*

"The wicked faery," said Roland, "who lives in the black tower."

From his tone of voice, she knew he was going to kiss her. And she did nothing to stop him as he lowered his weight onto her and kissed her with an unhurried lasciviousness which made her cheeks burn. She shivered and realized this time what his thrusting tongue was promising was in store for her.

"So beautiful," he murmured. Which was a lie. "I want you." Which was not a lie, she conceded, feeling him hard against her stomach where he rubbed and moved sensuously against her. For some unfathomable reason, Roland Vawdrey desired her something fierce.

"Do you want me, Eden?" he muttered, lifting his head. As usual, she felt herself almost dazzled by the proximity of so much male beauty.

She couldn't quite bring herself to answer, so instead she placed a hesitant hand against his shoulder blade. His molten gaze snapped to hers, and she saw him close his eyes as if savoring her touch. He couldn't really like it that much, surely? Without giving herself pause to think, she stroked her hand slowly down his spine.

He gasped, his eyes flying wide. *"Eden!"*

"Was that not—?"

He gave a brief shake of his head and swallowed. "Put your hands up over your head."

"What?"

"Over your head and keep them there."

"But why?" she asked even as she complied.

"Because," he murmured, "your touch overexcites me." It did? She pondered that piece of information. "You keep rushing me when I want to linger."

By touching him? she wanted to ask, but his actions were robbing her of breath. He'd pulled up her shift and was kissing all around her flat stomach. She was just taking a steadying breath when his tongue darted unexpectedly into her belly button, making her gasp. "Roland!"

He glanced up. "If that shocked you," he said richly, "then what I'm going to do next will turn your hair white."

Eden glanced down in alarm. He winked at her. He was joking. She relaxed in spite of herself. Then he kissed her between her legs. The same wicked kiss he had given her mouth. She gave a soundless shriek and tried to bounce up off the bed. He just used the momentum to get a firmer grip on her as she ineffectually flailed around.

"R-Roland!" she squeaked as his brawny hands held her hips in a merciless grip as he did inconceivable things with his tongue. Unable to watch, Eden closed her eyes with a whimper and gave herself up to the shuddering pleasure which had her arching her back and pressing into his mouth in an abandonment which shocked her to her core. Tears gushed from

231

her eyes, and she flattened her palms against the headboard, bracing herself against the onslaught of sensation.

For a moment, she hovered agonizingly tense on the brink before he tapped the tip of his tongue against part of her that throbbed, and she yelled out brokenly as he did it again once, twice, and on the third time she broke. And then it was a good thing he held her so tight, for her limbs were suddenly shaking and weak and she could do nothing but pant and sob and gaze up at the top of the wooden bed in speechless wonder.

Through it all, Roland held her firmly, his mouth working between her legs, his circling tongue drawing out the licentious pleasure until she lay still, her chest heaving and her breath ragged, her cheeks wet with tears.

"I can't wait," Roland said thickly, his hot breath still fluttering against her intimate parts, "until you react like that for my cock."

She was too wrung out to remonstrate with him over his lewd words. Instead, she just groaned as he hauled himself up onto his knees and crawled up her body, stripping off her shift. Now came the worse part, thought Eden with dread. Though she realized she'd have to suffer it without complaint now she was a wife. His manhood felt bigger than ever as it pressed insistently against her. Roland looked somewhat pained himself, she noticed as he settled between her legs. "This won't last long," he grunted. She hoped not. She stiffened as he probed her wetness there with his fingers and made an approving noise deep in his throat. Taking a deep breath, she passed her arms around his back.

He swore. "Gods, I'm not—let me inside first—I can't…" Eden blinked up at his confused panic. Catching his desperation, she opened her legs wider as he fumbled and swore. And then he was there, where he wanted to be, pushing inside her with an urgency that surprised her.

He had been very careful with her last time, but this time, he thrust all the way in, making her gasp as she braced herself. To her surprise though, she took him without too much discomfort. Before she could wonder too much at this, he had given her his whole weight, pinned her to the mattress, and was thrusting into her with a vigor he had not allowed himself before, murmuring disjointed words and groaning almost as if he were wounded.

"Roland?" she asked, half alarmed, half what? She scarcely knew. Only that she could barely catch her breath, and something about his wildness was strangely thrilling. She found she was pressing her thighs in hard against his hips, and holding her breath, her face hot, her chest heaving with the exertion.

His eyes locked to hers when she spoke his name, and the expression there made her breath catch in her throat. She almost felt as if time halted and hung suspended for a moment before Roland Vawdrey came apart completely in her arms, a heaving mass of muscle and sinew and seething lust.

In the aftermath, she held him close to her. He was breathing heavily and neither one of them spoke for several long moments.

Then Roland lifted his head. "One of these days," he said, not quite meeting her eyes, "I'll manage that part with a little more finesse."

Really? wondered Eden doubtfully. It was hard to imagine. And how could you even make such an act more dignified? It was so…base and primitive.

"You can do it now," he said.

"Do what?" asked Eden, mystified.

233

"Touch me."

Eden's mouth almost fell open. Why on earth would he want her to touch him now? "Oh," she said lamely. She placed her hands uncertainly on his chest. He gave that low rumble she was starting to realize was approval and dropped his head back onto the pillow beside hers, rolling onto his back, and taking her with him, so she lay half on top of him.

"More," he said gruffly, his eyelids dropping down over his eyes.

Eden tutted, and was disconcerted to see him smile. How could he look so…so…words failed her…*happy*? Even in her thoughts, she stuttered over that choice of word. It couldn't be because of her. His hand seized hers and stroked it over his chest. "Like this." Eden bit her lip. A week ago, if someone had told her she would be lying naked on top of a satiated Roland Vawdrey, stroking his chest, she would have called them a liar to their face. "Now kiss me," he said, interrupting her thoughts.

"What?" Eden faltered. She glanced around; the hour was hard to determine in their cupboard-bed. "It must surely be approaching daybreak," she objected.

He opened one eye. "How does that signify?" He sounded lazily curious, nothing more.

Eden ducked her head, tucking her hair behind her ears. "I just mean that, we'll soon have to rise."

"Not until you've kissed me, we won't. And make it a good one."

"What do you mean, *a good one*?" asked Eden indignantly.

His smile grew, though his eyes were closed again. "One that will fortify me for the day ahead," he explained. "Otherwise, I'll have to keep snatching kisses from you to keep me going."

Eden spluttered. "That's ridiculous!" Did he mean with tongue? she wondered distractedly.

"Now don't turn all stiff and starchy," he said, his hand sliding from her waist to rub her hip. "It won't work, not when I can still recall…"

Horrified at the prospect of what he might say next, she dropped her head and pressed her lips to his. Roland's hand on her hip squeezed gently, and Eden shifted slightly over him as she steeled herself for the next part. Bracing a second hand against his warm chest, she touched her tongue to his lips.

Roland gave a muffled exclamation. Squeezing her eyes tightly shut, she slipped her tongue fully into his mouth, and found both her hips firmly gripped as Roland sat up, dragging her into his lap. She squeaked and would have pulled her head back, but his hand was suddenly tangled in her hair, holding her plastered against him as he took the lead in their incendiary kiss, his tongue stroking insistently against her own. One of his hands grasped her backside firmly, whilst the other covered her breast. Finally, he dragged his mouth from hers and leaned his head back against the headboard.

"Fuck, Eden, not that good," he groaned. "Now all I can think about is being between your thighs again." Eden's face flamed. He shot her a speculative look. "I expect you're too sore though.

"Of course I am!" she stammered, dragging her gaze away from the blatant arousal between his legs. In truth, she was more tender than sore this time, but she certainly did not fancy

235

another round with the beast that very morning! It was indecent to even think of it!

He huffed out a breath, releasing her. Immediately, Eden scrambled off him and pounced on her shift, dragging it over her head to cover her nakedness.

"Sorry," he said ruefully, raking a hand over his face. Then he grinned at her. "But that was a *very* good kiss." He had no right to look so boyishly handsome when his behavior was so utterly brazen!

26

Roland kept a close eye on Fulco as they broke their fast. He was unnerved by the idea of him as some kind of bearded seducer. He would definitely be having a conversation with him at some point on the subject. How the devil was he supposed to go off and compete at the tourneys and leave his wife with such a manservant?

Fulco did not join them to eat this morning, having risen hours before and started on his work outside. Instead, he simply brought in a large platter of pickled herrings and salted stockfish, and then abruptly left. Parnell and Seth snuck through the door and insinuated themselves under Roland's bench.

"What's that one called?" asked Eden, pointing to the ginger dog wrapped around Cuthbert's legs.

"That's Nudd," Roland told her.

"Nudd?"

"It's an old name round these parts."

"I see." She seemed ill at ease this morning, and blushed whenever his gaze fell on her. Which was often. He found he didn't tire of the view.

"You should have called him Tod after a male fox," said Cuthbert. "He looks just like one. My granny raised a fox cub once. She found him half drowned in his den. Someone had killed his mam."

"What happened to him?" asked Eden.

"She still had him, last time I visited home." Cuthbert shrugged. "He stinks something awful though. His name's Nix."

"What's the gray dog called?" asked Eden. "The one who looks like a gargoyle."

A gargoyle? Roland lowered his butter knife. "His name's Dimon." He saw her repeat the name under her breath as if committing it to memory. For some reason that pleased him too. He noticed out of the corner of his eye that Parnell had abandoned him to appear at Eden's side. His tail thudded against the floorboards when she spoke to him in low tones.

"Should have called him Babewyn," said Cuthbert scornfully.

"I'll have you know," said Roland, "that my father considered him a vastly handsome animal and paid a goodly sum for him."

"Speaking of gargoyles, I forgot to tell you," said Cuthbert, looking up from his plate. "When I was in the village yesterday, I came across a Lady Orla Bernard. She was buying flax from old Simpkin when I was getting wool for your mattress."

"Who?" demanded Roland.

"That's who I was telling you about!" said Eden triumphantly. She turned to Cuthbert. "She is Fenella's sister-in-law, is she not?"

Cuthbert nodded. "That's right, and a right busybody, truth be told. There I was, minding my own business, when what does she do, but march over and demand to know 'who I was to be using up the village resources!' Simpkin, he was right put out about it."

Roland grunted. He'd just bet he was. Walt Simpkin would sell his own mother for a few coins.

"And did you tell her?" asked Eden, who seemed a good deal more interested in the tale than he.

238

"Aye," Cuthbert agreed. "She left me very little choice." He shot a furtive look at Roland and cleared his throat before addressing Eden. "She said she'd often heard the Lady Fenella speak of you. Said they'd be sure to call on you here and pay a visit."

"What? When?" Roland scowled. "You would think she'd wait for an invite!" She'd be waiting a long time, he reflected. But after all, they were newlyweds.

Eden seemed to take the news in her stride. "I have often heard Fenella speak of her also and would be happy to make her acquaintance." Then she seemed to remember her surroundings and looked a bit more uncertain. "I suppose I could receive her in the sitting room next door?"

Roland rolled his eyes. *What a damnable nuisance!*

After breakfast, he set off downstairs to go in search of Fulco. Cuthbert caught up with him in the disarming room afterward as he was pulling on his boots.

"Are we still bound for Areley Kings on the morrow?" he asked.

Roland's head snapped up abruptly. He'd completely forgotten about it. It was a fine purse to the victor at Areley Kings and not one he would lightly pass up on. "I'm not yet decided," he stalled.

Cuthbert gave him a knowing look. "You've doubtless had other things on your mind," he said with a faintly patronizing air. Roland ignored him. He had frankly bigger fish to fry.

He found Fulco carrying hay bales into the stables on his shoulder. "Fulco," he called. "A word."

His manservant grunted and disappeared into the nearest stall before reappearing and tilting his chin at Roland.

"What's all this I hear about you bringing women up to the Keep?" Roland asked without preamble.

To his surprise his manservant merely looked aggrieved. "I does my best, Master Roland," he sighed, shaking his head. "You ask Baxter, if I don't! Why, many's the time I've given 'em a tour of the old place. You come and take a look, my girl, I says to 'em. I'll show thee, there's nothing to be afeard of! But there, they always cry off not long after, saying the place gives 'em a bad feeling or some such nonsense."

Roland paused, revising the lecture about propriety he had been about to deliver to his blameless servant. "You don't leave them alone in the kitchen with Baxter at any point, do you?" he asked with misgiving.

"It'd be a fine thing if I didn't," said Fulco in an injured tone. "After all, it's not me that gives orders within the Keep."

Roland rolled his eyes. *Small wonder then!* "And none of the village girls will stay?"

Baxter sighed. "Course, it probably don't look the thing. Should be the housekeeper as takes on the maids."

"It's a shame you're not married," said Roland absently. "Your wife could have had the role of housekeeper."

Fulco blushed. "I don't say I wouldn't like to take a wife," he admitted gruffly. "But my mother has some very strong views on the matter."

"Your mother?" repeated Roland blankly. He cast a swift look at Fulco, who was at least three score years by his estimation.

"Aye, Master Roland. A good woman, my mother."

"Didn't she used to run the buttery here at one time?"

"That she did indeed. Before my father died."

"She lives with you now, I'll warrant."

"Aye," agreed Fulco. "She lived with my sister Annie for the first twelvemonth after the old man passed. But then, they fell out, on account of Annie's husband, Jeb. Then she moved to my sister Constance's household."

"Then they fell out?" guessed Roland.

Fulco rubbed his nose. "Aye, more's the pity. Mother didn't approve of how Connie's raising her young 'uns."

Roland cleared his throat. "And now she doesn't approve of you courting."

"That's about the sum of it," Fulco agreed sadly.

Roland cast his mind back to recall Mrs. Fulco, winced, and then hastily consigned the memory back to the back of his brain where it belonged. "Who was it you had your eye on before that?" he asked.

The other man opened his mouth, then swiftly shut it again. "No one," he mumbled, but his coloring was high, telling his lie.

Fulco was a damn poor liar, which for some reason cheered Roland up no end. It was hard to imagine him in the role of habitual seducer of innocents. "I'm off to Areley Kings on the morrow," he told him, slapping him on the back. "I'll be taking my squire with me and will be some four or five days."

Fulco looked alarmed. "What about my lady?"

"You'll have to wait on her," said Roland airily. "I daresay she won't give you too much trouble."

241

"It ain't my place!" he objected with spirit. "Who'll take care of things out of doors?"

"Well, I can't rely on Baxter," said Roland dryly. "He's a dyed-in-the-wool woman-hater."

Fulco looked appalled. "Th-there was one lass," he stammered. "As always said, she was up to the task." He looked pained.

"As maidservant, or your sweetheart?" asked Roland flippantly.

"Maidservant," huffed Fulco, looking scandalized.

"Then why haven't you hired her?" asked Roland suspiciously.

Fulco's cheeks were like two rosy apples by this point. "Because she's none too nice in her morals," he growled.

Roland's eyebrows rose. "Not fit for anything but rough work?"

Fulco shuffled his large feet. "I was mebbe a little harsh," he admitted. "I don't know of any real ill of her. Just that she has a teasing, provoking manner my mother never cared for, and she was widowed very young."

Roland frowned. "Don't like to bring this up, Fulco, but your mother doesn't approve of your sisters either. Do you go about casting aspersions on their morals as well?"

Fulco looked chastened. "I spoke out of line," he said.

Roland shrugged. "Well, maybe she's not ideal to wait on my wife, but beggars can't be choosers. If she'll brave the Keep, then send for her forthwith."

"Aye, Master Roland," he said gloomily.

"And look lively about it, man!" Roland ran back up the stairs to the Keep. Fulco quoted his mother far too much for comfort. He doubted any woman would take him on with such an

242

interfering mother-in-law. Feeling reassured about leaving Eden with him, he returned to back indoors in search of his wife.

For some reason, his thoughts were never far from her these days. He gave his head a slight shake. Doubtless that would soon pass, but for now he would not worry overmuch about it. Truth was, he felt a deep sense of rightness about installing her here at the Keep.

He had not lied earlier when he had said as much to her in bed. She belonged here, as mistress in a way no other woman would. He felt a fleeting pity for Fulco, who, no doubt, slept in a narrow cot every night without the comfort of a warm body at his side. *Poor wretch, he ought to wed.* He dwelled a moment on Eden's daring kiss that morning and felt his blood warm. While it had far surpassed what he'd hoped for, it wasn't going to fortify him all day. Not by a long shot.

He did not find Eden upstairs but unexpectedly in the kitchen kneeling on the floor over a large tub of soapy water. She was wringing something out. "What are you about?" he asked, peering over her shoulder.

"I only have one gown," she reminded him. "I'm washing out my shift and my veil."

Roland opened his mouth to say she ought to give it to someone else to do but stopped himself. No doubt, she would not relish the idea of Cuthbert or Baxter washing her undergarment. "Hopefully Fulco has found some girl in the village," he said, watching her screw up her nose. "What is it?"

"This noxious stuff Baxter gave me," said Eden, referring to the lye used for washing the laundry.

Roland snorted. "Come here," he said, pouring out a clean basin of water from a pitcher. "We had best wash it off your hands. It'll be too harsh for skin like yours."

She came to her feet. "It stings a little," she agreed, approaching him. "What is its substance?"

Roland smirked at her ignorance. "Ashes and animal fat, mostly." Eden grimaced as he placed her slender hands in the bowl and suffered him to wash the traces from her white skin. "You never laundered at Hallam Hall?" he observed. Eden shook her head. "You won't be expected to here either," he said firmly. "Today is the first and last time."

Eden looked up. "Who is the girl from the village?" she asked, looking anywhere but at him.

Roland reached for a cloth and set himself to drying off her fingers. "She's a widow," he said. "And very likely not suitable to wait on you, but she'll have to do for now." He replaced the cloth and put his hands to her waist, drawing her closer. "I need to speak with you. I've a tournament in Areley Kings coming up."

Her eyes flew to his. "When?"

"Cuthbert and I will need to set off tomorrow early."

She looked up at him blankly. "I see."

"We'll be gone likely three or four days. Maybe five."

"Five!" Eden looked alarmed.

"Will you miss me then, wife?"

"It's not that," said Eden with exasperation. "I have no books nor instruments for music! No loom for tapestry making. How am I to spend my days?" Roland felt a twinge of irritation. "Is

244

there even pen and ink for writing?" she carried on, heedless of his darkening mood. "What am I to do with myself?"

Roland shrugged. "I could see about ordering you some such things when I'm on my travels," he suggested.

"I suppose I could take walks, or ride if the weather permits," Eden said, distractedly glancing out of the nearest slitted window.

"Not too far," Roland cautioned. "And you'll need to take a couple of dogs for attendants."

Eden's eyes widened. "Do you get many strangers hereabouts?"

"You never know," Roland heard himself warn direly, even though it was very rare in this out-of-the-way spot.

"Castor still does not like me," Eden reminded him, looking ruffled. "I would only be able to rely on Parnell and Seth."

"Maybe it would be a good notion to show you the nearest paths this afternoon," Roland suggested, though he'd had no such intent just moments ago.

Eden perked up at that. "Could you show me the route to the village?"

"You would not go there alone," said Roland firmly.

"What if Fulco were to accompany me?" she asked. Roland remembered glibly telling Fulco that his mistress would not give him too much trouble and felt a pang of guilt. "Or maybe this girl from the village would be agreeable?"

"She might at that," he agreed. "And don't forget you're expecting a visitor." With a bit of luck, he'd miss having to meet their nosy neighbor.

Eden's aspect brightened. "Oh yes! The Lady Orla. That's true."

"I daresay you'll find plenty to occupy yourself with." For some reason, the notion did not overly please him. She should, he thought, pine a little for her absentee husband of one week.

Eden seemed oblivious to his displeasure. "Will we walk or ride?"

"Walk."

And walk they did, at least six miles in a circular route encompassing part of the woods and one of the neighboring slopes. Castor and Hector remained on guard, but they took the other four dogs with them, and they gamboled about as Roland threw sticks for them and encouraged them to jump into the stream.

"Won't they get muddy?" Eden objected as her favorite, Parnell, stood poised in indecision on a large rock, barking.

"They need a clean. Otherwise, someone will have to bathe them at some point."

Eden shrieked as Nudd shook his gingery fur dry next to her, splattering her with droplets of water.

"Here, Nudd." Roland whistled, leading him to green grass to roll in. The dog's tongue lolled out as he lay panting on the grassy bank.

"Don't you miss them when you're at the palace?" Eden asked curiously. Seth dropped a stick at her feet, and she gingerly retrieved it, wiped it with her handkerchief, and then threw it in the opposite direction. He bounded after it, closely chased by Dimon.

"Of course."

"Then why do you not keep at least one of them with you?"

"And break up the pack? The Keep's their home."

"It's yours too," she reminded him. "But you still have business at court."

"How would I even choose which to take? I don't have favorites like you."

Eden cast a reproachful look at him. "You said your father had a favorite," she reminded him. "And besides, you could take it in turns which dog you selected."

He shook his head. "A man may have many dogs in his lifetime. But a dog only ever has one master."

"What do you mean by that, I wonder?" she asked, taking the stick from Dimon, who had dutifully brought it back to her. Seth barked as she considered which direction to throw it.

Roland watched as she flung it with all her might, only for it to land a short distance away. Clearly, Eden's youth had not been spent following physical pursuits. "Try throwing it underarm next time."

"You mean, I suppose," she continued, ignoring his advice regarding stick-throwing, "that they are still your father's dogs? And that you would not like to split them up or take them from the Keep which is their home?" Roland found himself disconcerted. He had not consciously reasoned it out like that, and yet…she was not wrong. "That's foolish," she said roundly. "Your father left the Keep and the animals to you."

"Actually, he didn't," Roland reminded her without heat. "He left them to Oswald."

"And Oswald then bestowed them on you."

247

"True enough."

"It's hard to imagine Earl Vawdrey as master of this place," mused Eden, again perturbing him. She cast a sidelong look at him. "You're a better fit, I think." He thought she echoed his words from earlier unconsciously, but the notion pleased him all the same. "It's curious to think of the three of you as young boys living here," said Eden slowly. "You're all so very different. What were your mothers like?" Roland gave a start. "Of course you don't have to answer," Eden said hurriedly. "I did not mean to pry—"

"It's not that," Roland said, waving her apology aside. "It's just that I did not know any of them." Now it was Eden's turn to look surprised. "Oswald's mother was my father's first wife. She died in childbirth and Oswald was reared by a wet nurse. She was from the village and moved in, becoming my father's mistress. She was Mason's mother. Eventually she returned to her husband but left Mason here. I daresay my father had tired of her. He then married my mother, his second wife, when Oswald was eight and Mason seven years or thereabouts. Apparently, she was my father's favorite—he used to say she had a lot of spirit. I wouldn't know, she broke her neck in a fall from a horse when I was just a baby."

Eden looked disconcerted. "And your mother's people?" she asked.

Roland shrugged. "My father never suffered them to visit. Said her kinsmen were a lot of damn fools."

"You never met any of them?"

"Once I think, some years back. Her father was a country squire or some such. Dull as ditchwater. I didn't miss out on much." Eden smiled, but in a perfunctory manner. "Now you," he said softly.

"I suppose that is fair, but I've already told you about my ne'er-do-well sire. My mother died soon after he, and I was raised by my uncle. The rest you know."

"What rest?" asked Roland in dissatisfaction. "You've barely told me anything."

"About the same amount as you," she said defensively.

Roland blew out a breath. "I was the youngest son," he said. "My father's favorite and what else is there to say? I ran amok about these woods as a boy, became a squire at thirteen to my older brother Oswald. I came to court at fifteen and trained and was knighted at twenty."

"You were betrothed," Eden prompted him.

"What?"

"To Linnet."

Roland gave startled laugh. "Aye, that I was. My father betrothed me at twenty-one to Linnet Cadwallader. We never met, and shortly before we were to wed, I jilted her." He pulled a face. "Luckily, Mason was there to pick up the pieces."

"Luckily? Did you not try to get their marriage annulled?" Eden reminded him dryly.

Roland reddened. "I did," he admitted. "Not my finest hour."

"Why did you change your mind?"

She really wasn't going to let him off the hook. "Purely mercenary reasons," he said after a heavy pause. "Pettiness and greed."

She gave him an appraising look and was silent as he helped her over some stepping stones across a brook. "Does it never make things awkward? At family gatherings, I mean?"

Roland shot her a look. "Not really," he said. "Mason used to get a little het up about it at one time. But they've been married four years now and have three children. It's all water under the bridge." He whistled, and the dogs who had roamed on ahead came circling back.

"I hope—" Eden broke off, biting her lip.

"What?" Why did she suddenly look so troubled? he wondered.

"I only hope that Lenora is as understanding," she said, "about what I've done. Cutting her out, I mean, as your bride."

Roland did not speak for a moment. "She's sure to be," he responded carefully. "For she does not know me any better than Linnet did. Not really."

"My uncle said…" Eden began, only to break off again.

"Tell me."

"He said that if Lenora forgave me, then he would send on my things." When Roland did not speak, she carried on. "Though I suppose he would naturally send them to Caer-Lyoness, rather than here."

"It doesn't matter either way," said Roland dismissively. "I'll buy you new things."

"You misunderstand me. It's not so much my belongings," Eden said sadly, "as the knowledge that my cousin does not hold it against me. You see, we were very close growing up. Rather like your brothers, our ages were similar. When my uncle took me into his household, it was in the role of Lenora's companion."

"You were his niece," Roland reminded her shortly, "and should not have required any other role to secure his protection." It rankled to think of her as a poor relation at Hallam Hall. Having to justify her place there, as if she did not belong.

She looked surprised by his words. "I told you, did I not, that my father was a spendthrift and a gambler. My uncle had to pay off his considerable debts."

"I still fail to see how that is your fault."

Eden was silent a moment, pondering his words. "I always felt the need from a young age to prove to Uncle Leofric that I was not wild and ungovernable like my father. That I would not bring shame on the family name but was respectable and dutiful and good."

"You haven't brought any shame to his door," said Roland sharply.

"Only because you married me," said Eden in a slightly choked voice. When he made an abrupt move toward her, she flung out her arm to ward him off. "No, don't comfort me, I'm well. I just wanted there to be some frank speech between us."

"Then let me return in kind," said Roland. "When I woke up in that bed with you on that first morning, I wasn't angry. Not by a long chalk. So, let's have no more talk about you taking anyone else's place. It wasn't anyone else's. It was yours. Are we understood?"

Eden stared at him a moment, open-mouthed. And when he held out his hand to her, she took it.

27

Roland and Cuthbert left early the next morn, and Eden found herself sat at the window seat in the sitting room, waving them off.

Roland had made love to her again the previous evening, and he had taken his sweet time about it too. He had been tormenting and provoking and seemed to want something more from her, which she found alarming. At one point she had simply asked him to tell her what he expected her to say.

His hands had cupped her breasts. "'Yes, my lord and master' would be nice," he had sighed throatily. "But I'd settle for a measly 'yes, husband,'"

Eden had pressed her lips together and turned her head to one side. She certainly wasn't saying anything so ridiculous!

"No?" he had tutted, his voice warm and teasing. "Even in this little thing, you refuse to please me?"

To her horror, Eden had felt hot tears spring to her eyes and spill over. She'd blinked rapidly to try to banish them before he saw.

"Eden," he'd groaned. "Sweetheart."

Sweetheart, why did he insist on calling her that? She had given a choked sob, but Roland's lips had already been on hers, coaxing and sweet. She had let him comfort her with his soft kisses and his hands, stroking her back, encouraging her to respond to him.

"You know you please me, wife," he had said huskily. "None so well as you." His hands had roamed down her hips and pulled her flush against him. "Oh, Eden," he had sighed gustily, shifting his weight to press against her.

He had refused to be rushed. He had stripped them both entirely naked and turned her this way and that, petting and lavishing her body with his touch and kisses in some rather peculiar places. Brushing them against her ribs and the undersides of her breasts before turning her onto her stomach and kissing up her spine.

Strangely, his lips had avoided the usual spots. She had wondered if his jaw had been too stubbly to kiss along her neck or the valley between her breasts. When she had the chance, she reached out to touch his jaw with the backs of her fingers to check. At her touch, he had shivered, and his need had finally grown urgent enough to put an end to his tormenting explorations.

First, he had set her on her hands and knees and put his mouth to her again, making her yell and sob like an abandoned creature. Then he had mounted her from behind and driven into her until her arms had given out. In the aftermath, he had been very tender and affectionate, falling asleep with his face buried in the back of her neck as he had the night he had taken her virginity at Tranton Vale.

She watched as they disappeared down the hill, and sat for a moment, feeling rather forlorn. Parnell jumped up onto the seat beside her, and instead of remonstrating with him, Eden found herself wrapping her arms around his neck. He gave a small whine, and Eden sighed, laying her cheek against his curly coat.

She had already eaten, dressed, and braided her hair. The dogs had been racing between the Keep and the stables for the past two hours as Roland and Cuthbert had loaded up the jousting gear. Castor was still skulking outside, but Dimon, Seth, and

Nudd lay dozing by the fire which Fulco had lain for her. He entered the room now with a basket full of freshly cut logs.

"Fulco, are there truly no books at all to be had about the place?" Eden asked, looking up. She found it hard to believe there were none about the place.

"Books?" Fulco tugged his beard and looked uneasy. "Not much call for books around these parts," he said. At Eden's dissatisfied tut, he scratched his head. "That young Cuthbert found a mess of old paperwork when he dragged that old mattress out the box-bed to restuff it," he admitted grudgingly.

"Indeed?" Eden's ears pricked up. "Pray tell me, what did he do with them?" Fulco screwed up his eyes. "Please tell me you didn't use them to start the fire."

Fulco bridled. "I did not," he said. "'Tweren't my place to dispose of 'em!" Eden sighed in relief. "I think he threw them in that there old trunk, in the main bedchamber."

"I don't suppose," said Eden hopefully, "that you noticed what manner of reading matter they were?"

Fulco shook his head. "Don't got no call for reading," he sniffed.

A mess of paperwork. It didn't sound very promising in truth, but Eden still went to investigate once she was left to her own devices. She soon retrieved a half dozen scrolls, and to her excitement, three leather-bound books from the bottom of the trunk. The scrolls did not actually look so very old, and when she unfurled the first one, she was surprised to find meticulous diagrams of a structure that she recognized after staring at it a moment or two. Why, it was Vawdrey Keep.

There were copious numbered notes in a close cramped hand which she found hard to make out and lists of measurements

254

and calculations which seemed to refer to stone, clay, limestone, and chalk. Were these the plans for the building of the Keep? she wondered. But no, they did not seem old enough. She glanced up as the door squeaked open and found it was Parnell trailing after her. He flopped down on the rug next to her with a dispirited huff. Eden reached out and patted him before rolling her scroll back up and unfurling the second one.

She recognized the penmanship at once. The author of this one was clearly the same as the first. But this time she did not recognize the building which was on a much grander and larger scale than the Keep altogether, with two matching towers at either side of the main entrance. Her eyes scanned down the page with interest.

With a start, she noticed the page was initialed O.V. *Oswald Vawdrey*, she thought with surprise. She lowered the page a moment and returned to the first scroll. A quick examination showed her this one also bore the same initials. She seemed to remember that Roland said the wooden box-bed had originally been in Oswald's room, so that would make sense. She had no idea that the King's chief adviser had been so interested in architecture.

Discarding the first scroll, she returned again to the second one, and suffered a shock. For on closer examination, she realized in fact that it *was* Vawdrey Keep depicted after all. But Vawdrey Keep after extensive building work had been added onto it, including, she noticed with astonishment, a second matching tower. She gasped at the vision of how the place could look. It was truly inspired. And to think it sprang from the mind of Earl Vawdrey, she marveled. It was remarkable. Had he originally intended to be an architect rather than a politician?

The third and fourth scrolls were covered in diagrams showing the various chambers and quarters that the expanded Keep would provide both for family and servants' quarters. They were truly fascinating, and Eden wasn't sure how long she spent poring over them. The fifth scroll was wholly devoted to calculations of the materials involved in such a project. Eden scanned this with interest, but not much understanding. She wondered how old these plans were, and if the projections would still be valid or need updating in any case. After all, they must be over ten years old.

The sixth scroll was blank, and Eden folded this one up thoughtfully, thinking to use it for her own purposes of letter-writing. She had been putting off writing to her grandmother and Lenora, but that duty could not be shirked for much longer. Though what she could say by way of apology, she knew not. The prospect loomed heavily on her mind before she reflected there was probably no ink or writing implements to be had about the place in any case.

She returned the scrolls to the chest but took the books next door to her own bedchamber where she set them on a small table. She had five days to get through, she reminded herself. It would be no good if she squandered all of the reading material in one morning.

At midday she took Parnell, Seth, Dimon, and Nudd on a long walk. She called all the dogs, but Castor and Hector had only followed her a few yards from the Keep before turning back. They then posted themselves outside the tower as if standing sentry, but she could see their ears were pricked up as they watched the rest of them walking down the hill.

As she was retracing her steps, it was perhaps not surprising that she found herself going back over the words that Roland had spoken to her the previous day. She tried to imagine the three Vawdrey brothers as boys about the Keep. Oswald the heir, so secretive and reserved, hiding himself away with his books, and sketching out clever plans to transform his rather primitive birthright into something far more impressive. Not knowing he would one day discard it altogether, establishing a glittering career at court. Mason, baseborn and sleeping on a straw mattress in the attic room, who would ever have dreamed he was destined for a dukedom? And Roland, the youngest, his father's favorite.

She would never have imagined that under the swagger and the brashness lay...what? Eden broke off her thoughts abruptly, her steps slowing down. What was she thinking? After all, what did she know of Roland Vawdrey? Did she really imagine she had gained some unique insight into him this past week?

How could he simultaneously seem at once so much more straightforward, and yet so much more complicated than she would have ever imagined? Her thoughts strayed briefly to Roland's distress over his brother's supposed death. His refusal even now to take hostages in mock battle. Nudd yipped at her, and Eden picked up her pace.

Of course, the most astonishing words he had spoken had not been about his family at all, but had been when he had made that quite extraordinary claim that he had not been angry when he awoke that disastrous morning and found her in his bed. Like a changeling, she thought, then wondered if the dark faery-tale wood was having an effect on her. He had, of course, only said that to spare her feelings after she had grown overemotional. That had been unfortunate. Thinking of Lenora was when she was at her most susceptible.

Seth barked, and when she glanced down, sure enough he had brought her a stick. She retrieved it, and flung it underarm as her aggravating husband had suggested. In truth, it did go a lot further, curse him! She noticed that while Seth, Dimon, and Nudd took off after the stick, Parnell dogged her heels, keeping her well within his sights. She smiled to herself. Really, was it any wonder she had a favorite?

They were a good three hours, and Eden was just divesting herself of her cloak and mittens in the disarming room when Fulco came hurrying in. "She's here now," he said breathlessly. "Brigid Hamble. I daren't leave her in the kitchen with Baxter, not after what Master Roland said this morning. So, I've set her to cleaning out the dining chamber."

Eden blinked, wondering what exactly Roland had said about Baxter that morning. "Very well, Fulco," she said, wondering why he looked so distraught. "Thank you."

Fulco took himself off, muttering under his breath, and shaking his head. Eden arched an eyebrow at Parnell, who was watching her carefully. "What ails him, do you suppose?" she murmured. Parnell's tail thumped against the stone flagstones. The other three had all barged their way past Fulco and gone running up the stairs at the first opportunity, but faithful Parnell waited for her. They mounted the staircase and Eden even remembered the location of at least half of the trip steps.

The last one caught her out and she pitched forward, clutching at the door in front of her. *One of these days*, she thought. She practically tumbled through the door and found herself eye level with a young woman on her knees, scrubbing the floorboards with a brush.

"Not another great dirty-pawed beast!" she scolded Parnell, who eyed her coldly.

"You'll find we keep scores of them here at Vawdrey Keep," said Eden, straightening herself up, and dusting her skirts. "Where are my other dogs who came up before me?"

The girl suddenly grinned. "Don't you worry, milady. I opened that door and banished them to the other chamber. They're in there, snoring their great hairy heads off."

"Oh, good," said Eden. "I apologize for the muddy paws. We've been abroad for hours, and I did not think of it."

"Bless you," said the girl. "Looks like you'd be the first one in decades if you had, by the state of this place. I'm Brigid." She bobbed a curtsey. Brigid had a pleasant, open-looking face, with freckles across her nose, fair coloring, and extremely curly, sandy-colored hair which was escaping from her headscarf. Eden immediately took a liking to her.

"I'm very happy to meet you, Brigid. I understand that you are the bravest girl in all of Sitchmarsh."

Brigid laughed. "Well, I've been called bold-faced before, but never brave!" She cast an admiring look at Eden's fancy blue dress, which, quite frankly, had seen better days. "You must be the Lady Vawdrey. Mr. Fulco said you was as fine a lady as ever seen round these parts."

"How nice of him," said Eden in surprise. "I hope you will ignore whatever Baxter says of me. I'm afraid he is not half so complimentary."

"Oh, I knows Mr. Baxter alright," said Brigid with a gleam in her eye. "I knows him of old from the village. A right old curmudgeon. He don't have no time for the fairer sex, and no mistake."

"I don't expect he does," agreed Eden. "Do your family reside in the village, Brigid? Only your accent sounds more Aphrany than Sitchmarsh."

Brigid's eyes widened. "Fancy you recognizing that!" she said. "Mr. Fulco never said as you was well traveled."

259

"Well, I don't know about that," said Eden modestly. "But I have spent the past three winters at court in Aphrany."

If anything, Brigid's eyes grew wider. "Well, it's like this, milady. I'm Aphrany born and bred. But my late husband, Will, was from Sitchmarsh. He was apprenticed in Aphrany but returned to his home village and brought me with him." She shrugged. "I lost him three summers ago. Many's a time I thought about upping sticks and heading back to the city. But I never did it yet."

"Do you not miss the hustle and bustle of city life?" asked Eden. If Brigid was a city girl, maybe that explained her scorn for country superstition.

"Oh yes," said Brigid. "But I don't miss the pickpockets and the cutthroats and the swindlers. Least," she amended with a wink, "not much." Eden smiled. "But you mustn't stand about here in the draught, milady," Brigid said, jumping up. "If you're back now, I'll lay the fire and let Mr. Baxter know he's to set about your dinner."

"Thank you, Brigid," said Eden. In truth, she had a good feeling about the new maid's appointment. Which was why she was surprised to find Fulco hovering by her elbow as soon as she'd finished her supper, a glum expression on his face. "What is it, Fulco?" she asked, for Brigid had already taken away the trenchers and bowls.

He cleared his throat. "Just to say, milady, that if Brigid Hamble doesn't give satisfaction, you can tell me, and I will give her marching orders."

Eden frowned at him a moment. "If I was not happy with Brigid, I would not hesitate to tell her so myself," she told him firmly. "But as it happens, I think she will do very well indeed." Fulco could not have looked more astonished if she had announced that Brigid was her full-blood sibling. When he still stood there, looking at her doubtfully, she added in a dismissive tone: "You have done very well in appointing her." He finally took this as a cue to leave and did so.

Eden only managed an hour in the unwelcoming sitting room before retiring upstairs to her bedchamber. Brigid had lit the fire for her in there, and Parnell and Nudd followed up the stairs after her. With some misgiving she let them in with her and watched them settle in front of the fire with wide yawns. Eden got on with the business of washing and undressing for bed.

Once ready, she picked up the three books she had left on the table and her candle, and opened the small doors to the box-bed, clambering in. Looking about her, she found the handiest niche for her candle holder and stowed it there, above her head. Then she selected the uppermost of the three books which was a decent size with little metal clasps holding it shut in the shape of small, clutching hands.

To her surprise, after unfastening it, she found it was an illustrated storybook giving an account of the adventures of some knight she had never heard of called Sir Aguillerd. Eden's lips turned downward. She was not personally fond of chivalrous romances and the popularity of the insipid Sir Maurency of Jorde had spawned a slew of even more bland imitations.

Casting that one aside in disappointment, Eden reached for the second book, which was a red leather-bound tome which had the first few links of a chain still attached to its spine. It had clearly been part of a chained library previously, and Eden wondered where Oswald Vawdrey must have come across his few prized books.

The inside flap contained a rather nasty curse which said it would befall anyone who stole this book belonging to one

Jeoffrey John Nokes of Cantonville. Except that Jeoffrey John's name had been firmly scored through and Oswald Vawdrey's written above it in an audacious, bold hand. Eden's eyebrows rose. Well, she thought. Nothing bad had ever happened to Earl Vawdrey that she knew of. Then, she recalled he had been cut down in battle. Perhaps the curse of Jeoffrey John Nokes curse had proved effective?

When she prized it open, she found it was a compendium of beasts with an illustration and a paragraph about each one, listing their characteristics, virtues, and vices. Flipping through the book, Eden found the everyday creatures listed side by side with more fantastical chimeras.

On impulse she looked up "dog" and found: "Most loyal creature, faithful to its master, come what may. Distance cannot dim a hound's devotion. Be it mastiff or lapdog, its heart be of the same substance." There followed a drawing of a man lay on his deathbed and his dog's head flung back in a mournful howl. At his bedside sat a nun in holy orders. On her lap, a little white lapdog, who was looking up at his mistress with eyes only for her. Eden smiled, and pushed open one of the cupboard doors to check on the two dogs. In the glow of the fire, she could see their sleeping bodies, stretched out before the hearth.

Returning to the book, she spent only about an hour reading, before she found herself yawning, and her eyelids drooping. It must have been that long walk, she thought as the book slipped from her fingers.

She caught it but noticed it had fallen open at a page which was not fastened to the others but had merely been inserted into the pages. With surprise, she noticed that the illustration was that of a naked man. Her eyes opened wide. Whoever heard of finding an entry for man in a bestiary? "Ambiguous, and changeable creature with potential for either good or evil, sometimes both. Untrustworthy," Eden read in astonishment.

She stared at the page. Why had it come loose? she wondered, examining it closer. She turned it over. It bore no marks of binding. Returning to the drawing again, she blinked at the unflinching realism of the pen strokes. On the entry for mermaid, the sea creature had her breasts covered with a conch shell she was holding, but there were no fanciful flourishes or strategic fig leaves on this one.

Slowly, she came to the conclusion that this page was a good imitation of the other entries but had been added at a later date. She closed the book thoughtfully. But who had added it? Jeoffrey John Nokes or Oswald Vawdrey? Whichever one it was, they were an excellent forger, and held rather misanthropic views.

Suddenly she wanted to ask Roland's opinion. What would he be doing now? she wondered, blowing out her candle and rolling onto her side. She remembered the pavilion he had shared with his friends at Tranton Vale. *I always have the right bunk*, he had said, so they clearly always shared a tent between the three of them.

Would his friends Sir Edward and Sir James be asking him how he found married life? And how would he reply? She shifted about on the mattress. In truth, it seemed to her that he was adjusting to this life rather better than she was. She huffed and rolled onto her other side, thumping at the pillow.

When she contemplated her husband's return, her stomach lurched. No doubt he'd be wanting to commit outrages on her body again! She pressed the backs of her hands to her heated cheeks and frowned. She wasn't anxious for a repeat of *that*, she told herself briskly. *No, not at all.*

Her thoughts halted abruptly as an image of his face swam before her eyes, when he'd cried out her name the last time. Why had he done that? And why did she keep thinking of the transported expression on his face? And not only that, but he'd been *happy*. She knew it. Just because he'd lain between her thighs and committed "that act" with her.

It was very odd, but the suspicion entered her head that ballad singers and poets had it all wrong after all. Maybe they were just overcomplicating the whole thing? Of course, she knew full well that any beast in the field felt a compulsion to rut. That part was understandable, and she'd been forewarned as such.

The part she didn't understand was why he wanted to kiss and fondle her *afterward*. What possible purpose could that serve? All it did was make her feel confused and awkward when she remembered it now. She wished he wouldn't do it. Why could he not just roll off her and go about his business like everyone said men did! The way he acted was like he felt somehow closer to her because of a physical intimacy they'd shared, but that was nonsense!

She lay brooding over Roland Vawdrey for far longer than she'd ever admit before her thoughts flitted to her cousin. She must try to write to Lenora on the morrow. Then she made a list in her head of all the people she owed letters to. Lenora, Gunnilde, Fenella, her grandmother. She really must speak to Fulco tomorrow about a pen and ink. Or perhaps she should ask Brigid?

Her new maid seemed a resourceful girl, where Fulco could be a little surly and uncooperative. Gradually she drifted into an uneasy and fitful dream where the beasts started to crawl out from the pages of the compendium, large as life. Strange to say, it was not the lions or tigers that bothered her most, but the man, who still had no clothes on, and turned out to be Roland

Vawdrey. *Oh dear*, she thought, *is he really so untrustworthy?*
Then he held out his arms to her, and she walked straight into
them. Like a total fool.

28

The next morning, Eden woke to the sound of barking and to Brigid shaking her shoulder. Eden exclaimed and sat up in bewilderment.

"Quiet, you daft beast, do!" Brigid urged Nudd, who barked in her face again, unabashed.

To her surprise, Eden found herself sat on the hearthrug in her room next to the dogs. "What...?" She rubbed her eyes and looked at Brigid.

"Your bed not comfy, milady?" the maid asked, plunking her hands on her hips.

Eden crossed her arms, feeling a nip in the air. It was a good thing she'd been curled up with the dogs or she would have been chilled to the bone. "I must have been trying to quiet them and fallen asleep," she said awkwardly, and rose stiffly to her feet. She hobbled over to the washstand where Brigid was pouring her out a basin out of hot water. Her big toe throbbed. She must have stubbed it in the night. Eden glanced around nervously but could see no other sign of upset.

"Well, you won't be traipsing over the hills today, milady," said Brigid cheerfully.

For a moment, Eden thought she was referring to her pained toe, then she heard the sound of raindrops and glanced at the window. "No indeed," she agreed, seeing the steady downpour. She set about her ablutions. "How was your night's sleep?" she asked, turning to look over her shoulder at Brigid. "Are you settled in the servants' quarters?"

The maid looked pleasantly surprised by her enquiry. "Very comfortable, thank you, milady. I don't say my in-laws' house isn't pleasant, for 'tis. But their second son is lately married, and the place is full of bodies. My presence there..." She shrugged. "It's probably come to its natural end. They promised my Will they would take care of me, but he's been gone three years now, and there was no children to bind me to them."

"You were widowed very young."

"Yes," agreed Brigid, nodding her curly head. "Married at sixteen, widowed at nineteen."

Eden realized they must both be much of an age. "Married at sixteen..." she repeated. "Your in-laws still live in the village then?"

"My father-in-law is Hamble the miller," explained Brigid. "They've lived in these parts for generations."

"Like the Vawdreys," said Eden thoughtfully, wondering why there were no portraits in the Keep, or any personal touches. Maybe because the place had not had a mistress for so many years. And even when it had, for only very brief periods before some tragic fate befell them. Hastily, she changed the direction of her thoughts.

Brigid took the dogs down to let them out and Eden finished dressing and tidying her hair away. She had just finished pinning her braids securely into place when a great din was raised below with the dogs. "What now?" muttered Eden as she took herself down the stairs to the floor below.

Walking through to the sitting room, she approached the window seat and peered below. She could see Fulco remonstrating with Castor as he led away someone's horse. It wasn't one of theirs. Looking thoughtful, Eden walked back into the dining chamber where a fresh loaf and butter had been laid out for her. She buttered herself a piece of bread and was just pouring herself a cup of water when she heard the knock on the door. "Come in."

The door flung back and to Eden's surprise it was Castor and Seth who came barging in.

"You brutes!" yelled Brigid after them. "Your pardon, milady," she said breathlessly. "But I couldn't stop them!"

"It's not your fault," Eden assured her, eyeing the large white dog and the large brown dog respectively as they sat themselves on either side of her, staring with hostility at the door. Eden turned back and found Brigid ushering in a guest. Over her arm she carried a sopping wet cloak and hood which was dripping all over the floor.

"The Lady Orla Bernard has come to visit with you, milady," she announced with a curtsey.

Eden rose from her bench. Castor gave her a warning rumble. "Castor!" she remonstrated with him and curtseyed to her guest. "You must forgive our dogs, Lady Orla. I'm afraid they are unaccustomed to visitors and their manners are sadly rusty."

"It does not signify." Orla waved the apology aside as she sailed into the room. She was a tall, thin woman with a rather long nose and light brown hair. Eden thought she was aged in her midthirties or thereabouts. She envied her dark purple gown, which had a high neckline and had black velvet bands at the wrists and hem. She wished she was dressed in such a gown, instead of her frivolous ice blue which she was heartily sick of by now.

"Take a seat on this bench here, nearest to the fire where you can dry out," she urged Orla. "It is such filthy weather this morning. Will you join me?" she said, gesturing to the loaf. "There is sure to be some fish dish served at some point."

"I never eat before a light meal at midday," said Orla disapprovingly. "My mother used to say that only the infirm or the infantile should eat at daybreak. Or common workers, of course."

"Oh, did she?" asked Eden. "Well, she would not have been alone in that belief. It is the common opinion after all." She let that sink in before continuing. "We have a mutual acquaintance I think in the Countess Vawdrey."

"My sister-in-law," said Orla, arranging her skirts around her and looking smug.

"And mine," Eden reminded her.

"Quite, quite," twittered Orla. "You are lately married. I wish you joy, of course."

Eden steeled herself, waiting for Orla to make some comment about Lenora being the intended bride, but to her surprise, she did not.

"Fenella wrote to me about it, of course. She is very fond of Sir Roland, for all his faults." Orla looked about her. "Is he from home at present?"

"He is competing at the tournament at Areley Kings," said Eden, bristling in spite of herself at the mention of Roland's faults.

Orla clicked her tongue. "Menfolk! How childishly they play at these games of war!"

"You do not care for the tournaments, Lady Orla?" Contrarily, Eden, who had always despised them, now felt the need to defend the pursuit.

269

"Oh, I've never been to one," said Orla breezily.

"If you had," said Eden, "then you would not call it 'play.'"

"Pshaw!" said Orla violently.

Castor growled, and Eden was forced to put a hand out to lightly touch his head. He stopped the noise at once and Eden returned to her bread and butter.

"I see this place is still packed to the rafters with curs," said Orla with a loud sniff. "It's almost like the old baron were still rattling around the place!"

"Oh, there's always been dogs at Vawdrey Keep," said Eden mildly. "Did you know the late Baron Vawdrey?" She was curious in spite of herself.

"Oh yes, he was a well-known figure around these parts," said Orla.

A light knock was heard on the door, and Brigid sailed in bearing a dish of herrings. "Shall I fetch another plate, milady?"

"Well," mused Orla, "those herrings do smell rather delicious. Perhaps I will make an exception, just this once, dear Lady Vawdrey."

"I am honored. Please do, Brigid."

"I'm amazed you have female staff," said Orla, her eyebrows high. "The last thing I heard the place was shunned."

"Oh yes, I had heard tell of some rumors. Spectral hounds, was it not?" asked Eden slyly.

"Hounds? Oh no, my dear!" Orla lowered her voice. "Ghost brides of the old baron. They walk the place, wringing their hands and lamenting their premature deaths."

"Dear me!" Eden stifled a laugh. Orla looked shocked. "I'm sorry, 'tis only that I have been here several days now and seen not one spectral thing."

"Oh, well… I daresay it is a load of nonsense," admitted Orla, climbing down off her high horse.

"The baron was unfortunate to lose both his wives," Eden conceded.

"Both?" repeated Orla in surprise. "Oh no, I'm sure he had many more than that!"

"No, no," Eden corrected her. "He was married only twice."

"But surely…" Orla broke off and flushed. "Oh, I just remembered," she said awkwardly. "It is hardly nice to mention it, but some of those unfortunate women were…*lemans*!"

"You mean Mason's mother?" asked Eden calmly. "But she did not die. She returned to her husband."

Orla turned quite pink. "You mean she abandoned the sanctity of her marriage?"

"Apparently."

"Well!" Orla looked flabbergasted by this. "I am astonished that any man would take her back."

"Perhaps she was very beautiful?" hazarded Eden. "Beautiful people are often pardoned things that others are not."

Orla pursed her lips. "There is only one true beauty," she said piously. "And that is of the soul."

The door opened again, and Brigid plunked a plate in front of Orla, along with a knife and a spoon.

"Is she a village girl?" Orla asked loudly as Brigid exited the room. Eden thought she saw Brigid's shoulder hitch.

"Yes," she said. "One of the Hambles," adding in her mind, *by marriage.* Orla's company was not the most congenial, she thought, and wished it was Fenella sitting before her instead of her prickly sister-in-law. "Tell me, have you met Fenella's twin sons yet?"

"Not yet," admitted Orla, spooning herself some herrings from the bowl. "I invited them to visit with us for Midsummer's, but Earl Vawdrey is far too overprotective and has vowed Fen will not stir from their home for a sixmonth following her lying-in. It is too ridiculous."

"They are a most devoted couple," said Eden, pushing the butter dish in Orla's direction. Perhaps she would be more affable once she had eaten?

"Devoted?" repeated Orla shrilly. "He is quite silly about her. She can do no wrong in his eyes. Fenella has only to voice the smallest hankering for something and he delivers it up to her, tied with a bow. You should see her jewels! Her gowns! It's not really quite…well, *decent*," stressed Orla.

"And now she has given him two sons, he will be even worse, you mark my words." She dug her knife into the pat of butter. "By rights, of course, she should be installed here," she sniffed. "While he's at court. But no, he cannot bear to be apart from her, and instead buys her not one, mark you, but *two* town houses the size of cattle markets and fills them with baubles to keep her amused!" Orla shook her head. "She would do very well here, with her own people," she said peevishly. "I'm married to her brother, so I should know!"

"Earl Vawdrey is also from hereabouts," Eden reminded her.

"Oh yes, *him*," said Orla. "But he could not wait to brush the dust of Sitchmarsh from his boots. Always thought he was too good for this place, he did. With his fancy ways."

"He's gifted this place to Roland now," Eden told her and braced herself for a shocked reaction.

Orla's knife clattered down onto her plate. "He what?"

"Vawdrey Keep, he has bestowed it on Roland."

"His birthright?" squawked Orla.

"Yes."

"Given to the youngest son?"

"Yes."

"I never *heard* of such a thing!"

"It is certainly very generous."

"Generous!" repeated Orla. "Pah!" She tucked into her herrings, mumbling under her breath.

Eden thought she said, "You just wait till my Gil hears about this," but could not make out the rest of it. She did not think that Oswald Vawdrey would care overmuch what his countrified brother-in-law thought of his affairs but kept this to herself. "Do you know yet what names Fenella has given her boys?" she asked diplomatically.

"Names?" Orla looked puzzled. "Oh! I do not think they name them until they are at least three months, do they?" She looked vague. "After all, they are not kittens."

Eden frowned over this, which did not seem to make very much sense to her. It dawned on her that Orla was more than a little eccentric. Unless it was some rustic custom around these parts?

"I must ask, Lady Orla. Where do you make the bulk of your purchases?" she asked, attempting to steer her onto safer ground. "Would it be Pryors Naunton? I find myself in need of some necessary items for my wardrobe."

"Depends on what sort of items," Orla answered, cautiously dabbing her mouth with a napkin. "If it is fine work you require, such as gowns, cloaks, or hoods, then yes, you will need to go to the nearest city. If it is some plain work such as…*ahem*, undergarments, or even some woolen stuffs, then there is a woman in the village who can assist you."

"That sounds ideal," said Eden, thinking of some spare shifts. "If you would be so kind as to direct me…"

"Her name is Parva Osgoode. She resides next to the smithy," said Orla helpfully. "Tell her I sent you, and you will be assured of a welcome."

"Thank you so much."

Orla stayed another hour and made sure to stress how important she and her husband were in local circles. According to Orla, there were only two other families of import in the locality. The Fulchers and the Gisberns, who both lived half a day's ride away, though in opposite directions, and Orla doubted they would call without an invite. She explained that the Vawdreys had shirked all social responsibilities for the past decade at least and had much to make up for.

Once Orla had departed, Eden felt herself at something of a loose end. The rain had tailed off a little, but everything lay now very wet, and Eden feared her shoes would not be up to a long walk in such conditions. When Brigid appeared to poke the fire, Eden asked her about Parva Osgoode and her sewing services. Brigid said she could easily engage her to make up some shifts on the next shopping trip into Sitchmarsh.

Apparently, this usually took place on the first Wednesday of every month. By Eden's calculations that was in some six days' time. She nodded anyway, having no money of her own to bring this forward.

Instead, she asked Brigid to make enquiries if there was any ink or writing implement to be had about the place. She was not overly optimistic, but the maid returned within a half hour bearing a tray with two quill pens, a pen knife, and a bottle of ink.

Castor and Hector had taken themselves off to ensure Orla left the premises, but to Eden's surprise, they returned with Parnell and Nudd to sit in front of the fire as she set about the task of cutting down the quills to make the nibs usable. When this was achieved, she fetched the scroll of paper she had put away the day before and cut it up with the knife into four pieces.

She then set about writing a newsy letter, full of nonsense to amuse Gunnilde Payne. Her new friend was the easiest to write to, as she required nothing by way of apology or explanation.

She had covered both sides of the paper when she heard a great clamor go up from downstairs, which she fancied was Seth howling, accompanied by some frenzied loud barking from Dimon. The other four dogs all leaped up from where they were lay and started their own answering baying.

Eden covered her ears with her hands and got up from the table, making for the door which the dogs were all pawing and scratching at to get through. "Patience!" she admonished as they started shouldering the door as soon as her hand was on the bolt. She drew it back, and they burst through and poured down the steps to confront whatever intruder had dared to darken their doorstep.

Eden sighed, and took the steps at a more leisurely pace. She very much doubted she would receive two visitors in one day. Perhaps it was some traveler who had lost their way? When she reached the disarming room, she found Fulco dragging a trunk across the threshold, and looked at him enquiringly. "Quiet, ye villains!" he bawled over his shoulder at the dogs. Eden didn't even flinch. He looked back at her. "For you," he said, straightening up.

"For me?" He nodded. She looked down at it. It was a very large, handsome trunk, covered in leather with a nail head trim in an attractive design. For a moment, her heart had leaped with the hope it might have been her own trunk forwarded on from Hallam Hall. That would have meant her cousin had forgiven her after all. However, she did not recognize this trunk, which looked to be still smelt of newly cured leather and looked very expensive. "Was there no note or missive with it?"

"Messenger just left it like that," said Fulco unexpansively. "Want me to carry it upstairs?"

"Yes, please."

"Where to?"

"My bedchamber, I think." Eden glanced out of the door and saw a cart trundling back down the hill. The dogs had followed it partway but were now turning back and returning to the Keep. She followed Fulco up the steps, careful to leave enough distance so that if he was caught out by a trip step, she would not be flattened by the large trunk. When she reached the top, he was already setting it down.

"Messenger give me this too," he said, reaching for a leather cord around his neck which bore the key.

"Thank you," said Eden, taking it from him. Fulco nodded and left her to it. She did not waste any time, but instead knelt before the chest, unlocking it and lifting the lid. To her surprise, the first thing she saw was a swath of rose-pink satin. "But what is this…?" she puzzled, lifting out what revealed itself to be a pretty gown with a silver trim. She recognized this—it was Lenora's! Dropping it with an exclamation, she returned to the chest.

The next dress she drew out was of sea-green with exquisite gold detail. "This…" She broke off distractedly. She was sure this was one of Lenora's new gowns also! She recognized it from the last dress-fitting that Lenora had in Caer-Lyoness. She had insisted that Eden sat there while she selected the fabrics and had spent a small fortune on them. Uncle Leofric had only agreed to it as part of her betrothal wardrobe.

Eden's blood ran cold. Why would her cousin send all her new gowns to her? Was she saying, *Here you may as well take everything that is mine!* thought Eden with horror. Next came a gold gown, decorated with a pink rose motif all over the bodice and gauzy see-through sleeves.

Last came a pure white dress with a low-scooped neckline and sleeves so long they would no doubt touch the floor. Eden threw that on the floor along with the others and rifled through the rest of the chest looking for a note or letter from Lenora, but there was none. Only three fine shifts of exquisite lawn, which would mean she had no need of Parva Osgoode after all, a mass of silk stockings and veils in an array of colors, and an assortment of matching ribbon garters. Eden sat back on her heels and stared numbly at the finery. Then she burst into tears and found she could not stop.

277

29

Three Days Later

Roland dismounted and scanned the tower for any visible signs of his wife. Which was frankly ridiculous. What was he expecting? A flash of blue at a window, or her to come running with his name on her lips? Both were sadly unreasonable, given the fact most of the windows at the Keep were narrow arrow loops, and his wife was more likely to scold him than hang about his neck. He had no idea why this thought made him smile to himself either. "I'll send Fulco down to help carry the packs in," he told Cuthbert, who was leading the horses toward the stable.

"Aye," said Cuthbert knowingly. "You wouldn't want to keep milady waiting," he added with considerable cheek.

Roland reached into his saddle bag and extracted a couple of items before slapping Bavol on the rump and sending him after Cuthbert. He hurried up toward the Keep. They had been gone six days in all, as he had diverted on impulse to Pryors Naunton on a shopping venture. He had ended up having to buy a third horse to load up all his purchases. And that wasn't even the sum total of what he'd bought.

The furniture he had commissioned would be conveyed here at some later point. He wasn't quite sure what had come over him, but he was more eager to see Eden than really made sense. He exchanged some words with Fulco on the first floor, sending his manservant down to the stables.

Then he made his way to the second floor, where he found the dining chamber and sitting room both empty, and the fires unlit.

Hearing a foot on the stair, he wrenched open the door and surprised a curly-haired maid carrying down a tray. She faltered in her step, then gave him a hasty curtsey.

"Where's my wife?" he demanded.

"She's in her room, Sir Roland," responded the maid, recovering fast and guessing who he was.

"Her room? Is she ill?"

"No, sir," she hesitated. "Only a little melancholic, I think." At his stunned look, she added, "Doubtless missing you, sir."

But Roland was already climbing the stairs two at a time. It occurred to him, shortly before opening the door to the bedchamber, that he had not seen a single dog since arriving, something unheard of at Vawdrey Keep. Then he blinked uncomprehendingly at the sight in front of him.

All six dogs were dotted around the room, draped over chests, stretched out on the hearthrug, and even one—Parnell, the villain—lying across the bottom of the bed. Eden's feet were resting on him as if she were a living breathing tomb effigy. Castor, lying on top of a large handsome trunk, raised his head from his paws to look intently at Roland, then dropped it again and closed his eyes.

"Oh, you're back, are you?" asked Eden, lowering her book to look at him. She had the doors wide open to the box-bed and was wrapped in a blanket, one long braid over her shoulder.

"What's all this?" asked Roland with a sweeping hand gesture encompassing the whole room.

Eden shrugged. "It's been wet and miserable," she said and returned to her book.

Roland shrugged out of his doublet. "Here, Parnell!" he said sternly, and the dog grudgingly climbed to his feet and hopped down off the bed. He shot a dirty look at Roland as he opened the bedroom door and ordered loudly: "Out!" The dogs all came to their feet and reluctantly skulked over to the door. Shutting it behind them and turning the key, Roland crossed to the washstand and washed his hands, face, and neck in cold water there.

"We've a maid now," said Eden, her eyes still on the page. "You could ask her to bring hot water."

"Haven't got the time," answered Roland succinctly, stripping himself off and toweling himself dry.

"What do you mean, you haven't got the time?" asked Eden, frowning as he crossed the room toward her.

"I mean," said Roland, hopping nimbly into the box-bed, and pulling the doors shut behind him, "that I haven't got the time." He took the book from Eden's hands and tossed it over his shoulder as he settled over her.

"Careful with that!" chided Eden as he took her lips in a kiss he had been anticipating for *days*. His hands sought for the edges of her blankets. He tore his mouth from hers. "Give me your tongue," he urged, "like last time."

Eden's cheeks turned crimson. "Well, really—!" she spluttered.

"I haven't stopped thinking about it," he admitted thickly, dragging down the blanket. *Finally.* His large hand covered her breast, making out its shape.

"Don't tear my new shift, it's very delicate," Eden said irritably. "Your hands are cold."

"So warm me up then, you little shrew." She tutted, but fussed around, dragging the sheets up around his shoulders. "I meant with your body," Roland told her with a laugh.

"You were gone six days," said Eden accusingly. "Not four or five!"

Roland felt an unaccountable warm feeling spreading through his chest. He'd meant to join his aching body to hers as soon as possible, but now for some reason, he was inclined to tarry over exchanging words with her. *Unfathomable*. "Did you miss me then?"

"No!" huffed Eden. "I had better things to do, I assure you!"

"Did you?" He kissed her neck, moving her dark braid out of the way. He wanted her hair loose and falling around her shoulders. "The servants told me you've been moping about the place. Lonely and missing me." Gods, her skin was soft.

"They grossly exaggerated," Eden replied, but she sounded breathless and distracted as he lingered over the flickering pulse in her throat.

"I missed you too," he heard himself groan. "Gods, Eden, you've no idea." She caught her breath at that, and he pressed his advantage by taking her mouth again, and the kiss he'd wanted all along. They were both panting after that, and she finally seemed to catch his urgency. He squeezed her breasts. "Are my hands still cold?" he rumbled.

"N-no," she conceded, and he reached down between them, bunching up her shift, and cupping her between her legs.

"Gods, Eden," he whispered, stroking her most secret feminine place. "Your pelt here is velvety soft, I could pet you all day."

281

She squeezed her eyes shut. "Must you talk when you're doing such things?"

"Yes, I must," he said, though in truth, he could not remember such a compulsion before now. "I want you to talk back to me too."

She opened one eye. "Don't call it my pelt."

"What shall I call it then?" He slipped a finger inside her, and she made a muffled sound that made the blood pound in his ears. "Eden?" he prompted.

"I don't know," she gasped.

He closed his own eyes when he felt her get his finger wet. Rubbing his thumb through her curls, he added another finger, and she whimpered. "I want to put my mouth there," he admitted. "But you're already wet enough for my cock." Eden's eyes flew open. "Which shall it be?" he mused. "Will you promise to come on my cock this time? Like a good wife?" Eden's gaze back at him was blank and slightly glazed. "No preference?" he teased.

"Don't toy with me," she said, a tremor running through her voice.

He moved his fingers, and she gave a startled moan. "I don't think you mind as much as you make out." He slid his thumb lower to tease her hidden pearl. "You liked my tongue here last time," he said, tapping it.

Eden's eyes widened. "R-Roland!" she gasped shakily.

"Shall I do it again?"

She surprised him by rolling her hips. "*Please*," she murmured, and her hand flew from his shoulder to slide between them, catching his hand, and pressing it between her legs.

"Just my fingers?" he grunted. "You want them here?"

She nodded her head, and he pressed his thumb, applying the pressure she needed there. *Holy hells.* She went up like wildfire. Roland gritted his teeth, throwing his weight on top of her to pin her to the mattress. Her back arched. He kept his fingers deep inside her as she cried out, bucking against him, riding his fingers. His cock throbbed, feeling neglected, wanting in.

She needed to take her pleasure first, he reminded himself. He had only bedded her a handful of times. He had to take it slow and initiate her right. They had years ahead of them. Years for him to get it how he wanted it, with his cock deep inside her. This was about her wants, and what she needed for it to feel good. How long did it take virgins before they adjusted anyway? He had no idea.

When he felt her tremors subsiding, he thrust his fingers again, her tender flesh quivering around them, and she sighed. He kissed her brow, then her mouth, and she let him without murmur, tangling her tongue with his. Nice. Or it would be, if his cock wasn't about to explode. He jerked back his head.

"Eden." His urgent tone roused her from her languor. "My turn," he said and watched a certain trepidation enter her expression. She nodded her head though, licked her bottom lip nervously, and peered down between them. His cock flexed, almost as if the damn thing was trying to impress her.

She winced, and he could tell his size was not a source of pleasure for her yet. Still, she let her legs fall open for him and he took himself in hand, guiding himself where he most wanted to be. "Relax," he said, wishing he sounded more in control, less like he was imploring her.

He knew full well he'd been too rough last time. He poised himself at her entrance, letting his broad cockhead grow wet

283

from her juices, and sank into her until he felt resistance. "Please Eden," he breathed, closing his eyes. "Ah, gods." She pressed her thighs into his hips, and taking this as encouragement, he pushed until he found himself making progress again. "*Sweetheart*," he gasped as he slid deeper into to her tight, silky sheath. He shuddered, striving for control, his brow beading with sweat. He dug his fingers in the bedsheets as he slid the final inches until their pelvises were touching. For a moment, speech was beyond him. Then he spoke very carefully. "Is that—?"

"Yes," she said tightly, and he felt her take a deep breath and then release it, relaxing her limbs against him.

Thank fuck. He wasn't sure how much of this gently, gently approach he could stand. Tensing his muscles, he began to move, not as gently as he would have wished, but not as hard as he longed to either. Eden bore it stoically, and he seized her hips in his hands to haul her against him, showing her the rhythm he craved. When she attempted it independently, moving against him, striving to please him, his brain shut down and he thrust inside her until he came, roaring.

30

Roland woke suddenly at the sound of a falling log. Reaching across Eden, he pushed one of the box-bed doors open to survey the room. All was quiet. The fire needed stoking, but he didn't want to move. Eden was curled into him in a deep slumber, dead to the world. He frowned noticing the dark shadows under her eyes and swiped his thumbs under them. Had she been sleeping poorly without him then?

The notion made him feel a curious pang in his chest. Though, it was only fair when you considered how long he'd lain awake in his bunk of an evening thinking of her. His friends had teased him something fierce, saying they found him sadly changed, a staid married man now. Not that he'd cared.

He had caught them sending odd looks his way when he'd bought her trinkets from the hawkers, or casually dropped her name in conversation. Eden shifted, flinging an arm around his waist, turning more fully into him, and carefully, he moved his arm to accommodate her. Was that a bruise? Her shift had slipped down one shoulder, showing a purple mark on her upper arm. How had she done that?

He touched it lightly with the backs of his fingers, and she murmured against the pillow. He lay still, waiting for her to fall quiet again. She really was a most restless sleeper. Peering out of the box-bed doors again, he guessed the hour was not much more advanced than four or five o'clock. He really should wake her but was strangely loath to do so.

In the end he dozed back off himself and woke an hour later to find Eden watching him. She glanced hastily away as soon as she realized he was awake.

"What hour is it?" she asked, clearing her throat.

"It must be supper time, or thereabouts," he said with a yawn. "We may as well take our meal here, in our room." Eden turned her head to look at him suspiciously. "I'm tired from my journey," he pointed out reasonably. "And there's a perfectly good table in here we could use, for the two of us."

"It's true that it's draughty in that dining chamber," she agreed cautiously.

Roland smiled to himself, and when she went to wriggle out from underneath his arm, he suffered her to. "Don't trouble yourself getting dressed," he told her when she made her way toward the chair with her gown draped over it. Eden stopped and looked back over her shoulder at him.

"I brought you something you can just slip on over your shift. It's very unlikely you'll want to go abroad again today," he said with a nod toward the window where the rain was bucketing down.

"What did you buy me?" asked Eden. "A dress?" She sounded so suddenly hopeful, he felt a little sorry to disappoint her.

"A mantle," he corrected her. "Fulco and Cuthbert should have brought everything in by now."

"Oh." She hovered uncertainly, and he pulled himself out of bed and pulled on his braies, chauses, and tunic.

"I'll go, you stay here." When he returned twenty minutes later carrying packages, she was brushing her long, dark hair in front of the fire. "Here, for you. Open this one first and put it on. Fulco is bringing up more logs for the fire shortly."

The bundle was large, and when she unfurled it, Eden found a stunning mantle of navy brocade with a gold motif pattern. She shook it out. "It's beautiful!" she exclaimed.

"There are two slits to put your arms through," Roland showed her. The mantle was lined in a gold silk.

"Let me braid my hair first," she said when he held it out for her to put on.

"Leave it loose. It's only the two of us at supper." She acquiesced, and he helped her don the robe before passing her another parcel. "Open this one." Inside were some gold satin slippers for indoor wear. "Put those on too."

"You've brought me so many gifts…" she said awkwardly.

She hadn't even seen the half of them.

A knock on the door interrupted them, and Fulco came in bearing logs, Brigid following on close behind with things to lay the table. Supper was a simple meal of stewed rabbit with prunes and pearl barley served with onions and raisins. Roland suspected they were eating the same meal below stairs. He preferred his meat roasted but ate heartily all the same. Eden seemed to mostly toy with hers and slip titbits to whatever dogs had snuck in with the servants. He watched her covertly as they ate their meal. She seemed skittish and kept looking at him out of the corner of her eye when she thought he wasn't looking.

"Is there aught amiss with my face?" he asked her at one point.

She took a critical look. "Well, you've got a new bruise at your left temple, if that's what you mean." She took a sip of wine. "Did you lose again?"

"That's not—" He broke off in exasperation. "Why do you keep stealing glances at me like that?"

Eden stiffened and turned red. "I'm sure I don't know what you mean."

"And I did not lose," he said, narrowing his eyes. "And what the devil do you mean *again*?" Gods, it was a wonder he had any ego left these days, the way she kept battering at it!

Eden shrugged. "I thought from the way your friends spoke at Tranton Vale that losing was a regular feature of the tournaments."

"You thought—!" He broke off, giving her a baleful glance. He could see from the look on her face that she hadn't meant to intentionally insult him. Taking a deep breath, he decided instead to patiently set her right. "That's just how men are, Eden. They don't brag of their friends' successes, only glory in their defeats."

"Oh?" She looked skeptical.

He set his own goblet down. "Have you ever once heard me boast of Bev's success in the melee?" She shook her head.

"Yet that is where his strengths lie. He's very tactical."

"Why do you not compliment him on it then?" asked Eden, looking bewildered.

Roland snorted. "Like hells I would! As his friend, it is my duty to point out his woeful ability in the jousting and mock him about it at every turn."

"That seems rather…churlish," Eden responded hesitantly.

He could see she was using her words carefully, and he had an inkling she was going to say "childish" before hurriedly changing it. Appreciating the fact she was trying to avoid conflict for once, he shrugged. "It's different for men. Female

288

friendships are more…" He struggled, having never considered the nature of female relationships before.

"Nurturing?" suggested Eden helpfully.

Roland wasn't sure if that was right. He didn't think Eden's polite friendships were anything like as close as his brother-in-arms style kinship with Bev and Attley.

"They are," Eden insisted. "I make sure to always encourage my friends in their endeavors."

"Mmm." He made a noncommittal noise. He was sure that was true enough, but he still didn't believe she let anyone get close enough to be considered a true friend. He lifted his drink again and looked at her over the top of it. The strangest thought drifted into his head, that *he* wanted to be that close to her. Which was fucking ridiculous. Why would he want to be friends with his own wife? To disguise his confusion, he drained his cup.

"I've been thinking about my friend Gunnilde Payne," she was saying. "I am not convinced that her feelings are deeply engaged with Arthur Conway. After all, there are probably not that many matrimonial prospects in Tranton Vale."

Roland managed to dredge Gunnilde Payne from the recesses of his memory, but Arthur Conway meant frankly nothing to him. He assumed an expression he hoped showed the appropriate husbandly interest. "No?" he said, clearing his throat.

"For my part I think she could do a lot better than be connected by marriage to the Conways. I wonder if anyone suitable could be introduced to her when they come to court." She frowned as though considering a thorny problem. "How does a woman stimulate a man's interest?" she asked impulsively.

289

Roland, who had extended his own hand to refill his goblet, froze. "What?"

"I said, how does a woman capture a man's attention? So that he notices her as a woman, I mean," she explained, seeing his thunderstruck expression. "Or are you not allowed to tell me? Is it breaking some kind of male confidence?"

"Why are you asking?" Almost, he felt like he was swimming against the tide in this conversation.

"Gunnilde Payne," she said as though explaining something blatantly obvious. "She comes to court next month. I was wondering if perhaps one of your friends might...?"

His brow cleared and he let out a short laugh. "You're wasting your time there," he said, on confident ground once more.

"Nonsense," Eden told him briskly. "I'm quite sure these things can be cultivated. I mean," she hesitated a moment. "You only have to look at us."

Roland again felt completely floored by her conversation. "What the devil do you mean by that?" he demanded.

"I meant no criticism," she responded lightly though she blushed faintly. "I only meant that I would never have been the bride of your choice, that is all. And yet, in spite of that you... Well, you do not shun my presence in your...life," she said, and he knew full well she had been going to say "bed," but then decided it was too indelicate.

Roland was very quiet. He opened his mouth as if to speak and then closed it again without uttering a word. Gods, why was this so hard? "It's not something you can just conjure from thin air," he said with an odd tone to his voice that even he could hear. Eden looked set to argue the point. "And before you say I never noticed you as a woman, let me set you straight. I did."

Eden sighed. "I know you're trying to be gallant..." He snorted. "But we both know that is not true, and I'm not remotely offended by the fact."

"Eden," said Roland firmly. "We both know I don't have a gallant bone in my body!"

"Naturally you do not wish to put me out of humor with you," she stated mildly. "But I would truly prefer there to be nothing but honest dealing between us."

"Honest dealing?" he repeated. "Are you sure about that?" After all, perhaps honesty would be the best policy. He couldn't carry on tiptoeing around her like this!

"Quite," Eden told him. "I believe it is for the best."

"Very well then, but don't say I didn't warn you," said Roland, and she eyed him with surprise. "I always noticed you, Eden," he said simply. "Even when I thought you a shrill-tongued, stuck-up harpy, I wondered what you'd feel like underneath me."

Eden gasped. "But that's...absurd." She stared at him uncertainly. "You did not."

"Yes, I did."

"But..." Eden cast about wildly. "Why?"

Roland shrugged. "I don't know. You always intrigued me, I suppose. And when we kissed at Midwinter, that curiosity increased tenfold. And now you're mine, and there's an end to it."

She blinked at this several times, unsure how to respond. No doubt realizing what nasty creatures men were, when it came down to it. Now *he* was the one stealing glances at her. He

291

cleared his throat. "Tell me what you've been about these past six days, wife," he said, aiming for less contentious grounds.

"I've taken many walks with the dogs," she said in a stifled voice. "And read all the books I could lay my hands on."

"You found books?"

"To be precise, Cuthbert found them," admitted Eden. "Fulco saw him throw them into a trunk and I retrieved them."

"Didn't know we had any."

"I believe they belonged to your brother Oswald."

"I can well believe that," he grunted. "I bet they're as dull as ditchwater and all about politicking and such."

"One was about the government of kings," agreed Eden. "But the others weren't. And I found some building plans too," said Eden. "Which your brother drew up many years ago for extending the Keep."

"Oh aye?"

"They were vastly interesting," said Eden. "Although they would cost a fortune to carry out. He must be quite extraordinarily clever, I think."

Unaccountably, he felt irritated by all this talk of Oswald and his plaguey cleverness. "Anything else?" he asked, hoping to induce a change of subject.

"Orla Bernard called. She broke her fast with me."

"And did she spend the entire visit speaking of Oswald?" he asked sarcastically.

"She did mention him, naturally, as he and Fenella are our mutual acquaintances," said Eden. She paused then added, "She

292

said he is infatuated to an almost unnatural degree with his wife."

Roland lowered his wine with a frown. Was that true? Both his brothers were certainly very caught up in their wives. "Unnatural?" he repeated.

"She seemed to think so."

He shrugged. "My sisters-in-law don't seem to have any complaint." Eden apparently had no rejoinder for that. "What else did she have to say?" he asked grudgingly.

Eden bit the inside of her mouth. "Not much," she said. "She told me of a seamstress in the village and seemed surprised we had secured Brigid's service here."

"How is that working out?" he asked. "She and Fulco are not…clashing?"

Eden looked surprised by this. "Not that I've heard. Why should they?"

"It seems Fulco's mother does not approve of young widows," he answered evasively. "I fancy she's not overkeen for him to take a wife."

"It's probably just local prejudice against an outsider," said Eden with disapproval. "Brigid is from Aphrany, originally. You know how people can be." She could have a point, he thought, but made no reply. The silence stretched, though he did not notice it until Eden cleared her throat. "So how did your friends fare at Areley Kings?" she asked. "Sir James and Sir Edward."

"Neither acquitted themselves with much aplomb," he answered, both pleased she had bothered remembering their names, and irritated she had not asked after his success first.

"Attley crashed out of the first round of the jousting and Bev was on the losing side of the melee."

"And your protégé, Sir Renlow?" asked Eden. "Did he at least make it through in one piece?"

"I'd hardly call him my protégé," said Roland with surprise.

"Is he not?" Eden frowned. "I thought I heard somewhere that he was." She pondered this a moment. "I forget where. So, you do not encourage him to pursue the tourneys then? I thought it a little strange at the time."

"What do you mean?"

"That it would be most odd for you to encourage one such as Sir Renlow."

Roland frowned, placing his cup back down on the table. "How so?"

"I would have thought it obvious," said Eden, arching her elegant brows at him.

Something about her manner immediately irritated him. Doubtless she thought poor Renlow should be spouting poetry instead. "Not to me. Why don't you enlighten me with your superior knowledge on such matters?" he asked coolly.

Eden put down her spoon and regarded him censoriously. "At Tranton Vale, he was ignominiously defeated in the joust," she pointed out. "Then he was knocked unconscious and taken hostage in the melee." The slight pucker between her brows cleared as she recalled something. "I was told you paid his ransom that day so he was free to join the feasting. That was why I thought you had taken him under your wing. And after that he was defeated at the Challenge to Arms. Badly."

"And pray tell me, how do you think the likes of Kentigern, Orde, de Crecy, and myself started out?" asked Roland with an edge to his tone. "Do you imagine we sprang forth as fully developed fighters and tacticians in our first season?"

"Well, I would certainly hope you showed more natural talent for it than poor Sir Renlow," she retorted.

"I've seen competitors spit out a tooth, shake off a concussion, and lash broken fingers to a lance," said Roland harshly, then paused, but she said nothing. "I *know* Renlow has what it takes because he is unflinchingly brave. Doesn't matter how many times he gets knocked down, he'll get back up, and one of these days, mark you, he will start winning."

"Sir Renlow?" she asked incredulously.

He gave a short, curt nod. "He is utterly fearless."

Eden stared at this, before rallying. "Or utterly stupid," she said.

Roland drew back his chair, getting to his feet. "Skills can be learned," he said. "Courage can't."

"Where are you going?"

"To check on the horses."

"Surely Fulco can do that," Eden pointed out, two spots of color appearing on her cheeks.

"I need some fresh air." He was disappointed, he realized. Which made him as stupid as she clearly thought he was. He'd known all along that Eden was stuck up and haughty. She'd made no secret of the fact she preferred intellectuals to knights. Why did it feel like such a slap in the face then? It made no earthly sense. It dawned on him that Eden was still speaking. He stared at her impatiently.

"If I said aught that offended you—" she was saying.

"You didn't," he cut her off, striving to sound bored, but merely coming off as rude. "I would have to value your opinion in order for it to offend me."

Eden gasped. "And *this*," she said, "is precisely *why* I don't understand the way you carry on in the bedchamber!"

"What?" Now Roland felt his own face heating.

"Why do you keep pretending I'm someone else come bedtime?"

Roland stared at her. "Pretending you're—?" Words failed him. "I'm not pretending you're anyone but you," he retorted.

"I don't believe you."

"Why would I?" he asked, mystified.

"Because…" Her face reddened. "We don't value each other's company or opinions. We're not *friends*. Yet as soon as we're in the bedchamber you…you keep *kissing* me." She lowered her voice over the last two words as if they were somehow indecent.

And he must be as twisted as she was, because for some reason, that made his blood course faster. He kept his face impassive, but it was a struggle. "So?" he asked. "You're my wife, aren't you? Funny sort of husband I'd be if I didn't even kiss you first."

Eden looked back at him with frank skepticism.

"What do you expect me to do?" he demanded. "Just lift up your skirts and have my merry way without even a kiss first?"

When she appeared to consider this, he felt winded. "N-no," she said after a moment. "I understand the kissing and such before. I'm talking about afterward. It seems…superfluous."

"Superfluous?" he echoed blankly. He knew not why but he was finding it hard to concentrate. He felt like she'd kicked him right in the chest. "Well, now you've told me," he heard himself respond. "Rest assured it won't happen again." He threw his napkin down with a hand that shook slightly. He had a bitter taste in his mouth.

He had been victorious at Areley Kings, but any warm glow from that now abruptly fled. Which was also foolish, as he had a large purse of gold and a new trophy out of it. What did he care if his cold bitch of a wife didn't want his kisses? He rubbed his chest distractedly as he moved away from the table.

"Wait." Eden had half risen from the table, her expression tense. "I just meant…it feels strange, that's all," she finished lamely.

"I see."

"So, you won then?" she asked with an air of desperation, and it dawned on Roland with horrible clarity that she could see she had hurt his feelings. How was that even possible? He was Roland Vawdrey, and no one had had the power to do that in years. Realizing he was still rubbing his chest, like she had inflicted a physical wound, he abruptly dropped his hand. "At Areley Kings," she rambled on. "The jousting or the mock battle thing?"

"Melee," he corrected her automatically, though continuing this nightmare conversation was the last thing he wanted. He just wanted to get away. "Joust," he said shortly, answering her question.

"You won both?" she asked in confusion. "Well, that's very impressive."

He snorted. Gods, now she was trying to bolster him up! Could this get any worse?

"What? Everyone agrees you're very good."

"I only won the jousting, Eden," he said irritably.

"Oh, well, that's still…" She trailed off. "What went wrong in the melee, do you suppose?" she asked brightly.

Roland regarded her with almost open-mouthed incredulity. "No one expects to win both! And even if they did, I'm not about to talk battle strategy with *you*!"

"I'm just trying to make a little pleasant conversation between us," she huffed.

"Well, don't bother!" he bit back. "I find your conversation *superfluous*." With that cutting rejoinder he flung out of the room, slamming the door behind him. It would have been more satisfying if he didn't suspect she was surprised he even knew what the word meant!

Eden Montmayne, thought Roland savagely as he descended the stone steps, was without doubt the most infuriating woman in the unchronicled history of infuriating women. No doubt, he thought, she'd soon correct him if he ever shared that suspicion. The bloody woman always had plenty to say, no matter what the subject matter! He was slightly disturbed by the fact he was now anticipating what she would say though.

His footsteps slowed. When had he started doing that? He *never* did that. Other people's opinions were largely a matter of indifference to Roland. Certainly, they had no consequence regarding the way he acted. Not that they would now, he thought with a hasty scowl. She was a shrew of a bride, and he must be stark staring mad to have—what?

He pulled himself up short. Wanted her? Well, that was ballocks. He'd been coerced into taking her to wife, he reminded his errant thoughts uneasily. A sarcastic response in his own head irritated him, telling himself he never stopped panting after his own wife. When the hells had he started upbraiding himself? He frowned, diverting his steps toward the stables.

Besides, she was an ungrateful harpy, not wanting his kisses. He must be the only man in the kingdom who hankered after her cruel lips! Gods! He rubbed his jaw distractedly. And why didn't she want his attentions, damn it? He was her husband. And by his reckoning, he hadn't been all that contemptible in the role. Had he even once taken her to task for trapping him into wedlock? Not even once!

He'd accepted the consequences of his actions with practicality. No reproaches had passed his lips, even though the little wretch had the nerve to look as sick as a dog throughout their entire wedding ceremony and even tried to flee in the aftermath! He snorted. And then she'd got the brass neck to begrudge him her lips!

It was the least she could bloody give him, he thought, walking on with an injured air. When he thought about the rank ingratitude, it fairly took his breath away! He was the King's champion! Maidens dropped their handkerchiefs, and other things, in the hopes of enticing him, and his own wedded wife was asking him not to kiss her after he'd ploughed her. It was beyond all reasoning, he thought darkly. It was pointless even trying. He kicked an abandoned pail as he entered the stables. It made him feel a little better, but not much.

31

Roland was never going to kiss her again. Eden paced the room distractedly as Brigid cleared away their supper things. She felt a little sick. She wasn't really sure how things had deteriorated so quickly over supper, or why she had persisted in such a completely *fruitless* line of conversation.

Good grief, it was almost like she had been trying to needle him. She covered her mouth with her hand and turned sharply on her heel as she ran over the conversation in her head. Where had it all gone so badly wrong? Her steps slowed a little and she frowned, remembering the blaze of emotion she had felt when he had described Sir Renlow as "utterly fearless." She had been pierced with the strangest regret and longing at his words. No one would ever describe her in such glowing terms, she thought, closing her eyes briefly. Little Miss Perfect who always strove never to put a foot wrong, but somehow ended up disgracing herself anyway.

And how extraordinary that Roland Vawdrey should consider the strange figure of Sir Renlow as the perfect fledgling knight. He really was full of surprises, this husband of hers. A pity then that she had gone and willfully filled him with disgust for her, she thought, biting her lip. So far from the brave Sir Renlow was she that instead of welcoming Roland home and attempting to build some kind of mutual respect between them, she had instead flung every dark doubt and secret fear she harbored about their ill-fated marriage in his face. *Oh well done, Eden.*

"Milady?" asked Brigid hesitantly.

Eden sharply turned her head. "Yes?"

"I didn't catch what you said."

Eden made a quick movement with her hands. "Nothing to signify," she said hurriedly. Had she spoken aloud? Then to her embarrassment, she felt the floodgates open and tears coursing down her cheeks.

"Oh, milady!" Eden shook her head, but when she tried to reassure her maid, all that came out was a sob. "The great brute, what did he say?" asked Brigid indignantly. She plunked down the tablecloth she had been folding and ushered Eden into a chair.

"He—not his fault—mine," gasped Eden, mopping at her eyes with a napkin.

"Hah—likely story! And you been missing him so, these last few days too!" she tutted. Eden took a jagged breath. No, that wasn't right. Had she? "Menfolk!" exclaimed Brigid with great loathing. "If you knew what I had to contend with, that oaf, Fulco! Huffing and puffing at me, and never taking his beady little eyes off me."

"Oh dear," quavered Eden, glad of any distraction from her own woes. "You're not leaving us, are you?"

"Leaving?" snorted Brigid. "I should say not! It'd be a fine thing if I let such a great lummox drive me out, now I've found somewhere I belong."

"Oh, good," said Eden shakily. She wiped her cheeks and rallied herself. "Someone will have to speak to Fulco. Is he waiting for you to put a foot wrong then?"

Brigid gave her a wry look. "Something like that," she murmured. And strangely enough, she blushed.

"Roland says that his mother is likely poisoning his mind against any marriageable women."

"Is that so?" asked Brigid with interest. "Well, good luck to her with that!" She nudged Eden conspiratorially. "He is a fine figure of a man when all's said and done, and not so many of them about. There'd be plenty of lasses in the village glad to have him."

At Brigid's wistful tone, Eden looked up. "But not you?" she asked curiously, then felt contrite. "I'm sorry, you don't have to answer that. I didn't mean to pry."

Brigid laughed. "I did cast my eye his way at one time, as it happens," she admitted. "But I came on too strong for the likes of Fulco. He'd have preferred if I'd played the bashful maiden, rather than the brazen widow." She clicked her tongue. "A shame, but there 'tis."

"I daresay a bashful maiden would never hold her own against his mother," said Eden.

"You may have something there, milady," agreed Brigid and they both smiled at each other. Eden's smile was rather watery. "There now, that's better. Shall I fetch you a posset, milady?"

Eden opened her mouth to reply when they both heard the dogs start up barking below.

"Whatever's gotten into them now?" said Brigid vexedly. "It surely can't be a visitor at this hour?" She hurried to the door, and when she flung it open, Eden thought she could hear unknown male tones below. Brigid looked back at her with wide eyes, evidently having heard the same strains of muted conversation. "I'll be back directly when I've found out what it's all about, milady," she said and disappeared.

Eden stood uneasily in the center of the room. Who would call at this hour in such an out-of-the-way place? She had just gone to retrieve her book from the shelf in the box-bed when she heard a hurried step on the stair. She turned to face the door as it burst open, and Roland stood framed there. "What is it?" she asked, catching sight of his expression.

"You'd better come down," he said grimly.

32

Roland had not spoken to her on the staircase, but when she followed him into the sitting room, she found it seemed full of strangers, and checked on the threshold. She looked about her in bewilderment and realized it was only two men dressed in the manner of knights.

"Eden," said Roland. "This is Sir Palmerston du Vrey and Sir Symond Chevenix of the King's guard." The two knights stood by the fireplace stepped forward and bowed to her. "They have come to accompany you back to Caer-Lyoness, at the request of the Queen."

"The Queen?" Eden blurted and then, "*Me?* Why?" She looked searchingly at the two knights. Sir Symond was the younger of the two and he stared glassily past her shoulder while Sir Palmerston cleared his throat before averting his eyes. She turned back to Roland.

"It seems," he said heavily, "that the Montmaynes have lodged a complaint with the Queen about certain irregularities with our marriage."

"My family has?" Eden heard herself ask in a high-pitched voice she hardly recognized.

Sir Palmerston coughed. "That is correct, Lady Eden," he said.

"Which I find extraordinary," continued Roland coldly, "when you consider that your uncle and guardian acted witness at our wedding."

Sir Palmerston cleared his throat. "It is the Lady Dorothea Montmayne who has petitioned the Queen." Roland looked blank.

"My grandmother," explained Eden with a sinking heart. She'd petitioned the Queen? "She surely has not left Hallam Hall!" she faltered, groping about for a chair to sink in. Roland caught her firmly under her armpit and lowered her into a seat, for all the world as if she were an old woman. In truth, she had come over a-tremble.

"Lady Dorothea is at court now," Sir Symond informed her with a nod.

"I can scarce believe it! She has not been to court in twenty years!" Eden muttered, more to herself than anyone else.

"She is accompanied by her granddaughter, the Lady Lenora," added Sir Symond, earning a glare from Sir Palmerston.

Eden looked up in dismay. "Is—is Lenora a petitioner too?" she asked with a catch in her voice.

"We are not at liberty to tell you any more at present," cut in Sir Palmerston firmly. "But you must leave with us at first light, my lady." He glanced at Roland. "By royal decree."

Eden felt herself go at once hot and then cold all over. She felt Roland's hand press down on her shoulder, and realized he was still stood by her chair. She took a deep breath. "I see," she said and forced herself to look up at Roland. He was still looking rather foreboding in the flickering firelight and had not spoken for several moments. *He will be glad to see the back of me*, she thought blankly as she tried to gather her wits about her. For some reason, it was proving difficult. She was finding it hard to catch her breath.

"If we are to leave at daybreak," Roland said with deliberate emphasis on the *we*, "then you must be our guests tonight at Vawdrey Keep." Eden turned her head sharply to look at him. "We will have beds made up for you. I'm afraid they will be in

305

the servants' quarters as we are still in the process of refurbishing the place."

Sir Symond turned rather red. "You don't seem to appreciate the nature of our mission, Sir Roland—" he started stiffly.

"That would be very good of you, Sir Roland," said Sir Palmerston, cutting across his companion loudly. "And perhaps a bite to eat, sir. If it's not too much trouble?"

"Of course," said Roland. "I will have supper sent up for you directly." He held his hand out to Eden, and she took it hastily, and found herself dragged to her feet. "And now to bed with you, I fancy, with such an early start in the morn."

Sir Symond opened his mouth to speak, but Eden saw Sir Palmerston deliberately step on his foot. He muttered something out of the corner of his mouth, which sounded like "Don't be such a bloody fool, lad!" but she could have been mistaken.

Roland whisked her out of there without another word and saw her up the steps to their room. "I'll be back presently," he said shortly. "Lock the door and be sure to open it only for me."

Eden nodded and hurried to comply. She had washed and undressed by the time he had returned. He brought Parnell and Castor with him, and after letting them in, she got straight into bed. She had no words and no earthly idea what to say about her predicament.

She listened to the sounds of Roland washing and shedding his clothes and then his footsteps approaching the bed. He blew out the candle then climbed stealthily through the doors, and Eden felt him settle beside her.

She waited a few moments with her eyes open, but he did not speak. After a while she closed them and waited for sleep that did not come. Instead, she lay awake, thinking about her grandmother and Lenora and what awaited her at court. Eventually, she must have drifted off to sleep, for the next thing she knew she was being shaken awake by Roland, who was already up and dressed.

"If you rise now, I'll send Brigid in to help you dress and pack up your things."

"Things?" repeated Eden blankly, but he was already crossing the room. "Wait!" She sat up. "You're still coming too? To court?" she asked and rubbed her eyes.

He nodded curtly. "Of course," he said and left. Eden got out of bed and presently Brigid bustled in carrying hot water for her to wash. As Eden set about her ablutions, her maid flung back the lid of the chest and started lifting out the gowns which Eden had stuffed back in there.

"Which will you wear today, milady?" she asked once she'd laid the four gowns out. She ran a hand over the gold dress with the pink roses. "I've never seen such dresses." She cast an admiring glance Eden's way.

"They're not mine," Eden told her. "They were made for my cousin's bridal trousseau."

Brigid looked doubtfully from the fine gowns to Eden and then back again. "You and your cousin must surely be of a muchness when it comes to size," she said. "They look as if they were made for you."

"I don't wear colors," Eden said flatly.

"But your blue gown is so pretty!"

"That was not made for me either," said Eden. "But for Lady Payne. I prefer myself in somber shades. They suit my personality better."

Brigid shot her a surprised look. "I find that hard to believe, milady. You look so well in nice things. 'Tis plain, my master thinks as much," she said, glancing at the blue and gold robe Roland had brought her back from Areley Kings.

Eden had no reply to make to that. "As to which I'll wear," she said, "I have no preference. The blue is being cleaned, I think."

"If you've no preference, then I think this rose pink would look very well," said Brigid.

Eden donned a clean shift as Brigid exclaimed over the brightly colored stockings. She passed Eden a pair which were sky blue with gold ribbon garters. "Just pick out the plainest veil," Eden recommended as she saw her hovering over one covered in fancy ruffles and pleats. Brigid pouted and selected one with a delicate floral border.

Once dressed it seemed to Eden that she looked like she was dressed for a banquet, rather than a day's traveling. She really did look the image of a frivolous courtier, she thought despairingly. Still, there was nothing for it; she owned nothing sensible. Instead, she sat down and arranged her braids as best she could, securing them in a roll at the nape of her neck before Brigid helped her pin the veil over the arrangement.

"I'll pack your things while you break your fast below," Brigid assured her.

Eden looked back from the doorway. "Thank you, Brigid." She stood a moment, watching as the young woman busied herself folding the fine chemises and stockings that had been intended for Lenora. Was this the last time she would see Brigid? Her heart heavy, Eden made her way down, realizing she did not even have to look now or count the stairs as she went. She had, in fact, mastered the trip steps.

The table had been laid with toasted bread and butter and a platter of salted fish, but no one else was seated yet there. Eden made a quick meal, and it was only as she was finishing up that Sir Palmerston and Sir Symond made an appearance. She thought she heard one of them exclaim before the door opened.

"My lady," mumbled Sir Palmerston with a bow before he was seated.

Sir Symond appeared to be limping slightly. Eden wondered if he was a victim of the staircase or a dog bite. She had noticed that none of the dogs were attendance and wondered at it. Where were they all? Were they with Roland? And where was her husband? Her stomach lurched. And how much longer would he continue in that role?

They embarked on their journey as soon as their escorts had finished their morning repast. Their party was dour and uncommunicative, and that included Eden, who retreated into her thoughts. The only one who seemed relatively merry was Cuthbert, who brought up the rear. Nothing could put a damper on his spirits for long, and Eden suspected he was happy to return to the city.

The only thing that brought her any comfort was that Roland brought two of the dogs along with them, Castor and Parnell. When they took infrequent breaks, Parnell leaned heavily against her legs. Even Castor periodically checked on her before returning to his master's side.

The first night Eden found she was expected to sleep in a separate bedchamber to the others, who it seemed would bunk down in a communal room. Sir Palmerston was apologetic

309

about locking her in, but firm, and she was led to understand he would be remiss in his duty if he did not take this step. Roland was stony silent on the subject, simply directing her to take both dogs with her when she retired. On hearing the key turn in the lock, strangely, her first thought was that at least this way she would not be able to sleepwalk any further abroad than this room.

She readied herself for bed, pondering how Sir Symond had reacted the previous night and realizing that he had meant to separate them sooner. Was their marriage to be declared invalid? How would she fare at court if she was to figure as a prominent player in such a scandal?

Could she bear all the gossip and conjecture if it was about her? Court had always been her happy place. She had always felt secure in the circles she moved in there. Was that to be ripped away from her? And if so, what would she do? Her hands and feet felt clammy as she considered being returned to her uncle. Would he even accept her back in such disgrace?

She remembered his irate face the last time she had seen him and felt anxious. His only option would be to bury her at Hallam Hall, perhaps as her aunt's companion. Eden shuddered, thinking of Lenora's discontented mother. Perhaps he would be merciful and bury her in a convent instead.

It was perhaps not surprising that she couldn't settle in the strange surroundings. In the end Parnell jumped up onto the bed, a heavy weight across her legs. This seemed to do the trick, and she managed to get some rest in the early hours of the morning.

The second day's traveling was not much different to the first, except it grew warmer the further south they traveled. The sun was high in the sky, and Eden shed her mittens and drew back the hood of her cloak. They covered a good many miles, and on the second night, Eden managed to sleep a little better from sheer exhaustion.

On the third day they reached Caer-Lyoness. To Eden's alarm, they were forced to wait at the south gate for an armed escort. Was she under arrest then? Her eyes flew to Roland's, but his own were shuttered and gave nothing away. As she watched, Sir Palmerston drew him aside and they had some quiet conversation that Eden could not hear.

Sir Symond moved alongside her, an expression of officiousness on his face that immediately irritated her. If he could get away with it, she realized, he would march her into the castle and throw her at the Queen's feet like a prisoner! She directed her coldest, haughtiest look upon him and was pleased to see his face flush as he turned away.

At long last a group of soldiers with lances marched out of the gate, and Sir Palmerston stepped forward, offering to help her dismount. Eden refused his help, though she thanked him politely after climbing down from Christobel.

"My horse—" she started, but he preempted her.

"—will be taken to the royal stables immediately, my lady."

She took a deep breath and looked back at Roland. He was looking right at her, although he and Cuthbert were still on horseback. Were they going to leave her here then? It seemed only she would be delivered up like some sort of captive! Her bosom swelled with indignation.

"Take the dogs," said Roland curtly.

Eden opened her mouth to argue, but then changed her mind. After all, she needed all the friends she could get. Instead, she inclined her head stiffly, and at his order, both dogs bounded to her side. Sir Palmerston eyed them a moment doubtfully, but then offered her his arm. She placed her hand on it, the guards fell into place on either side of them, and Eden found herself marched into the royal palace. She had never thought herself a fanciful person, but almost, she could imagine herself clad in chains.

To Eden's surprise, she was not taken to the Montmayne quarters as she'd expected, but instead directly to the Queen's apartments. Sir Palmerston's smart rap on the door was answered by Jane Cecil, the Queen's latest favorite. Eden felt herself bridle, though in truth, Jane kept her eyes tactfully diverted. The courtiers they had passed in the corridors had not scrupled to stare.

"Do come in, the Queen awaits," murmured Jane, opening the door to let them in. "My orders are only to admit Sir Palmerston," Eden heard Jane tell the others behind them, and was gratified to imagine Sir Symond's displeasure at being left out. She turned back, only to make sure the dogs were let in, but Castor and Parnell were already barging past the surprised-looking lady-in-waiting in their hurry to catch up with her.

Queen Armenal was sat in a low, ornate chair before the fire. She was dressed in a muted bronze-green dress which suited her olive complexion and dark hair well. She held her hands out at once to Eden. "Dear child," she said loudly. "We are most relieved to see you returned to us." Unsure if the Queen referred to court or the "royal we," Eden curtseyed low and then clasped both of the Queen's beringed hands in her own. "Do sit. You are doubtless fatigued from your journey."

Jane wordlessly took her cloak as Eden seated herself and listened to the Queen warmly thank Sir Palmerston for his services, politely hoping it was not too arduous a task she had set him. Sir Palmerston assured her it was his pleasure to serve

312

his Queen and then bowed low to both of them in turn and backed out of the room.

"It is funny, is it not, to think his family used to be one of my most furious critics," mused the Queen, watching the door shut after him.

"Indeed?" asked Eden politely. She was distracted by Castor and Parnell, who had taken the opportunity to freely roam about the elegantly furnished rooms, pawing and sniffing at whatever took their fancy. "Here!" she called sharply. "Excuse me, Your Majesty," said Eden. "Castor! Parnell!" Her voice rang out authoritatively, making the unfortunate Jane jump. "Come to me!" The dogs looked up, their ears pricked, their eyes alert as they returned to her. "Sit!" They settled at this, though Parnell circled twice before collapsing with a sigh.

"What large, unwieldly beasts!" exclaimed the Queen. "I had no notion you were fond of such uncouth, powerful creatures. Still," she added slyly, "you have now survived several weeks as a Vawdrey, so perhaps it should not surprise me overmuch."

Eden looked up sharply, but the Queen was smiling urbanely. She did not like to point out it was not quite three weeks she had been married yet, but instead reached out and patted Castor, who looked likely to start barking wildly at any minute.

"Ah, Jane!" said the Queen as Jane Cecil approached, bearing a tray of refreshments. "Such a treasure, is she not? I don't know how I would do without her. She is the only one I can depend upon not to abandon me for a husband." The Queen sighed forlornly, and Eden realized this was a barb with a new target. The Queen used to say that about her—Eden.

Not anymore, it seemed. Jane had thoroughly replaced her in the Queen's affections. She wondered, not for the first time, at Queen Armenal's fondness for the pale, rather insipid Jane.

Everyone knew her far more attractive sister, Helen, was the King's mistress. Eden doubted very much that the Queen was ignorant of the fact.

"Will you take wine or mead?" offered Jane, setting down her burden and reaching for the silver goblets.

"Wine, please," said Eden, glancing at the beautiful view the Queen's apartments afforded over the palace grounds. By the position of the sun in the sky, Eden estimated the hour was no more advanced than five o'clock or thereabouts. She found herself devoutly hoping that Roland had not left her here, and gone back to Vawdrey Keep, abandoning her to her fate.

The thought caught her off guard. Had she become accustomed then, to this husband of hers? It had been such a short amount of time relatively, she reminded herself dazedly. Why did it seem so odd being back here at court in her old life?

"No doubt you are still reeling from the events of the past few weeks, no?" said the Queen smoothly as Jane poured her wine. "We are all giddy, in truth, is that not so?" When Jane Cecil only answered her with a discreet nod, the Queen tsked. "Eden will not thank us to hide from her the truth. There has been *much* whispering in corners." She nodded. "But yes, it has been *intolerable.* And so, I have told the King. It is an insult to me, for one of my ladies to be an object of such infamy."

She settled back in her seat as Eden tensed, leaning forward in hers. "I daresay," said the Queen with an airy wave of her hand. "That brother of his, the Lord Oswald Vawdrey, could have drawn over it the veil most discreet, if he had not been hampered by that execrable Sir Christopher…"

"Uncle Christopher has been at court?" asked Eden with dismay.

The Queen looked heavenward. "I do not mean to be overly censorious of your family, my very dear Eden," she said serenely, "but this Christopher Montmayne…" She gave a grimace of distaste.

"I know," said Eden without thinking. "My own father was said to be much worse though."

The Queen gave a startled burst of laughter. "Really?"

Eden felt herself turn pink. She was never usually so frank. "Yes, my father, Godwin Montmayne, was the black sheep of the family. Uncle Leofric was the only respectable one."

The Queen looked thoughtful. "How interesting! Perhaps, the Lady Dorothea, she was too strict. Boys are hard to raise, or so I hear," she sighed. "If one allows them to run wild like savages, they grow up as such. But then if one keeps them to the path that is so straight and narrow—also savages, but deceitful ones! Sometimes I am very glad that I have only the stepson. If he turns out to be the bad lot…" She shrugged. "I cannot be held to account."

Eden thought fleetingly of the absent prince who was being raised apart at some country idyll and wondered at the Queen's attitude. She thought of the woods and hills around the Keep that Roland had roamed over as a boy. On the whole, she thought raising them like honest savages might have better results. She surfaced from her thoughts with a start, realizing the Queen was still addressing her.

"—I hope that will not be too much of an inconvenience to you," she was saying smoothly.

"I beg your pardon, Your Majesty?"

"I was explaining your living arrangements while the hearing it is ongoing."

"Hearing?" repeated Eden blankly.

The Queen smiled at her. "My poor dear. It must be very distressing for you. But you must take heart. Your grandmother, she wishes for you the best. If it means the scandal, then that is what must ensue. She will not tolerate you being coerced into a distasteful union. This she told to me herself."

Eden gasped. "So, the hearing…?"

The Queen gave a nod. "It is to determine whether this marriage, it should stand."

It turned out that Eden was to remain in the Queen's apartments in a shared attendants' room with Jane Cecil during the goings-on. The hearing would be held over three days and testimonies would be taken from various witnesses. Eden listened with a sinking heart to the plans laid out before her.

The Queen was to preside over proceedings, and it seemed she was looking forward to them with great relish. It would start on the morrow. Anticipating the event, Eden found she lost all appetite for the delicious supper that had arrived from the royal kitchens. She felt sick, and not just of stomach, but of heart.

33

Eden scanned the packed audience room. She could see every leading courtier crammed in from pillar to post, save one. Where was Roland? In the end, she gave up all pretense of looking dignified and craned her neck, turning in her seat. He was nowhere to be seen! Eden tried to fight down the rising panic. Had he gone back to Sitchmarsh then? Had he left her?

Her heart pounded in her chest. She could feel her breathing grow shallow. She had spotted her grandmother, Lenora, and her uncles sat near the front. She had also seen Sir Oswald Vawdrey, head to toe in black. He had that habitual smile playing about his mouth, but she did not believe for one minute he was as relaxed as he looked. After all, was he about to perjure himself before the Queen?

Then she remembered that someone had once told her that chief adviser to the King included another role that wasn't so openly discussed. That of chief spymaster. Perhaps after all, lying wasn't going to be a problem for Lord Vawdrey. She had just slumped back in her seat when she noticed the blond head of hair next to Oswald. It was Cuthbert! She sat up again but looked in vain for Roland. He was not there.

She felt lost and without an anchor. She wasn't a Montmayne anymore, and yet, she wasn't now a proven Vawdrey either. She had no one! She didn't even have the dogs as she had been forced to leave them in the Queen's quarters. Forcing herself to take a deep breath, Eden mustered some composure at least. She had always been able to fall back on her self-possession. It could not abandon her now.

A hush fell over the room, and Eden realized the double doors down the other end had opened, and the Queen was swooping in, resplendent in a glinting purple gown with underskirt and full sleeves of gold. She wore a purple coif cap and gold veil to match. Glancing down at the sea-green gown of Lenora's that she *had* felt overdressed in, Eden suddenly felt modestly arrayed. Queen Armenal was dressed to capture the eye, and she had certainly achieved her aim, as her audience was captivated by her appearance.

The Queen arrived at the front of the room, and a page stepped forward to help her climb the steps to the dais. Once she had mounted the platform, she wasted no time, but approached the front to address the crowd in her commanding voice. "My lords and ladies, gentles all—welcome!" She beamed and scanned the full room with every evidence of approval.

"We are here today, as you are all aware, to hear the case for and against the validity of the marriage that took place last month, between Sir Roland Vawdrey and Lady Eden Montmayne. Statements will be given by various witnesses so that I may determine whether it is null and void or legally binding. I would ask that you keep any noise to a minimum so that we may hear what the various speakers have to say."

A murmur of assent went up from the crowd, and Eden twisted her hands in her lap. The Queen consulted a piece of paper that was passed up to her by a clerk. "The first witness that shall testify will be the Lady Dorothea Montmayne." A loud, excited muttering went up as the Queen walked to the back of the dais and elegantly sank into her throne there.

Eden's mouth felt dry as she turned and watched her grandmother walk stiffly down the middle of the room. She wore a dark fawn velvet gown trimmed with white fur and pearls. Her iron-gray hair was swept up into an elegant matching coif and she wore a wimple giving her the full matronly effect.

Her eyes were hooded, her expression grim. She dipped into a rather old-fashioned curtsey which may or may not have been due to the stiffness of her joints. Then she took the seat that was pointed out to her near the front by yet another page, who wore the royal Argent colors of blue and gold.

"It was you, was it not, Lady Dorothea," began the Queen in her clear, carrying voice, "who first approached us regarding the authenticity of this marital union?"

Lady Dorothea inclined her head. "It was," she assented.

"And why was it that you felt impelled to appeal to your sovereign for intercession on this matter?"

"I had many pressing concerns," said her grandmother dryly. "Not the least being the clandestine manner in which the ceremony was performed. I was not present, despite being under the same roof at the time. It was conducted at an ungodly hour, with very few witnesses."

She paused while this was digested. Then added, "I do not believe my niece was consenting." There was a clamor of noise at this. Eden closed her eyes briefly. "I believe she was coerced," continued Lady Dorothea calmly. "And to add insult to injury, she was *not* the intended bride in this agreement between our families. Sir Roland Vawdrey was contracted to another."

The buzz of whispers that greeted this was very loud indeed. Eden heard her cousin's name on several tongues, but when she steeled herself to glance in Lenora's direction, she found her looking as detached and tranquil as ever. Nothing, it seemed, could disrupt Lenora's poise.

"These are serious allegations indeed, Lady Dorothea," said the Queen soberly. "I count at least three possible impediments."

She looked across at one of the clerks who was making notes with his quill pen. He gave a firm nod of agreement. "Could you oblige us by elaborating further on why you believe the ceremony was *clandestine* in nature?"

"Certainly, I can," replied Lady Dorothea magnificently. "My son Leofric told me the banquet he was hosting was a betrothal feast only. Not," stressed Lady Dorothea, "a wedding feast. He told me it was for *his* daughter, Lenora. Why then, the following morning, was my *other* granddaughter hastily married off in some obscure manner and spirited away without even so much as a farewell to her kinfolk?"

Eden felt her heart race and had to struggle not to cover her face with her hands. Had her uncle not given his mother any explanation for what had occurred?

"Was no explanation offered to you by Sir Leofric?" the Queen asked, echoing Eden's unspoken thoughts.

Lady Dorothea's mouth twisted. "The explanation I was treated to was *inconceivable* in every way and an insult to my intelligence, as well as my granddaughter," she said bitterly.

The Queen paused while the audience made of that what they would. Eden felt the tips of her ears burn. She could quite imagine that there were plenty of rumors abroad after her uncle Christopher had been spreading malicious gossip. She clutched her skirts between nerveless fingers and dared not look toward her uncle.

"Perhaps," said the Queen loudly, "you could instead explain to us why it is that you do not believe the Lady Eden would have been a willing participant in such nuptials?"

Suddenly Eden felt glad that Roland was not present for this. She stared at her grandmother in horror, waiting for the words that would fall from those thin lips.

"Indeed, I can. When we conversed prior to the betrothal feast, we discussed quite frankly Sir Roland's unsuitability as a bridegroom."

Eden stiffened. *Oh no.* She racked her brain, trying to remember their conversation. What had she said? She did not think she had been so very insulting about Roland's fitness for marriage. After all, she had been trying to be diplomatic and not to worry her grandmother.

"When you say 'we'…?"

"Eden and myself," clarified Lady Dorothea.

"And do you remember," asked the Queen with a gleam in her eye, "what qualities the two of you found particularly lacking in Sir Roland?"

Lady Dorothea pursed her lips. "I do not remember the specifics," she said. "But I distinctly remember we were of one accord in our wishes. That Lenora should wake up and realize he was not the man for her before the marriage took place."

The Queen nodded slowly. "I see," she said. "But just because Eden did not think that Sir Roland would make her cousin a good bridegroom, it does not follow that she would rule him out as one for herself."

"My granddaughter has *never* admired that manner of man," said Lady Dorothea grandly. "She has always had refined and artistic tastes." She looked down her rather long nose and fixed Eden with a gimlet eye. Eden blushed and looked away. "It is unthinkable that she would desire such an ill-made match."

"I see. Thank you, Lady Dorothea." Eden forced herself to watch as her grandmother jerkily rose from the chair and then stalked back to her original seating place. "I think next," said Queen Armenal, her voice rising above the babble, "that we should talk to the alleged jilted bride, the Lady Lenora."

This caused a furor among the masses. Eden turned her head and stared with the rest as Lenora rose from her chair, a vision of feminine beauty with her pink and white complexion, her cornflower-blue eyes, and her golden ringleted hair. Many sighs were heard around the chamber as she made her way to the front and curtseyed gracefully to the Queen. She wore a very simple gown of the palest pink, and a wispy veil fluttered about her, concealing nothing. She looked like an angel.

"Fair Lenora," said the Queen. "Your legendary beauty has not dimmed one whit as a result of such infamous treatment, I find."

"Oh no," said Lenora, opening her eyes very wide. "I have known for months that Sir Roland only had eyes for my cousin. He never wanted to marry me."

"Nonsense, child!" burst out her grandmother, Lady Dorothea, angrily from the crowd. "Why you persist in this tale is beyond me! I have explained this to you many times…" She broke off angrily when she noticed her words were creating quite a stir in the audience with several people craning their heads to look at her.

"For shame!" Eden heard one courtier hiss. "Trying to browbeat the fair Lenora!" tutted another. Eden winced, but looking back at her cousin, found her looking utterly unruffled by the interruption.

"He never wanted to marry me," Lenora repeated clearly, and their grandmother turned quite purple with chagrin.

"Thank you, Lenora," said the Queen brightly. "It is fascinating to see things from a different viewpoint. Then this feast…?" she suggested. "It was not a formal betrothal feast between your two families as everyone thought?"

"Oh yes," said Lenora. "But not for me. For Eden." Her words caused a scandal among the assembled courtiers. Lenora waited patiently for the noise to die down. "I offered my cousin the lend of my new silk gown and my pearls for the occasion." She turned her head and looked directly at Eden. "Is that not so, Eden? And my jewel-encrusted toque."

Eden nodded feebly. She did not feel up to mentioning that the toque had been filled with kittens at the time.

"But how sweet of you!" exclaimed the Queen indulgently. "You must be very fond of your cousin, I think."

"Oh yes," said Lenora, turning her guileless eyes back to Eden. "She is like my sister, really. Although my father never treated us as equals, that is how I have always regarded her."

"You were not raised as equals?" the Queen asked, sounding surprised at the turn Lenora's testimony had taken.

"Oh no," said Lenora. "Otherwise, she would have had her own pearls and silk gown, would she not?"

"Quite," murmured the Queen. Then seemed to give herself a little shake. "So, you would have us believe that Eden's ensuing marriage with the King's champion is *not* a matter of enmity between the two of you at all?" asked the Queen.

"Oh no," said Lenora mildly. "Why should it be?"

Eden's palms were clammy, so she reached down to wipe them on her borrowed skirts. She felt suddenly dizzy and disorientated. Could Lenora really believe that? About Eden still being like a sister to her? And that she had not usurped her place as wife to Roland? She looked so…so imperturbable and sedate, it was hard to believe she was not wholly in earnest.

A sudden hush fell over proceedings, and Eden turned to find that Oswald Vawdrey had stood up from his seat.

"Earl Vawdrey?" said the Queen, turning to look at him. "You have something pertinent to contribute at this point?"

He smiled a wintry smile. "As to that, I hardly know. But it was I that approached Sir Leofric regarding the betrothal arrangements in the first place," he said, and then smothered a yawn. "I beg your pardon, Your Majesty. I am but recently a father…"

A smatter of laughter broke out from the onlookers.

The Queen's smile turned a little brittle. "But of course," she said, and Eden wondered if the Queen did not appreciate sharing the spotlight with a player of his magnitude. There was a sort of assured style and grace about Oswald Vawdrey, which only very few possessed. He was tall and lean and dressed all in midnight black. You could almost overlook his self-possession if you did not know any better. Eden had a feeling it was woe betide you if you did. His keen eyes roamed now over the key players, and when they fell on her, his head tipped to one side, and he looked speculative.

"Well, if you would be so good as to share your information with us now, Lord Vawdrey," the Queen prompted him, sounding a little impatient. Eden knew there was no love lost between the two of them, which was mostly due to politics.

Oswald made his way unhurriedly to the front of the hall, and Lenora returned to Lady Dorothea, who now wore a look of frozen outrage. Lenora did not look even remotely fazed as she sat down beside her.

When Oswald spoke, his voice was surprisingly full-volumed. "My brother Roland asked me, as head of our house, to approach Sir Leofric Montmayne with a view to discussing the proposed marriage approximately two months ago. It was some couple of weeks before our paths crossed, and we were able to discuss terms regarding the proposed joining of our houses. Once we had talked over a few preliminaries, we were able to proceed to the point of arranging a formal betrothal feast at Hallam Hall."

"If I might just stop you there, Lord Vawdrey," the Queen interrupted him, holding up one elegant forefinger.

"Of course, Your Majesty," he responded politely.

"We seem to have raced ahead, Lord Vawdrey," she said reproachfully, "and skipped the most relevant point."

"We have?" He frowned and turned to the audience with a small bow. "Do forgive me."

They laughed, and the Queen looked annoyed. "Which one of the Montmayne girls," she asked, dramatically sweeping a pale, graceful arm in an arc, "was the prospective bride? That is the question!"

Oswald Vawdrey looked totally astonished by her query. He looked about him with supposed incredulity. "Why, as to that, there was simply never any doubt in my mind. It was entirely apparent who was my brother Roland's intended, and had been for several months by this point."

There was a murmuring in the crowd, and Eden knew they were discussing that infamous Midwinter kiss. For the first time, she felt no burning shame about the gossip. That kiss seemed…well, almost *innocent* now!

"And to be clear," said the Queen with a tight smile, "you are referring now to…?"

"I refer, of course," he responded gravely with a small bow in her direction, "to the Lady Eden." A positive buzz went up after this.

"If I might appeal to you all for quiet!" trilled the Queen, and the hubbub died down with seeming reluctance.

One voice could still be heard protesting though, and Eden turned her head to look at her uncle Leo, who was bleating like a bullfrog.

"Ah, Sir Leofric," said the Queen tolerantly. "You *would* seem the logical person to speak next."

34

"But did Lord Vawdrey actually say the word *Lenora* in his request?" persisted the Queen some five minutes later. She wore a faintly frustrated air, for Sir Leofric had turned out to give a very poor account of himself. He was defensive, apt to ramble off the point, and quick to take offence at any perceived slight.

"Yes!" burst out Sir Leofric. Then he appeared to waver. "Well, only consider for yourself," he said indignantly. "He said 'you have in your charge…' something along the lines of 'the power to bestow a flower of womanhood.' Something of that sort. Well obviously, he was talking about Lenora. Everyone knows she is called the Flower of All Karadok." He looked around with a smug look on his face, but after a moment or two seemed to realize that he had not given the assurances everyone had expected. Indeed, the noise from the crowd was getting quite loud again.

Earl Vawdrey stood up from his seat in the audience. "Pray forgive me, Sir Leofric," he said mildly, and everyone went immediately silent. "May I first commend you on your powers of recall and your honesty. You are part right at least. I made no mention of the words *daughter* or *Lenora* in my request, and I did in fact say the words *your charge*."

He let that suggestive phrase sink in as everyone started up their whispering once again. "And that is because," he said politely, "I was speaking of your ward, your niece the Lady Eden, all along. As for the flower remark, I'm afraid I did *not* know that was one of the Lady Lenora's sobriquets. She has so very many." He bowed low to Lenora, who gave him a dazzling smile.

Sir Leofric's eyes were almost bulging out of his head. "Why I—I—I…" He cast about wildly. "Well, that is what I took him to mean!" he protested feebly. "Never even occurred to me he could mean Eden!"

"It never occurred to you he could mean Eden?" repeated the Queen sharply. "I *see*…" She turned to the crowd and frowned as they all started clamoring. "Now that is very suggestive, is it not?"

It was not long after this that proceedings wound up for the day and a very subdued Eden was escorted back to the Queen's chambers with Jane Cecil. The Queen had gone to the King's apartments to take supper with him, so Eden assumed it would just be an awkward dinner with her and Jane.

She wished she could warm up to Jane, but for some reason, they were both very reserved with each other. To her surprise, they had no sooner shut the door behind them than a knock was heard upon it. The dogs went mad, and Eden was forced to drag them both by their collars into the next room as Jane answered it. Eden scolded Castor, who was the instigator, until his ears lay flat, then she released them and returned to the outer chamber with both of them close on her heels.

To Eden's astonishment it was her good friend the Lady Fenella, Countess Vawdrey, along with the Lady Linnet, Duchess of Cadwallader. They were also both her sisters-in-law. Neither had been present at the day's official proceedings.

"There you are!" Fenella beamed, coming toward her at once. Eden immediately ran to her friend, and they embraced. "My word, don't you look pretty!" Fen exclaimed. "Let me get a good look at you. What a pretty gown! How well that sea-green color suits you! You look just like a nereid!"

"I could say the same for you, you're positively glowing," Eden told her in a choked voice. She was touched Fenella had not dwelled on her pallor, or the dark rings under her eyes. Her friend by contrast looked extremely well. "Motherhood is clearly agreeing with you."

"Oh yes," said Fen with a proud smile. "We're all thriving, all four of us." Eden's smile was strained. She hardly knew what to make of Fen's husband, Oswald Vawdrey, these days. "And I have brought Linnet with me to welcome you to the family."

"It's been an age since I last saw you, Eden. How lovely to see you again!" said Linnet with her sweet smile.

Something was definitely different about Linnet, Eden thought distractedly as she kissed the freckled redhead on the cheek. Then she noticed the loose-fitting gown and fuller figure and realized Linnet must be expecting again. "And you too." She screwed up her eyes, trying to remember how many children Linnet and the Duke of Cadwallader already had.

"Oh this," laughed Linnet. "It's a pretty fabric to be sure but cut like an old sack. Still, it will expand with me, so it's good for comfort." She placed a hand on her bump.

"Congratulations," stammered Eden, unsure if she was supposed to offer them so soon. Perhaps that was why neither had been present? Fenella had only been delivered of her twin boys some two months ago, and Linnet was clearly in the family way.

"Thank you. Shall we sit?" The three of them moved toward the table where Jane was directing a servant to place the dishes. "This all looks excellent, what a treat," said Linnet with easy grace, and she and Fenella exchanged pleasantries with Jane, who soon seemed to relax and look less ill at ease for intruding on a family party.

329

Eden managed to make a better meal than the previous evening when everything had tasted of ashes and was secretly relieved when Jane rose as the last course was cleared away.

"If you ladies will pray excuse me, I will retire to the other room. My head aches sadly this evening and I would do all the better for a lie down with a damp cloth across my brow."

They all disclaimed at this tactful retreat, but Jane was firm and bowed out of the room only moments later.

"What a discreet young woman," said Linnet approvingly. "I predict she will go far at court."

"She already has done rather well," pointed out Eden, and then immediately felt contrite.

"Oh, you must not mind so much, Eden," said Fenella quickly. "Indeed, now you are a married woman, you will not have so much time to devote to the Queen's service."

Linnet murmured in agreement. "We are all devoted to the Queen, of course," she said painstakingly, "but there is no denying that she is rather demanding and best served by an unmarried lady, I would say."

Eden hesitated, not liking to bring up the fact she might very soon be restored to the status of single lady, depending on the outcome of the hearing. "I met your sister-in-law at Sitchmarsh," she said instead, turning to Fen with a rather forced brightness. "Lady Orla Bernard."

"Oh, how lovely!" exclaimed Fen excitedly. "Did you meet my brother, Gilbert, also? Or visit my old home at Sitchmarsh Hall?"

"No," explained Eden regretfully. "Orla kindly called on me, but I did not get the chance to return the visit, although she did most cordially invite me."

"Oh no, of course," tutted Fen sympathetically. "Such a pity and so tiresome for you! This silly misunderstanding!" She pressed Eden's hand. "Oswald is most put out on your behalf."

"It is not the most propitious start to your wedded days," agreed Linnet. "But after all, Mason and I suffered something not dissimilar, and our marriage made a full recovery from the experience."

An awkward silence drifted over them as they reflected on the fact Roland had also been involved in that appeal for an annulment, but that time as a petitioner.

"He was not there today," burst out Eden, unable to hold it in any longer. Her chest rose and fell. "Roland. He did not attend the hearing." Her words sounded devastated, but she was too shattered to be embarrassed about that right now.

Eden and Fenella exchanged glances. "My dear," said Fen kindly. "Did you not hear?"

"Hear what?" asked Eden hoarsely. But she already knew. He had gone home. Without her.

"Roland was summoned to the King today and stripped of his position as King's champion."

Eden dropped her napkin through nerveless fingers. "*What?* No! I—I heard no such thing!" She stood up and then sat back down again in agitation. "I can scarcely believe... I mean, why did no one tell me? I thought... That is, I quite imagined..." She gulped, stared at the tabletop a moment, and then, to her embarrassment, burst into tears.

"I daresay no one wanted to distress you unduly," said Linnet kindly as the storm abated. She passed her a handkerchief as Fenella patted her shoulder. "You are going through quite enough as it is, without anything else to worry about."

"Is he very upset?" Eden sniffed, looking up at Fen's and Linnet's concerned faces. "Have you seen him today?"

They both nodded. "He's not terribly upset," Linnet said quickly. "About the title, I mean. In truth, I do not think he cares two rushes for an honorary title."

"Once I heard him complain that all it did was distort the odds so that it was not worth wagering on him any longer," said Fen with a small laugh.

But Eden found she could not even muster the smallest of smiles at this. He hadn't left her. He had been stripped of his title. Because of her.

"Eden…"

Eden waved her hand awkwardly. "Speak of something else," she said hoarsely. "I beg of you."

"This seems like a funny thing to say," sighed Fen, "but being involved in an annulment case is something all three of us have in common. Indeed, I think it must truly be a Vawdrey thing."

Linnet gasped, lowering her goblet. "That is true!" she said with a stunned look at Fen. "I forgot that Oswald had your first marriage annulled."

Fen nodded sagely. "I was thinking it this morning, but I didn't like to say so to Oswald. He's so sensitive about the subject. You know how they can be." She pulled a face.

Linnet laughed. "Only too well." They both turned to Eden.

"Roland and I have not even been married yet a month," she reminded them when they seemed to be waiting for her agreement.

"Oh, but I am sure you have his measure by now," said Fen. "And I am so pleased, for it seems long overdue to me that Roland was settled."

"Er, yes," said Eden feebly. "I think we are—um—we *were* doing our best, although, it is rather an adjustment to make, don't you think? To being a married person?" she confided in a rush. "And yet, strangely, I thought at times that Roland seemed to make it almost without conscious effort!" She looked helplessly from Fenella to Linnet. "Whereas I—" She broke off, looking down at her hands.

"I think," said Linnet thoughtfully after a pause, "that Mason found it more difficult to adjust than I did. But he took to it beautifully once we were over the initial stages." She turned expectantly to Fenella.

"Oswald definitely took it all in his stride," said Fenella cheerfully. "Even though I had been married before, I was the one flailing around like a panicked hen."

Eden huffed out a breath, and Linnet surprised her by reaching across and patting her hand. "Perhaps," she suggested tentatively, "Roland took to married life easier because he was ready for it."

Eden sat back in her chair. "You mean because he had decided to offer for my cousin?" she asked flatly. It seemed pointless to keep up the subterfuge. She was sure both Fenella and Linnet must be fully in their husband's confidences.

"Oh but…" Fenella looked up quickly. "That's not right. It was you that Roland wanted. Right from the outset."

Eden shook her head with reluctance. "I expect Lord Vawdrey wanted to spare you the details, in case you would worry about it as my friend. You had not long been delivered of your twins at the time."

"Oh *no*," said Fenella vigorously. "You're quite wrong there. Oswald keeps me fully up to date when it comes to family matters. I was confined to my bed for the last few months of my pregnancy, and he came and joined me every evening for cozy chats. We liked it so much that we still do it now," said Fenella complacently. "He reads his paperwork in bed beside me." Eden tried and failed to imagine the immaculate and precise Lord Vawdrey retiring early to bed to sit beneath the covers with his wife, chatting over his day. She looked uncertainly at Fenella, but her friend was looking entirely sincere. "He told me from the very first, when Roland asked him to approach Sir Leofric for your hand, and then updated me every step along the way of negotiations."

Eden's jaw dropped. "Forgive me, Fenella, but that just isn't right. You must have misunderstood…"

"There was never any question that it was Lenora," Fenella insisted quietly. She looked to Linnet for support.

Linnet fiddled with the pear she was slicing with a small fruit knife. Looking up, she cleared her throat. "Well, Mason did seem to be under the impression that the intended bride was to be Lenora initially," she admitted awkwardly. "But after the business at Hallam Hall, he told me that Oswald seemed vastly pleased with the outcome, and he did say he wouldn't be surprised if it was the one he had intended from the very offset."

"Of course it was." Fenella frowned. "After all, Oswald saw Eden and Roland embrace at the Midwinter feast. He knew they were destined to be together. And, so did you, Linnet." She prompted her sister-in-law when she looked blank. "Remember? What Baron Vawdrey said to you on his death bed?"

Linnet's confusion fell away. "Oh that," she said enthusiastically. "Yes, Father was very insistent that Roland was to marry a girl of sense and not some feather-brain."

"You see," said Fenella, turning to her triumphantly.

Eden bristled. "Lenora is not a feather-brain."

Fenella and Linnet exchanged glances.

"She's not!" insisted Eden. "People just don't understand her, that is all."

"Well, in any event," said Fen glibly, "you were the one that Oswald intended for Roland all along. I know that much."

There did not seem to be much point dwelling on the whys and wherefores of it all. Eden felt tired after the day she'd had. Instead, she sat back and listened as her two sisters-in-law gleefully shared with her tales of the early days of their own marriages.

"Mason told me that I should mix with our neighboring families," said Linnet with a droll look. "As apparently, he did not have time to sit with a wife of an evening. Then when I went ahead and made plans to visit the Jauncey family, he suddenly forbade me from setting foot on their estate!"

Eden frowned. "Did he explain why he changed his mind?"

"Never," snorted Linnet. "In fact, he told me I could see who I pleased as it made no odds to him. Then slammed a lot of doors, gave me an armed guard, and told me he shouldn't have to come looking for me when he returned home of an evening."

Eden stared at her friends as they both dissolved into laughter. She couldn't see what was funny about a male acting so unreasonably.

"Oswald told me as his wife, I could return to Sitchmarsh and pick back up with my day-to-day life in the country with very little material change," said Fenella with a breathless laugh. "Then, a few days later, he turned around and said he'd changed his mind, expected me to become a courtier, and declared, quite coolly, that he expected me to ingratiate myself with the Queen and become one of her ladies-in-waiting!"

Eden blinked. "He changed his mind?" she repeated incredulously.

Fen nodded. "That's husbands for you!" She shrugged, her eyes alight with mirth.

Linnet wiped her eyes. "They're so funny sometimes!"

Eden watched them both and wondered if she was mad, or they were. Compared to how his older brothers had behaved, Roland seemed almost reasonable as a husband. She shifted in her seat as Linnet and Fenella exchanged more fond stories of their spouses acting inconsistently. Was this really just a part and parcel of married life?

She bit her thumbnail now, and wished she had been more conciliatory with him, and not told him she did not want his kisses! Why had she done that? Fenella was telling the tale of how Oswald had gone ahead and had her previous marriage declared null and void simply because he did not like the idea of her being another man's wife.

Linnet followed this up with some story about Mason unblushingly upping the number of children she had promised him whenever it suited him. Eden sank further and further down into her seat. Roland's brothers sounded like nightmare husbands in comparison to him!

35

Roland woke to a heavy weight across his legs and the sound of off-key whistling in his close vicinity. He poked his head out of his blanket and glared blurrily at Cuthbert, who was clattering around with water and clean cloths. Then he looked down to find Castor lay across his legs, his massive head resting on his front paws. Castor cracked one eye open to look at his master and then shut it again. "What are you doing here?" Roland asked, reaching down to rub the dog's ears. Castor yawned.

"The Queen sent for me to fetch him to you," said Cuthbert, breaking off his tune.

"What?"

"He wasn't playing nice with her other lady-in-waiting."

Roland sat up. "Explain."

"Lady Eden is sharing a room presently with Lady Jane Cecil." Roland pulled a face. He thought it a bit rich that someone else got to sleep in the same damn bedchamber as his wife. "Castor objected most strongly to the sleeping arrangements."

"Is that so?" Roland asked, absently patting the dog.

"The Queen said Parnell could stay, but this one had to be returned to his master."

Roland grunted. "Did you see your mistress?" Cuthbert nodded. "And?" he prodded with annoyance.

"And what?" asked Cuthbert. "She was scolding Castor up a storm. Then soon as I went to take him, she was hanging round his neck, crying her eyes out." He shrugged. "She was likely tired," he added fairly.

Roland eyed the large white dog who did look a bit sheepish, now he thought about it. "Ah well, not really your fault, my boy." Castor thumped his tail against the bed.

"How do you make that out?" spluttered Cuthbert. "He had that Lady Jane pinned against a chest of drawers, screaming fit to raise the dead by all accounts. The guards rushed in thinking there was an attempt being made on the Queen's life!"

Roland shrugged, supremely unconcerned. "I don't agree with the sleeping arrangements either," he said, climbing out of bed.

To his surprise, Roland found two occupants already in the adjoining room. His brothers were seated at the table. "Cuthbert never said you were here," he commented, pulling out a chair. Castor darted forward, straight under the table.

"Good morning to you too," said his brother Oswald dryly. "Was that Castor?"

Roland ignored the question, for he could see the dog was already sniffing in welcome at Oswald's boots.

"Of course we're here," thundered Mason. "By all accounts I'm likely to be called for a witness. Yes, Castor, it's me," he said, holding out his hand for the dog to sniff. "I still haven't heard how events turned out yesterday," he said, turning to Roland.

"No good asking me," said Roland. "I wasn't there either." He turned in his seat. "Where's Cuthbert with the food—?" he started, but the door opened and in hobbled Meldon, the old family retainer who now lived with Oswald. He was bearing a large salver.

"Meldon! How are you, you old rogue!"

"Meldon gets a warmer welcome than his own brothers, mark you," complained Oswald.

"Better'n what I hear you are, Master Roland," grumbled Meldon censoriously. "What's this about you getting your wife confiscated?" He clattered down the dish of salted fish and bread.

"Don't remind me," said Roland darkly.

"Just a temporary measure," said Oswald airily as he reached for the butter. "And we'll soon have it sorted out."

Meldon sniffed and pulled out a cloth to polish up the knives. Castor poked his head out from under the table. "You never brought the dogs from the Keep here with you?" asked the old servant in startled tones.

"Only the two of them," said Roland, buttering a piece of bread.

"Well, I only hopes they're better behaved than when the old baron had 'em!" Meldon tutted.

Roland cocked an eyebrow. "Doubtful. Castor's already been expelled from the Queen's chambers."

Meldon cast his eyes heavenward as Mason demanded details. Once the story was told, and chuckled over, with much fuss made of Castor, Mason turned to his younger brother. "I hear you've had something else confiscated," he said bluntly.

Roland frowned. "What's that?"

"Attley told me you're no longer the King's champion."

"Attley? When did you see him?" asked Roland, brightening. "Is he at court?"

"He and Ned Bevan arrived this morning. I daresay to offer their support."

"They will be called as witnesses," Oswald corrected Mason.

"Attley and Bev?" echoed Roland. "What the devil do they know about anything?"

"They competed at Tranton Vale, did they not? Where you spent the days immediately following your wedding."

Roland snorted. "Aye, and what of it? Do you mean to tell me—?" He broke off distractedly. "I can't believe you've allowed all this to happen!" He glared at his brother.

Oswald spread his hands wide. "I? What makes you think I was instrumental in any of this?"

Roland glared at him. "Everything's down to you in this bloody palace, and everyone knows it!"

"You flatter me," said Oswald, dabbing a napkin at his mouth. "But if I could have delayed this exercise I would have. You have not been wed long enough for us to be assured of its outcome. After all, it's been little more than three weeks."

Roland sat up straight in his chair. "Our marriage is valid," he said loudly. "And if I was allowed to speak, I would tell them so!"

"You will be permitted to speak on the third day, and not before that," Oswald told him. "Have you heard that the King is sitting over today's events?"

"The King?" Roland looked startled, and not pleasantly so.

"Is that a bad thing?" asked Mason, who had been watching Roland with interest.

"He was in a rare temper with me yesterday," muttered Roland.

"Yes," sighed Oswald. "He did not want to dismiss you as his champion. It always puts Wymer out of sorts when he is forced to do something he does not want to."

341

"He acted like he wanted to clap me in the stocks!"

"I daresay he did," said Oswald. "The Queen has been plaguing the life out of him. She was most put out to lose Eden. Most put out indeed."

"Aye, well," said Roland belligerently. "She'll have to reconcile herself to it. And so will he!" He looked up and caught Mason's smirk. "What?"

Mason shook his head and crossed his massive arms. "Naught," he said with a short laugh.

"The Queen's most annoyed to be missing out on today," warned Oswald. "So, no doubt she will have put a flea in the King's ear this morning already. Tread carefully."

"Queen Armenal won't be there?" asked Mason.

"*No* ladies will be there," emphasized Oswald. "Not even Eden."

"Why not?" spluttered Roland, who had expected to have a glimpse of his wife at the very least.

"It was decided it would be too indelicate for ladies' ears," said Oswald. "Today will be delving into the wedding ceremony and the aftermath." Roland groaned. "Precisely," said Oswald.

36

"Get on with it, man!" barked King Wymer, glaring through beetling brows at Sir Christopher Montmayne. "Spit it out if ye've something to say!"

Eden's least favorite uncle bridled but could hardly protest when answering his sovereign. "I proceeded with the others to the best guest bedchamber," he said stiffly. "The door was locked, but with the help of the steward and Sir Roland's two brothers it was forced." He paused, screwing his face up.

"What I saw there shocked me, shocked me to the very core. A scene of licentiousness which I had never dreamed of seeing in the hallowed halls of Hallam." The King snorted, and Sir Christopher looked affronted at the amused ripple that ran through the audience. No doubt, if the audience had contained ladies, he would have had the scandalized reaction he had anticipated.

Among the lords, knights, and barons however, his words were not having the effect he desired. "My niece, Eden Montmayne, was lolling abed with Sir Roland, and both as naked as babes!" His jowls shook with horror. "'Twas plain what had transpired the night before, and what grievous step their illicit passion had led them to take," he intoned piously.

"I see," said the King, his eyebrows shooting into his fair hair. "And—er—Sir Roland offered no excuse or denial of the scene you witnessed?"

"Not he!" burst out Sir Christopher indignantly. "Indeed, in spite of his night of sin, he still evinced a shamefully amorous and lusty state for her!" A gust of laughter went up from the crowd, and Roland shifted in his seat. "I scarcely knew where to look, Your Majesty! Never had I—"

"Yes, yes, I'm sure," said King Wymer brusquely. "And then?"

Sir Christopher drew himself up, pursing his lips. "My brother Leofric and Lord Vawdrey had some words about how to restore my niece's honor." He cast a nervous look in Mason's direction. "I—er—attempted to remonstrate with my niece upon the gravity of the situation but was prevented by Sir Roland's kinsman."

"Which one?" asked the King with a flicker of interest.

Sir Christopher fiddled with the links of his belt nervously. "The Duke of Cadwallader," he admitted. Heads swiveled in Mason's direction. His brother looked entirely unperturbed, Roland noticed.

"And then?" prompted the King impatiently.

"Sir Roland climbed out of the bed and shoved me from the room, shutting the door in my face," Christopher finished in an injured tone.

"And where was the Lady Eden at this point?" enquired the King.

"She was still abed, Your Highness."

Wymer sat up in his throne, a frown on his face. "Do you mean to say the pair of them were left to their own devices again, sequestered in the guest bedchamber?" he asked incredulously. "Not the smallest effort having been made to separate them or take your niece back?"

"I—er—well," Sir Christopher stammered lamely. "Yes, Your Highness."

"Both of 'em," said the King sarcastically. "Still 'naked as babes'?"

"Er—yes," admitted the unhappy Sir Christopher. "Naked as the day they were born."

"Extraordinary! Oh, sit down, man!" he said impatiently, and scanned the crowd until his eyes fell on Mason Vawdrey. "Cadwallader," he said grandly. "Best have your account next, I fancy!"

Mason made a stoic and unshakeable witness. He corroborated the facts without any embellishment, and his fierce stare made sure his statement was not punctuated with any crowd reaction. They did not dare.

The King digested his account broodingly before steepling his hands at his square jaw. "What I don't understand," he said slowly, "is this. The host's niece was found in Sir Roland's bedchamber." Roland felt himself tensing. Oswald laid a hand on his arm, giving a tiny shake of his head. "It seems to me that the Montmaynes were glad to rush through a quick wedding to set things to rights." Mason gave a short nod of agreement. "The lady was heretofore of impeccable character and reputation," conceded the King. "But why did the Vawdrey party not balk in any way at the way things turned out?"

"Why should we?" rumbled Mason in his deep voice. "When it was evident this was the very outcome my brother desired." There was a crowd reaction to that. Mason did not acknowledge it, but the King's hand shot up to quiet the murmured voices.

"What makes you so sure of that?" asked the King sharply.

"I heard him say it with my own ears," said Mason firmly. "At the feast the night before. He said they were presenting him with 'the wrong one' and he would not take her to wife. When I

345

asked him what possible objection he could make to the lady, he answered she was not the one he wanted. He said, 'She is not Eden.'"

At that, the muted voices rose in a great swell. Roland felt himself flush. Had he really said that? Mason's bold gaze told him that every word was true. He felt strangely elated. Perhaps he wasn't such a stupid bastard after all, when he let his baser-self rule on instinct alone? He had been consumed with Eden Montmayne, and what's more, he had been celibate in the six months since she had kissed him and made him hers. It had been his thinking-self that had thought to put an end to his struggle by marrying the prettiest girl at court, like he had always intended. His thinking-self was a fucking idiot. He had no patience with him. His blood ran cold at the idea he could have wed anyone else. But then he remembered that he had stated quite clearly at the feast that he would take none to wife, save Eden. That reassured him, and he could breathe easy again. He wished Eden could have heard that. Though not any of what her idiot uncle had come out with. One day that bastard would pay for talking about Eden being naked in a roomful of men.

His brother nudged him again. "Did you hear who has been called?" he murmured in an amused voice.

"No." Roland looked up quickly and saw Cuthbert sauntering unhurriedly down the middle of the room as if he had not a care in the world. "You jest."

But he did not.

"I see," said the King, nodding his head sometime later, a smile tugging at his lips in spite of himself. "And what—uh—what made you suspect that your master was—ah—employing artifice on the journey?"

346

The King was not the only one enjoying Cuthbert's testimony. The crowd was, immensely. Roland felt his face grow warm.

"Her horse was fine, Your Majesty," snorted Cuthbert, "and showed no symptom of lameness." He cast a knowing look at the audience, who laughed into their sleeves. "He just wanted her on his horse, up before him." He nodded sagely. "It was obvious, even to someone of my tender years."

Roland winced, closing his eyes briefly. When would this come to an end? He cast a resentful look at Oswald, but his brother was smothering another yawn. If anything, Mason was more sympathetic to his plight, he thought crossly. But maybe that was because that poor bastard had been through someone trying to annul his marriage. *Him.* He supposed, uneasily, that one of these days he ought to try to make that up to Mason. The thought had never really occurred to him before.

He listened with excruciating embarrassment as Cuthbert detailed how Roland had kept Eden locked in an inn bedroom with him for a night, a day, and another night before he would consent to continue their journey to Tranton Vale. By all accounts, he reflected, he was coming across as an extremely lecherous husband when, truth be told, they had not even consummated their marriage by this point! He squirmed inwardly as Cuthbert repeated a couple of the landlady's choice remarks which had their audience rolling in the aisles.

"I'm going to kill him," he murmured out of the corner of his mouth.

"You'll not touch a hair on his head," Mason told him firmly. "Strictly speaking, he's still part of my household, and only with you on loan."

"Well, you can have him back directly!" Roland grumbled. "The little wretch!"

347

After Cuthbert, Roland's friend Sir James Attley bore witness to how Roland had brought Eden along to their pavilion at Tranton Vale and bade them to raise a toast to his marriage.

"And how was his manner?" barked the King.

"His manner, sire?" asked a startled Attley, who clearly had hoped to get away with talking facts rather than opinions.

"His manner. One of your oldest friends, isn't he? Surely you can gauge his mood. Was he resentful, surly—how did he seem to you?"

Attley looked dismayed. "He—er—he seemed—er…" He stared down at his feet a moment and took a deep breath. "Jubilant, sire," he said at last. "Elated, proud. He was showing her off like he'd won some great prize." Attley scratched his neck. "He—er—sat her on his lap, and not just in the pavilion with us, but at the banquet too," he said, looking embarrassed. "And—um—called her *sweetheart*." Attley turned a dull red when people started up whispering again. "At the banquet he fed her from his plate, and they shared a loving cup."

"Hmmmm." The King narrowed his eyes at him. "Did he make no mention of the circumstances of taking her to wife?"

"He just said he'd changed his mind, sire," said Attley simply.

Sir Ned Bevan backed up his friend on these details when it was his turn, and additionally, he told of how they had walked in on Roland kissing his new bride on his bunk on the following afternoon. He was a lot less flustered than his friend and told the tale in a straightforward manner that went over well with the audience.

"In your opinion, did your friend seem resentful at being trapped into a hasty marriage?" asked the King.

"No, Your Majesty, he did not," said Bev decidedly. "He looked like he could scarcely bear to let the lady out of his sight." He hesitated, and the King picked up on it immediately.

"Yes, Sir Edward, you have something to corroborate this claim?"

"I do," said Bev, raising his chin. "The next day, the victor of the joust, Lord Kentigern, awarded the tourney garland to Lady Eden. When he heard of it, Roly—your pardon—Sir Roland flew into a jealous rage, the like of which I have never seen him display before."

"Indeed?"

"He was quite white about the mouth. Almost immediately, he determined to drag her off to Vawdrey Keep like a possessive husband."

Roland kept his eyes straight ahead as he felt both his brothers turn to look at him with interest.

"Humph," said the King. "Where he's kept her closely guarded ever since," he said irritably. "Shall we adjourn for some refreshment?" The guards at the far end opened the door and a buzz of conversation rose up toward the rafters. "Can't think what Armenal expects me to do about all this," Roland heard the King say plaintively to one of his advisers. "It'll be a miracle if she isn't with child already from what I've heard!"

37

Eden spent a very strange second day at the palace. Not long after breaking her fast, she received a missive from her grandmother, Lady Dorothea, formally requesting a farewell meeting. Queen Armenal, when apprised of it, encouraged her to receive her grandmother in the Queen's own sitting room.

"But yes, of course, Eden. You must see your grandmother before she leaves. Send your reply with my page. Jane can sit in the antechamber with a book or some needlework to give you some privacy. As for myself, I am going hawking presently." She refused to take no for an answer.

A half hour later, Lady Dorothea was ushered in. She was dressed as if for travel in a somber gown of charcoal gray. After seeing her seated before the fire, Jane tactfully withdrew with her book.

"You're going back to Hallam Hall then?" Eden asked nervously. Her grandmother did not answer, and Eden sat in the chair opposite her. "I wrote you a letter," Eden added after a moment's heavy silence. "Actually, I wrote you three."

Her grandmother sat very still. When she spoke, her voice was harsh. "I understand you have been fraternizing with the Vawdrey family, despite your own flesh and blood being kept at bay." She shot an accusatory look at Eden.

"I have not seen my husband since I arrived here at court," Eden answered. "Though it is true, I did see my sisters-in-law yester'een."

"Yet you did not see fit to send for your own cousin?" Lady Dorothea did not wait for Eden's answer. "Is it too much to hope you have not been taken in by your *new* friends?"

"Fenella has been my very good friend now for many months," Eden answered quietly.

"Well, far be it from me to offer any advice to my own granddaughter!" huffed Lady Dorothea. She glared at Eden. "I want to know what happened," she said distinctly. "And I don't want any of this *rubbish* Lenora has seen fit to spout at me. I thought, from you at least, I would get plain dealing." She broke off her words with a gesture of impatience. "Out with it, child! Come, did someone put you up to it?"

Eden stared. "No." *Such as who?* she wondered.

"You thought you'd set yourself up as some sacrificial lamb then, is that it? To spare your cousin?"

Eden gave a shocked splutter. "Of course not!" Her cheeks turned red. "My sense of duty never extended that far!"

Her grandmother narrowed her eyes at her. "Then I cannot understand you."

"I would have to have been a complete fool to even think of such an idiotic scheme," Eden pointed out.

"You'd rather I thought you out to snare a husband for yourself, would you?" Lady Dorothea's eyebrows rose. "Was it Leo's plan? I want to know. How on earth did *you* of all people end up in bed with the King's champion?" snapped Lady Dorothea.

Eden fell back breathless in her chair. "Stop it, Grandmother!"

"It's no use playing coy if that's the story you're sticking to, my girl!"

Eden noticed the haggardness about her grandmother's features and the tension in her tall, thin body. She had not been to court in twenty years, and yet she had dragged herself here to try to demand justice for her granddaughter who she had believed had

351

been wronged. Even if it meant dragging her family name through the mud. "He—I mean, Roland—has been very…*good* about it," she said, avoiding Lady Dorothea's pale blue eyes.

Her grandmother's thin hands twitched in her lap. "If you've nothing else to say on the subject, then I will take my leave of you," she said coldly.

Eden's eyes darted to her face, which was an outraged mask. The older woman swept suddenly to her feet. "Wait!" she said, throwing up a hand. "If I tell you…" She gulped. "You will not… You must not…"

"If you cannot find it in your heart to trust me, your own kinswoman," said her grandmother vehemently, "then…"

"I walked into it," said Eden. "You remember my old affliction, when troubled? How I…used to walk. In my sleep." She covered her face a moment with her hand. Eden heard a rustle and peeped through her fingers. Lady Dorothea had dropped back into her seat, her face white as chalk.

"No," she whispered. "Eden, you could not have!"

"I'm afraid I must have," she replied tonelessly. "I've been over it in my head time and again. There can be no other explanation." She swallowed. "He—he was uppermost in my thoughts at the time. We had discussed him that very afternoon, as you remembered. How we hoped Lenora would come to her senses and not go through with it." She broke off a moment.

"Of course, Uncle Leo always put his most honored guest in the yellow bedchamber, I would have known that instinctively. He was very drunk that night, and would not have woken when I let myself in." Her grandmother's face, when she steeled herself to look at it, was horrified. "I could not think straight the next morning. We were discovered, it was all such a living

352

nightmare. I felt so unwell and unlike myself. I was confused, I had no defense or idea at that point what had even happened. When I realized later, well… You can imagine how I felt. Guilty, utterly wretched to find I was, in fact, the author of my own undoing."

Lady Dorothea rose to her feet and walked to the fire a moment, where she stood staring down at it. "I hardly know what to say, Eden," she said awkwardly. "I had no idea you still did this childish thing."

"I've only recently restarted," said Eden tonelessly.

"You have done it again since?"

"At least twice," she admitted. "And probably would have done so more than that if it were not for—" She broke off, not wanting to admit that Roland would throw a leg or arm across her to still her unquiet slumbers.

"What an unhappy start to wedded life," said Lady Dorothea. She returned to her chair. She sighed heavily. "You say he has been kind to you?" she said after a moment's pause. "Is it too much for me to hope that is the truth? He must have been exceedingly angry when you confessed, my girl, and nothing you can say will convince me otherwise."

Eden hesitated. "I—I have not confessed," she said, raising her chin.

"I beg your pardon?"

"I have not confessed," she reiterated, clasping her hands together in her lap. "I tried to have a frank discussion with him on the subject, but somehow…it did not go to plan. We ended up quarrelling. I got extremely emotional. It's hard to explain."

Lady Dorothea tipped her head to one side. "Quarrelling," she repeated.

"Oh yes. We quarrel and bicker, and then afterward, well…" She broke off again feebly. "He does not seem to really bear grudges. It's almost seems as if it clears the air."

Lady Dorothea cupped her chin in one hand and regarded Eden thoughtfully. "Your grandfather and I had some lively spats in the early days of our marriage," she said vaguely.

"Really?" Eden was startled by this information.

"I hope you don't think I'm intruding, Eden," her grandmother said. "But what exactly does Sir Roland imagine motivated you to climb into his bed?"

Eden sighed. "He thinks I decided to entrap him into marriage," she said simply. "But for some reason, that did not give him a disgust of me like you'd think. He seems to…rather like the idea that I wanted him that much." She felt her cheeks turn quite pink at her grandmother's regard. "He's ridiculous sometimes, and I've given up trying to understand him."

Her grandmother gave a short, startled laugh. "Have I been worrying over nothing?" she asked shrewdly.

Eden looked away. "Possibly. Do you think I ought to discuss the sleepwalking thing with him?" she asked.

"What do you think?" Her grandmother sounded curious.

"I think it would make him feel sorry for me," said Eden abruptly. "And I do not want that."

"I see."

"Do you?" Somehow Eden doubted it. "The thing Roland admires most in all the world is bravery," she said suddenly. "I suppose I would like him to think me brave, rather than an object of pity."

Her grandmother did not speak for several moments, and when she did, Eden was taken aback.

"I'm going home," Lady Dorothea said. "To Hallam Hall. In a month or so, when you have set everything in order here, you and your husband can invite me to stay with you, and I will accept. Then I will get to see these quarrels for myself."

"Very well, Grandmother."

"Come and kiss my cheek and wish me a good journey." Eden complied. "It seems your in-laws mean to draw a veil over the whole unfortunate business of the betrothal feast," she said with a sigh. "On reflection, I can see that would be the best thing for all involved." She tapped Eden lightly on the cheek. "Do not go running away with the idea that Roland Vawdrey is so very philanthropical or chivalrous in his consideration toward you."

Eden hesitated. "How do you mean, Grandmother?"

"It stands to reason. If he was not angry to find you in his bed," she said dryly, "it was because he wanted you there in the first place."

38

Eden saw her grandmother out and then returned to the sitting room. A packet of letters awaited her attention, and she untied the ribbon that tied them together without much enthusiasm. The first was from a Mr. Childers who was one of the artists she supported.

He was a very gentle and earnest man of middle years who had been employed writing the same ballad for as long as she'd known him. This time he had sent her three verses he had extensively rewritten and had plunged into these without much by way of greeting. Luckily, she recognized his sloping handwriting before she got to the illegible signature.

She set this aside and turned to an irate letter she had to read through twice before she could make head nor tail of it. It seemed that the poet the Dowager Duchess of Rand had agreed to sponsor was very upset at the treatment he had received from her. Other than that, and an obscure charge of "wanton theft of intellectual property," Eden was not sure what else could be drawn from it.

The letter was signed R. Lewen. She cudgeled her brain but could not bring R. Lewen to mind. Casting that aside, she came next to a very agreeable letter from Gunnilde Payne and lost herself catching up with what her new friend had been up to. Gunnilde's narrative held a wistful tone, and Eden thought things must have seemed a little flat at her father's house after the tournament was done and dusted.

To Eden's surprise she only mentioned Arthur Conway once in passing, and Eden guessed that the friendship between their two families had not had any great resurgence since. Eden lowered the letter and thought a moment. In her estimation, her friend deserved considerably better. She wondered what she could do for her when the Paynes came to stay at court as planned. Could she introduce her, for instance, to one of Roland's well-connected friends?

Before she had pondered too long on the eligibility of his acquaintance, she reminded herself of the uncertainty of her own wedded status. By the time the Paynes arrived at court, there was a very real chance she herself could be unmarried and in disgrace. A sharp knock at the outer door roused her from her glum thoughts, and she heard Jane Cecil conversing with one of the guards out in the corridor.

Suddenly the door to the sitting room opened, there was a whirl of turquoise silk and blond ringlets, and it shut again. Her cousin, Lenora, was stood with her back against the door, a determined look on her face.

"Should we take a walk, do you think?" Lenora suggested brightly. "We could take your oversized hound," she said, looking at Parnell.

Eden blinked at her. "That might be a good notion," she agreed cautiously, and glanced at Parnell, who was still lying at her feet.

"Has Grandmother told you she is leaving for Hallam Hall?"

"Yes, she told me. Will we need cloaks, do you think?" Eden asked, glancing at the window.

"No, 'tis a fine afternoon."

"Then I will just go and speak with Jane…"

"Oh, but we can chaperone each other, surely?" said Lenora hastily.

Were they to have some frank speech between them? wondered Eden. She hoped so, however painful it might prove. Jane Cecil voiced no objection to the cousins taking a turn in the gardens, and they slipped out by a side door into the Queen's rose garden.

"Does he not need a halter or some reins?" asked Lenora, eyeing Parnell doubtfully as he bounded joyfully across the neat walkways.

"He's not a horse," Eden pointed out mildly.

"He's practically the size of one."

"He is rather large," Eden agreed. Parnell sniffed and rooted in the tidy hedges as Lenora hooked her arm through Eden's and they walked slowly along the path.

"Why did you never reply to my letter?" asked Lenora suddenly. "You were no doubt very cross with me, and you had every right to be," she continued in a rush of words. "Only…I did hope for some word from you."

She turned her head and fixed her eyes on Eden in unspoken appeal. "Indeed, I acted in what I believed and *still* believe to be for the best." Eden blinked. *What?* "In truth I don't blame you for not responding to my letter. It must have been a terrible shock to you and—"

"What letter?" Eden asked.

Now it was Lenora's turn to stare. "The letter I asked Lord Vawdrey to give to you, after you had departed Hallam Hall on your wedding morn."

"But…Lenora." Eden frowned. "I received no letter from you."

"What? No letter?" Her cousin looked stunned. Then another thought struck her, and she seemed more assured. "Of course, your memory of that day will be quite sadly fragmented."

Eden nodded. "That is true. I was feeling most unwell," she agreed before frowning again. "But how do you know that?"

"'Tis a common aftereffect," said Lenora with a wave of her hand. "But Lord Vawdrey assured me there would be no long-term repercussions."

"I'm afraid I don't quite understand—" Eden began with a terrible feeling of foreboding. "Aftereffect of what?"

"The drug," said Lenora impatiently.

"What drug?"

"The drug I slipped in my wine, you remember? I asked you to drink it for me, as I did not care for it."

Eden came to a halt. "Lenora, what are you telling me?"

"Had you not already deduced that you and Sir Roland were drugged?" asked Lenora, her eyes opening very wide. "I felt sure that even without my letter you would have worked it out. After all, how else did you imagine it happened?"

Eden stared at her. "Drugged? Are you—? But—?"

"Both of you were drugged," said Lenora simply.

Oh, my gods. "But *why*?"

"Oh dear," said Lenora. "My letter explained it so much better for me. Let us go and fetch it for you." A certain fire entered her eye. "I mean to ask Lord Vawdrey exactly what he meant by not letting you have it!" She grabbed Eden's arm and started towing her along the path.

"Now?" squeaked Eden.

"He must still have it," Lenora tossed back over her shoulder. "I want you to read it."

Eden looked about for Parnell, who had been distracted by a passing butterfly and was foolishly gamboling in the shrubbery. His massive head swiveled toward her, and he galloped after them.

"I can scarcely credit it," Lenora was muttering under breath. "I am most put out!" And indeed, she looked it. Of course, on Lenora, anger showed as a deeper rose in her cheeks and an extra brilliant shine to her eyes like blue topazes.

"But couldn't you just tell me what the letter said?" Eden asked breathlessly as they rounded the path that skirted the long gallery. The guard there fell back, and they passed through the door unhindered.

"You don't understand how long I agonized over writing that note," said Lenora. "You know how poorly I express myself in general."

They were striding along the corridor now toward the officials' corridor. Eden supposed Lord Vawdrey must have a large study here. She looked about with interest.

"Excuse me?" Lenora hailed a nervous-looking clerk. "We are looking for the office of Lord Oswald Vawdrey, chief adviser to the King."

He directed them to the very end of the corridor, and when they reached that room, Lenora rapped loudly on the door. It was answered by a rather chubby young man with pale eyes and thinning hair, who introduced himself as Lord Vawdrey's private secretary, Bryce. Eden recognized having seen him often in Lord Vawdrey's wake.

His discreet gaze passed over her, and he admitted them both to the antechamber, directing them to be seated. He stared a moment at Parnell, as though unsure of his own eyes, then clearly decided to ignore him.

"His lordship is currently in an audience room with the King," he said, tactfully diverting his eyes from Eden.

"Yes, we know it is day two of the hearing," said Lenora graciously. "But from our experience yesterday, we know there are breaks for refreshment and such." She waved a hand. "Could you please have a message taken along to him that Lady Lenora Montmayne wishes to have a word with him about a most pressing matter? And that his sister-in-law Lady Eden Vawdrey awaits him."

Bryce gave a small cough, and then sat at his desk. He thought a moment and then wrote a couple of lines on a small rectangle of paper. Then he rang a bell. A page darted in from another small room. They had a whispered conversation and then the page made off with the paper.

"Can I offer you ladies anything while you wait?" he asked politely. Eden was impressed that he did not stammer or stare in Lenora's presence. In truth, he wore a rather monkish air, so perhaps that was not to be wondered at. His office was scrupulously tidy, and when they assured him they were not in need of anything, he returned serenely to his work.

It was some quarter of an hour later that Oswald Vawdrey showed up at his offices, tall and dark and clad head to toe in unrelenting black. He paused on the threshold, bowed briefly at both ladies, had a quiet word with Bryce, and then ushered them into his rather grand inner sanctum.

His office was huge with a painted ceiling of the celestial heavens. Parnell padded around it, sniffing at furniture, until he found a spot under a table that he took a fancy to and curled up in it. In happier times, Eden would have been glad of the opportunity to peruse the extensive bookshelves and the large maps, but not today.

"You will, I hope, excuse my brevity," he apologized urbanely. "But the King has only granted me a brief respite." He gestured them toward chairs and seated himself behind his desk. "Did Bryce offer you some refreshment—?" he began, but Lenora cut him off.

"Why did you not give my cousin the letter I gave into your keeping for her?" she demanded.

Eden watched Oswald Vawdrey's expression grow instantly guarded. "My dear young ladies…" he started lightly.

"You specifically promised you would deliver it to her!" Lenora persisted, slapping one dainty hand down on his polished desktop.

Only by the faintest quirk of his very black eyebrows did Oswald Vawdrey betray any surprise at Lenora's uncharacteristically animated behavior. There really was a very strong family likeness between the three brothers, thought Eden distractedly. Though Oswald was a lot less brawny than his two younger brothers, he had the same dark good looks and height.

Of course, to her mind, Roland was the better looking. Mason's features were too harsh, and Oswald's too smooth, whereas Roland's were just right. "Your letter?" he mused after an infinitesimal pause. "Ah yes, I seem to recall now. You *did* hand me a letter." He looked regretful. "Alas, that morning at Hallam Hall was so chaotic, I fear…"

"You forgot!" choked out Lenora. "How *could* you?"

Eden reached across to touch her cousin's sleeve. "Lenora," she said soothingly. "Calm yourself. This is not like you…"

"Calm myself?" Lenora wheeled around on her. "How can I be calm, Eden? Knowing what you must have thought? Knowing how you must have felt… My gods!"

Eden passed an arm around Lenora's shoulders, and shot a look of bafflement at Oswald Vawdrey.

Lenora turned impulsively to her. "You thought I would blame you, did you not? You thought I would be upset?"

"Naturally, I was worried—"

"But that was so unnecessary!" burst out Lenora. "And it truly makes me angry to think of us being out of accord!" She turned back angrily to Oswald. "And all because of you!" she said accusingly.

He held up his hands appealingly. "If there has been any discord between the two of you, allow me to bear the blame—" he began.

"Discord?" echoed Lenora in disgust. "She is like a *sister* to me! Do you not understand? There is no one whose opinion matters to me more!"

Oswald seemed to consider this a moment. He reached for a silver chain around his neck, extracted a key, and then unlocked a small drawer in his desk. From this he withdrew a folded paper which he offered across the desk to Eden. She took it from him and unfolded it.

My dearest, Lenora had written.

Do not be out of reason cross with me. In truth, if I have offended, it is the fault of listening to your strictures rather too well. I am acting for once without self-interest. Indeed, it is

363

your interests which I have put first. I love you, Eden, and want what is best for you. Too long you have played the poor relation at Hallam Hall. I want you to have nice things, steadfast social standing, and to be mistress of your own home. Father would not have matched me to Sir Roland Vawdrey if he could not provide all this and more for a wife.

If it has not occurred to you already, then I must confess that I alone am the author of your disgrace. Please believe, it was not a decision that I took lightly. I know how much you value your reputation and virtue. Pray do not smart regarding your fall from grace. You will scarcely credit it, but in my experience, people do not warm overmuch to paragons of virtue.

In mitigation of my behavior, please believe my motives were not just in your interest. Sir Roland is sick for love of you. I am not the only one to have noticed it, so it is not merely a figment of my imagination as you thought. If you could only see the way his eyes follow you, the way you are his sole focus when you are in the room, then you would believe it too.

He is yours, and now I have delivered him. The rest is up to you.

Your ever-loving Lenora

Eden read the letter through twice, her mind reeling. She lowered the letter with trembling hands into her lap and stared unseeingly at the large window at the other end of the study.

"Please try to understand, Eden," begged Lenora with tears in her eyes. "I meant to act for the best. You were both being so sadly stubborn. I knew I had to do something rather drastic."

"Drastic!" echoed Eden in a croaky voice. "My gods!"

"Yes," Lenora concurred. "Nobody would ever believe I had it in me."

"But how did Lord Vawdrey factor into this?" Eden asked, glancing over at Oswald, who was watching them both with interest.

"Pardon?" Lenora looked momentarily disconcerted. "Oh, I simply asked him to pass along the letter—"

"No," cut in Eden. "No, that won't do, Lenora, I'm afraid."

"You think me lacking the ingenuity, of course, but as I said in the letter, the scheme was of my own making…"

Eden held up a finger. "The drug," she said.

"From a hawker I met outside the cathedral," said Lenora quickly.

"But you said, 'he assured me there would be no aftereffects,'" Eden reminded her.

Lenora licked her lips. "I meant the hawker, of course."

"No. No, I do not believe you would dose me with a drug you had bought from a hawker. Besides, you said 'Lord Vawdrey assured me.'"

Lenora's expression was chagrined. "Oh bother!" she exclaimed. "Maybe I am as dim as everyone thinks me!"

Eden glanced again at Lord Vawdrey, who had a smile playing about his lips. "The truth, if you please," she said crisply.

"The truth is," interjected Oswald smoothly, "that your cousin and I found ourselves of the same mind on this matter. I, too, felt that drastic action was required to spur my brother into taking the right course of action. He had been, quite frankly, mooning over you for months. Since that kiss you shared at Midwinter…"

Eden made an involuntary movement. "But alas, Roland has never been...shall we say, very *self-aware*?" Eden felt herself bristle at the criticism. "It's true, you know," he said regretfully. "It's actually something of a family failing when it comes to matters of the heart. All three of us brothers had something of a blind spot in this regard. We stumble around in the dark with our feelings when we should be dragging them out into the open sunlight. At least, until we find the right woman." He gave his first genuine smile. "Then it all falls into place."

Eden sat reeling. "But how did you even hatch up such a scheme? How could you drug your own *brother*?"

"The Lady Lenora and I simply found ourselves stood next to one another at some function and started talking," Oswald said reasonably. "As like-minded people do, we found our common ground and our discussion bore fruit."

Eden didn't believe that for a minute. She imagined him sidling up to Lenora and planting the seeds of the dastardly plot into her cousin's mind. But perhaps Lenora had been ripe for such mischief, she thought, looking back at her cousin, who was regarding her with anxious eyes. Who would have dreamed that Lenora would act thus?

"I can scarcely believe all this," she said, closing her eyes. "All this time, I thought I sleepwalked myself into Roland's bedchamber." A stunned silence greeted her words.

"That did not occur to me," said Lenora, looking upset. "You have not done that for years!"

"Is Roland aware you thought as much?" asked Oswald, looking intrigued.

"No," said Eden, slumping in her chair. "He simply thinks I set about entrapping him."

"He would, of course," sighed Oswald.

"Pompous thing!" cried Lenora indignantly. "Well, one good thing can come of our confession, and that is that you can set him right at once!"

Oswald winced. "Perhaps you could postpone such a confrontation, until after the hearing has concluded?" he suggested.

Lenora turned her blue eyes on him. "You don't think we should take the opportunity tomorrow to confess all to the Queen?"

Oswald looked pained. "I do not think that would be at all constructive," he said cautiously. "Unless..." He left a pause. "Annulment is the outcome you are hoping for, Eden?"

Eden gave a start. *Annulment?* Her hand flew to her mouth, and she stared down at her feet.

"Are you very unhappy, dearest?" asked Lenora, looking even more distressed. She twisted her handkerchief in her lap. "I vow, I will *never* try to help anyone ever again! I wrought far less damage when I thought only of myself!"

Eden opened her mouth, but before she could answer, Oswald Vawdrey spoke.

"It is a shame," he said thoughtfully, "that you were not permitted to hear the testimonies given this morning to the King. They would have set your mind at rest a little, I think. People have such very strange views about women's delicate sensibilities."

He hesitated. "Is there any point that I could qualify regarding the evidence I gave yesterday to the Queen?" he offered. "I think you should know that when I said Roland never once

367

spoke your fair cousin's name in connection with the betrothal, I spoke the truth. Your name, however, has been on his lips many a-time in my hearing. And since that Solstice Eve, I would say almost constantly."

He gave her a shrewd look as Eden's cheeks grew pink. "I do not wish to be indelicate, my dear," he said ruefully, "but I think you should know that at Hallam Hall, Roland told me quite categorically that he would not marry Lenora, solely for the fact she was not you." Eden stared at him. "I would swear on my life," he said quietly. "And if you do not believe me, you may ask Mason. He himself gave this information to the King in a sworn statement this morning. And he is not so adept at lying as I."

He smiled at her again. "I for one am extremely happy to have you in the family. And I am not the only one. My wife is thrilled and Linnet also. One of my father's last wishes was to see Roland married to a woman of character and sense."

Eden looked to Lenora, but she did not look remotely offended. "Lenora has a good deal more to her than just a pretty face," she retorted, and meant it.

"I am sure that is true," Oswald conceded with a nod to Lenora. "But I think even she would agree she would not have brought Roland to heel."

"He does not need bringing to heel," Eden responded tetchily. "He's my husband, not my hound!"

Oswald turned his head aside and covered his mouth as if to suppress a sneeze or cough. Eden felt an uncomfortable suspicion that he was smothering a laugh. "Of course," he agreed hastily. His face, when he turned back, was quite composed, but his eyes were still alight with laughter. It crossed her mind that her dear friend Fenella must have her work cut out for her with this man for a husband.

"I think I will just go and take a look out of the window," said Lenora decisively, and she stood up and wandered in that direction.

Eden could only suppose her cousin was trying to be tactful. She looked uncertainly to Lord Vawdrey to find him still watching her. "I saw your plans for the Keep," she said awkwardly.

"My plans?" He sounded startled.

"Yes, for the expansion and a second tower."

"Good gods," said Oswald Vawdrey, and for the first time she could see she had taken him aback. "He never kept them!"

Eden looked at him enquiringly. "The old baron?" she guessed.

His unseeing gaze refocused on her. "Yes, my father," he said slowly. "I presented them to him, rather pompously, as a gift when I was twenty or thereabouts. I was vastly proud of myself." His lips twisted wryly. "Alas, he was not ostensibly impressed or grateful. He believed me an impudent puppy to want to improve on perfection. I thought he would have consigned them to a fireplace years ago. He certainly never mentioned them again. Well, well, wonders will never cease."

"I expect he *was* impressed," said Eden, feeling strangely sorry for a younger version of Oswald. "I can hardly see how he could fail to be. I thought they were inspired." She looked at him searchingly. "Roland is terribly proud of Vawdrey Keep as well, he must have got that from his father, I think. Did you want to be an architect then?"

"What? Oh no, it was just a little project to while away the hours. Having spent time at Vawdrey Keep, you must realize how one must find ways to keep oneself occupied."

"If I'd had my books and my music I daresay I would have been vastly contented there," said Eden defensively. "It is a very beautiful part of the country with many spectacular views." Noticing he was watching her keenly, she shifted in her seat.

"I think, with your encouragement," he began tentatively, "Roland would not be averse to making improvements to the old place. You might not think it, but he has managed to amass a surprising amount of wealth beating his opponents to a pulp in the field." He pulled a face. "And he is not noticeably hampered either by sentiment or pride when it comes to melting down his trophies to add to his coffers."

"While it's true that my husband routinely melts down his trophies," said Eden, spurred into making a defense, "I think you're quite wrong to attribute this to a lack of sentimentality." She paused. She didn't want to betray any of Roland's secrets, but she could surely point out something which any onlooker was free to observe. She eyed Oswald doubtfully. "Have you never noticed that Roland is one of the only knights who declines to take hostages during the melee exercise?"

Oswald's eyelids flickered, and he tipped his head to one side, a faint frown on his face. "You clearly attach some significance to the fact, sister?" he said mildly, but she could see his eyes were watchful, despite his relaxed pose.

"I do, quite frankly," she answered him. "How could I fail to, given what happened at the battle of Adarva."

Oswald's expression tightened, and she could see her directness did not please him. Good gracious, did he really expect her to tiptoe around the issue like some kind of diplomat? "He was only fifteen at the time," she persisted, "and thought he'd watched you die. Then he found out afterward you were a hostage—"

Oswald waved a hand. "Yes, I am aware of what happened, Eden," he said dryly. "None so well as I."

She took a deep breath. "Is it any wonder, then, that he has no taste for the practice? Even though his greatest rivals in the field—Lord Kentigern, Sir Garman Orde… They all do it, as a matter of course. If all Roland cared about was coin," she persisted doggedly, "then he, too, would hold his vanquished foe to ransom. But he does not."

"Out of deference to me, you think?" asked Oswald lightly, but she could see the idea had affected him. He rose from his chair and crossed to the fireplace, looking down at it a moment. "I did not realize that hostage-taking was so widely practiced at tournaments these days," he said finally without turning his head.

"Well, no, how could you?" muttered Eden. "When none of you actually go to watch him compete?"

He turned his head at that, and looked at her a moment, his expression curious. Then his lips quirked, and he looked, Eden thought, rather pleased. "We have been most remiss," he said gravely. "You are quite right to pull me up. Tell me, which tournament would you recommend we attend as a family en masse?"

Eden was quite sure she did not manage to conceal her surprise at this, though she tried. "But surely, you are aware of the King's royal tourney in two months' time…?" she began.

"Ah yes, of course. And who knows, we may even see him reclaim his title!" he said with relish. "What an excellent notion, my dear Eden."

She hesitated. "Are you not worried I may tell Roland that we were drugged?" she asked frankly.

Oswald leaned back in his chair. "He would be furious on your behalf, of course," he said thoughtfully. "But on reflection, I believe he would forgive me for his treatment. Eventually." He gave a small smile. "After all, I made sure he married the right girl."

39

Lenora accompanied Eden back to the Queen's apartments, and they sat awhile in the window seat while they threw out random questions at each other as they naturally occurred.

"Well, but who carried me into Roland's bedchamber?" Eden fretted, sitting suddenly bolt upright.

"Lord Vawdrey, of course, but I was with him the whole time, so you need not worry about the propriety."

"And who removed my dress?"

"Me, of course," answered Lenora complacently. "My turn. What did you think when you received my trunk?"

"That you were furious with me," admitted Eden. "Did you truly pick out these dresses intending them for me?"

"Of course," said Lenora. "And very well you look in them too, instead of dressed like an old crow."

Eden nudged her and Lenora laughed. "You could have my own things sent along to me now," Eden suggested.

"I'm afraid those old dresses have been donated to the poor," said Lenora virtuously. "To atone for your elopement."

"They have not!"

"Will you tell Roland that he was drugged?" asked Lenora curiously.

"I'm not sure," sighed Eden. "It would only cause disruption between him and his brother. Poor Fenella would not like that. Besides, he really doesn't hold it against me that he thinks I tricked him. If anything, he sort of admires it."

"I don't understand how you can't tell him." Lenora frowned. "Are you in love with him? I already know he is with you."

Eden pressed her lips together a moment. "We quarreled before the summons arrived from the Queen," she admitted. "It could not have come at a worse time."

"What did you quarrel about?"

Eden sighed. "It won't make much sense if I even try to explain. You see, there's this knight called Sir Renlow…"

Lenora listened with her chin resting on her palm. "You're right, it doesn't make any sense to me," she admitted. "But I've no brains to speak of."

"I also told him he should not kiss me so much," said Eden awkwardly, and turned bright red.

Lenora's eyebrows rose. "I hate it when they try to do that," she admitted, and Eden remembered what their grandmother had said about Lenora's dislike of ardent suitors.

"I don't," she confided. "At least, not when it's Roland. I just said that because… I don't know. I wanted him to reassure me that I wasn't just a warm body to him. Does that make sense?"

"A warm body?" Lenora repeated blankly.

Eden lowered her voice. "I know that he likes the…intimacy of the marriage bed," she said, wishing she did not sound so prim. "But I don't know if it makes any difference that it's me…" She trailed off miserably. "I'm not expressing myself very well."

"Oh dear," said Lenora. "Poor Roland." Eden gave her a startled look. "Did you not read my letter?" Lenora chided her. "He's been *longing* for you for months. The looks he was casting at you, even someone as disinclined for love as I could

374

read them quite plainly." She looked at Eden in surprise. "You read all that poetry, cousin. Can you really not tell?"

Eden puffed out a breath. "I've been thinking that poetry isn't much like the real thing at all." *Sir Roland is sick for love of you.* She cast a sidelong look at Lenora. "Do you really think he was lovesick for me?"

"I still think he is," said Lenora. "He won't be cured until you love him back."

"Do you think Lord Vawdrey spoke the truth when he said that Roland said he would wed none but me?"

"I do," said Lenora. "But it doesn't really matter what I think."

Eden reached across and clasped her cousin's hand. "Yes, it does," she said.

They sat for a moment in silence. Lenora squeezed her hand, and they both looked up as the door opened and Jane ushered in two guests to the sitting room. Eden grabbed at Parnell's collar, for he had bounded up at the intrusion.

It was Lady Harriet Portstanley and Lady Winifred Hawes, two serious-minded members of court who moved in scholarly circles. They had come, they said, to invite Eden to the poetry reading in the small gallery which they were sure she would not want to miss. As Eden had been instrumental in setting up these same poetry readings, it felt strange to be receiving an invite. Still, she thanked them for their consideration, and though Lenora pulled a face and cried off, Jane kindly intimated she would be happy to accompany her.

She had not explicitly been told that she could not leave the Queen's apartments alone, but it had been heavily implied. The four of them went along to the small gallery and sat and listened to the gathering of patrons and poets who had assembled there.

Eden enjoyed herself for the most part and had a flattering amount of people tell her she had been sorely missed among their number.

One of the less enjoyable factors was a small number of people present who were not regular members at all but seemed to be there simply on the off chance of catching sight of her. They took the opportunity to gawk at Eden and talk to one another throughout the poetry.

In the old days, Eden would have had stern words with them, but now she felt less certain of herself. Sat clothed in one of Lenora's frivolous bridal gowns, she felt most unlike her old self. A mere month ago, no one would have dared point and whisper about her in her presence. Now it seemed like something she would simply have to get used to, until the next scandal came along to replace hers.

At one point, she did level a censorious gaze in their direction, but it just had the dubious effect of dissolving them into giggles. Eden pursed her lips and went back to ignoring them.

Toward the end of the gathering, she fidgeted in her seat, wondering if it might be a good idea to simply slip away now before she was collared by anyone wishing to grill her. She touched Jane Cecil's arm, and to Eden's relief, Jane seemed to catch her meaning quick enough.

They both rose to their feet and started edging quietly toward the door. In fact, Eden thought they had got away with it when they managed to open and close the heavy door behind them, effecting their escape. She breathed a sigh of relief as the two of them started down the corridor, only to find her way barred by an irate gentleman waving a parchment in her face.

"Three weeks!" he yelled. "And nary a word! Secure a patron, they said! All your troubles will be over, they said!"

Eden flinched and stared at him. Dimly, she remembered him as one of poets from the group. She glanced back at the door to see if they had disbanded already, but no one else had emerged.

"You don't even remember me, do you?" he said accusingly.

"Mr.—er—Lewen," ventured Eden as things clicked into place. So, he was the one who had written her the angry letter. Jane had drawn tactfully to one side of the corridor and was trying to look like she was nothing to do with them.

"I'm vastly flattered," he remarked sarcastically.

"Of course I remember," said Eden smoothly. "You secured the patronage of the Duchess of Rand, I think? A couple of months ago, at one of our meetings."

"Oh yes!" said Mr. Lewen with a short, sardonic laugh. *"Her!"*

Eden paused. "I'm afraid I don't quite follow you—"

"Took my life's work she did!" he huffed, tears springing to his eyes. "Said she would be in touch with me forthwith, and then what do I find?" He swung wide an arm and covered his eyes tragically. "She's carried it off to her middle son's seat in the country with her! Without even sending me word!"

Eden hesitated. "Is it your only copy she has taken?" she asked, not without sympathy. He was certainly very distressed. "I am sure I can find the direction of her son's estate and write to her there—"

"It's one hundred and fifty pages, madam!" he screeched, pulling at his lank hair. "How many copies do you think I have?"

Eden drew herself up, adopting her firmest, most no-nonsense manner. Clearly expressing any sympathy for Mr. Lewen in his current frame of mind was a misstep. "As I said," she said briskly, "I will certainly speak to the duchess, and—"

Mr. Lewen wheeled around, blocking Eden's path with his body. He flung his skinny arms wide, preventing her from brushing past him. "That's what you say!" he said wildly. "But when? *When?*" The last word was practically screamed in her face.

Eden pursed her lips together. He was going to cause a scene at this rate. She glanced past him, but no one else was yet in view. She was sure she did not have much time before the poetry gathering broke up and there would be plenty of spectators. "Please collect yourself, Mr. Lewen," she said coolly. "I realize this has being a trying time for you, but—"

"Oh, do you? Do you really?" He gave high, bitter laugh, and Eden heard an edge of hysteria with a sinking sensation in the pit of her stomach. "What would the likes of you know about my struggles?" he demanded shrilly, his voice shaking with emotion. "You couldn't have the faintest notion, madam!"

Eden braced herself as he stepped directly into her space, bringing his face close to hers. "You're absolutely bloody—" His words finished with a startled yelp. Eden felt a whoosh of air, and something passed before her eyes. When she blinked and refocused, Mr. Lewen was pinned to the middle of the wall, his legs dangling beneath him. Eden turned her head and found Roland Vawdrey glaring down the length of his muscular arm at the poet whose tunic he held bunched in his fist.

"What the fuck do you think you're doing?" he asked softly. Eden gasped, thinking for a moment he was addressing her. "Answer me!" His voice rang out sharply, and he slammed the unfortunate man back against the stone wall for emphasis. Eden stared as Mr. Lewen's mouth opened and closed like a fish. "What's that you say?" Roland barked, narrowing his eyes.

378

"Let's have it. The reason you think you can speak to *my wife* in that manner?" His voice had dropped again, but somehow the softly spoken words seemed even more ominous. Mr. Lewen's terrified gaze darted to Eden in unspoken appeal.

"You know this man?" Roland turned his head to look at her.

Eden cleared her throat. "Mr. Lewen is a poet of some renown," she said.

"Is that so?" His words were clipped and hard.

"Until today," she forced herself to add, "he has always conducted himself in a courteous manner."

"Indeed?" Roland's gaze was fixed on the cringing poet's face. "And why was today any different?"

When Mr. Lewen remained dumbstruck, Eden cleared her throat. "Unfortunately, Mr. Lewen has suffered a disappointment with his patroness, the Duchess of Rand."

"A disappointment he saw fit to vent on you," said Roland in a cold voice, his steady gaze fixed on the man dangling from his fist. "Apologize," he added harshly.

"My apologies, good sir," gabbled Lewen hastily.

"To my wife, fool."

"I do implore you for forgiveness, Lady Eden," begged Mr. Lewen.

"If I ever hear you've been disrespectful to my wife in such a manner again," said Roland in a curiously expressionless voice, "you will not like what happens."

Mr. Lewen gulped, then nodded his head jerkily. Roland released him, and he fell to the ground, clutching his throat and wheezing. "It won't happen again, I assure you," he gasped.

"I should hope not indeed," responded Eden gravely. She turned back to Roland, who was stood watching her with a narrowed gaze. Was she imagining it, or was there a faint gleam of challenge in those eyes? "Thank you," she said. For a moment, she thought he looked surprised, but then almost instantly it was gone.

Mr. Lewen lurched off on shaky legs, and they both watched his retreat.

"I think that the meeting will be disbanding any moment," said Eden with dread. Jane had come forward and was looking awkwardly between the two of them. "Jane," she said, "I think it would be advisable for us to move from this place before everyone emerges."

"I agree," said Jane hastily.

"Would you object to my husband accompanying us down as far as the lower gallery?" Jane hesitated, looking torn. Clearly, she had received some directive about keeping them apart. "Please," appealed Eden. "We will stay in your view at all times."

Jane swallowed, two spots of pink color appearing on her pale face. "Very well," she said and fell in step behind them.

Eden placed her arm on Roland's and faced forward. "You do not mind accompanying us?" she said when he did not move at once. That seemed to spur him on, and they started walking. She stole a sideways look at him, only to find he was doing the same thing to her.

"H-how did it go today?" she asked with a faint air of desperation. "With the King?"

He cleared his throat. "It was…interesting," he said, though it sounded like he substituted that word for another.

Eden regarded him anxiously. "Did you get to speak?"

He shook his head. "Apparently, neither of us can until tomorrow."

Eden noticed she was fretfully plucking at his sleeve and pulled herself up. "Sorry, were you on your way somewhere just now? Have I dragged you away from something important?"

"Eden—"

"Yes?" But Roland did not speak, and unable to bear the silence, Eden decided on impulse to simply plunge ahead with what was on her mind. She took a deep breath. "I've been thinking about…everything you said, and the only conclusion that I can draw is that I am the absolute opposite of Sir Renlow. In fact," she carried on recklessly, "I'm a totally spineless coward. All I care about is appearing perfectly composed in front of others. You included. I can't even imagine competing, week in and week out, in front of crowds of people, suffering humiliation after humiliation. And getting no encouragement, save from the likes of you, paying his ransom. You're right. He must have incredible inner resilience and strength."

She steeled herself to brave a glance at Roland's face. He looked rather stunned. She swallowed. "In future, I mean to take Sir Renlow as my role model," she said, her cheeks burning.

This last part seemed to startle him into speech. "Eden…"

Before he could continue, and she lost her nerve, she plunged on. "I'd been tormenting myself about that kiss I gave you for the past week. Because I felt like I made a fool of myself. You didn't expect me to give you that sort of kiss, but I misunderstood you. It wasn't appropriate…" She gripped at his arm, unable to think what to say next, her face aflame.

"The kiss was perfect, Eden," he said sharply.

"And so, I said all those stupid things, because…" She gasped, tilting her head upward to discourage the wetness she could feel in her eyes. "Because I was too much of a coward to tell you how I really felt…which was sadly conflicted and…a little depressed in spirits after being left alone for so many days…"

Roland gave an exclamation and turned to look over his shoulder, as if checking Jane Cecil still followed them a few paces behind. By the muffled but exasperated sound he made, Eden knew she was.

"I'm well aware that I acted like the w-worst sort of harpy after you thoughtfully brought me all those gifts back from Areley Kings," Eden continued wretchedly. "But I—"

"Eden," he said quietly, yet firmly, interrupting her. "You are too hard on yourself. I had no idea…" He reached for her hand and applied pressure to her fingers. "This is not your fault. It's mine."

"So, you…you will kiss me again then?" she asked anxiously.

"Eden…" he said with a sharp inward breath. "You little wretch, what are you trying to do to me?"

She feared she had totally lost track of the conversation now. "But you said, 'rest assured it won't happen again,' and I surmised from that—"

382

"I was fuming," he said in a low, tense voice, "at the idea you did not welcome my kisses."

"Oh," she said softly.

"I had *no* intention of ever stopping kissing you," he continued hoarsely. "That was just my hurt pride talking."

Eden leaned further toward him. He adjusted his hold to squeeze her hand. "It was my hurt pride that made me say those things too," she admitted with a small, choked laugh. *Sir Renlow*, she thought. *Sir Renlow, Sir Renlow, Sir Renlow.* Then she spoke. "I wish you could kiss me now."

He made a strangled sound in his throat. "Can you slip away later?" he asked in a low voice. Eden's eyes widened. "I'd come to you," he carried on, "but I understand you're sharing your bedchamber with another."

"With Jane," she clarified. "But I don't quite know how I'd manage to slip away. Unless…" She thought of Lenora and bit her lip.

"Yes?"

"Perhaps I could enlist Lenora's help?" she whispered. "My grandmother has returned to Hallam Hall today, but my uncles will likely be in the Montmayne quarters."

"Come to me," said Roland. "Mason and Linnet are staying with Oswald and Fenella tonight at their house in town."

"Did they not invite you?" asked Eden, feeling stung on his behalf.

"I'm not good company right now. For anyone save yourself." He spoke the words with a faint trace of self-consciousness and heightened color in his cheeks, which made him look very boyish.

383

Eden told herself firmly that she was *not* enchanted by this bashful side of Roland. "If I don't manage to get away," she said in a low voice, glancing over her shoulder for they had reached the Queen's quarters, "what will we do if they try to say our marriage is unlawful?"

"Fight it," he said grimly, "with every weapon at our disposal."

Instead of feeling miserable, Eden felt a sudden reckless joy. She nodded, unable to think of appropriate words in response. The guards were standing to attention, and Eden waited reluctantly for Jane to catch up with them. As she withdrew her hand from his arm, he caught it and pressed it to his cheek a moment. Eden curled her fingers to feel the faint stubble on his jaw. Then he dropped her hand and walked away. Eden watched him all the way to the end of the corridor before she turned and entered the Queen's rooms.

40

In the end Eden simply sent a message to Lenora via one of the Queen's pages.

Dear Cousin, would it be possible for you to invite me to dine with you tonight in your chambers? It would be lovely to catch up with your news, and I would consider it a particular favor if you would invite our mutual acquaintance Lady G, who I quite long to see.

The page sped off carrying her note, and though she had initially been pleased as punch by her ingenuity, Eden had no sooner sent it than she started doubting that Lenora would catch her meaning. Lady G referred to Lenora's cat, Griselda, and Eden's intention was that Lenora would see the supper request for the mere nonsense it was, and realize she was instead asking for her help in some subterfuge.

However, so fond was Lenora of her cats that Eden feared she might not find anything amiss with her letter, even though the whimsical tone was most unlike Eden's usual manner! She paced about, wringing her hands and fretting that she would not manage her escape from the Queen's confinement that evening. The Queen arrived back from her ride and changed into a charming outfit of peacock blue. Eden tidied her hair and changed into her rose-pink gown. When she emerged, the Queen was reading a note which she passed to Eden.

"Your cousin invites you for supper," she said. "It might be a good idea for the two of you to clear the air, though I had hoped you might sing for me after supper. I have Viscount Bardulph dining with me this evening." Eden noticed a fleeting look of dislike cross Jane's face before she suppressed it. *Interesting,* thought Eden. *Jane does not like the charming viscount!* "Never mind," sighed the Queen. "Jane dear, you must read for us instead after supper."

"Viscount Bardulph does not care for my reading voice," pointed out Jane without any expression. "He said I have a nasal inflection, if you recall, Your Majesty."

"Nonsense!" said the Queen heartily. "He merely teases you. This is the problem with unmarried women," she said, turning to Eden. "They do not understand what teasing creatures men can be."

Eden felt a sudden sympathy for Jane. "It is likely because he is not used to our accent," she said. "Viscount Bardulph is from the Western Isles, is he not?" Jane's answering look said she wished he would go back there, and soon.

"That is so." The Queen nodded. "He is my countryman."

"Will you dine with your family this evening?" Jane asked Eden in a deliberate change of subject.

"Oh…yes," Eden replied. "My cousin writes she will call for me at seven."

Lenora arrived promptly at seven, and even exchanged a few words with the Queen. Eden was amazed at her cousin's self-possession. There was nothing furtive or nervous about her manner, and when Eden whispered her plan to her as they proceeded to the west wing, she did not even blink an eyelid.

"Of course." She nodded placidly. "I thought it would be something of the sort. I can return for you in three hours."

"I hope it is not a great imposition," Eden fussed nervously. "What will you do if a guard were to arrive for me, or something of that sort?"

Lenora shrugged. "I daresay I should think of something," she said vaguely with an air of assurance that quite staggered Eden.

"You must not worry," Lenora said glibly. "Just make sure you are ready to return with me at ten o'clock."

"I will." They had arrived at the Vawdrey rooms, and Eden kissed Lenora's cheek and knocked faintly at the door. It opened immediately. Parnell, who she had brought with her, jumped up at his master in excitement. Eden heard Castor bark from inside, and the next thing she knew, she was whisked inside, pressed back against the door, and thoroughly kissed as Roland turned the key in the lock.

A loud woof startled them both as Castor came bounding over to welcome her and Parnell. Roland grudgingly made room for the large beasts, milling around them. "Hello, hello there, Castor. I knew they would be pleased to see one another. Lenora is calling back for me in three hours," she said as Roland propelled her to a chair by the fire. He sat down and pulled her into his lap, kissing her again until she was breathless and clinging to him.

"Do you know what's going to happen on the morrow?" she asked as soon as she could draw breath.

"Not really," he admitted. "I think everyone who wanted to put in their two pennies has now done so. Mason caught me up on the first day and today seemed like much of the same."

"What did he make of it?" Eden asked.

Roland exhaled noisily. "He scarcely knew what to make of it," he said, rubbing the back of his neck. "And neither did I, hearing his retelling."

"Lord Vawdrey and Lenora *swore* that I was the intended bride," marveled Eden, lowering her voice. "Listening to them, I almost believe it myself."

Roland looked at her then glanced away. "Mason said the same thing," he muttered.

"What's wrong?"

He flung his head back and rested it on the back of the chair. "You should have been," he said, closing his eyes. "If I hadn't been so fucking blind about my own feelings. I never exchanged more than a half dozen words with your cousin."

Eden slipped her arm around his neck. "Don't be upset," she said, pressing in close to him. His jaw remained tense, even when she dropped a kiss on it. "If you *had* asked my uncle, I would just have said no. Screamed it, actually. Then run for a convent," she said seriously.

His eyes flickered open, and he grudgingly smiled. "I'd still have had you, all the same," he said.

"Yes," she whispered and kissed the corner of his mouth, where it turned up. "And today? Who was there?"

"Your uncle Christopher," muttered Roland. Eden tensed. *Oh no.* "Mason and *Cuthbert*," Roland continued with disgust.

Eden drew back to look at him uncertainly. "Really?"

"Little swine has gone to Oswald's tonight. Making himself scarce."

"Anyone else?"

"Attley and Bev."

"Oh dear," said Eden. "I don't think your friends approve of me."

"Well, that's where you're wrong," said Roland, his thumb circling her hip. "It seems they had my measure from the start. I like you in this dress," he said. "But I still want to take it off you. Can I?" Eden wanted to ask what his friends had said for him to get that impression, but Roland was kissing her again and demanding her wholehearted participation. When she wound her arms around his neck, he gave a deep growl of appreciation. Eden drew back in alarm. "No you don't," he said, tightening his arms about her. "Not after tormenting me like that this afternoon."

"Tormenting you?" she asked uncertainly.

"Telling me you wanted me to kiss you when I couldn't."

"Oh." She smiled at him. "But I did not say that to torment you. I thought you would be pleased." Noticing his expectant air, she reviewed his last few sentences in her head. "Yes, you can. Take my dress off me, I mean."

She had no sooner uttered the words than he swung her up in his arms. "Stay!" he said firmly to the dogs who had jumped to their feet. They both dropped back down by the fire and Parnell rolled onto his side.

"I expect they are missing the others," observed Eden ruminatively. Roland said nothing, just shouldered the door open. He carried her inside, and Eden looked around with interest. "I miss our box-bed," she sighed.

"Did I tell you I ordered another?" Roland asked, setting her on her feet and spinning her round so he could start unfastening her laces.

Eden looked back over her shoulder at him. "For here?" she asked with surprise.

"No, for Vawdrey Keep. It's a lot bigger and grander, with carving and lots of shelves for books and sconces for candles and things."

"Sounds nice," said Eden.

"I ordered us new bedding too. With our initials." He tugged at her bodice and then maneuvered it down to her waist. "I should get one for here too though," he reflected. "That's a good idea." With a few more short pulls, her skirts dropped to the floor, and Eden stepped out of them.

"This bed looks fine though," Eden said, walking toward it as Roland started hurriedly divesting himself of his own clothing. She had only just slipped under the covers when he bounded in beside her and started pulling her shift up over her head. Once they were both naked, he pulled her into his arms, and they lay still a moment.

"Naked as babes," Roland murmured.

"Pardon?"

"I've heard that phrase several times today."

"In what context?" puzzled Eden. Then she exclaimed, "About us?"

He laughed against her neck, tickling her. "Yes," he admitted. "This reminds me of when I first woke up on that morning. Though it's not entirely right." His tone was teasing, and he rolled onto his back, pulling her on top of him. Then with one hand he palmed her breast, the other coming to rest with great familiarly against her bottom. "It was more like this."

For the smallest moment, Eden considered telling him they had both been drugged that night. But then she realized it would completely ruin his playful mood. "I remember, your hair smelled nice." He sniffed it now. "Your skin smelled nice." He buried his nose in her neck and breathed in there with every sign of pleasure. "And you sure as hells *felt* nice," he carried on, giving her a good squeeze. "But the oddest thing was, when I realized it was you…"

"Yes?" Eden prompted tensely.

"I had the strangest feeling in my chest," he mused. "At the time I couldn't identify what it was."

"A sort of sick feeling?" suggested Eden in muffled tones against his shoulder.

He gave a short laugh. "No, *not* a sick feeling."

"What then?"

He cleared his throat. "It felt like a sort of overwhelming sense of well-being. Like…a huge weight had been lifted from there. Somehow it felt like everything had come right with my world. I was *glad.*"

Eden felt like all the air had been sucked from her lungs. She lay a moment like a stunned fish before trailing her hand to rest over his chest a moment. "Here?" she asked.

He shifted her hand to the left so it lay over his heart. "More like…here."

Eden thought of Lenora's words. Maybe in some obnoxious Vawdrey male type way, he *had* been pining for her. She lifted her head to look at him. *Glad.* He said he'd been glad to wake up and find her in his arms, she thought, her head reeling. *Glad.*

To find himself obligated to wed her? She felt her body trembling. It couldn't possibly be true, could it?

"Cold?" he asked in concern, crowding around her at once, rubbing his palm up and down her back. Eden found herself glancing uneasily at the door. "No one's going to burst in, sweetheart," he assured her. "We'd hear the dogs first."

That was true enough, and Eden relaxed a little. "I wish we were back at the Keep," she said wistfully.

"Really?" He sounded pleased.

"Don't you?"

"I don't mind," he said. "So long as…"

Unable to hear any more sweet words so soon, Eden leaned forward and kissed his lips. He said her kiss had been perfect last time, so she kissed him again boldly, and with tongue. Roland groaned into her mouth, hauling her body more firmly against his own, which strained against her with bunched muscle and hard need. Eden grasped his shoulders and let herself relax against him.

"I don't like poetry," Roland Vawdrey whispered. "But I do like you, Eden." He was tracing his fingertips over her hips. She shivered. Although his body felt tense and primed, his actions were lazy and unhurried. "And you don't like tournaments, but you do like me." He tugged one of her hands down from his shoulder back to his chest. "I want your hands all over my body." His words were thick with desire now. Experimentally, Eden ran her hand over the warm skin of his muscular chest. His eyes darkened and his chest heaved. He definitely liked that.

"Oh, Eden," he whispered.

Why did he keep doing that? Speaking her name with pleasure? It scrambled her brains and turned her to a puddle of mush. She gazed down at him. "I thought of another weapon at our disposal," she said breathlessly and let her hand wander lightly down his flat belly. He held very still and made a noise of startled pleasure when she made out the shape of his maleness with her hand.

Roland sucked in his breath. "My cock?" he asked, looking confused.

Eden blushed violently. "No! Yes…" she corrected herself. "I mean, well…" She lowered her voice. "You could put your baby in me."

For a full minute, he didn't utter a word. "What?" he asked finally in a strangled voice, breathing hard.

Eden glanced down in alarm at his violent reaction to her words. He seemed to have swelled to an enormous size and thrust more firmly into her grasp. "Um…well…" Eden was forced to adjust her hold. "It…was just an idea. I probably didn't think it through…"

"Say it again, Eden," he urged her huskily, his grip on her hips tightening.

Her eyes returned to his, and her cheeks were scarlet. "I thought that, well, one way around our marriage being annulled would be for there to be, a—um—well, a legal impediment to their nullifying…"

"Say. It. What. You. Said. Before."

"You could put your baby in me," she repeated wide-eyed.

He breathed in once. Twice. Then his glazed eyes seemed to refocus on her. "Gods, Eden." His voice was so gravelly she could barely recognize it. "Do you want that?"

"Yes…" she said, feeling a little alarmed by his reaction.

"Tell me then," he urged, his nostrils flaring.

"Well…"

"Tell me to put my baby in you."

"Roland," she squealed as in one swift motion, he rolled her onto her back and loomed above her.

"I can't wait," he said shakily as he settled between her legs. "Gods. I could spill right now."

She helped him by wriggling around underneath him, her legs wide, until he was poised exactly where he needed to be. His excitement seemed to be transferring to her. Eden felt wild and edgy with some kind of driving need. "Roland?" she asked uncertainly. He stilled, his eyes flying to meet her. "Please," she whispered, licking her lips.

"Anything," he vowed, though he was trembling now. "What do you need? My fingers? My mouth?"

"Put your baby in me."

He thrust, and Eden had to stifle a cry with the back of her hand. He was lodged so deep, her eyes watered.

"Eden?"

"I'm not crying, all is well," she assured him, and to her surprise, found it was. She looked back up to find him watching her in pained enquiry, sweat beading on his forehead. "You can move now," she said.

He grabbed her knee and pushed it out to the side, pinning her open to him as he withdrew and then thrust again. "Gods, I'm never leaving you again," he groaned.

"What do you mean?" asked Eden, bracing a hand against the headboard.

"Taking you with me." He planted his other hand against the mattress in an attempt not to crush her with his ardor.

"T-to the tournaments?" stammered Eden, who was finding it hard to follow the conversation whilst his hard body jostled against hers.

"Everywhere."

Eden opened and closed her mouth. It would probably be as well to put an end to the conversation, she thought. They could always return to it at some later point. "Very well," she said, "husband."

His head snapped up and he locked eyes with her. They both gasped when part of him seemed to swell further still inside her.

"Eden," he whispered, dropping his head down onto her breast. Everything inside her where he was sheathed was fluttering. "Say it again," he whispered.

"What?" she asked, confused at the odd sensation.

"Call me husband. Say my name." He rocked his hips, making her gasp this time. "Do it, Eden."

She licked her lips. "Roland," she whispered.

"Yes," he grunted, rocking hard against her.

"Husband." It came out like a whine this time. Why was that?

"Fuck." He spoke the expletive so clearly, her eyes flew wide. "Are you—?" His eyes were boring into hers. "Eden?"

What? Eden turned her face away in confusion. It couldn't possibly feel good, could it? "I—I'm not sure—" She gasped again. It wasn't a good idea to try talking when everything felt so strange. She tightened her grasp on Roland's shoulders and felt his deep murmur of appreciation vibrate right the way through her.

Suddenly she couldn't get close enough to his big body. Her legs wrapped around his hips; she could feel herself tighten around his man-root so tight that she felt alarmed. She arched up into him, straining, reaching for she knew not what, but suddenly desperate to achieve it.

"Oh gods," Roland groaned. "Yes, like that, sweeting." He thrust into her, and Eden yelped, but from pleasure this time, not pain. She gripped on to him so tight, she was sure he would object. Instead, he just flexed his body against hers harder. "*Finally*," he breathed. "I knew… Gods, I just knew you'd be like this."

"Oh! Oh, Roland!"

"Tell me," he ground out. "Now."

"I—I hardly know!" she gasped. "It feels *so*…inside me," she babbled.

"Good? Tell me it feels good to you, Eden."

"You feel so…*good*."

"Yes," he gritted out. "Yes. Every time now, I'm going to make sure you feel good like this. As good as you feel to me."

Really? She made him feel that good? Running her hands over his bunched and flexing muscles, she could feel his strength and

396

resolve as his body labored above hers. She felt bold and daring, like she could not get enough of touching his warm skin.

"Yes!" she whimpered, sinking her fingers into his shoulders, and arching up into him. "Please, Roland!"

She watched his eyes smolder. "What else?" he demanded.

Eden gazed up at him helplessly. She wrapped her legs around his back, clutching him tighter to her. Why wasn't he moving like she needed him to?

"Eden? What else am I to you?"

She refocused on his tense expression. What was he to her? She cast about wildly. "H-husband?" she ventured.

A look of vast satisfaction spread over his face. "That's right." He rewarded her with a few hard strokes that had her keening against his shoulder. When his pace slackened, threatening to stop again, a frustrated Eden dragged her hands down his back to his buttocks and gripped him tight.

Roland uttered a strangled oath and started moving his hips in earnest. "If you want me gentle, you need to ease your grip," he warned.

With a reserve of strength she didn't know she possessed, Eden squeezed him even tighter, using all her strength to haul him against her.

His body shook. "Gods, Eden, if you knew what you did to me—" His words broke off as he crushed his mouth to hers. And then, he was pushing her back into the mattress, driving her into it. Their bodies were a tangle of pulsating need, with their limbs moving together with one purpose. To lose themselves in each other's body.

Eden cried out when she found herself taken in a tidal wave of sensation and crashed against the rocks, coming apart in a thousand pieces. Only to find herself safe and in one piece once again, clinging to her anchor, which was Roland Vawdrey. He dropped his head and roared into her shoulder when his own wave broke. Eden's hand flew to catch hold of the back of his neck, clasping him to her.

By the time she came out of her stupor, she was lying sprawled over his chest, like a limp rag. Roland Vawdrey was on his back beneath her, breathing steadily. She should roll off him. If she could muster the energy. Was this what it had felt like every time for him? No wonder he was always clamoring for her.

She cracked an eye open but could not quite bring herself to move. One of Roland's hands was tucked behind his head at the pillow, the other resting on her lower back. He was lying still, as if asleep, but something told Eden that if she tried to extricate herself, he would have something to say about it. She closed her eyes and gave up the battle before it had even begun.

"Sleep a while," he murmured. "I won't let you sleep too long."

"Lenora returns at ten, don't forget," she said and yawned.

41

It was only half an hour later that Roland heard the door to their apartments open. He tensed immediately, and Eden grumbled into his shoulder. The dogs, however, did not bark, and he recognized his brother's low tones. *Shit*. A sharp rap on the door startled them both. "What do you want?" yelled out Roland bad-naturedly.

"It's me," said Mason's deep voice. "Come out and have a drink with us."

Eden gasped and clung to him, so he stroked his hand down her side. "Shh, it's fine, love," he assured her.

They dressed hurriedly, speaking in snatched whispers. He helped her back into her dress and craned his head toward her as she told him in murmurs that she had felt very low after receiving her cousin's trunkful of clothes. How she had feared that all was lost between her and Lenora but now it seemed they had made it up and everything was resolved.

He frowned over her reading of the gift of clothes from her cousin. It seemed to him that she had put the worst interpretation possible on it, but he hesitated before saying anything to put her out. He believed he was growing damned tactful as a husband. "Well," he said, "that's good all is resolved betwixt the two of you, in any event."

She also repeated the fact her grandmother, who had instigated this whole hearing mess, was heading back home, something Roland had not really absorbed earlier. This news he also managed to accept without an explosion of righteous wrath, but when he stepped back to survey Eden, he suffered a setback to his new equanimity. "You can't go out looking like that." He scowled.

"What do you mean?" Eden frowned, turning to look at him. She patted the pink gown she had just hurriedly donned, clearly thinking she looked perfectly respectable.

Roland snorted. "They're not seeing you like that, Eden. Only I get to see you like that."

Her hands flew to her hair. "Do I look untidy?"

"*Untidy* is not the word," he said dryly.

"What is then?" she asked.

"*Tumbled*," he answered with great restraint.

"Tumbled?" She turned to arch a brow at him. "Does that mean what I think it means?" He smirked. "Disgraceful," she said lightly, and smiled. He felt her smile right down to his bones. "You must have a comb somewhere hereabouts," she said. "Do you remember," she added with a hint of shyness, "how I borrowed your comb at—" But he had rounded the bed and pulled her firmly into his arms again. *"Roland?"* This time when he kissed her, he was gentle, but unhurried. When he finally lifted his lips from hers, she sighed. "That was a good kiss," she said, and looked up at him through her eyelashes. "A *very* good kiss."

"*Good* is not the word," he said gruffly. "Besides, all kisses with you are good." It was nothing more than the truth. She smiled again at that, completely unaware that he never said things like this. Never even thought them. Then again, Eden Montmayne wasn't exactly famous for her smiles. Yet here they were. Him spouting sweet words, and her smiling.

If anyone thought they were taking her from him, they were vastly mistaken. There was no chance in hells he was giving her up. Not now, or ever. She was his and so she would remain. It would take more than a royal decree to alter that fact. He shied away from what this meant, and instead led her to the door of his room and dragged back the bolt.

She caught his arm before he opened the bedchamber door. "What will your brothers say?" she whispered, looking worried. "About my having been here tonight?"

"If they've any sense of self-preservation, they won't say a damned thing," he answered grimly, and swung the door open, taking her hand and leading her out into the sitting room.

Oswald and Mason Vawdrey were both sat before the fire, and though their eyes widened at the sight of Eden, they wisely said nothing, except to utter a polite greeting. She murmured back in kind, and Roland led her to a chair set slightly back from the others. Then he kneeled at her feet and helped her on with her stockings and shoes.

The dogs thrust their noses at her over the arms of the chair and she stroked their muzzles. "Does it distress you that your grandmother has left already?" he asked as it suddenly occurred to him. He kept his voice low, reluctant to have his brothers overhear their private conversation, but no doubt the bastards could hear every word.

"Not as much as it ought to," she admitted, pulling a face. "She's seldom at court, and I'm used to only seeing her when I'm at Hallam Hall, which is not above twice a year these days." She hesitated. "It does make me happy that she cared enough about me to cause all this fuss," she confided in a rush. "Even though it has caused you and your family a good deal of inconvenience—"

"Eden," he interrupted her. "When all this is over and done with…then I'll appreciate it too. I just can't right now, that's all. We'll invite her to Vawdrey Keep." He winced. "When we've made it a bit more habitable."

"What's wrong with the Keep?" asked Eden defensively.

"Well, for a start, there's no mattresses in the guest bedchambers," he pointed out dryly. Then his eye caught on a piece of paper on the floor, which he retrieved. The sloping hand was unfamiliar to him, and he stared at it in bewilderment for a moment or two.

Eden looked up from where she was fussing with Castor. "Oh, I think that's mine," she said. "I must have slipped it into my sleeve cuff to finish reading later."

"Yours?" Roland lowered the letter with a heavy frown. "Who wrote this to you?" he asked with a sudden deadly calm.

"Mr. Edwin Childers," responded Eden readily enough.

"Childers? Who is he? What the hells does he mean by addressing you as 'Mistress, whose every word leads my heart to throb inside my breast'?"

Eden gave a startled laugh. "He's not addressing me." Her expression turned grave, seeing he was not amused. "He's a poet. That is merely three verses of his epic poem he has revised."

Her guiltless manner calmed him a little, but still he returned to the piece of paper with displeasure. "Tell him to write his poem on a separate damn page next time," he said. "I don't appreciate such sentiments being scribbled in the body of a letter sent to my wife."

Eden straightened up at this, looking serious. After a moment's heavy pause, she nodded. "I will."

"I understand that this stuff is important to you, Eden," he said gravely. "But there need to be rules. I can't have men accosting you in corridors and writing you love notes. I'll end up killing someone."

"What sort of rules?" she asked warily. "Is this about a private correspondence or attending poetry meets?"

"You can continue to do both," he said with extreme trust and generosity, if he did say so himself. "But I need your word you'll tell me if anyone oversteps any boundaries."

She breathed out. "Very well," she said.

"Very well, what?"

Eden looked disconcerted. "Very well, I promise?" she ventured uncertainly.

"Very well, *husband*," he stressed.

Eden opened and closed her mouth on a no doubt tart reply. "Very well, husband," she said meekly, surprising them both.

Roland turned his head sharply when he heard what sounded like a stifled chuckle from the vicinity of the fireplace. Both his brothers swiveled hastily back to face the fire. He returned to Eden, who was seemingly oblivious to their avid audience.

Hesitantly, she reached out and took one of his hands in hers. "Thank you," she said, robbing him of all breath. "For understanding when something's important to me."

He looked down at their clasped hands a moment before taking a deep breath. "Of course," he said, wishing devoutly his bloody brothers weren't drinking in their exchange.

He twisted his hand and interlaced their fingers. "This time tomorrow night," he said, "all this foolishness will be over, and we can get on with our lives. Our married lives," he stressed, leaving no room for her to get the wrong impression. "Together."

She nodded, and a light knock was heard on the door. The dogs both bounced up, but he managed to clamp Castor's collar. "Quiet, boy!" Her cousin had arrived for her. *Already.*

42

"So, it is true then, that you nearly strangled some poet this afternoon?" commented Mason as Roland closed the door after seeing Eden and Parnell off.

"Eh?"

"Cuthbert heard it from one of the pages."

"Come and sit with us," directed Oswald, gesturing to a chair.

"Where is Cuthbert?" asked Roland, dragging a chair toward the fire. He slumped down in it feeling heavy of heart. When Oswald went to pour him some wine, he waved it away. "I want a clear head on the morrow."

"One cup won't fog your head," Mason pointed out. "Unless you're Oswald." Roland just shook his head. "Cuthbert's out making merry with the other squires," added Mason. "No doubt fleecing them out of their pennies at cards or dice."

"And telling them salacious gossip," added Oswald. "You and Eden really are doing the current rounds at court. He will be dining out freely on that tale for many a week." He replenished Mason's goblet of wine and poured himself and Roland water.

Roland shrugged, unconcerned. Castor came and lay at his feet.

"That dog recognizes you as his master," said Mason. "He's not looking for Father anymore. How is all at the Keep?"

"Baxter's mad as ever. Fulco's mother means to keep him unwed. We've a new maid from the village named Brigid. I need to buy…" He waved a hand vaguely. "Hangings and draperies and such."

A heavy silence greeted his words. Looking up, Roland saw his brothers regarding each other with raised brows. "What?" he asked.

"Did our little brother first list *people* above possessions?" asked Oswald.

"Did he just bring up the subject of Fulco and his lack of a wife?" chimed in Mason.

"Did he just mention *curtains*?"

"Fuck off, the both of you," said Roland without heat. He took a sip of water. "All is fine, but I need to spruce up the place now I've a wife to keep happy."

"I'm very pleased to hear it," said Oswald. "I knew you were the man for the job."

"I never would have thought Eden Montmayne was the woman for it though," admitted Mason.

Roland found himself bristling.

"I disagree," said Oswald. "Though I do wonder…" He turned to Roland. "Has it ever crossed your mind, little brother, that Eden looks set to become a very formidable female indeed, once she's had a few years to adjust," he added thoughtfully, "from the role of poor relation?"

Roland's frowned cleared. "Oh aye," he agreed absently. "You should have seen how she ripped into the wife of that Lelland fellow at Tranton Vale. Reduced her to tears. Not," he added, "that she didn't deserve it."

"Oh, I'm sure," murmured Oswald.

"You sound almost proud of it!" Mason observed, swigging his wine.

"So what if I am?" demanded Roland. "A man wants a wife who can hold her own and defend his corner."

"Very true," agreed Oswald hastily. "And after all, our father always wanted you to marry a woman of character."

"Did he?" asked Roland with a flicker of interest. "First I've heard of it. He always told me he judged a wench by the broadness of her hips."

"It's true he came to wisdom lamentably late in life," sighed Oswald. "But he did achieve it in the end."

"I predict your marriage will have never a dull moment, brother," said Mason with a wry smile.

"Well, it hasn't so far," agreed Roland. "But if you mean I'll lead her a merry dance, you're quite wrong." He glowered at his brothers, who were watching him with interest. "For I mean to be a very good sort of husband."

"Do you?" asked Oswald. "Well, that's an excellent start."

"You don't need to tell me that," said Roland. "I'm already far and away ahead of the both of you in that respect."

"How so?" Mason frowned, plunking down his cup.

"Well," expanded Roland, "you intended to saddle Linnet with a couple of brats and carry on much the same as always. And as for you," he said, turning to Oswald. "You meant to send Fen into the country and forget you even had a wife!" Both his brothers stiffened. "It took you both a couple of months at least before you realized you wanted to keep them by your side."

"At least we never nearly married the wrong one!" pointed out Mason defensively.

Now it was Roland's turn to look pained, but Oswald gave a small cough. "No, no, he's quite right. He adapted a lot faster to wedded life than we." He regarded Roland curiously. "How long did it take incidentally? Before you were reconciled?"

"Soon as I woke up, of course, and found her in my bed," replied Roland smugly. "Turns out I'm a lot smarter than we all thought."

43

Eden had never felt so on display as when she walked into the audience chamber the next morning, her head held high and her back straight. She had performed music, sung, and recited, and even danced for a viewing audience and felt less conspicuous than she did now. Every head turned her way, and a loud whispering rose up to the rafters, increasing in volume.

The Queen was directly ahead of her, dressed in a gown of glittering emerald green. But it was not Queen Armenal who everyone stared at, it was Eden. She wore Lenora's most dazzling betrothal dress of gold, festooned with pink roses. It was a ridiculous confection of a gown, but strange to say, Eden recognized she looked well in it.

Lenora's maidservant, Hannah, had been sent along to dress her hair, so it had been like old times. Instead of her customary hairstyle, Eden had instead requested the same arrangement she had worn at Tranton Vale, with a section of her long black hair left loose down her back, and only the front part taken up and braided into a coronet.

Then, she had a gauzy gold veil attached to the back of the braided section to flutter at her middle back. Looking at herself in the glass that morning, although she had felt sick with nerves, she had thought, *I am too young to wear black. It is right there should be color in my life.*

As she marched after Armenal now, she caught Lenora's eye in the front row. Her cousin clapped her hands together in delight to see her wearing the gold dress. Eden permitted herself a small smile of welcome at Lenora, ignored her uncles, and allowed the page to discreetly direct her to a seat at the front.

The Queen mounted the steps to the dais to join King Wymer, who already sat in his throne, looking rather impatient to get proceedings started. Eden kept staring straight ahead, though of course, her heart thudded against her ribs, and all she really wanted to do was scan the crowd in search of Roland.

"Well, well," said the King, raising his voice and beckoning to a plump scribe, who hurried over. He turned to Queen Armenal, and they exchanged a few words. He gave a short nod.

"We are pleased to have arrived at this third and final day in deliberations over the marriage of Sir Roland Vawdrey and Lady Eden Montmayne," he said loudly. "We have now heard several statements from witnesses and parties involved. My consort, Queen Armenal, will now sum up our findings."

The Queen nodded portentously as she waited for the buzz of conversation to die down. "It is undeniable," she began sternly, "that this marriage did circumvent the proper order here at court, where both parties occupied prominent positions. The correct applications to our royal personages were not made. I was deprived of a most valuable lady-in-waiting. The King was deprived of his champion. Such behavior is not to be tolerated. It could even be argued that such a hasty marriage constituted conduct unbecoming in a courtier, setting an undesirable tone for our court."

She let these serious words sink in, her gaze taking in the multitude of courtiers who had gathered to hear the judgment. "My feeling is that the Montmaynes did obfuscate the matter of which bride was requested, though whether that was done willfully or through genuine confusion is not so clear."

There was a loud murmuring at this, and the King glared furiously at Eden's uncles, who immediately snapped their jaws shut. "It could therefore be justifiably claimed that Sir Roland acted in frustration that night, finding himself pledged to the

410

wrong Montmayne. The testimony of his two brothers, and Lenora Montmayne herself, bear out his dissatisfaction for the way things played out at the betrothal feast."

"Remember, my dear," cut in the King peevishly, "that Vawdrey has already been punished, when I stripped him of his position as my champion."

"That is true enough," agreed Armenal, looking thoughtful. "And there was no mention of a dowry being presented to him." She looked to Sir Leofric for confirmation of this, and he looked extremely uncomfortable before giving a quick shake of his head.

"I care naught for a dowry," said Roland loudly, and Eden jumped to find him only a few seats away to her right.

"The withholding of one could be considered an additional punishment," pointed out the King blandly.

The Queen clapped her hands. "Enough! I am decided," she announced in ringing tones. "His Highness the King has kindly agreed the sentence is mine to dispose in this instance, as it is I who have suffered the greatest injury." Eden blinked at this and did not dare look in Roland's direction. "I have given this matter great thought, and having taken Lady Dorothea Montmayne's complaint into consideration, I think the best way forward would be to suspend the match for one calendar month. During this time, Sir Roland will think how best to woo the Lady Eden in a manner fitting for a chief lady-in-waiting to the Queen. If, at the end of this period, the lady accepts his suit, then they will receive our blessing in the royal chapel."

A loud buzz of exclamations spread throughout the hall until the Queen raised a hand for silence. "Do you accept my judgment, Sir Roland?" she asked archly.

Eden waited calmly for Roland to object, but when he spoke, his words stunned her.

"I do," he said simply.

Eden turned her head to stare at his handsome profile, and then turned back to the Queen, her fingernails digging into her palms. She had been expecting him to object, to rail at her pronouncement. Indeed, if he cared in any way, she told herself, he would argue back against such a ruling. Which meant he must be indifferent. She felt mortified at his lack of reaction. Suddenly she was finding it hard to even breathe.

"You have something which you would like to say, Eden?" suggested the Queen.

Eden felt her face grow hot. "I have something to say to my husband," she admitted tightly. "If I can still address him as such!"

The Queen's eyebrows shot up, but she nodded and waved a hand obligingly.

Eden stood up from her chair and took a few steps forward and then turned around to face him. Roland looked back at her a moment, then came to his feet and walked forward also.

Eden waited until he drew level with her. Then she faced him down, her chest heaving with indignation. That he should not stand up against this measure cut her to the quick. It was outrageous! Monstrous, even.

"Now, love, don't take on so…" Roland started placatingly. Clearly picking up on her mood, he closed the distance between them. "I only mean…"

Eden snatched away her hand as he reached for it, feeling suddenly extremely angry. "If you imagine for *one minute* I'll

412

be sneaking to your bedchamber again, you're vastly mistaken!" she flung in his face.

"Again?" barked King Wymer behind them. "Hah!"

Eden ignored them, her furious gaze still on Roland's face.

"Wife…" Roland started again, his reasonable tone infuriating her.

"I think not!" said Eden crisply. "If we are back to mere courtship days, then you can hardly call me that!"

"Eden," he said loudly. "Don't misunderstand me—"

"Oh, I won't! Don't worry!" she retorted bitterly. "Not again!"

At that, he gave a suppressed sound of irritation, and taking another step toward her, seized her forearm, dragging her into his embrace. She tried to resist, but her satin slippers did not grip the flagstones, and he was a lot stronger than she was in any case.

Dimly, Eden registered the fact that benches were scraping along the floor as people craned in their seats to get a better view of them. Close by was the sound of a crash as one bench overturned altogether. She found she didn't even care; she could not tear her gaze from Roland's even if her life depended on it.

"Stop being a little shrew," he growled at her, his fingers tightening around her upper arms. "Do you want me to kiss you in front of everyone?"

Eden had already opened her mouth on a retort when his words registered with her. "Wh-what? You wouldn't *dare*!"

A look of amusement crossed his face. "Oh, Eden," he murmured. "I do love you." The background noise faded, and

413

time stood still. Everything else was just…irrelevant. Roland's lips came down on hers and he kissed her. Not angrily, but thoroughly, and with complete conviction that it was his right.

When she stopped resisting him, his arm slipped around her, holding her firmly against him. "My love," he whispered in her ear, his words alight with laughter, "that was so indiscreet, it was actually worthy of a Vawdrey." His shoulders shook with laughter. "I think in future, Renlow needs to take you for a mentor in fearlessness."

Eden, realizing she had been rather impolitic, looked back over her shoulder in trepidation at the Queen. Roland's arm was tight around her waist. She found herself clutching at the front of his doublet. She took a deep, fortifying breath, but before she could even utter a word, noticed the King was addressing the Queen in an urgent undertone.

"I think you'd better climb down off your high horse, Armenal," he was recommending tetchily. "The lady is clearly not pleased with your notion, not pleased at all. What's the point in punishing the fellow further? That's all I ask. Seems pointless if you ask me. He took her undowered and lost an honorary title, seems to me that should be the end of the matter."

The Queen leaned against one arm of her throne and regarded Eden thoughtfully. "Now this is a strange turn of events," she said. "I must confess myself at a loss. Your reactions are quite the opposite of what I expected." She tilted her head to one side. "Perhaps if you explained why it is you would have no objection to following my ruling?" she said, turning to Roland. The room hushed at once, and you could have heard a pin drop.

He cleared his throat, though did not release Eden. "In truth, I am not proud of the way I conducted my courtship of my wife," he said, flushing slightly. "This gives me the chance to set that to rights."

Eden held her breath. He wanted the opportunity to woo her? She was still reeling from this as the Queen turned to her. Suddenly, she realized she had not even responded to his declaration that he loved her.

"And now, Eden, why do you *not* wish to take this month-long hiatus from married life?"

This was it. Her opportunity to be as fearless as Sir Renlow, she thought. "Because," Eden said in a clear, carrying voice that even those spectators at the back could hear, "as a wooer, Roland Vawdrey may have been indifferent. But as a husband, he is without peer. I love him, and I will have no other."

The room erupted into chaos. And Roland kissed her. Again.

Epilogue

Two Months Later, the Royal Tournament, Caer-Lyoness

Eden reached up again to check the garland of flowers was sat
straight upon her head. She still couldn't quite believe that
Roland had presented it to her in front of everyone as
Tournament Queen. Or that she had taken it. The applause from
the audience had been quite deafening. She knew there was a
stupid smile on her face, but she couldn't seem to banish it.

She glanced over at her husband. He was stripped down to his
braies and chauses now and washing his hands in the basin
Cuthbert had left out for him. She caught the direction of his
gaze, flickering over her, before he plunged his hands back in,
and started rigorously scrubbing his face and neck.

For a moment, she had almost thought it was his lascivious look
he was casting her way. The one he habitually wore before
pouncing on her. But they were currently in a pavilion, in a
field outside the palace and surrounded by courtiers. So, she
must surely have misinterpreted his look, she thought. Maybe,
after all, she wasn't the expert she was starting to feel on the
various moods of Roland Vawdrey.

"Well," she announced with a sigh of satisfaction, examining
the fine gold bowl that Roland had been presented with, along
with the return of his "King's champion" accolade. "You did it.
You're the victor. Lord Kentigern was as dust beneath your
feet. You are once more the King's champion." Roland smirked
as he reached for the soap leaves but gave no other discernable
reaction. "You will be pleased to hear I've finally sorted my

itinerary for the next week while we're here at court," Eden rattled on.

"Tomorrow morn, I have a music recital in the Queen's chamber. I shall take my harp. Then in the afternoon I have a meeting with my fellow ladies-in-waiting, followed by a poetry reading in the lower gallery." She looked at him expectantly. "What say you to that?"

"Good," he said after a moment's pause. "Good." He was running a drying cloth now over his shoulders and upper body.

"So, which do you think you'll attend?" asked Eden politely. "The harp performance or the poetry reading?"

He seemed to consider this. "Harp. But I'll be returning to the quintain directly after you perform."

She nodded at this, then seemed to absorb his words. "Really? The quintain? Will you be back at practicing again so soon?"

"Yes," he said. He had got through today's proceedings remarkably unscathed. "But more importantly, will you be dancing again any time before we leave?" he asked, casting his towel away.

Eden shook her head. It turned out that Roland genuinely liked to watch her dance, but not if there were any gentlemen involved in the performance. In that case, he was sure to watch very closely, and Eden's partners tended to get rather flustered under his hostile regard. "No, I am merely teaching some steps to others on Thursday."

"Well, you need to give some of the other maidens a chance," he conceded. "When you dance, everyone else is thrown into the shadows."

"'Tis only you who thinks so," said Eden, who still got a little flustered when he spoke thus. She set down the golden bowl carefully. "And then, we travel to Chilbury on the following Monday for the next tournament, where I will cheer you on from the crowd." She turned to examine the rest of the things scattered on the table, lifting one of his gauntlets.

"How do you even lift your sword—?" she began when suddenly she felt her hips seized from behind and Roland's warm breath on her neck. He buried his face against the side of her throat and dragged her back against his front. Before she could stop herself, Eden let out a surprised squeak. "Roland! What do you think you're doing?" But he didn't want to talk.

His fingers were in her hair, tugging her face to turn toward his. So, she had not misinterpreted that look after all! He kissed her until she was breathless, and then spun her around, and lifted her up to sit on the edge of the table. Eden's eyes widened. "Roland—" she said, casting her eyes toward the entrance of the tent.

"The dogs are posted there," he said, kissing her neck, his hands busy pushing her skirts aside. "All six of them. They won't let anyone interrupt us."

"We're out of doors," she reminded him in scandalized tones.

"We're in a pavilion," he pointed out, and he tipped his head back to look at her. "Will that fellow Childers be at the poetry reading?" he asked with a sudden frown. "When he dedicated that ballad to you, you blushed."

"Well, it was a very great compliment he paid me," Eden replied.

"Let's get this straight, wife. I'm the one that makes you blush. Me. Your husband. No one else."

She looked at him gravely. "Mr. Childers is fifty-five and balding," she pointed out gently.

"I wanted to kill him."

"I'm not in love with Mr. Childers," she said firmly. "So kindly do not murder him." He said nothing. Eden tried again. "We simply have a shared interest and a similar taste and appreciation for the arts—"

"Eden," he interrupted her. "You're making me feel murderous toward him again."

Eden broke off her words to look at him in exasperation. "The one I love is you. If you were to award the tourney crown to another, then I would understand that you were paying a great compliment to that lady, and I would not…"

"That won't arise," he said crisply. "As I'm never going to give the tourney crown to another."

"What?"

"I'm only ever going to give it to you from now on."

Eden paused, scanning his face. "Are you in earnest?"

"Deadly."

She took a couple of unsteady breaths. "Fine, I won't accept any more poetry dedications."

They kissed, and Eden was quite lost in his embrace. When he pulled back again, she made a sound of protest.

"Unless…" he said, sounding frustrated. "Does that mean you will lose status somehow? As a patroness."

Eden looked up at him in mingled amusement and exasperation. "Not really." She pulled a face. "Poetry is not a sporting event. Though I suppose there is some prestige attached…"

"Very well, then," he huffed. "They can still dedicate poems to you."

"Roland Vawdrey," she said with a sigh and laid her hand against his cheek. "You are such a considerate husband."

"Open your legs then," he recommended breathlessly.

"Oh, very well!" Eden said, but she wasn't even convincing herself with her show of reluctance. He stepped between her legs, and she had to bite back an answering sigh.

"How can you be so—?" he asked thickly.

"What?" she asked.

"Tart, yet sweet," he said distractedly.

"What?"

"Like a piece of fruit."

Eden looked at him incredulously. "A piece of fruit?" But Roland was kissing the tops of her breasts. "It's perhaps as well you've never tried to write me a poem," she observed. "I suspect you would be very bad at it."

"As bad as you at jousting," he agreed, and she ran her fingers through his dark hair.

"All this," he said greedily, dragging down her shift to expose her breasts, "including this perfect bosom, is mine." He cocked an eyebrow at her as if daring her to argue with him.

Eden regarded him solemnly as he waited. *Perfect bosom?* "Yes, yes," she said indulgently. "It's all yours."

"It's going to turn so red here, from my attentions," he said with satisfaction, and ran a possessive hand over her tender white cleavage.

Eden gasped. "Did you not shave just now with your razor?"

"No." He shook his head.

"*Why not?*" she squawked. He usually did without fail.

"So everyone can see at the celebratory feast tonight," he said wolfishly, "that you are a woman who is thoroughly desired by her husband."

"Roland! That's absurd!"

He shrugged. "I disagree," he said calmly. "You have to give me some dispensation if I am to tolerate all your fawning admirers."

"Fawning—?" Eden broke off. "You're hopeless," she said with a sigh, relaxing back on her elbows against the tabletop. "Are you really going to bestow on me all your tournament crowns?"

"Of course." He was kissing now between her breasts with exquisite care.

"It will look most particular of you," she warned him, her hand flying to the back of his neck to cradle him at her bosom.

"I don't care, everyone knows I'm mad about you. No one will be remotely surprised." That was probably true. Sometimes she worried that people laughed, he acted so smitten around her, but Roland didn't seem to care one whit.

She had amassed more jewelry in the last two months than most ladies in a lifetime. She had glittering brooches and necklaces and rings to rival even the Queen's. Most of them had sapphires, as Roland said they matched her eyes. Their wedding had been blessed last month in the royal chapel with the King and Queen in attendance, Lenora, her grandmother, and all of Roland's family, including Cuthbert.

"I took those plans into town yesterday to see about getting the work started on the Keep."

"Really? So that's where you went! I was afraid you'd gone to commission more baubles for me." A guilty look flitted across his face. "Roland, you didn't!"

"You haven't got a diadem," he said in justification.

Then she realized what he'd said. "Oswald's plans to expand the Keep, you mean?" she gasped.

"Yes."

"But—"

"We'll need more room about the place," he pointed out. "There will doubtless be children before long, and probably more dogs... Fulco and Brigid have become handfasted," he reminded her. "They're likely to start a family soon. And Baxter even has a helper now word's getting out the place isn't haunted. Besides, you liked them, didn't you? The plans?" He pulled back to look into her eyes. "Eden?"

She nodded her head, unable to form words, just blinking rapidly up at him.

"We can afford it," he said. "Even your uncle insisted I took that dowry in the end. Mind you, I think your cousin shamed him into it." He frowned. "Shall we do this back at the palace, sweetheart?" he said, looking about them ruefully. "This was probably not my greatest notion. Oswald and Mason and everyone will all be expecting us to emerge..."

She wrapped her arms around his neck, drawing him down to her. "Your whole family watched you win," she reminded him.

His gaze drifted over her face a moment, then up to the garland on her head. "And saw you crowned," he added.

"Yes."

"Shall we go and join them, my love?" She shook her head. "No?"

"Not yet," said Eden. "First I want you to do that thing you promised."

"Which thing, my wicked faery?" His eyes grew warm. "Give you a baby?"

"Oh, I think you've already done that," said Eden lightly. She watched the emotions flit over his face: surprise, delight, elation.

"Really?"

"Really."

He laid a hand on her still flat stomach and rested it there a moment. "I can scarcely believe it," he whispered.

"I know," she whispered back. "It should be due next springtime."

Roland cursed. "What was I thinking? That building work should have been started a couple of months ago at least!"

"All will be well," Eden assured him with a gurgle of laughter. "You're panicking."

"What if it's twins? They do run in the family."

"We spend half our time at court!" she reminded him contentedly.

"I want everything to be perfect." He frowned.

"And it is," she told him sagely. "But right now, I want you to untidy me, and make it clear that I'm a very desired wife."

Roland's gaze turned dark. "That, my fearless lady, will be entirely my pleasure."

"But you must have a care not to dislodge my crown," Eden cautioned him teasingly. "I'm very fond of it, for 'tis proof of my husband's regard."

He eyed her a moment with a mixture of amusement and tenderness. "This is merely the first of many," he reminded her. "Now come and kiss me, Faery Queen."

"You've been spending too much time with Baxter," she laughed. But she kissed him all the same.

THE END

If you enjoyed this book, please consider leaving me a rating on Goodreads, Amazon, Bookbub or wherever else you leave your reviews. I would be very grateful.

You can find my website at: www.alicecoldbreath.com where you can sign up for my monthly newsletter and find out what I am up to.

Also, please do check out some of my other stories!

Many thanks, Alice.

If you want to read more about the Kingdom of Karadok, then the next book is Mathilde's story. Book one in The Brides of Karadok series.

Wed by Proxy

Thrice wedded, but never bedded, Mathilde Martindale has long lived in the shadow of her indomitable mother, and meekly done as she was told. Until one day, she decides to become mistress of her own destiny and leave the royal court to find her own path.

Married by proxy, Lord Martindale has never even met his bride of three years. Wed as part of a peace treaty, he bitterly resents the mercenary wife who cares only for wealth and prestige. And then he meets her.

www.ingramcontent.com/pod-product-compliance
Lightning Source LLC
Chambersburg PA
CBHW020830030726
47496CB00001B/176